Introduction

Black Widow
Half French and half Arapaho, Co... trapper as his bride and forced to lea... her husband is murdered, Collette i... flees into the wilderness. There she cr..... paths with a washed-up cowboy named Wyatt Kelly. . .in a race for hidden treasure.

Finding Yesterday
Justin Fairbanks, a young Civilian Conservation Corps recruit, is trying to escape his troubled past. Raised by his abusive, drunkard father, Justin learned to drink, steal, and "raise Cain" from his youth—until the car he was driving hit and killed the local pastor. Though Justin played tough on the outside, the incident shattered him. When the pastor's daughter arrives unexpectedly at the camp, Justin is forced to face what he left behind. And Lia must decide if she can forgive—and just how much.

After the Ashes
Friends and firefighters Thomas Walks-with-Eagles and Alicia Sanchez are from dramatically different backgrounds. Thomas is an Apache Christian from a reservation in Arizona; Alicia grew up with shocking abuse in Juarez. Their relationship takes a deeper turn when they're called to fight the 1988 fire in Yellowstone. But as the fire blazes out of control, doubt and the deadly inferno threaten their future.

Kamikaze
Researcher Taka Shimamori and park ranger Jersey Peterson haven't hit it off well. Jersey is threatened by Taka's blabbering scientific-ese and resents his brief commitment to Yellowstone. Which is what most people have done in her life—come and go. Taka wishes Jersey would let down her hardened guard, but she's made it clear that people, especially from his background, can't be trusted. Then a renegade group of poachers threatens the park, and trusting each other means more than ever. . . .

YELLOWSTONE MEMORIES

FOUR-IN-ONE COLLECTION

JENNIFER ROGERS SPINOLA

BARBOUR
PUBLISHING

Print ISBN 978-1-61626-745-2

eBook Edition:
Adobe Digital Edition (.epub) 978-1-62029-692-9
Kindle and MobiPocket Edition (.prc) 978-1-62029-691-2

Cover design and illustration by Kirk DouPonce, DogEared Design

Published by Barbour Publishing, Inc., P.O. Box 719, Uhrichsville, Ohio 44683, www.barbourbooks.com

Our mission is to publish and distribute inspirational products offering exceptional value and biblical encouragement to the masses.

ecpa Member of the
Evangelical Christian
Publishers Association

Printed in the United States of America.

Dear Readers,

If you've ever ached, like I have, for wide open spaces, shimmering geysers, waterfalls, fields of wildflowers, ice-cold lakes, and giant saw-toothed Rocky Mountains capped with snow, then you'll find yourself in awe of Yellowstone National Park. The first time I saw it as a college student—the farthest I'd ever traveled away from my Southern home in rural Virginia—I was overwhelmed. So different from the gentle ripples of the Blue Ridge Mountains and green farm fields of my childhood. Yellowstone, with all its vast and towering splendor, was love at first sight. And that love has never left me.

I couldn't wait to take you on a trip to Yellowstone—past and present—and introduce you to some of the quirky, flawed characters who might have crossed its borders over the years. Yellowstone attracts all kinds: artists, students, park rangers, vendors, firefighters, researchers. Each from different backgrounds, different families, different stages in life. And each one brings his or her own web of problems. Of hurts, of disappointments. Of joys and brokenness.

Which is where our Lord comes in.

To heal, to speak truth, and to bind up the wounds in His own unique way. Speaking in a personal voice to each struggling soul and taking us on a journey. A journey to healing. A journey that leads to Him.

I hope you'll hear His voice as you read.

And I hope you'll catch His whispers as you walk through His masterpiece of Yellowstone, the land I loved dearly from my first step off the bus.

For He makes our deepest dreams come to life—even those we never thought possible.

I know because He's brought me back. After moving from Japan to Brazil, I now live in the beautiful Black Hills of South Dakota, surrounded by Ponderosa pines and mule deer and rugged slate-blue mountains. Just a few miles from the Wyoming border, and a couple of hours away from Yellowstone National Park.

Almost fifteen years after my first trip to Yellowstone, and I have come home.

May God use these stories to bring you home to Him. Thank you for reading.

Jennifer R. Spinola

P.S. The Thoen Stone and the legend of Black Hills gold I've written about in this book is real by the way! If you're ever in Deadwood, South Dakota, stop by the Adams Museum and see the real sandstone carving. And look me up—I'm not far away!

BLACK WIDOW

Dedication

To Roger and Kathleen Bruner, my friends,
Bass Pro Shop partners, and writing confidantes.
None of this would ever have been possible without ya!

Chapter 1

1891

Whoa, there, boy—easy. Easy," Wyatt Kelly whispered, tightening the reins as Samson eased his way through the squeaky stable gate in the shadows. "Not a sound. Shh. That's it." He clucked softly and pulled the large stallion to a stop, listening. Straining for any sound in the chilly, moonlit night.

A weak shiver of dry grasses rattled together in the wind, a skeletal and foreboding sound. The distant flutter of an owl's wings, the faraway squeak of a field mouse. All cold and autumn-chilly under a brilliant, frost-white moon.

The same bright moon that had hid its face in a mournful sliver the day the Cheyenne murdered his family so many years ago. Leaving their bodies crumpled on the prairie grasses and skinny Wyatt Kelly bawling his eyes out. Shaking in terror.

The only thing he'd brought with him to his uncle's ranch as a lonely child was his father's mare and gentle, loyal Samson, her only wobbly colt. Wyatt had spent his younger years crouched in the stable, talking his lungs out to Samson.

And Samson listened, blinking great liquid eyes.

The only part of his family, save the distant and skeptical Uncle Hiram, that remained intact.

"That's it, Samson," Wyatt whispered, pulling on the reins. "Quiet, old boy. We'll be back before you know it." He pulled off his cowboy hat to hear better as he turned back toward the ranch house, which lay darkened with night, its windows black.

He held his breath as he flicked the reins slightly, urging Samson ahead, step after silent step. Wincing with each slight patter of gravel under Samson's massive hooves or the faint groan of leather saddle and reins. The clink of metal stirrup against boot, the squeak of the chilly lantern handle.

Wyatt's palm turned clammy against the cold barrel of his

Winchester rifle as he eased Samson past the log smokehouse and barns, keeping his head down and reins taut. Past the ranch hands' quarters and the long log fence, cold wind fluttering his black coat around him like a shroud. Wyatt didn't trust any of the ranch hands—none of the stable boys or Irish washerwomen. Not the sour-faced cook who turned out apple tarts and hearty stews. And especially not the mysterious Arapaho girl who'd come from a French trapper's colony in Idaho, all her Indian beads and braids hidden under her bonnet and demure white-and-blue cottons. Her cool demeanor unnerved him; Uncle Hiram swore a married girl that young and alone looking for work must be up to no good. After the gold, even.

And yet she trained horses like nobody he'd ever seen. "Jewel," folks called her—for no one really knew her name—brushed and braided and combed manes and tails, hauled feed and scrubbed troughs, poured water and broke the skins of ice that formed across the surface of the water barrels on frosty mornings. Wyatt and the stable boys would pause, mesmerized, as she trained and saddlebroke the wildest, most cantankerous colts from the end of a slim leather tether—moving in graceful circles, her long skirts and shawls swishing and beaded necklaces making a bell-like clinking, like iced branches in the winter wind.

But not even Jewel had a clue where he was headed tonight. He hadn't spoken a word—just slipped out to the ticking of the mantel clock, lifting his rifle from above the fireplace.

If only he could get to Crazy Pierre's old homestead in time to find the gold.

First. While everyone else—his uncle, the Crowder brothers, gold-thirsty prospectors—slept soundly, blissfully ignorant. Stumped once again by Crazy Pierre's insane old ramblings.

But not Wyatt Kelly. For once in his life, he'd figured something out.

Wyatt's hands trembled as Samson clipped softly down the ridge and through the grasses, leaving the ranch behind in crisp stillness. He lit the lantern, making spiny shadows across the prairie hills, and urged Samson to a slow trot as the giant teeth of the Rockies bit into the horizon. Vast and ghostlike.

Keeping his hushed secret with silent, brooding eyes.

Crazy Pierre DuLac's ramshackle cabin, its roof cracked open from a windstorm, lay just over the stream and beyond the ridge—just a few miles from the Yellowstone National Park boundary. Nestled just down the ridge from Uncle Hiram Kelly's cabin, where Wyatt forked straw and scrubbed stalls and hated the stench of cow manure and dust—and, frankly, his life in general. After all, there wasn't much else he was good at, except reading dusty legal volumes, taking care of Uncle Hiram's lousy bookkeeping, settling his uncle's debts, and trying not to let the prize bull gore him.

"A silly bookworm," Uncle Hiram grunted when he saw Wyatt sitting over one of those heavy legal books or volumes of agricultural sales, peering down through his glasses and moving his lips in quiet thought. "That's what you are. You're not your father, Wyatt—that's for sure. No sir. Amos Kelly was a real man. A real man with hair on his chest."

Wyatt would bristle to himself and pretend not to notice, dipping his pen in ink and scratching out a few notes about syllogistic fallacies and mathematical equations to show the rise in wool prices versus the growth in corn equity. Trying to hide the embarrassing bloom of red that spread over his face.

But not for much longer.

Crazy Pierre, rumors whispered, had buried all the gold he'd bought from the Indians for a pittance about fifty years ago. Gold nuggets the Sioux probably stole from Ezra Kind and his bunch after they panned a wagonload of it out of ice-clear rivers in the Black Hills back in 1834—and left a frantic message for help carved in sandstone.

A fellow named Thoen found Kind's message in South Dakota in 1887, giving authenticity to the theory that the gold was real—and plentiful.

Wyatt clucked to Samson and paused to let a screech owl flap out of the way, reining in the horse when he reared slightly. He slipped his hand in his coat pocket and unfolded a battered sheet of ledger paper where he'd penned Ezra Kind's message from the Thoen Stone as accurately as he could:

Come to these hills in 1833 — Seven of us — Delacompt — Ezra Kind — G. W. Wood — T. Brown — R. Kent — Wm. King — Indian Crow — all dead but me, Ezra Kind — killed by Indians beyond the high hill — Got our gold. June 1834 — Got all the gold we could carry — our ponies all got by the Indians — I have lost my gun and nothing to eat and — Indians hunting me.

"All the gold we could carry." Wyatt repeated the words to himself in a whisper, trying to imagine the sheer quantity of gold that would weigh down seven full-grown men. He shook his head, mentally adding zeros to his wildest numerical dollar value.

Locals said that two winters after Ezra Kind scratched his note into rock, Pierre met a group of Sioux Indians hauling a frayed burlap sack full of glittering nuggets up to a trading post in Montana.

Twelve new long rifles, a thick stack of cast-off wool army blankets, and the pocket watch he'd swiped off a dead banker sealed the trade, so the legend spun—and the Indians handed over the loot to Pierre. After all, what good was a bag of glittering rocks when winter snows blew into the drought-thin teepees and the buffalo had been driven so far southeast by the Chippewa that hunters brought home little more than prairie dogs?

Pierre, in his infinite wisdom, celebrated his purchase with a drunken bar brawl in Cody. When he woke up in his straw-tick bed a few days later, he had no idea how he'd gotten home from Cody—or where he'd buried the gold.

Snows fell heavy across the northeastern corner of Wyoming during the hard winter of 1836, and March passed before young Pierre finally dug out of his cabin and tried to find where he'd hidden his stash.

And for fifty solid years, Crazy Pierre dug holes all along the East Fork River.

Lending credence to the fact that he might have been. . .well, just plain daft.

~∞~

The local folk had long given up the idea of finding the gold—if there ever was any gold at all—since fifty years was a long time for loot of that magnitude to sit around. But just before the US Army took over Yellowstone National Park, which lay just across the creek from Pierre's place, rumors began to spread that old Pierre had hit pay dirt. Or *found* it.

1886—a mere five years ago.

Folks spotted him in the saloons swilling whiskey like a madman, exuberantly buying up land and horses and dropping wads of cash. When he heard that the army had taken over the park and vigilantly hunted down poachers, Crazy Pierre boarded up his cabin, sent a sealed letter off to some relatives in the Northwest, and died in a bar fight over a card game in Deadwood, South Dakota, three weeks later.

Leaving everybody scratching their heads over the gold.

Crazy Pierre indeed. Wyatt carefully folded up the paper and slipped it back in his pocket, fingering the rusty metal key ring that clinked against the lining of his coat. Brilliant Opportunist Pierre was more like it. Folks said the pocket watch he traded the Indians didn't even work right—and the glass casing was broken.

And now, if his hunch and the battered old keys told the truth, Wyatt was about to find out.

He eased Samson under a stand of low-growing trees and quietly dismounted, turning his head this way and that to listen for any sound of mountain lions or coyotes—or worse, intruders. But he heard nothing save the wind in lonely trees, rattling thin branches against the crumbly sides of Pierre's cabin.

"Wyatt?"

He jumped, fumbling with the keys and dropping them in the underbrush. He jerked up the lantern and swiveled his head around but saw no one but Samson. Samson whinnied again nervously and pawed the ground—an eerie sound.

"Shh, old fella." Wyatt patted Samson's graying head as he snatched up the lantern, leaving his rifle tied to the saddle. "We'll be quick. You'll see. I'll be in and out of here in a few minutes, if the coffer's where I think it is." He turned back at Samson's grunt of disapproval and stroked the sleek brown flank, whispering sweet nothings in Samson's velvet ear. "And you'll get your oats when we're done. I promise."

Wyatt scrabbled in the dried grass and moss for his keys, scolding himself for being so clumsy. Why, just yesterday he'd dropped them in the stable, and it had taken him hours to frantically track them down— under a clump of straw and mud. Wyatt Kelly, the most accident-prone man alive—who once nearly bashed his head in by stepping on a garden rake.

Wyatt tucked his Colt revolver tighter into his holster and stepped over snarls of ancient roots as he strode toward the cabin, holding up the lantern. He leaned close to the broken window, darkened with age, breathing in the dank, musty smell of old boards and forgotten rooms.

Mice-eaten panels and a caved-in roof.

A shudder passed through Wyatt with tingly horror as he passed his light on dusty cobwebs, which hung from the ceiling in opaque sheets, quivering in the breeze from the broken windows and roof. He trembled slightly, leaning against the mossy shutters for support.

Spiders. The thought of slender arachnid legs churned the long-eaten brisket in his stomach, making him wish he'd gone to bed without dinner. But if stalking through spiders' nests is what he had to do to find Crazy Pierre's gold, so be it. Wyatt loosened his collar, feeling nervous sweat prickle under his hat.

So long as he could keep the blood in his head and put one boot in front of the other.

Wait a second—was that a light from inside? Or merely the reflection of his own lantern? Wyatt forced his glasses deeper on his nose and leaned closer, squinting against broken glass to see better, and felt a brittle tree root give way under his boot. When he scrambled to his feet, banging his shoulder against a crooked shutter and nearly bashing the lantern against the stone-and-log wall, the light had vanished.

Wyatt turned the lantern this way and that against the shattered glass, feeling a nervous ripple down his spine.

"Calm down, for pity's sake," he scolded himself, annoyed at his shaking hands and clammy cheeks. "It's your own reflection, man. Pull yourself together and get in there before Kirby Crowder does."

Wyatt squared his timid shoulders and marched around to the front of the cabin.

Well, well. What do you know. Wyatt tamped the smooth soil at the base of the old door with his boot, that tense quiver traveling down his spine again. *Pierre's had visitors. And recently.*

The last time Wyatt had come to the cabin, windblown soil and leaves covered the threshold, piling up so deeply over the old ruin of a door that he'd had to shovel before it pushed open—and even then with difficulty.

A strand of torn cobweb inside flickered in the lantern light, blowing.

His heart thrummed as he pushed the door open with a long and plaintive creak, wishing he'd unstrapped his rifle and brought that with him, too. He held the lantern in one hand and swiped at cobwebs with the other, observing the mess: The chimney lay in ruins, a stack of broken and charred stones, and the floor had heaved and cracked from tree roots.

Making the ancient table tilt and smash into the wall. An old branch still hung from the gash in the roof, splitting the ceiling open. Wyatt looked up through frosty wire-rimmed glasses, holding his breath, and saw starlight.

A rough stone staircase led down to the old root cellar, its chilly interior dank with age. Lantern light splashed down the uneven steps in bright slants, glowing against old broken barrels and glass jars. The bright red hairs on the back of his neck tingled with the eerie sensation of being watched—and yet he saw no one, heard no breath or movement.

Wyatt swiped the lantern back and forth, making shadows slant and bend, but the root cellar remained wordless and clammy. Gravelike and silent.

And then—a bump, a sound. A scurrying.

He froze on the last step, motionless. Stilling the squeaking lantern handle and swinging globe with his free hand.

But as he swiveled around, his wobbly lantern beam illuminated nothing but empty, dusty shelves. Old barrels and feed sacks in the corner. An ancient pair of boots. Wyatt kicked one, and a mouse darted out of the boot and into a crevice in the wall.

Wyatt shuddered, jumping back in disgust.

An abandoned Smith & Wesson revolver gleamed back from an empty shelf, which lay sticky with cobwebs, and Wyatt picked up the revolver in surprise. No dust on the barrel, and the stock looked well kept and polished.

Why had it been left behind? A relic from a gold digger a few years past, forgotten? It couldn't have been Crazy Pierre's. Not in such good shape, with no dust or rust.

No matter. There was no time for speculation. Not now, when he stood so close to the box that had eluded him for years.

Wyatt dropped the revolver back on the shelf, feeling his fingers tremble with excitement. He counted the rotten oak shelves, measuring over exactly two feet, and then pried out a loose board from the floor below. Then another. The next board split in his hand, crumbling with a tinny sound onto something beneath the boards.

His heart stood still as the lantern beam illuminated a dusty box.

An ancient wooden box with rusty metal braces and a lock just the right size to fit a key in Wyatt's hand.

Wyatt knelt down, his hands shaking so much he nearly dropped the precious keys in his sweaty fingers, and inserted the first key into the lock. This key ring was nearly as valuable as the gold; he'd found it with the infamous initials carved in the rough metal: PDL. *Pierre DuLac.* Or in local Wyoming vernacular, Crazy Pierre.

A rusty key ring to match the coffer. The missing link everybody'd been looking for. Men would kill for this.

He tugged and jiggled, but it held fast.

He pulled out the key and tried another and then another, but still the lock refused to budge.

Wyatt tried each of the keys again, one after the other—grunting and straining at the lock.

And. . .nothing.

Wait a second. Wyatt jerked up the key ring and shook it in the light. Three keys? He thought there were four.

Weren't there. . . ?

Wyatt counted again, feeling the color drain from his face.

At that exact moment, he heard a sneeze. A distinct bump, coming from the dank recesses of the room behind the cluster of barrels and feed sacks.

Wyatt scrambled to his feet, stumbling twice, and pulled his Colt from its holster.

"Come out now," he ordered, trying to make his voice sound sterner than he really felt as he cocked the hammer. "Or I'll blow all those barrels to bits."

Silence.

Wyatt moved closer, his boots shuffling on the hard-packed earth. A cobweb tickled his neck, and he slapped at it, trying to keep his teeth from chattering. Kirby Crowder was probably crouching back there with his posse, waiting to pump him full of lead and gunpowder.

Men had died over gold. Ezra Kind's whole group of prospectors back in 1834, including a Crow scout, had probably been murdered by the Sioux in an attempt to keep the gold in the Black Hills. And the likes of the Crowder brothers—and whatever scum they'd dug up from bars and gambling outfits—sure wouldn't think twice about slitting Wyatt's throat for a chest of gold.

Wyatt steadied the gun and eased a step closer, kicking at one of the barrels. "Come out with your hands up, or I'll shoot."

His hand on the trigger flinched, palms sweaty.

And before he could pull it, a shadowy figure rose slowly from behind the barrels, casting a terrible shadow.

Wyatt thrust the lantern forward, heart pounding in his throat.

Chapter 2

Jewel?" Wyatt leaped back, feeling the blood drain from his face as if he'd seen the ghost of Crazy Pierre himself. He reeled, light-headed. "Uh...Miss Jewel? Ma'am?" he corrected, trying to recall his manners as a thousand disbelieving thoughts hit him at once.

Take off your hat, Wyatt! For pity's sake. Wyatt scrambled for his brown leather cowboy hat with his free hand, gun wobbling, and clumsily dropped the hat on the floor.

"What," he stammered, "in thunder's name are you doing here?" He cleared his throat, all nerves and shaking fingers. "Ma'am?"

Wait. Shouldn't he translate? The girl spoke as much English as her ridiculous Indian pony. Arapaho, maybe, the few words he knew— or French or something? She came from a French trapper's outpost in Idaho. That much he knew, from all his wasted tutoring sessions back at Uncle Hiram's cabin—mainly trying to pry her knowledge of the gold.

But his dry mouth couldn't form any words. Couldn't think.

On a good day at the ranch he could barely meet her eyes, so graceful she was—so darkly mysterious, so confident. Oh, how he envied her ease and confidence—her uplifted chin and sparkling black eyes, meeting his for a fleeting second over the Bible pages or across the stable.

And his gaze would flutter away in embarrassment, landing on his boots or the table, or on her simple wedding band. Scurrying off like a field mouse before she noticed the ruddy glow in his freckled cheeks.

Jewel raised her head from behind the barrels, her earrings glittering in the light from the lantern, and said nothing.

"Answer me, miss, or...or..." Wyatt couldn't finish his own sentence, trying to keep the gun level and make his lips move. "Why are you here? At my uncle's, and at Crazy Pierre's?"

He blinked, feeling sweat break out on his forehead under his hat. Her appearance made no sense. His uncle's Arapaho horse trainer who bungled all her verbs and couldn't understand a lick of English? In Crazy

Pierre's root cellar at midnight? Black spots swirled before his eyes, and he reached out a shaky hand to steady himself against a brittle shelf.

Jewel lifted her chin in an almost haughty manner. "My given name is Collette Moreau," she said coldly in perfect English, standing up to her full height. Hands raised. "But you may call me Jewel like everyone else. What are *you* doing here?" She nodded to the floor. "And you may get your hat."

Wyatt stared then fumbled on the dirt littered floor for his hat. He slapped it back on his head at a crooked angle.

"I'm. . .I'm looking for something," Wyatt stammered, strangely unnerved by her calm and even accusatory demeanor. For pity's sake. He was the one holding the gun!

He jabbed the gun barrel forward, trying to keep a steady grip as his palms perspired. "How did you find out about this place?" *Wait a second.* "You speak English?" Wyatt stared, openmouthed. "I thought you could. . . could barely get out a sentence."

His mind reeled as he recalled hours and weeks of tedious tutoring, trying not to fall asleep at his uncle's brawny oak table while she stammered over the simplest of words in the thick family Bible. He'd lean his stubbly red-bearded chin in his hand and yawn, pulling off his glasses to wipe bored tears from his eyes.

"That fool girl can't speak a word of English," Uncle Hiram had said after she left, rocking back in his chair and making the wooden slats of the chair groan in complaint. *"Figures. Redskins are awful slow at learning. Which is why you've gotta work your hardest to get anything she knows outta her. You hear?"* He swept an arm around the golden-hued room. *"This is a fine ranch, Wyatt, but we'd be sitting on a gold mine if she led us to that treasure. Why, we'd be kings. You know that?"*

Now here Wyatt stood, trying to remember how that same tongue-tied girl—who had stumbled over his broken French and questions about the gold with blank eyes—had just spoken in flawless English.

"But I thought. . ." Wyatt blinked at her through crooked glasses.

"Of course I speak English." Derision flashed in Jewel's eyes. "I did go to school, you know—the mission school where I grew up—and I worked for an English doctor for a while. I've heard and understood every word you've said since your uncle hired me on the ranch. And as for the intelligence of my people, why don't you let me give you a lesson in Arapaho nouns—since you think you're so smart?" Jewel moved closer.

"Truth is, you can't even say the name of my pony correctly, and I've told you dozens of times. You pronounce all the consonants wrong, and you've absolutely no tonal distinction whatsoever."

She put her hands down slowly and moved, as if in defiance, from behind the barrel. Sweeping her long skirts and shawl with graceful ease.

Wyatt took a step back and kept himself between Jewel and the revolver on the shelf, trembling. "So this is your gun," he said, finally finding words. He picked it up and stuffed it in his belt. "And that must have been your light I saw. Now get your hands up, or I'll. . .I'll shoot!" He gulped the words down, ashamed. He'd sooner put a bullet through Uncle Hiram's prize stallion than this wisp of an Indian girl who worked tirelessly, frosty dawn to blue-cold evening, without complaint.

Then again, she'd probably shoot him first if she got the chance.

Jewel made a swipe for her revolver and then put her hands back up. "Of course it's my gun. You think I'd be foolish enough to ride off the ranch at night without a firearm?" She tossed her head. "You startled me. I didn't have time to grab it before you came down the stairs."

Wyatt opened and closed his mouth. "So. . .you know." His words came out hoarse. "You know where the gold is."

Jewel tipped her chin up. "As if I'd tell you."

The gun wobbled in his hand as he took another step back, strangely terrified by her fearlessness. "I mean it! I'll shoot!" he stammered, gripping the stock with two hands to keep it from shaking.

"No you won't." Jewel crossed her arms as if in defiance. "What clues can I give you if I'm dead? That's what you've been after the whole time, isn't it? With your ridiculous questions about Pierre DuLac that you thought I couldn't understand?" She pushed the gun aside. "And you've got a spider on your head. Hope it's not a black widow. One bite can disable or even kill a man."

"A. . .a what? A spider?" Wyatt scrubbed at his head in a panic with the crook of his arm. "You're lying."

Jewel shrugged. "Suit yourself. Odds are it's a black widow though. They nest in dark and undisturbed places just like this."

Wyatt wavered, and nausea rose in his gut. "Where is it?" He dropped the lantern on a shelf with a clatter and slapped his forehead, nearly dropping his gun. "Get it off me, will you?"

"Give me the gun." Jewel calmly held out her hand, rings sparkling. "Before you shoot yourself."

He hesitated, his chest heaving. How could she possibly know he hated spiders? His deepest, darkest, most tightly kept secret that he'd kept from everyone, including Uncle Hiram. What was she, some kind of a mind reader, intent on humiliating him beyond reason?

"You're lying." Beads of sweat broke out on Wyatt's forehead, and he leveled the gun at her, trying not to think of webs and crawling legs. "Put your hands up."

"If you say so." She fixed her stare on his forehead and raised her hands about two inches as if in mocking. "Black widows use a poison that paralyzes the nervous system of the body, you know," she added. "Which causes incredible swelling and pain. In fact, in just five minutes after the initial bite, the venom spreads to—"

"Cut it out!" Wyatt slapped at his head again in agony, doing a little dance.

"I'm warning you." Jewel held out her hand again. "Don't complain to me if you shoot a hole in your foot and can't walk to the doctor to get an antidote."

"Fine." Wyatt smacked the gun in her hand, trying not to hyperventilate. "Get it off me, will you?"

Jewel took the gun and leveled it at him. "Thanks." And she kept the gun trained on Wyatt, spreading out her skirts to kneel on the cold dirt floor in front of the wooden chest.

Wyatt shook out his hat and hair and then slowly turned to Jewel. "You were bluffing about the spider," he croaked, watching in horror as she produced a key from the folds of her skirt. No, two keys. His eyes bulged behind crooked glasses. "Why, I ought to...to..."

"To what?" Jewel aimed the gun at him. "Hands up, please." She wagged the barrel of the gun. "And don't bother trying to use my Smith & Wesson. It's empty. See for yourself. I used five rounds on a pack of coyotes on the way over here."

In a quick second Wyatt raised his head and pictured poor Samson hobbled to a tree by his lead, fending off half a dozen coyotes—while he poked around in Crazy Pierre's basement.

"Coyotes, you say?" He glanced upstairs nervously. "Did you kill them?"

"I'm an excellent shot, Mr. Kelly." She raised an eyebrow. "Samson's fine. I'm sure of it."

Wyatt swiveled his head back and forth between Jewel and the cellar door, mouth open in question.

"How did I know you were thinking of Samson?" Jewel's tone softened, tender almost, and she gave the faintest hint of a smile. "I've seen you in the stable, Mr. Kelly. You might not be so good with roping and branding, but you love that horse. You'd do anything for him, wouldn't you?"

Wyatt felt his fingers quiver on her revolver, nearly dropping it, as that humiliating blush of heat climbed his neck.

The gun. The gun, for Pete's sake! Wyatt fumbled with the barrel, showing an empty chamber. Six hollow clicks. "So you are out of rounds. But. . .but lying about one thing, Mrs. Moreau." He stood up straighter and forced himself to meet her eyes. "There's no spider. And you stole my key."

"Of course I stole your key, since you were so kind as to leave it carelessly lying around in the stable. And"—she shot him a cool look— "it matched the one Pierre sent my husband."

"Your *husband*?" Wyatt sputtered, trying to straighten his glasses and nearly knocking them off. "That's who Pierre sent the letter to?"

"Thing is, you need two of his keys to open the lock." Jewel ignored him, holding both keys together. "See how they interlay?"

Good heavens. Wyatt craned his neck to see the pattern in the keys, which made a rough "PD" in dull metal. *Pierre DuLac. That son of a gun.*

"I didn't know there was a fourth key," Wyatt muttered, humiliated at being duped.

"What did you think, that Pierre would carry around the missing key to the coffer in his pocket while the US Army was tromping right past his house?"

"The army?" Wyatt scrunched up his face. "What are you talking about?"

"Yes, the army." Jewel raised her eyes boldly to meet his, endlessly black in the flickering light of the lantern. "Didn't they settle the borders of the national park while he was still living here?"

"What are you, a history expert?" Wyatt snapped, feeling like a simpleton.

Jewel ignored him. "And Pierre wanted for all kinds of crimes? What a ridiculous idea. He was smarter than that. He planned to come back to his cabin once the army backed off, and he sent the key to my husband for safekeeping. Intending to get it later."

"Your husband," Wyatt repeated in a hollow voice, feeling doubly duped. He took a chaste step back, putting his hands up so as not to touch her. "A Moreau."

"A *DuLac* Moreau."

"Well, you're overlooking something, Jewel. Collette Moreau. Whoever you are." Wyatt pointed a shaky finger. "I knew Crazy Pierre myself. I used to haul wood for him. And key or no key, you won't find the gold in that chest." He gestured with his head. "I saw him bury this. There's no gold inside."

"Liar." Jewel jabbed the gun at him.

"Don't believe me? Pick it up yourself. It's too light to hold gold." He scooted the wooden chest with his foot, and it moved easily. "And Crazy Pierre had far more gold than would fit inside a little box like that. Savvy?" He shot her a triumphant look. "But I have a hunch there's something inside that'll tell us where to look—and I bet I can interpret Pierre's clues. I met him, remember? You didn't."

Jewel shook the chest furiously, and Wyatt watched as her bright eyes dimmed and her lips turned downward. She sat back on her heels and rested her chin in her hand.

"Maybe you're right." Jewel swallowed and looked up, her long braid falling over her shoulder. "But I have something you don't."

"My key?" Wyatt took a step closer, his fingers curling into fists.

"And mine." She clinked them both together. "Plus the actual letter Crazy Pierre sent my husband with instructions."

"Give me my key back." He held out his hand.

"No." She hid the keys in her skirt pocket. "And I've got the gun, so I give the orders here."

They were stalemated. Wyatt stood there silently a moment, wondering if he should offer peace or try to grab the gun. He flexed his fingers and then made a swipe for the gun.

Wrong choice. Jewel turned the barrel on him in a liquid second, her dark eyes flashing.

"My uncle was right about you," Wyatt spluttered, slowly putting his hands up. Feeling hot, angry blood pump in his veins. "That's why you came here looking for work, isn't it? So you could pick us off one by one after you steal all our clues to find the gold?"

"Your uncle said that? Well, that's certainly ironic." She aimed coolly at him, and for the first time Wyatt's heart pulsed with real fear. "You've both been trying to get as much information as you can from me about the gold, but you've forgotten one thing."

"What's that?" Wyatt licked his lips, wondering if he could dart up the stairs or if she'd really shoot.

"That I've been doing the same thing with you."

"But. . .but you've no right! My uncle *hired* you!"

"He hired me to train his horses. Which I've done. Exceedingly well, I might add, on such a meager salary and without heat or running water in the bunkhouse." Jewel took a step closer. "Have you ever slept a night out there? It's pure misery in the winter. The place is full of rats."

"Still." Wyatt shivered, chilled by the images of scurrying mice and Jewel aiming at his nose. "Taking a job to smoke us out is wrong. And by taking the key, you've stolen from me."

"It's not your key. It belonged to Crazy Pierre." Jewel sniffed. "And why are you hiding it from your uncle? Skulking around here at midnight instead of telling him what you're doing?"

"Because my uncle can't keep a secret to save his life. He'd tell everybody in town about the key, and I'd be shot by a dozen gold diggers trying to strike it rich." Wyatt's pulse burned. "And what business of yours is it anyway? It's certainly more my key than yours."

"It was Crazy Pierre's key, and you stole it from him."

"I didn't steal it! I found it. There's a difference." Wyatt took a step forward. "I was in Deadwood, South Dakota, buying horses, and I found it in the stable grounds. Pierre died before I could return it to him."

"Really." Jewel smiled as if in amusement.

"It's the truth, I tell you! Why would I lie?"

She studied him a moment, her dark shadow quivering against a pitted wall in the flickering lantern light. "So you *found* the key." She narrowed her eyes. "Even if I believe you, it makes no difference. I also *found* it in the stable when I happened to be sweeping up. You dropped it there like refuse, did you not?"

"Irregardless, the key was my property!" Wyatt jabbed a finger at his chest.

"Irregardless?" She cupped a hand over a laugh. "That doesn't even make sense, Mr. Kelly. It's *regardless*."

"You're wrong!" He raised his voice, sweat prickling under his hat. "I think I know English."

"Well, I think I know prefixes. And it's wrong."

Wyatt felt his fists clench in fury. Of all the nerve. "Listen, miss," he growled, trying to think of an argument that would catch her, corner her, into letting him go and handing over the letter. "That key was protected in the domicile of my uncle, and I'll have you arrested!" He waved an arm for emphasis, bluffing the first thing that came to mind. "The last time a no-good Indian stole something from one of the ranchers in this part of the state, the sheriff had him hung. You hear me?"

Jewel paled visibly in the lantern light.

"I'll have you arrested and taken before a magistrate before daybreak!" Wyatt leaned forward and tried to look menacing. Making it up as he went along. "Why, I know all about you. All about your. . .your sordid past. You thought I wouldn't find out, but I know everything—and I'll tell it all to the judge!"

Jewel swallowed, and the revolver shook in her hands.

What on earth did I say? Wyatt's jaw dropped in surprise.

"You don't know anything about me," she hissed, taking a step closer and holding the gun out with both hands.

"I know everything." He didn't back away, determined not to lose the upper hand—no matter how he'd come by it. "And if you kill me now, it won't be the first time. You'll hang for it!"

"If you kill me now, it won't be the first time?" Wyatt halted, horrified. What did he mean by that? That it wouldn't be the first time she'd killed Wyatt? How utterly ridiculous. What, did he sleep through grammar school? He gripped his head in both hands, wondering how he managed—by sheer, bumbling luck—to mess up everything.

"Fine. Take it." Jewel thrust the revolver at him so swiftly he nearly dropped it. "You don't turn me in, and I won't turn you in. Deal?"

"Uh. . .pardon?" Wyatt craned his neck to see through smudged glasses.

"Let's just start over—you, Mr. Kelly—and me, nobody of any consequence." Jewel flipped the corner of her shawl around her shoulder, a movement that should have resonated carelessness but did not. Instead, Wyatt noticed her eyes take on a terrified cast like a deer startled by an intruder.

"As business partners. Fifty-fifty. Everything secret. Do you agree?" She knotted her hands behind her back, and Wyatt saw them trembling.

"Fifty-fifty?" Wyatt felt the weight of the revolver in his hands, like an idiot, and quickly spun it around to face her. "Are you crazy? You lied about the spider. How can I trust you with anything?"

"Oh no. I didn't lie about that." Jewel gazed up at his forehead. "It's. . .still there. And I'm quite sure it's a black widow." She leaned forward, squinting. "Yes. Red hourglass."

And at that exact second, Wyatt felt something stir his hair. Something thin and tiny, like the brush of an insect leg.

"You were going to let it bite me." Wyatt gazed at her in accusation, his chest heaving. He'd hurled his hat and glasses across the room before clawing at his leather vest and stomping senselessly at the fleeing black speck.

Now Jewel crouched near his fallen glasses, trying to bend the crooked frame back into shape.

"A black widow, Mrs. Moreau. Really. How can I partner with you after that?"

"You were going to shoot me." She wiped the glass lens on the hem of her skirt. "I figured it was fair."

Wyatt didn't respond, checking his hair again with a shaky hand. "Partners," he muttered, turning up his lip. "How can I partner with the likes of you?"

Jewel coldly handed him his glasses, her warm fingers brushing his briefly. "How can you afford not to?"

Wyatt took the glasses with a terse nod of thanks and tried to straighten them on his face, his heart beating dizzy-fast again. Was she threatening him? After all, Jewel had obviously done something in the past that frightened her—something that made her want to forget it. Had she stolen something bigger than a key or. . .killed someone? The only bluff that made her take notice was the law. The magistrate.

Which meant. . .

Hairs stood up on Wyatt's neck as he studied her there in the dim lantern light. The keys in her hand, glinting, and her downcast eyes. The sparkling beaded earring that caught the light in colorful spots, next to the graceful curves of her neck.

"Who are you?" he whispered, holding up the lantern to see her better.

"Jewel," she replied in mocking tones. "You know my name."

"That's what people call you. But that's not your real name."

"Collette Moreau. You know that, too." She raised her face defiantly. "An Indian and a woman who can't be trusted, and who couldn't possibly learn the English language. What else do you want from me?"

"Tell me more." Wyatt didn't know if he was asking or ordering, but he couldn't pull the lantern away from her face. "Who are you? Where do you come from?"

He warily set his Colt down on a shelf next to a collection of dingy, dust-covered bottles. "Tell me the truth." He hung his thumbs in his belt loops and glanced at her, shifting his hat nervously on his head.

Jewel's head came up, and she studied him in silence.

"Look." Wyatt crossed his arms. "Everybody has a thing or two to say about you in town, and around the ranch, but nobody really knows the truth."

"The truth." Jewel gave a sad half laugh and looked away, putting her hands on her hips. "Is that what they really want?"

Wyatt swallowed, and the scarlet bandanna around his stubbly throat felt tight. "It's what *I* want."

"Why?"

He scuffed the heel of his boot in the dirt, shrugging his shoulders. "Nobody even knows your real name. Except. . .well, me. Why is that? Why are you hiding?" He waved an arm around the root cellar. "Digging around in the dirt in a cabin at midnight?"

Jewel didn't answer, twisting her wedding ring back and forth on her finger. "If you must know, I am Arapaho and French," she finally said in a tender tone, her gaze seeming to go right through Wyatt as if not seeing him at all. "I'm the daughter of an Arapaho chief, born in an Arapaho village just outside the border in Nebraska." She swallowed and looked down at her hands. Her delicate fingers, now worn from cold water and harsh soaps. "I was sold as a bride to a French trapper in Idaho when I was a young girl."

It took Wyatt a second to register that Jewel hadn't answered his question. Did she share her real name because she. . .trusted him? On some level? A wash of heat spread through his chest, and he blinked faster.

Of course not. It was probably all part of her twisted plot to pull the wool over his eyes, like everything else. He shifted his position against the shelf, keeping his gaze focused on his boots.

"How young were you?" he asked gruffly when she said no more.

"Fourteen years old."

Wyatt's hands clenched against the shelf, trying to still the angry throb in his heart at the thought of a fourteen-year-old slip of a girl being bought and sold like a mare—worse, like one of Uncle Hiram's prize cattle—for a few gold coins or some blankets.

"So what are you doing here in Wyoming?" he finally asked, clearing his throat.

"I am Hagar," she replied. "From the Bible you taught me at your table."

"Huh?" Wyatt shook his head to make sense of her words. "I mean, ma'am? Pardon?"

"Running from great injustice and much suffering." Tears gilded the corners of her eyes as she fumbled with the keys, knotting her fingers together. "I need this gold. Please. Help me find it. There's enough for both of us, if the legends about Crazy Pierre are true. And I have reason to believe they are."

"What do you mean you *need* the gold?"

Jewel turned, and a shadow covered part of her face. "I can't tell you why. But I need it. My life may depend on it."

Wyatt crossed his arms. "Well, I need the gold, too, you know."

"You? For what?"

He hesitated. "To pay back an old wrong," he said quietly, his hands clenching into fists. "I've been planning it all my life. And I'm so close now." Wyatt squeezed his eyes closed, scarcely daring to breathe. "So close I can almost feel it. After all these years, maybe I'll finally make amends for my father's death."

Jewel regarded him quietly. "I'm sorry about your family, Mr. Kelly." She spoke so softly he had to lean forward to hear well. "I know you miss them."

Emotion quivered in Wyatt's chest, and he feigned a cough to cover it. Pretending he hadn't heard. "So how can I know you're telling the truth about your. . .your story?" He gestured with his arm. "You could be spinning a yarn, for all I know."

"So could you. And to answer your question, you'll just have to trust me."

"What if that's not good enough?"

"The truth is all I have, Mr. Kelly." She spread her hands wide. Cracks showed on the tips of her fingers. And before she could cover it, he noticed an ugly scar running the length of one brown forearm when her long wool sleeve fell back.

Jewel faced him there in the darkness, eyes glazed with sorrow, and something stirred in Wyatt's gut. *She* has *spoken the truth.*

"Well, come on then." Wyatt stuck his revolver back in his belt and reached gruffly for the wooden box. "We'd better get out of here. We'll take it with us and open it in daylight. What do you say?"

"Fine. But don't even think of opening it without me." Jewel picked up her darkened lantern and held up his, which threw gold across the dusty wood of the box. "Fifty-fifty. You keep the box, and I keep the keys." She patted her pocket. "Partners, right?"

Wyatt lifted the box, and something rattled inside. Sliding around the inside of the box with a tinny metallic sound. He tucked the box under one arm and paused to let Jewel go first, tipping his hat by habit, and then he took the stone steps two at a time. Unspeakably grateful to leave behind the musty root cellar, which crawled with spiders and reeked of sour pickles.

As soon as he reached the top, he heard voices.

Two men's voices, filtering from the woods into the broken ruins of Crazy Pierre's house. Distant torches flickered against the trees in glances of light and shadow, splintering in long stripes against the crumbling log walls.

"Of all the rotten luck!" Wyatt hissed, ducking under the low cellar doorway and furiously brushing away cobwebs. "They've caught up with us."

"Who?" Jewel took a step back toward Wyatt.

"The Crowder brothers. They're ruthless. They'll kill us both." He put a finger to his lips.

"There are two of us and two of them. We're matched."

"Naw." Wyatt stroked his chin as a wave of nausea flitted through his stomach. "Not against the Crowders. They're crazy, both of them—and they carry more lead with them than a whole infantry. Why, I've only got a few more rounds. We're finished, you know that?"

"Can we make it outside?" Jewel stumbled over a sunken piece of flooring and caught herself against a rough-hewn chair.

"Nope. They'll see us for sure if we waltz right out the door." Dull glass in the single window sparkled in sharp shards, and the opening was too small to squeeze through without cutting himself to ribbons.

Jewel held his glowing lantern behind her to block the light. "Hurry, then. Get back down to the root cellar."

"No way." Wyatt shuddered at the thought of spiders. "There's no way out of that cellar. If they find us, we're done for. Quick!" He pushed her back, feeling his hands turn cold. "Put out the lantern."

"Give me my gun back." Jewel held out her hand.

"What?" Wyatt spun around. "It's empty! You said so yourself."

"I've got an extra round or two." She jingled her skirt pocket. "And besides, you're not exactly the best shot. I've seen you out on the ranch, Mr. Kelly. With all due respect, you can't even shoot a magpie."

Wyatt scowled, feeling his cheeks burn in humiliation. "Are you crazy? I'm not giving you your gun back."

"What, you think I'm going to stand here and let them shoot me? I'd have been in and out of this place ages ago if it weren't for you."

"You might shoot me in the back of the head and take ol' Pierre's chest for yourself."

"Better than getting run through with one of Benjamin Crowder's knives. He's not very accurate, you know."

"Fine. Take it." Wyatt pulled her Smith & Wesson from his belt and slapped it in her hand. "Satisfied? Now douse the lantern and hide behind something. Quick."

Jewel reached out greedily for her revolver. "Try not to leave footprints in the dust. Walk like my people do when they're stalking game: on the sides of your feet. Not the sole." She jerked her head up. "I bet you left boot tracks all across the floor when you came in."

Wyatt swallowed nervously.

"You did, didn't you?"

Jewel lifted the lantern for a quick look and then sighed and shook her head. As soon as she'd clicked a handful of bullets into her revolver, the inside of Pierre's cabin turned to clammy darkness.

Chapter 3

Yellow light gleamed in one of the windows, illuminating a dusty maze of cobwebs and broken boards. Wyatt flattened himself against the wall beside the crumbly chimney. Hardly daring to breathe. Jewel ducked under the rotten table.

"Get back," she whispered, whacking his toe with the stock of her (heavy) revolver and making him jump. "Your boots are sticking out."

"Get back yourself!" he snapped. His toe smarted where she'd smacked it. "I can't squeeze in here any tighter."

"Well try. You want to get us killed?" Jewel tugged a broken board against the chimney and angled it over his boots.

Torches flickered, and Wyatt heard the whinny of horses. The clink of metal as someone lit lanterns and the stench of kerosene.

A figure clad in a long coat pushed open the wooden door, his lantern light shining across the ruined layers of log and stone. "I know it's gotta be around here. That's what the ol' dog said, didn't he?"

Wyatt ducked his head as he recognized Kirby Crowder's voice, and his eyes watered from the dust. He moved just enough to rub his nose against his shoulder, hoping to goodness he didn't sneeze. He'd spent all spring sneezing as a child when the wild grasses bloomed; twenty-five years hadn't changed his allergies and wimpy sensitivities much. When the dust blew across the Wyoming plains, he swelled up like a porcupine.

"Fella's lyin' through his teeth." Boots clomped against boards. "Why, I oughtta. . ."

The room grew utterly still, and Wyatt was pretty sure he knew what they were seeing: his boot tracks in the dust leading straight to the root cellar. His chest heaved with nauseated panic.

"By cricket." Wyatt heard Kirby's boots scuff the wooden planks as he squatted down, and something like heavy leather holsters groaned. "Somebody's been here. Looky this."

"Down to the root cellar, I reckon."

"You g'won down and see, and I'll wait here a spell." Kirby lowered his voice. "See if he comes back—whoever he is."

Wyatt eased his head around the side of the chimney to see if by some miracle he and Jewel could outmatch Kirby in weapons, but he needn't have. A shift in Kirby's stance and the clanking of heavy holsters confirmed that, yes, Kirby would shoot the daylights out of Wyatt if he even tried to draw his revolver.

Kirby cocked his shotgun, and the sharp, metallic click echoed through the cabin.

Benjamin's boot clatters faded down the stone steps, and Wyatt heard him holler. "There's a hole busted in the floor. Reckon they've already took it?"

"What do you mean, a hole?" Kirby must've leaned under the cellar door to see because his lantern light abruptly died into a cold shadow. "We got here before that Bradford sucker did, that's for shore. Ain't nobody else who'd know what that old Injun told us."

"Well, somebody's pulled the floor up." Benjamin's voice echoed, low and eerie. "There's a space underneath, but ain't nothin' in it."

The cabin silenced, and Wyatt felt himself convulse with a sneeze. His chest shuddered as he pressed his nose closed, and Jewel elbowed him hard in the shin. So hard he almost cried out.

Wyatt thought he saw Kirby march to the door to check outside, holding out his lantern, and then the image dissolved into watery stripes. His mouth scrunched closed. His nose tickled.

And he sneezed.

Exploded, rather.

Twice. So violently that he rocked backward, banging his head against the wall and knocking off his hat. A startled pigeon flew from the broken section of roof overhead, wings flapping.

"What in tarnation?" Kirby growled, stalking over in Wyatt's direction and hoisting his rifle. "Come out now, whoever you are, or I'll blow you to bits!"

Wyatt tried to move, but his lungs stifled, and his nose itched. He slid to his knees in misery, fumbling to keep his hold on the revolver. His glasses fell off, clinking against his boots. And he opened his mouth to sneeze again.

When he opened his eyes, Kirby lay sprawled on the floor and Jewel was raising a heavy wooden plank to swing again. Benjamin hollered and fired a shot behind her, but she ducked. The bullet glanced off a rotten section of log, making a chunk crumble from the wall.

Instead of swinging again at Kirby, Jewel whirled around and brought the plank square across Benjamin's middle without any warning, doubling him over. His lantern clattered to the floor, and she wrestled the pistol out of his hand, knocking his hand into the wall until he cried out in pain.

He lunged after her, but in a quick second she'd cracked him across the skull with his own pistol, knocking his hat off and bringing him to his knees. He struggled to get up, and she laid him out with another blow to the head. Ripping his other revolver from his belt and kicking his rifle down the cellar stairs with a clatter. Just in time to turn the pistol on Kirby, who was scrambling to his feet. Both hands grabbing at pistols in his holster.

Wyatt stood there, the revolver clenched in his hand. His knees knocking and eyes watering. Unable to take his eyes off Jewel's quick and fluid movements. If he had any doubts about her ability to kill, she'd removed every one.

"Why, you little cur!" Kirby turned the barrel of his shotgun around and swung at Jewel with such great force that he struck the wall, splintering the heavy wooden barrel of the gun. Shooting two rounds into the wall behind Jewel with the pistol in his left hand. "Who are you anyway?"

Jewel ducked, cocking Benjamin's pistol and leveling it at Kirby's head. "Don't worry about who I am," she retorted. "Drop your gun."

Do something, you idiot! Wyatt scolded himself. *Don't let Kirby Crowder take down a woman!*

Wyatt blinked swollen eyes, remembering how his burly father had thrown himself across his mother and two sisters for protection, wrestling five Indian braves as they tried to drag him away. The wagon burned, bristling with arrows; the prairie grasses sputtered with flames. When his father's great head finally slumped, bloodied, Wyatt counted six arrows sticking out of him—and two gaping bullet wounds.

His blood trickled down into the smoking prairie grass, a terrible rust-red.

And when they came to haul away his body and kill the others, his father lifted his hand one last time: plunging his dagger square into the Cheyenne brave's chest. Even after they carried away the wounded brave, blood and spittle leaking from his mouth, they couldn't pry the dagger from his father's dead fingers.

Wyatt had buried his face in his mother's side and bawled, terrified.

"You're certainly not your father," everyone said to Wyatt with a shake of the head. As if he wasn't smart enough to figure that out himself. Uncle Hiram thought him a fool and a skinny excuse for a ranch hand.

Wyatt felt a pang sting through his chest as he looked down at his slim, freckled hands, bony in the moonlight from the broken roof. Not great and strong and calloused from hard work like his father's. No, he was scrawny Wyatt Kelly: a twenty-five-year-old who could barely see and whose flaming red hair and glass-blue eyes had been so exotic—so alien—that the Cheyenne warrior who raised the spear to take his childhood spared him out of pity. But mainly fear.

The same fear that kept them from slaughtering the rare white buffalo. "Sacred," they called it. "An omen."

A spectacle was more like it.

And such was the reason that Wyatt even lived.

Instead of pulling the trigger, Wyatt eased backward, letting a shadow obscure his face.

Before Wyatt could plan a move, the unbelievable sound of horses' hooves thumping on the ground outside the cabin jarred him upright. He heard shouts, saw bright lights.

Sidekicks. We're done for. Wyatt squeezed his eyes closed and tried to imagine how it felt to die—and what would happen after Kirby's bullet knocked him into the proverbial Kingdom Come. Was there really a heaven and hell like the family Bible depicted in those stuffy old picture plates? Or was it just lights-out, and nothing more than eternal darkness? Sort of like being locked in Crazy Pierre's root cellar for eternity?

Oh God, no. . . . Please. Anything but that.

"This is Major Marshall from the Yellowstone National Park cavalry," barked a voice, echoing through the half-open door. "Kirby Crowder? Benjamin? I know you're in there. Come out with your hands up, or I'll fill you both full of bullets."

Wyatt opened one eye.

The window shutters flung open, and two soldiers stood there in full uniform, light from lanterns and torches blazing against their brass buttons and cocked revolvers.

"You've been poaching elk and bison off national park property,

Crowder. And about two dozen mule deer. We've been tracking you for miles. You so much as fire one shot, and we'll take you down."

Wyatt saw Kirby freeze, his pistol aimed at Jewel. Benjamin, who'd roused himself and started to climb to his feet, stood shakily.

"Better come on out," another stout voice rang out. "There are six of us here, and we'll shoot you if we have to."

By jingle. He's right. Wyatt felt his breath go out in a shaky spasm. The army ran Yellowstone now, and they were vigilant about cracking down on poachers. The last fellow who got caught poaching bison red-handed wound up in the guardhouse at Fort Yellowstone before he could reload his musket.

"You're surrounded, Kirby," called the major. "I've got men on every side of this place."

Wyatt heard whispered curses and stamping feet, and both Crowders frantically rushed around the room, probably looking for an exit or a place to hide.

The cellar. If either of the Crowders holed up down there, it could be days before the army got them out. But Wyatt couldn't move, couldn't breathe.

Over the ruins of a broken table, Wyatt saw Jewel meet his eye, giving him a slight nod toward the basement.

Me? Wyatt looked behind him to see if she were gesturing to someone else. *She wants* me *to block the cellar?*

Wyatt licked his lips, sizing up the shadows and shapes in the room, and then suddenly leaped around the chimney, scrambled over stones, and ducked through the cellar door. He slammed the door shut behind him, trembling as he tugged the latch to hold it closed.

"Wait a second—another one?" Kirby roared from the other side of the door, jerking it hard. "Who's this? He looks like that scrawny Wyatt Kelly fella, if I didn't know better."

Boots clattered on the floor, and bright light flooded the crack under the door. "Time's up," barked the major. "Kirby, Benjamin, drop your weapons and get your hands over your head before I count to three, or I'll shoot you where you stand."

"You, half-breed," Kirby rasped. "I'll be back, you hear me? I know where the gold's at, so don't bother getting in our way."

The major spoke again, his tone harsh and strident. "Now, Kirby." Wyatt heard someone kick the front door open followed by the sound of booted footsteps and metallic clinking of weapons.

"There's somebody else hiding in here, too," bellowed Kirby in a hoarse voice, banging on the cellar door so hard it rattled Wyatt's teeth. "And I aim to find out who it is."

"I don't care if it's Crazy Pierre's ghost. All I care about is you and your deadbeat brother. It's three in the doggone morning, and I'm sick of chasing you." Wyatt heard the major cock his revolver. "One. Two."

Kirby's guns clattered as they hit the floor.

The US Army. The national park. Reality seemed to fade, ripple, as Wyatt sank to his knees.

Yellowstone, they called the park—where thunderous falls roared over a yawning chasm of volcanic rock and sulfur steam boiled up from the ground like a watery furnace. Scalding water bubbled and spurted, sometimes hundreds of feet into the air—and shimmering pools of acid carved wildly colored rings and chambers into the rock like glazed Indian pottery.

Jim Bridger and other explorers had written about "petrified birds and trees" and "waterfalls spouting upwards," all stinking of volcanic smoke, but most folks thought they were weaving tall tales. Bridger, however, spoke the truth. Wyatt had seen the geysers himself as a skinny kid, prodded along by an impatient Uncle Hiram who wanted to show him the pits of "fire and brimstone" where he was sure the devil lived. And where "boys who disrespect their elders go, too, when they die," Hiram had added, giving an evil cackle.

Wyatt had stared, horrified, into a shimmering basin of searing water, heat bubbles breaking on its steaming surface—recalling the black-clad street preacher in Cody who'd wept and shouted about hell, hanging graphic paintings of lost souls in a smoke-filled agony that looked an awful lot like Yellowstone.

As the mists on the geyser pit lifted, Wyatt peered deep below the shivering water to an underwater pool of clearest crystalline blue—so blue the color hurt his eyes. Beyond it, streaks of red-gold and green intertwined like strands of multihued cliffs against a cobalt Wyoming sky.

"Uncle Hiram," he'd said, pointing. Breathless. "How could the devil make those colors? They're so beautiful, don't you think?"

Hiram had leaned forward, scrunching his craggy brow. "Dunno,

Wyatt. Mebbe he got bored there in hell. Ain't nothin' to do but burn."

Wyatt said nothing, gazing over the railing and wondering if Uncle Hiram and the street preacher were right, and the devil made it all. Or if both of them were wrong, and by some sort of divine, comic irony, God had made the whole thing.

Wyatt had just turned to follow along the rickety boardwalk when a long snort at the far edge of the wood made him turn his head. And there, not thirty feet away, stood a colossal, full-grown bull bison—chest-deep in the hot springs, steam clouding all around him like heavenly stained glass. Two sharp horns curved toward the sky in reckless splendor.

The biggest animal Wyatt had ever seen. So strong his sinews stood out under his massive brown hide in taut lines, shaggy fur mounting around his enormous head like a king's chain mail battle cloak. Daring anyone to disturb his respite on such a cool morning.

The bison stamped his bushy feet, shaking the water into colored rings, and waded a pace or two deeper. Mockingbirds and meadowlarks parted; aspens cringed. He snorted again and tossed his magnificent head, horns gleaming. Breath misting over the water. Huge and defiant eyes caught Wyatt's in an insolent gaze of absolute fearlessness, should Wyatt dare to challenge his majesty's peace.

Wyatt backed up, white-faced, and scrambled up the boardwalk to call for help.

But no one had noticed the bison. Wyatt stopped, peering over his shoulder. The big beast turned his head away from Wyatt, silent and aloof.

And Wyatt said nothing. Dry-mouthed. Keeping the secret to himself, a fluttering of pressed-down excitements too wonderful to voice.

But as he rounded the forested bend, seeing nothing more of the bison but a cloud of steam through the aspen leaves, Wyatt knew one thing: No devil had made Yellowstone.

It had to be God.

❧

Someone tugged open the cellar door, and Wyatt looked up at Jewel's silhouette against stars in the open roof. Crazy Pierre's dark and ruined house curved around her, silent.

The stench of sour pickles wafted up from the root cellar, and Wyatt thought suddenly of spiders.

"Are you all right?" Jewel knelt down and lit the lantern. The glow warmed her face and cupped hands.

Wyatt tried to raise his head, but it felt heavy.

"Mr. Kelly?" She shook his shoulder. "They're gone. You can come out now." She held up the lantern. "You should have covered me better, you know that? If it were up to you, I'd be dead by now. I think our deal should be more like sixty-forty, not fifty-fifty. But you did keep them out of the cellar. I suppose that counts for something."

Something twinkled over her head, like a spider dangling from a silken thread.

"Did you shoot the buffalo, too?" he murmured, feeling a giddy blackness in his head. "I hope not. It'll take more rounds than you've got in your revolver anyhow."

And Wyatt put his head down on the top step.

Chapter 4

Wyatt flipped the Bible page and fixed his glasses, trying to look calm and nonchalant, as if he didn't care a bit. "So you really think I fainted, Mrs. Moreau?" He watched Uncle Hiram in the rocking chair by the fireplace, dozing. His fingers steepled together and eyes closed.

"You did faint. I didn't know you were so. . .sensitive."

"I'm not sensitive." Wyatt felt heat flare in his cheeks.

"And afraid of spiders."

Wyatt scooted his chair back in a huff, blood pulsing in his face. "That's enough. Read the next Bible story, will you?" He glared over at his uncle again, wondering if he'd been bats to invite Jewel back for tutoring. But he needed to speak to her about the gold—and by George, Wyatt wasn't the sort of fellow to slink around the ranch alone with a young girl—married or not—making the ranch hands whisper.

Jewel looked up at him with a slight smile. "It's all right, you know that?"

"What's all right?" Wyatt's brow still made two angry lines.

"To be afraid of things. To be. . .well, just like you are. There's nothing wrong with that."

Wyatt bristled, turning the pages of the Bible faster than necessary. He scrubbed a fist along his cheek, scruffy with patchy red, and hoped he could hide the blush. "Are you going to read or not?" he asked crossly.

Her gaze probed him with gentle curiosity before turning to the Bible before her. "'Now faith is the substance of things hoped for, the evidence of things not seen,'" Jewel read aloud over Hiram's snores, her words clear and beautifully strong. "'Through faith we understand that the worlds were framed by the word of God, so that things which are seen were not made of things which do appear.'"

"Does that make sense to you?" Wyatt stifled a yawn.

"Not really." Jewel blinked at the lines of type, following them with her finger. "Do you have faith, Mr. Kelly?"

"In what?"

"In God. In the truth of the Bible."

"I. . .I don't know." Wyatt squirmed uncomfortably. "Faith in any-thing seems a little impossible to me. Although I'm always interested in the truth."

"I know you are."

"You. . .what?" Wyatt scratched his red hair uncomfortably.

"I can tell you're a man who seeks the truth." Jewel leaned back and regarded him coolly. "Of course, I could be mistaken. But people do say you keep your word."

Wyatt lifted an eyebrow. "I'm not sure anybody around here has a good word to say about me."

"You're quite mistaken, Mr. Kelly." Jewel leaned forward boldly. "You want to hear truth? You could do so much more with yourself if you stopped trying to be someone you're not."

"Pardon?" Wyatt's jaw slipped.

"You've got a good head on your shoulders and your own good gifts and strengths. You don't need your uncle's approval or anyone else's."

Wyatt stared, sputtering for words. "How dare you speak that way about my uncle," he managed, his heart beating fast in his chest. "He's your superior. Your boss. He hired you."

"I never said not to respect your uncle." Jewel raised her voice slightly. "He's a good man, Mr. Kelly, and he deserves your respect—and mine. He's raised you and looked after you his whole life. But he doesn't own your future, and you certainly owe it to yourself to discover what you can really accomplish if you stop comparing yourself to someone else."

"Are you crazy?" Wyatt bristled. "I don't compare myself to anybody!"

"Yes you do. All the time."

"Who?" He scooted his chair forward, making an ugly rasping sound. Uncle Hiram stirred, his snores sputtering.

Jewel folded her hands and glanced up at the faded tintype photograph of Amos Kelly on the mantel. "You know who," she whispered.

Wyatt abruptly got up from the table and fidgeted with something on the shelf, trying to straighten the plates with quivery hands until he knocked them together. When he sat down again, he polished his glasses a long time without speaking and then growled, "You sure do speak your mind," and stuck his glasses on his face at a twisted angle.

"So should you."

"You're wrong about all of it, you know that?" Heat climbed Wyatt's neck. "Completely wrong."

"No I'm not."

"That's enough!" Wyatt shut the Bible and pushed it to the side of the table, his fingertips shaking with anger. "Look. If you want to talk about the gold, then talk. Otherwise we're done here tonight. Got it?"

"Fine." Jewel met his eyes without flinching. "Go ahead. You start."

Wyatt shuffled his feet irritably under the table, glancing over at Uncle Hiram's sleeping figure. "All right then. What do you think of the contents of the box?" He dropped his voice to a near whisper. "Do you think Crazy Pierre really buried it, or did someone else take what he'd originally left and replace it with something else?"

"You said you saw him bury it."

"I did, but that was years ago. Somebody might have dug it up since then." Wyatt rubbed his forehead with his fist, letting his temper cool down. And keeping his father's photograph out of his line of vision. "If it was Pierre, what was he thinking leaving nothing in that box but a rusted old set of spurs?"

"And his letter to my husband doesn't help much: '*Le trône de solitude dans la lumière de la lune.*'" Perfectly accented words rolled off her tongue like kisses. "'Throne of solitude in the light of the moon,'" she translated. "But it makes no sense to me. Pierre said something about looking under the whiskey jug if my husband was too dense to figure it out."

"Under the whiskey jug." Wyatt rested his chin in his hand. "That's pretty cryptic."

"Not only that, but Pierre wrote that letter over four years ago. Even if he left a specific whiskey jug, maybe down in the root cellar, it would almost certainly be gone by now."

"So what next? I don't get the spurs or the letter. A throne is where a king sits. Something royal? Expensive?" He raised his palms in frustration. "Or something up in the sky, like. . .like a constellation. Is that what he meant by solitude and the moon?"

"Maybe something related to a horse, then, because of the spurs?" Jewel played with the Bible page.

"Is there some. . .horse-shaped constellation?"

"What? No." Jewel stopped another laugh with her palm, and Wyatt glared.

"I'm just trying things, you know," he grumbled. "You could at least be civil."

"Wait a moment." Her smile faded. "Pegasus. The winged horse."

"Why, you're right." Wyatt ran a hand over his jaw in surprise, thinking. "No, *I'm* right. The big square in the winter sky."

"Could the big square be a box? Like the box we found?" Jewel gasped. "And one other thing. A horseshoe could look like a moon. A crescent moon."

Wyatt studied her briefly, the candle flickering between them. A bead of wax slipped slowly down, melting into a molten ivory pool.

Jewel actually hadn't shown him the letter. Who knew if she'd told the whole truth—or even part of it? "Is there anything else in the letter, Mrs. Moreau?" he asked carefully. "Anything at all?"

Jewel didn't answer, twisting the wedding band on her finger.

Wyatt crossed his arms. "You're keeping something from me, aren't you?"

"Should I?" She eyed him with a suspicious look. "If I tell you everything up front, you could figure it out and take the entire stash yourself."

"Me?" Wyatt pointed to his chest, openmouthed. "I'd never do that."

"How can I believe you?" Jewel held his gaze. "No shrewd treasure hunter shows the landowner the full map before she asks permission to dig." The candle flame flickered from her breath.

Wyatt crossed his arms over his chest, narrowing his eyes. "You promised me fifty-fifty. That was the deal. And that means you tell me everything." He raised an eyebrow. "Partner."

"How do I know you've told *me* everything? Prove it, Mr. Kelly."

"I gave you my word, and that should be enough." He leaned across the Bible. "You admitted yourself that I'm a man of my word."

They regarded each other across the table, and neither spoke. A log snapped in the fire, sending up showering sparks. Outside the house, the wind rattled a loose shutter, which banged and groaned.

"So long as you doubt me, how can I trust you with any evidence I find? Or my ideas, or. . .or anything?" Wyatt banged a fist in his palm for emphasis. "Fact is, I don't even know who you are. What's to ensure me you won't take what I say and run off with the treasure yourself?"

"Nothing. Do you trust me?"

Wyatt studied her, his jaw tight. "Maybe. Maybe not."

"So you don't know for sure."

He picked at his nails in the lamplight. "I'd like to," he said finally, lacing his calloused, freckled fingers together. "But how do I know if you trust me? I could ask you the same question."

"Neither of us can know anything for sure." Jewel reached across the table and touched the corner of the Bible, nearly brushing Wyatt's hand. "But I'm learning a bit about faith from this book—and faith never asks me to believe foolishly or throw all my caution to the wind without counting the consequences."

Wyatt quickly put his hands in his lap. "Why, you don't mean to tell me you believe what's in here, do you?" Guilt crept up his spine like a spider skulking in Crazy Pierre's root cellar.

"Maybe." Candlelight flickered on Jewel's face, more earnest than Wyatt had ever seen her. Eyes clear and dark like a winter sky, sparkling with starlight. He looked away, pretending to study a knot in the pine-log wall.

"You think faith never asks you to believe foolishly? Look at Abraham." He flipped the Bible back to Genesis. "God told him to move to a new land—a land He hadn't even shown him—and ol' Abe packed up without a second thought. If that's faith, then forget it. It's not for me."

"No. You're missing it." Jewel pushed the Bible closer to Wyatt, and her voice took on a reverent tone, almost husky—like the one she used when training horses in her native Arapaho. "God moved with Abraham one step at a time, never asking more than His just due. You're right that God told him to move to a new land—but when he did, God blessed him. God promised him a son, and Abraham believed and waited years until it happened." Jewel smoothed the page with her finger. "God didn't throw everything at him all at once. He allowed Abraham to learn who He was, little by little, so that Abraham could make the hard decisions in the end."

"Huh." Wyatt scratched his head.

"I admire that. It took great courage on Abraham's part to believe, but also on God's—to wait and patiently reveal His character over time."

Wyatt massaged his temples, feeling like he'd just stepped in a noose. "You said you were Hagar," he said, switching subjects slightly. "How am I supposed to know that whole story isn't a lie? I don't know if I can trust you to tell the truth. About that or anything else."

"Maybe you can't." She arched a dark eyebrow. "But you can do what Abraham did."

"What, pack up and move?" Wyatt felt his patience wearing through, like a threadbare patch in his overalls.

"No. Wait and watch my character. Then you'll know whether or not you can trust me."

Wyatt leaned his elbows on the table and shook his head. "You're a Christian, aren't you?" His lip turned up slightly. "You've been pretending the whole time, just like you did with English. Why, I bet you know this whole book inside and out. Maybe you're even a missionary." He set his jaw. "Am I right?"

"What? I'm not a Christian." Jewel folded her arms. "I'm not anything. I don't know what I believe." Her eyes seemed, for a moment, sadly empty. She looked away, firelight flickering on the lines of her face. "I don't follow the gods of the Arapaho anymore. I fasted every year during the Sun Dance, and all my life I prayed to the Creator of the Arapaho who speaks through eagles. But I felt nothing. Heard nothing. Almost as if I'd died and my spirit ceased to exist."

Tears shimmered briefly in Jewel's eyes, and she blinked them back, keeping a stoic face. "When I heard the priest at the mission school speak about Jesus, the ice in my heart began to melt. And I longed to read the Bible. To soak up the stories and learn about the God who spoke not through eagles but through people, through His Son Jesus—and from His book."

Her eyelashes trembled closed. "But as soon as I learned to read, my father sold me to my husband, who neither approved of women reading nor listened when I asked for a Bible." She rubbed at a scratch on the wooden table with slender fingers. "I asked God, if He existed, to let me hear His Word for myself and see if it was true."

She looked up briefly. "And then you asked me to study English. With this." Jewel passed her hand over the pages of the Bible.

Wyatt realized he was gaping and closed his mouth.

And you only offered to teach her because of the gold. Shame on you. Wyatt shifted uncomfortably in his chair, guilt weighing so heavily on his heart that he could hardly breathe. He stared down at the slats in the wooden table until colored lines glowed behind his eyes.

The wind rattled the window shutter again, and Jewel jumped.

For the life of him, Wyatt couldn't think of a single word to say about the Bible. So he simply closed it and pushed it to the side, trying to bring his mind back to the gold. "Did the letter say anything else you feel comfortable telling me?" he asked in a gentler tone.

"It didn't say much at all, Mr. Kelly. It was a short letter. Just the key and the note, and my husband thought it funny."

"So your husband seemed to understand the letter?"

"Not at first. But after a day or two he picked up the letter and read it again, and he laughed."

"Wait a second." Wyatt looked up suddenly. "Why didn't your husband go after the gold then, if he knew Crazy Pierre died? He had the clues, and he figured out where Pierre hid the gold."

Jewel scooted back in her chair, pressing her lips together. She didn't reply.

Something awful thumped in Wyatt's chest, like the Cheyenne war drums on the field where his father died.

"Mrs. Moreau?" Wyatt leaned forward. "Your husband. Why didn't he go after the gold? And where is he? Why do you never speak of him?"

The clock on the mantle struck, and Jewel flinched. Her fingers twisted together, shaking like a leaf in the winter wind. "It's late, Mr. Kelly." She abruptly rose to her feet, sweeping her long skirts from under the table. "I think I've had enough studying for the evening, if you don't mind. Good night."

"Wait." Wyatt scraped his chair back. He crossed the room in fast strides and stood with his back to the door, throwing his arm over the latch.

"Let me leave, please," said Jewel in cold irritation, attempting to duck around him. "I've told you everything you need to know." She reached defiantly over his arm to rattle the latch.

"Why won't you tell me?" Wyatt kept his hand over the latch. "You've already told me your real name and the details about the letter. Why do you need to keep hiding?"

"I thought you said you knew everything about my past." She raised her face to his boldly, but her cheeks had paled. "You're the expert, right?"

Wyatt's heart quivered in his chest, trying to remember what exactly he'd said to call her bluff. Something about the magistrate—and something about her sordid past. "I know enough. But I'd rather hear the truth from you—and not from everybody else in town."

Jewel fingered the latch but didn't move to open the door, even when Wyatt finally stepped aside. "So they're talking about me here, too?"

"A little." Wyatt cleared his throat. "Yes." He crossed his arms over his chest.

"Do you believe them?"

He scuffed his boots on the pine floor, listening to Uncle Hiram snore in his chair. Wind whistled around the sides of the log house, rustling grasses.

"I see." A line in Jewel's slender neck bobbed as she swallowed. "So you do believe them. Your actions show it."

"My actions show no such thing. I want the truth, and that's all."

"Why? Why do you want to know about my husband so badly?" Jewel turned to him, so close he could see the outline of each dark eyelash. "His whereabouts have nothing whatsoever to do with the gold."

"Because I won't partner with you if you're doing dirty work for someone else. And that's final."

Jewel's eyes widened in what looked like surprise—and perhaps even relief. "I'm not blackmailing anyone, or stealing, if that's what you're suggesting." She swept an arm toward Wyatt. "How do I know about you? How do I know you're honest and not working against the law yourself?"

"Because I've got nothing to hide." Wyatt spoke gently. "You talked about character earlier, Mrs. Moreau. Ask anyone about me and they'll tell you everything. No secrets."

Dark strands of hair had come loose from Jewel's braid, falling in soft lines around her ears, and he longed to brush them back from her smooth forehead. But he stuffed his hands in his pockets instead, hoping the rush of color stayed out of his face.

"Then why do you care where my husband is? What business is it of yours anyway?" Jewel's cheeks glowed an unusual pallid pink, and for a second she looked small and vulnerable there against the rough pine door. Clad in the blue-and-white cottons of a people not entirely her own and gossiped about by townsfolk she'd never met.

"Listen to me, miss. If I'm going to work with a criminal, I need to hear your side before I make up my mind." Wyatt leaned forward.

"So you can turn me in?" Something in the way she said it held a warning. A fearful quiver but with a dagger beneath.

Wyatt's heart pounded in his throat, and he breathed through his nose, trying to keep calm. Thinking through his words. "I don't want to." He spoke gently, meeting her eyes. "I truly don't."

He reached out and put a hand on her arm, trying to still the frightened look in her eyes. "Tell me. Where is your husband? You wear his ring." He gestured to her plain silver band. "Where is he, then?"

Jewel glanced down at his pale hand on her arm, but she did not pull away. "Will you believe me if I tell you the truth?"

Wyatt licked his lips nervously and then nodded.

"Fine then." Jewel closed her eyes. "My husband is dead."

Chapter 5

Wyatt lay uneasily in his bed, unable to sleep. Every whistle of wind around the corner of the house haunted him, and the steady creaking of the pine floor made him jump. All his rusty red hairs standing on end.

If Jewel had killed her husband—a sinister guess when he put the ugly pieces together—then might she not just as easily kill him, too? A business partner with fifty percent of the goods she'd like to have all for herself?

She'd already gotten the key from him. What purpose could he possibly serve her now?

Wyatt fingered his Colt revolver under his pillow and wondered, with a tight pinch of his stomach, if he should warn Uncle Hiram—and maybe get Jewel off the ranch before she struck again. Not long ago a disgruntled cattle driver in Buffalo had set fire to an entire ranch, taking the lives of six ranch hands and nearly killing the ranch owner himself.

Is that why Jewel had taken the job? To seek out all the information she could about Pierre's gold and then get rid of the evidence?

Black widow indeed. Wyatt pulled his revolver from under his pillow and checked the chamber then loaded in an extra round. He put the gun down and flopped back on the bed in misery, staring up at the darkened plank ceiling. He didn't want to think the worst. Not at all. Not about Jewel, with her earnest black eyes and long scar on her forearm.

After all, she'd trusted him with her name—her story. Even the contents of her private letter. Why would she deceive him now?

Or maybe the whole thing was a lie. What if her name was not Collette Moreau after all, and she was merely stringing him along—hook, line, and sinker?

Because goodness knows, he wanted to believe her.

Badly.

So much so that his stomach curled into a quivery knot, and he felt the blood rush up his neck, pulsing in his throat. He saw her standing in Crazy Pierre's root cellar with tears in her eyes, her fingers briefly brushing his as she handed him his glasses. Her dark head bent over the Bible.

She was different, this strong-minded Indian girl, from the giddy, empty-headed females he'd seen in Cody and Deadwood, swilling whiskey and banging on cheap player pianos. Fanning their ample cleavage with feather fans and giggling over ignorant jokes.

"You've got a good head on your shoulders and your own good gifts and strengths," Jewel had said at his Uncle Hiram's kitchen table.

And something deep inside him wanted desperately to believe that, too.

The courthouse in Cody—that's where he needed to go. He'd make up some excuse for Uncle Hiram and leave first thing in the morning. His motives were twofold: First, to request a map of the area from five years ago, when Crazy Pierre would have written the letter. And second, to ask a few questions about a certain Collette Moreau, otherwise known as Jewel.

"Mornin', Clovis. Got any news for me today?" Wyatt tipped his dusty hat and leaned against the counter. A stripe of sunlight glanced off the polished wooden desk, making his sleepy eyes wince. His room at the boardinghouse in Cody had been cold and dirty, and metal bed slats poked him in the spine all night long.

"Well, well, well. Look what the wildcat drug in." Clovis peered at Wyatt through tiny wire spectacles, which reflected the dirty window glass and city street lined with hitching posts, empty with late fall. He grinned and leaned over to shake hands. "Wyatt Kelly. Ain't seen you in a while. How's that ranch? And that uncle of yours?"

"Oh, fine. He's thinking about investing in sheep these days."

"Sheep, huh? They're a lotta work, you know. Well, I don't have any news for ya, unless you count the drunkard who got thrown in jail yesterday for walkin' the railroad track." He chuckled together with Wyatt. "What brings you to town?"

"Nothing much." Wyatt rubbed his fingers together to warm them from the cold. "But listen, I need a favor." He glanced over his shoulder and lowered his voice, leaning both elbows on the counter. "I need some maps of the land around, say, East Fork River or thereabouts—on the other side of the Shoshone reservation. Older maps." He scratched his shoulder and stretched. "How far back do you go?"

"Old maps? Why, you ain't prospectin', are ya? Or fightin' with somebody over boundary lines?"

"Don't be silly." Wyatt straightened his hat and tried to produce a posture of ease, slouching against the counter. "I'm just looking for a couple of places is all."

"Well, now, let me take a look. I'll be just a minute." Clovis adjusted his glasses and disappeared into a storage room, rummaging and pulling out boxes, and finally returned with his arms full of stuff.

"Looky here." He dropped some dusty papers on the counter. "See if this is what you want." He smoothed a paper with wrinkled hands. "Here's a copy of the map drawn by the Hayden Geological Survey came through the area back in 1871. All the rivers and geological features and such, and some sketches, too, if you'd like to see them."

1871. Back when Crazy Pierre was still digging holes like a mole. Wyatt straightened his glasses to see better.

"And here's a later map of the Yellowstone River area back in '81. East of here a bit. Why, close to your uncle's ranch, probably." Clovis carefully handed him a print. "Lotta details and such. The railroad lines and some businesses. Even some private property."

"Let me take a look at that." Wyatt pulled the paper closer.

He made space at the counter for an elderly man in a suit and studied the map, his eyes running over the lines and contours. Following the names with his finger. He read the tiny type from top to bottom and back up again—pausing only at a little place about ten miles from Pierre's cabin, up in the mountains. About twenty miles from Yellowstone, up against a mountain ridge.

"Clovis," Wyatt pointed to a square on the map as Clovis shuffled under the counter, "what's this place here?"

"That?" He squinted then took his glasses off and stuck his face closer. "Why, that's old Crescent Ranch."

Wyatt sucked in a sharp breath, feeling his pulse pick up. "I remember that place. They had an inn, didn't they? A boardinghouse or something?"

"Sure they did." Clovis ran a hand over his balding head, his hairs grown as long as possible and combed over with some kind of waxy pomade. "Forgot what it was called now. Water in the well dried up and had to close everything up. Never rebuilt."

The room seemed to shimmer suddenly as if through heat waves. "The inn had a big chair in the entranceway, didn't it? Made of deer antlers or something?"

"Moose." The white-haired man in the suit leaned toward Wyatt at the counter. "Antlers from a prize moose, and the rest elk."

"You remember it." Wyatt faced him.

"Sure I do." The man's eyes were nearly opaque, like pale blue ice. He turned a knobby cane as he spoke. "That chair stood more than six feet tall—and my father killed the prize moose himself. Nobody's ever seen a bigger moose in these parts."

"Do you remember the name of the inn?" Wyatt held his breath.

"Of course. The Monarch Inn. After the butterfly." The man blinked, and those pale blue eyes seemed to drift away. "I was a boy when they built it."

Monarch. Throne. Crescent. Wyatt held on to the counter with shaky hands. "Do you know what's there now—in the place where the inn used to be?"

"What do you mean?" The man's face twisted in a sort of confusion. "There's nothing there. The whole place was boarded up like a ghost town. Been empty for years."

"Anything else, Wyatt?" Clovis carefully stacked the maps together.

"Just one thing." He tugged at his suspenders uncomfortably, not sure how much to say. "You ever hear about a fellow named Moreau? From Idaho?"

"Moreau. Moreau." Clovis passed a hand over his thin scalp, patting his long hairs into place. "French fellow, ain't he?"

"That's the one."

"A fur trapper, if I remember correctly. Mink and ermine. Made a good living up there with his kinfolk."

Wyatt turned toward the window as Clovis talked, pretending to be absorbed in a man hitching up a cart along the street. Light snow blew in thin gusts like goose down, floating and whirling.

Clovis kneaded his chin with his knuckles as he thought. "Augustin Moreau, you mean? If that's the man, sure. I've heard some talk about him."

"What's the word on him?"

"Word? He's been dead for three years."

Wyatt's heart seized up, and he felt as if the blood had stopped pumping. Turning his fingers to ice. "What, was he shot?"

"No. Bludgeoned with a metal stovepipe on Thanksgiving Day." Clovis stuck his head closer. "Funny you should ask because just the other day the sheriff asked if any of us had seen an Indian girl in town. An Arapaho, I think. A young girl, he said, and pretty—looking for work. Said they were searching for her back in Idaho, and a few folks thought they might've seen her in these parts."

"Arapaho are good-lookin' people." A thin cowboy with cold-red cheeks and tawny, overgrown whiskers looked up from the doorway. "Tall and stately, with the nicest features you ever saw. They say the Ute Indians like to steal Arapaho wives."

Wyatt swiveled his head back and forth between the cowboy and Clovis, his mind an incredulous blur. "Why are they looking for the girl?" His heart beat so loudly he could hardly hear. "What's she done?"

"There's a bounty on her head." Clovis put the stack of papers back in a drawer and closed it. "They say she killed her husband."

Chapter 6

Wyatt stalked through the stable in a fury. His hair hung a filthy red under his battered hat, like muddy river clay—messy with wood splinters and sweat and soil. "I give up, Mrs. Moreau. I mean Miss Moreau. Whoever you are." He crossed his arms stiffly, furious breaths heaving in his chest. "There's no gold."

"Excuse me?" Jewel looked up from raking through mounds of dirty hay, her fingers pink from cold.

"Either somebody's taken it already, or Crazy Pierre's a liar." He heaved a ragged sigh of frustration. "Or maybe both."

"No, both is impossible." Jewel set the rake against a gate and offered Wyatt a stiffly dried cloth she'd hung after washing. "If he's a liar, then there's no way someone could—"

"You know what I mean." Wyatt scowled. "I'm in no mood for parsing verbs now, if you don't mind."

One of the young stable hands paused, feed bucket in hand, and Wyatt glared at him until he scampered out of sight. Then he took the cloth and sponged his dirty face, borrowing a bit of water from the water trough to moisten the cloth and scrub his filthy boots.

"Well." Jewel wiped her hands and leaned the rake against the log wall. "It sounds like you've made up your mind." Her breath misted like a fine veil, dissipating slowly.

"Look. I'm tired of these games." Wyatt snatched his hat and banged it against his boot to knock off the dirt. "I've been digging all day long, two days straight, and nothing." He slapped the hat back on his head. "Show me the letter now, or I'm calling it quits."

"You've been digging?" Jewel put her hands on her hips, and her cheeks flushed. "You didn't tell me."

"You haven't showed me the letter yet!" Wyatt flung out his arms.

"You should have told me where you thought the gold was, and we could have discussed it together. But you disappeared for five days

53

without telling anybody where you'd gone, and what was I supposed to think?" A flicker of hurt flashed across her face, but she covered it quickly, picking up the rake again and pulling it across the stable floor in staccato strokes.

"Look." Wyatt put both hands up, trying not to look at her. Those flushed cheeks and red-and-blue beaded earrings glittering under her dark hair. "I didn't intend to do any searches without you, all right? It just happened. I was in the right place at the right time, and what was I supposed to do?" A vein in his neck pulsed. "Ride all the way back here to the ranch and ask your permission?"

"So. . .it just 'happened.'" Jewel kept her back turned. "I'm not sure how that's supposed to work. Have you ever heard of one partner digging without the other?"

"Jewel. Listen." Wyatt strode across the stable and grabbed her elbow. "Miss Jewel," he faltered, reddening and dropping her arm. Horrified at his own boldness. "Ma'am. I apologize." He ducked his head and scrubbed his dirty forehead with the palm of his hand, trying to gather his words and his sense. "I heard a few things in Cody, and I thought I'd check 'em out. The old Monarch Inn on the Crescent Ranch? Ever heard of it?"

"No." Jewel smoothed her sleeve where he'd touched her and continued raking.

"It had a big chair that locals called the 'Throne.' But there's nothing there. Absolutely nothing." He looked out over the stable, shaking with exhaustion and frustration. "I wasted my time."

"Look here, Mr. Kelly." Jewel advanced toward him, pointing her finger straight at his chest with such spunk that he involuntarily put his hands up. "You shouldn't have done anything without telling me first. I think I know where the gold is, and you didn't bother to ask."

"You know?" Wyatt stumbled backward, knocking his hat sideways against a plank.

"I thought of it after you left, and it makes perfect sense. But you haven't told me why you went to Cody."

He straightened his hat and kept his eyes averted. "On business."

"Whose business?"

"Personal business."

"Fine. Don't tell me." She folded her arms. "But don't expect any clues from me either, if you're not willing to tell me everything, fifty-fifty. You can figure out where the gold is on your own. But I think I know."

She turned to walk away, and Wyatt just stood there, hands on his hips. "They're looking for you, you know," he called after her. "I thought you'd appreciate it if I told you."

"I beg your pardon?" Jewel whirled around.

"In Cody." Wyatt dropped his voice and took a step closer. "You know why."

Jewel's face went pale, and she clapped a hand over her mouth. "You told them, didn't you?" she whispered. "You told them I'm staying here."

"I didn't tell them anything." Wyatt kicked the mud off his spurs against the hard floor, still angry.

Jewel blinked as if confused and drew back, nearly dropping the rake. She lunged for it, catching the handle before it clattered to the floor. "You. . . mean you didn't tell them I'm here?"

"Of course I didn't." Wyatt tossed the cloth over a wooden gate. "What was I supposed to say? 'The girl you say killed her husband is working at my uncle's ranch—come and get her'?"

"They'd drag me out of my bed."

"Doggone right they would." Wyatt took a step closer, his hands clenching. "And I'll be honest. I don't know what to think of you." He pointed a shaking finger at her, hoping the ache didn't show too much in his eyes. "But let's get one thing straight. You stay away from my uncle, hear me? If anything happens to him, so help me, I'll call the local sheriff and have you dragged off to the gallows."

"I'd never touch your uncle." Jewel spoke so softly Wyatt could barely hear.

Wyatt sized her up, arms crossed. A lump swelled in his throat so tightly he had to breathe deeply through his nose.

"Don't you think I would have done something already if I'd planned to? I've been here more than two years." Her eyes filled suddenly, and she looked down at the straw-covered floor, kicking at it with a high-buttoned boot. "And I didn't kill my husband. It's a lie."

Wyatt didn't answer. He stuck his hands in his pocket and looked away, clenching a muscle in his jaw.

"You didn't turn me in." Jewel raised her head, her expression changed to one of gratitude, almost humility. "That speaks more of your belief in me than anything you can say."

"I haven't said anything," Wyatt snapped, kicking a bit of straw with his boot. "I just want the truth, and that's it."

Jewel studied him a moment, not speaking. A gust of wind blew snow flurries through an open window in the stable, and she shivered.

"It's in the outhouse."

"The outhouse? What's in the outhouse—the truth?" He scrunched up his forehead. "What in the Sam Hill are you talking about?"

Jewel glared, shushing him fiercely with a finger to her lips. "Crazy Pierre's outhouse," she whispered. "I think I've figured out the riddle."

Wyatt threw his arms up in disgust, ready to turn and stomp away, when the words fell across his memory like snowflakes: *"Throne of solitude in the light of the moon."*

Moon. Crescent. *Outhouses sometimes have a crescent moon carved in the door.*

"Of all the. . ." Wyatt's face bleached, and he snatched off his hat and whacked a post with it, not sure whether to laugh or kick something. Two horses backed and reared in indignation, and Jewel scolded him, rushing to calm the horses.

"You're telling me ol' Crazy Pierre left his gold in a doggone privy?" Wyatt stalked closer.

"Throne of solitude." Jewel shrugged with a smile. "I guess they don't call him crazy for no reason."

Wyatt considered this a second, letting out a snort of laughter. "He was eccentric all right. A strange fellow. But there's no way under the sun I'm digging into somebody's privy—I don't care how long he's been dead."

"Not under, over." Jewel spoke in hushed tones. "The rest of the letter said this: *'Deux pieds en bas et lèvent les yeux.'* 'Two feet down, and look up.' Do you understand?"

"Exactly. Two feet down. I already told you, I'm not digging up a john. Got it?"

"No, no, no!" Jewel shook her head furiously. "You're not listening. Two feet down. You're thinking measurements. Crazy Pierre was thinking *feet*." She lifted the hem of her skirt to show her boots. "These." She pointed. "In an outhouse, you put two feet on the floor."

"And then 'look up.'" Wyatt's voice dripped wonder. "So. . .up in the rafters?" He felt his eyebrows nearly touch his hair. "You think it might still be there?"

"I don't know. But I'd like to find out."

Wyatt faced her, his breath huffing as his mind whirled through the possibilities. Ticking off all the crazy clues one by ridiculous one.

"The spurs in the wooden box," he said hoarsely, resting a hand on his forehead. "They had crescent moons."

"Like an outhouse door." Jewel stood so still that Wyatt could see a stray snowflake catch in her hair as it blew through a crack in the log walls—a tiny white sparkle among gleaming black, like a lone star. He felt the sudden urge to reach out and brush it away, but instead he stuffed his hands in his jacket pockets.

"Let's go then." Wyatt reached over the wooden post and patted Samson's shiny neck.

"Now?"

"I'll tell my uncle you're indisposed for the evening." Wyatt straightened his hat. "First one to Pierre's gets dibs."

Jewel's eyes glowed. "I'll beat you there."

Chapter 7

Light snow whirled around Wyatt as he scrambled off his horse. He threw a wool blanket over Samson's back and gathered up his lantern, rifle, and shovels. A brooding sky hung in blue-gray layers over the pines, like translucent paper.

"Come on." Wyatt looked over his shoulder, the cold wind nearly blowing his hat off. "I don't like the way these clouds are rolling in. Looks like a snowstorm."

"If the gold is up in the rafters, it shouldn't take long." Jewel slid off her sleek Indian pony's back, her long black hair blowing. She'd tied it back with a simple velvet ribbon; Wyatt was amazed at its length and thickness. The women in Cody would pay big bucks for a wig made of hair like Jewel's.

"But do you really think an old outhouse could support the weight of, say, a hundred pounds of gold?" Wyatt finished tying Samson and shouldered his things, forcing his eyes away from Jewel and into the gray distance past Pierre's house. "And if there's as much gold as he said, it would weigh a lot more than that."

"Depends on the outhouse, I suppose." Jewel ducked her head into the wind and walked side by side with Wyatt. "The structure and the design."

Wyatt shook snowflakes off his glasses and snorted. "If it's really there, old Pierre was crazier than I give him credit for. Or smarter. Nobody in their right mind would hide gold in a privy—and nobody in their right mind would look for it."

They rounded the corner of the old cabin, and the front door creaked in the wind, swinging slightly open. Wyatt hushed, listening for footsteps or voices. "That old place gives me the creeps," he whispered, moving closer to Jewel. "I guess we are really crazy to do this."

"Maybe so." Jewel set her lips in a determined slant. "But I'm not giving up now—maybe never. I need to find this gold. I have to. It's more important than you can possibly imagine."

Wyatt looked sideways at her, lifting a thick spruce branch for her to walk past. His shovels and rifle clinked together, hollow and metallic.

"What's so important?" he asked. "Why do you want the gold so badly?"

Jewel hesitated a moment, her eyes briefly meeting his. "I need it to start over." She rubbed her nose, which had reddened in the cold. "Nothing more."

"Start over?"

"You know what they say about me. That I killed my husband. But I didn't. I give you my word." Her eyes glittered, but Wyatt couldn't tell if it was tears or wind that made them fill.

"Did you have any reason to want to kill him?"

"Many." Branches snapped under Jewel's boots.

Wyatt drew back in surprise but said nothing. The wind rattled bare tree branches together like skeleton fingers, and Jewel lifted her long skirts to step over a fallen limb.

"But I didn't kill him. His death was mysterious all right—but I didn't do it. Although I think I've figured out who did."

"Who?"

"Someone who wanted the letter."

A shiver of cold fear tingled Wyatt's spine. "But you've got the letter. Do you mean somebody might be looking for you now?"

"Possibly. My husband wasn't exactly tight-lipped about secrets," she said, passing the lantern to her other hand and accepting Wyatt's arm to pass through a thicket of briers. "A little whiskey, a hand or two of cards, and he couldn't keep a secret to save his life. He spoke about the letter a week before he died, and that same week some men ransacked our house—apparently looking for the letter."

"So you think one of them did it?"

"Of course. It's pretty obvious to me, but no one would listen." Jewel shrugged. "His whole clan had always disliked and distrusted me for being *Indien d'Arapaho,* as if that made me less than human. So when he died, everyone blamed me without a second thought."

Wyatt paused and surveyed the forested stretch outside Crazy Pierre's homestead, scanning the trees for anything resembling an outhouse. His breath fogged and faded like the thin hope of comfort Jewel must have felt back in Idaho among the trappers.

"Why do you still wear his ring then?"

She shot him a dark look. "I assure you, Mr. Kelly, that a woman alone in this part of the country is far safer if she wears a ring than if she doesn't. I'm surprised you didn't think of that yourself."

"Sorry." Wyatt scratched his neck, ashamed. Until now he'd thought of Jewel mainly in labels: Indian. Female. Hired hand.

But under it all, she was painfully vulnerable. Just like himself, but perhaps more so.

"Did. . .did you love him?" Wyatt asked in a near whisper, barely managing to speak the words. He kept his burning face turned toward the cabin, shivering under his thick leather coat.

"I beg your pardon?" Jewel twisted around to see him.

He shouldered his shovels and rifle uncomfortably, and everything clattered together. "I'm sorry." He felt heat flood his face in racing pulses. "It's none of my business. Forgive me."

Jewel brushed strands of hair from her eyes with her free hand. "Did you ask me if I loved my husband?"

Of all the fool things for me to say. "I truly apologize." Wyatt rubbed his face in his calloused palm, eyes scrunched together in embarrassment. "Forget I said anything, will you?"

"No, I did not love him." Jewel's steady gaze caught his. "Ever."

Wyatt remained as still as a blue spruce, not daring to speak or even to breathe.

"He treated me as nothing but property, Mr. Kelly. I was bought, sold. He wasted our money on whiskey and women, and he beat me. Quite severely at times. Once he might have killed me if I hadn't defended myself with a pitchfork." She ran her hand over her forearm—the one where Wyatt had seen the long scar.

In a blinding second Wyatt remembered Jewel in Crazy Pierre's cabin, raising the blunt end of the pistol stock to swing at Kirby Crowder with surprising force and agility. *But she did not pull the trigger.*

"Why do you ask?" Her cheeks were red with cold.

"Huh?" Wyatt turned, too shy to look at her. "Why do I ask what?"

"If I loved my husband." Jewel turned her eyes on him, their darkness keen and penetrating.

Wyatt paused a moment, his chest rising and falling under his coat with his breath. Afraid to speak, to ruin the hush. "Did I ask that?" he stammered, painfully aware of what a short distance separated them. A foot? Six inches? Jewel's breath misted, dissolving into thin air near his cheek.

"You did."

Wyatt looked down at his boots in reddened humiliation, twisting the lantern handle and trying to come up with a reason that made any sense at all. "I. . .I have no idea."

"No one's ever asked me that before," Jewel whispered. "Thank you."

Then she reached out boldly and gave his cold hand a gentle squeeze.

⁓⊛⁓

"Over there." Jewel pointed as they tromped through fallen pine branches and autumn-thin leaves. Snow gathered in white patches in the crooks of tree trunks.

"What's over there?" Wyatt had to force his attention away from her, willing the wild hammering of his heart to slow down. Straightening his knocking knees.

"The outhouse, Mr. Kelly."

He could still feel the fleeting warmth of her fingers against his. "Oh, that." Wyatt swallowed and crossed his arms, trying to feign nonchalance. "You're right. It sure looks like a privy to me."

Jewel strained on tiptoe to see better. Not that she was short. In fact, she came all the way up to Wyatt's chin—not a mean feat for a girl. The Arapaho were tall and stately, great warriors, and Jewel must have come from hardy stock.

"The outhouse has a stone base, Mr. Kelly. Will you look at that." She caught her breath. "And a crescent moon carved in the door."

"By gravy." Wyatt stroked his jaw. "That stone base might make it sturdy enough to hold a stash of gold, if the rafters are built sturdy. And it's solid pine log. You just might be right." Wyatt looked over at her. "You're not too squeamish to peek inside a crazy old man's latrine?"

"As I recall, I wasn't the one scared of spiders."

Wyatt scowled and pretended not to hear.

The outhouse stood in a thin stand of trees, not far from an old barn. It was a simple structure, with log walls and a peaked roof. A few shingles had come off over the years, but otherwise the outhouse probably looked much the same as when Crazy Pierre spent his days digging up the forest.

Snow blew in fast flakes as Wyatt attempted to pry the outhouse door open, tugging on the swollen wood. Jewel put down her lantern and pistol and helped Wyatt pull, and the bottom of the door creaked open, scraping across soil. Wyatt stuck his boot inside the crack and leaned against the door, easing it wider for her to duck inside.

"Do you see anything?" Wyatt struck a match and lit the lantern wick. He pushed the door wider with his shoulder and held up the lantern, straining for a glimpse of the rafters over Jewel's head. "It's boarded over." Wyatt's heart leaped. "And the board's buckling in the middle. Can you see that?"

"Look at the wood he used." Jewel leaned her hand on Wyatt's shoulder and stepped up on the wooden seating platform, avoiding the cavernous dark hole. "It's a different wood type than both the structure and the door. Here." She reached for the lantern and shined it on the joint between the wall and the ceiling. "It looks like heavy barn board."

"And nailed up in a hurry. It's a bit crooked, unlike the rest of the structure." Wyatt felt around over his head.

"See the nails over there? They're starting to pull out."

"Braces." Wyatt's voice came out in a hoarse whisper. "By George. He put braces and trusses in here."

Jewel shivered, and her teeth chattered together. "It's got to be the treasure."

"I'll break it open." Wyatt reached for his ax.

"And let it all fall through that open hole?" Jewel gasped, pointing at the shadowy toilet opening in the platform. "If you break the ceiling and rafters open, all the gold will crash down on top of us." She tapped the wooden seating platform with her foot. "You know this thing isn't very sturdy, right? And there's an open pit underneath that's probably been. . . shall we say. . .well used over the years?"

"I get it, I get it!" Wyatt stuck his head through the creaky wooden door and peered up at the roof. "We can hack the roof open, but there's no way I can crawl up there myself. I'll have to boost you up."

"All right." Jewel put her things down and pushed past him. "Hurry though. This snow's coming down hard."

Wyatt bent down and locked his fingers together. He waited for her to step, first one pointy, high-buttoned boot and then the other, and then he boosted her up. Jewel grabbed at the edge, her fingers clawing at shingles, and Wyatt pushed her up to the roof.

Jewel steadied herself on the rough shingled peak, her wool skirts fluttering in the wind, and reached for the ax. She brought it down hard at an angle, turning her face as splinters flew from the boards and shingles. Then again. Two brittle shingles cracked and tumbled off in pieces.

"That's it—keep going!" Wyatt shielded his eyes as heavy white flakes melted and beaded on his glasses. "Do you see anything yet?"

Jewel braced herself again and swung the sharp ax blade, and Wyatt heard the thump of metal cutting into wood. She hacked a few minutes, splitting open a crack, and then brought the ax down with a mighty whack.

The boards split open, and broken chunks of wood rolled down the shingled roof and into the grass.

Wyatt strained his head excitedly. "What's up there?"

"I don't know." Jewel bent and put her face to the crack and then shook her head. "It's dark, and the snow's coming down too hard. Let me open it up a bit more."

Wyatt watched Jewel's steady brown hands and felt a stab of shame at the way he'd spoken of her, tried to use her. Why, he and his uncle hadn't done much differently than her French trapper husband, who viewed her as property to be beaten.

Jewel's lips moved, her face turned toward him—and Wyatt realized she'd said something.

"Pardon?" He shook the snow from his hat.

"I said there's something here." Jewel's voice was sharp, urgent. Triumphant. "An old burlap sack full, bulging and tied at the top with twine. And. . ." She sucked in a gasp. "Something's glittering through the place where the burlap's worn through."

Chapter 8

Wyatt tried to speak, but his mouth felt dry, like he'd swallowed straw. "You're serious." His hands shook. "You're really serious. What's in the sack?" Wyatt tugged on the side of the outhouse roof as if to pull himself up, desperately wishing he could see.

"It's the gold," Jewel whispered. "Pounds of it. Nuggets of all sizes. I've never seen anything like it."

She reached into the hole in the roof and then reached down toward him with cupped hands. Dribbling a rain of gold nuggets into his outstretched palms.

Wyatt turned the gold over in his fingers, speechless. Snow sifted down on the pile of gleaming nuggets in white streaks, sticking in ornately pronged flakes and then melting into tiny water beads.

"We've. . .we've found it," he whispered. "So Ezra Kind wasn't bluffing about the gold—and the Thoen Stone's real. I can't believe it. I never thought. . ." Wyatt glanced up at Jewel. "You were right about the outhouse thing."

"A wild guess." She tucked her neck and shivered in the wind.

"A good one." Wyatt looked down again at the gold in his hand. Funny thing though—it didn't look much like gold at all. He sifted it in his fingers, watching the light gleam on the dull, brownish edges of mottled nuggets, like dirty cracked corn. The kind he might fling to his uncle's chickens without a second thought.

And to think this yellowish stuff was the metal of kings, of ancient currencies and Egyptian tombs.

He could buy a new suit now—a new team of the best horses—the best oats for Samson—repair the wagon—help Uncle Hiram pay off the rest of his cattle. Start a sheep business. By jingle, he'd run the sheep business! And books—the best books—new ones! He'd have a collection. No, a library!

And the land. . .oh, the land he'd longed for nearly all his life.

Beautiful Cheyenne prairie that had nestled just out of his reach—occupied by the murderers who'd taken his family away from him. Not for sale exactly, no—but for the right price, even the US Cavalry would. . . ahem. . .negotiate.

He'd dreamed of the deed, the feel of the paper in his hands. The persuasive argument in favor of US interests, with all the right words and loopholes. The smirk of satisfaction as the judge signed his name in black ink: *"Land ceded to the United States Government, supervised by Mr. Wyatt E. Kelly."* The bang of a gavel.

He'd have his revenge after all—the last say.

Long-lost wishes and thoughts swelled up in Wyatt's throat in giddy delirium, nearly choking him.

Jewel was straining at something in the hole in the roof, pulling and twisting, and Wyatt barely had time to react when she heaved a heavy sack at him. He threw the handful of nuggets in his coat pocket and grabbed the sack before it bowled him over.

"Watch your aim, will you?" Wyatt grunted as he lowered the hefty sack to the ground. It slid sideways into a fat, lumpy pile, the threadbare patches on the sack nearly ripping open.

"You try balancing on a roof and handling a bag this heavy," Jewel shot back.

"Well, just warn me next time." Wyatt knelt and pulled at the top of the sack. Images spun through his mind: the abandoned inn outside Cody. Gold nuggets dripping through his fingers like yellow sawdust. His patched trousers, and a fat pocket full of heavy nuggets.

Time seemed to stop; the neck of the bag slipped open in a blurry haze.

"You're not going to faint again, are you?"

"What did you say?"

And Wyatt looked up in time to see a black circle opening over his head, swallowing him whole.

⁂

"You're really something," Jewel was saying from the top of the outhouse.

Wyatt looked up from where he leaned against the log side of the outhouse, head bent. One arm against the wall for support.

"What's wrong with you? Have you always been this. . .uh. . .fragile?" It sounded like she was going to say the word *weak* but slipped in a substitute at the last second.

Wyatt bristled. "I'm fine, okay?" He stood up shakily and wiped his face. "Just a little vertigo is all. Why's it such a big deal?"

Jewel scooted down the outhouse roof and dangled off then let herself go. She dropped to the ground next to Wyatt and refolded her wool shawl. "It's not a big deal. It's just. . ." She shrugged and brushed the snow from her hair. "You're different."

"I'm who I am, all right?" Wyatt snapped. "I get overwhelmed by things, I guess. Too much emotion and not enough guts. Is that what you're trying to say?"

"I never said that." Jewel pressed her lips together, and streaks of snow fell past her face like shooting stars. "I like who you are, Mr. Kelly. The most honest man I've ever met." She raised her face boldly to his. "And you've got plenty of guts. We wouldn't be here if it weren't for you."

Wyatt knelt by the sack, not looking up at her. Incredibly thankful the brim of his cowboy hat hid his burning face. "Of course not," he fumbled, trying to pick up a couple of gold nuggets and dropping them clumsily in the grass. "You'd have figured it out already and been halfway back to wherever by now." He looked up at her with a plaintive, hollow gaze. "I guess that's what you're going to do now that you've got the gold, isn't it?"

"Maybe." Jewel knelt next to him and opened the mouth of the sack, sifting her hand through the nuggets.

"I thought so." Wyatt scooped up the scattered nuggets and dropped them lifelessly in the sack. "I guess I always figured you'd go back to your people someday." He swallowed, barely peeking over the brim of his hat to see her. Wishing he had something to offer her—to make her stay.

But she was a rich woman now, and she certainly didn't need him. Hurt seared under his breastbone, startling him.

Jewel didn't answer, turning a golden chunk between her fingers. "I said maybe," she corrected him softly, almost sternly. "But probably not. If you want to know the truth, I've already been back to Nebraska." Jewel dropped her gaze and tied the sack shut. "And it didn't work."

"What do you mean it didn't work?"

"I'm not one of them anymore, if you can understand." Jewel tucked her cold hands inside her shawl and shivered, looking positively frozen. "I lived with the French community in Idaho for years, and I'm not who I was before. I don't understand Arapaho ways like I used to. I walk differently, dress differently, even eat differently now. I've forgotten many of the old ways."

"You could learn again, I guess." Wyatt tugged on the sack of gold, the weight making him stagger off balance. Keeping his face turned away.

"I don't know if I could or if I'd want to." Jewel bent over and helped him catch a bulging corner. "I'm different now, and sometimes there's no going back. They didn't accept me and my new ways, just as they didn't accept my French mother before she died. Only this time I was viewed as a deserter, a sellout. Like an ordinary white woman who left her Indian heritage behind."

"Wait a second." Wyatt grunted, hefting the sack to the other arm. "They sold you in marriage! How can they call you a deserter?"

"Marriages and treaties have been part of our culture for generations. My marriage was no different." Jewel's boots left tracks in the snow beside his. "But they expected something impossible—that I return to them the same way I left, when I was fourteen. It can never be done."

She gave a soft sigh. "It's like Abraham in that Bible of yours, Mr. Kelly. Try as he might, Abraham could never go back to Ur."

"Of course not. He'd moved on."

"More than that." Jewel turned briefly to face him. "He'd come face-to-face with the living God, and he would never be the same." Her breath misted. "Truth and character, Mr. Kelly, cannot be undone." Her breath let out a frosty puff. "But I guess you don't have a clue what it feels like to have no home, do you?"

"Me?" Wyatt chuckled. "You think I call my uncle's ranch 'home'?"

Jewel looked up swiftly, as if in surprise—and Wyatt shook his head. "Don't get me wrong. My uncle's cared for me since I was a boy, and I'm grateful to him. I respect him as my uncle, and I will until the day I die. But I'll never fit in there. He thinks I'm a nobody—with no potential." He paused to scratch his red head under his cowboy hat. "And he's probably right. Truth be told, there *is* no place for me to go, Miss Moreau. I've lost my parents. My sisters." He swallowed, and his throat seemed to swell two sizes. "The only people I've ever truly loved in my whole life. What kind of God would do that to a boy, I ask you?" He sent a severe look Jewel's way. "Since you're so enamored with this God of Abraham?"

Jewel spoke so softly Wyatt almost couldn't hear over the quiet crunch of her boots. "The same God who gave up His own Son for you," she said, looking up briefly. "Without sparing Him or holding anything back. That's the way I see it, anyway."

Wyatt nearly dropped the bag of gold. He grunted and fumbled for it, mumbling something about the burlap being too old and too damp, and pretended not to hear her. He tramped his way through the spruce boughs toward the horses, trying to push away the image of the family Bible on Uncle Hiram's table. The words and lines, burning deep into his heart. Resonating suddenly, like the gentle thunder of wind in the pines.

"So what are you going to do, then, with your share of the gold?" he finally asked, gruffly changing the subject and feeling inexplicably ashamed. After all the years that Bible had gathered dust on Uncle Hiram's mantel, had he ever once cracked it open of his own accord?

"I'll use the gold to take me as far as I can go and build my own homestead. Far from Wyoming, where people are hunting for my life."

"You're right about the 'hunting for your life' part." Wyatt set down the heavy sack, groaning, and stretched his back. "So do you want to divide up the gold now or wait until we get back to the ranch? I swear I'll give you your share."

"You can stop saying that, Mr. Kelly." Jewel touched his arm lightly. "I believe you."

"Oh. Well, thanks." And he stood there like an idiot, not even moving to pick up the sack. Hands in his pockets and face hot as a griddle. Opening his mouth to say something—anything—that might make her stay at the ranch a little longer.

To forget Nebraska or her own homestead for a while.

"Let's pack it on my pony, though," she said, shivering as the wind changed directions slightly. "Bétee's saddlebags carry more than yours, and she has more space. I ride bareback."

"What?" Wyatt fidgeted in his pockets. She might as well have asked for the moon; he hadn't heard a word she said. "Sure. Whatever you say." He stepped over a clump of snowy roots and opened the pony's worn saddlebag flap.

"What about you?" Jewel helped him tighten the twine at the neck of the sack, and they lifted it together. "You've never told me what you plan to do with the gold."

Wyatt didn't answer, and his face darkened. "Catch that end, will you?" he grunted, straining to hoist up the gold to a saddlebag. "This thing's awfully hard to lift without splitting the burlap."

"So you won't tell me." Jewel shivered again, and this time her lips took on a purplish sheen below reddened cheeks as she helped him shove the sack in the saddlebag. She hopped from one foot to the other, blowing on her hands to warm them.

Wyatt took a long time adjusting the gold in the saddlebag and shaking it out to even the weight. He squeezed the saddlebag closed after three tries and strained to strap it shut then fiddled with the clasp on the buckle. "My father was killed by the Cheyenne," he said in a taut voice, not looking up. "I've hated those people all my life."

Jewel hesitated, straightening the blanket under her pony's saddle pack, which gaped at the stitches from the weight of the gold. "I'd probably hate them, too, if they killed my father."

"I loved my father." Wyatt's knuckles bulged as he squeezed the strap. "More than anything. And they killed him. Not only that, but they butchered my mother and sisters, too. I lost everybody. Everything." He shook his head. "I've got nothing left but my uncle, and he thinks I'm a shrimp. A nobody. A good-for-nothing who will never make anything of his life. And he's probably right."

"Says who? Why do you think you can't compare to your father?"

"He was a big man. Strong. Brave and bold." Wyatt scuffed a boot angrily on the grass. "I'm none of those things. Never have been. I'm a homebody. A...a guy who faints when he sees a spider." He shook out the pack to make more space. "I had tuberculosis as a child and was always this feeble, sickly thing. It'll never change."

"You don't have to be a copy of your father, Mr. Kelly, to be like him." Jewel poured a handful of loose gold into the pack. "You can follow his path in your own way."

"What path? I'm no good at anything. My father had built his homestead, produced three children, and arm wrestled grizzly bears by the time he was my age. He cut our cabin out of the woods, right under the noses of the Sioux, and made a hearty living doing whatever he pleased. If I lived my whole life, I couldn't be half the man he was." He straightened his hat. "I can't shoot. I can't really do anything well."

That was an understatement. The last time he'd shot at prairie dogs on the ranch, he'd wasted fifteen shots and not hit a single one. He did manage to shoot a window out of one of the barns, though—and Uncle Hiram pitched a fit about that.

"But there's one thing I've been planning almost my whole life."

"What?" Jewel took a step toward him.

Wyatt hesitated, fidgeting nervously with the leather fringes on his vest.

"The truth, Mr. Kelly." Jewel crossed her arms. "I'll find out soon enough anyway. You might as well tell me."

Wyatt sighed. "Listen, miss. I don't expect you to understand, but I know for a fact those Cheyenne who killed my parents—or their relatives—are sitting on a windfall of coal and natural timber. I've been studying the books for years, and that one little piece of prairie's got more than enough resources to keep the US government happy for years. I'll manage the land, and they'll be delighted to hire me for such a fair price." Wyatt stuck his hands in his pockets. "I'll finally make something of myself, after all these years. No matter what my uncle says."

Jewel's eyes narrowed. "On the backs of the Cheyenne. If they resist, the army will slaughter them, and you know it."

"On the backs of the people who killed my family." Wyatt stuck his neck forward. "And isn't that what you told me? To use my skills and discover my gifts?"

Jewel's eyes snapped with unexpected fire. "On the backs of the people who were here *first*," she corrected. "And you know that's not what I meant when I spoke about your gifts, Mr. Kelly. Not that I condone slaughtering your relatives in any way. But answer me this—is there any chance the Cheyenne you speak of had been displaced from their original homeland already? Perhaps more than once? After years of broken treaties and failed promises?"

"Of course not." Wyatt waved his hand in irritation, but he did not meet her eyes.

Her voice turned cool. "You're sure about that? Because I've heard an entirely different story. And when your family is starving and you've been driven off your designated land and hunting grounds not once but three times—all the while cooperating peacefully and signing treaties that ultimately meant nothing—it makes for ugly politics."

Wyatt crossed his arms stiffly, a vein pulsing in his neck. "You've said enough," he snapped, his words coming out thin and taut. "I get it. The Cheyenne and Arapaho help each other out, don't they?"

Jewel ignored his question, taking one step closer. "What would you do, Mr. Kelly, if your family was starving and the Cheyenne took away your land three times? Each time they found gold, or coal, or something else of value, they canceled the treaties they'd agreed on and forced you off your land—sometimes in the middle of winter?"

"I'd take them all out, one by one." Wyatt's hands clenched with anger. "If I could shoot worth a lick, that is."

"Well then." Jewel crossed her arms. "Consider that a partial explanation of what might have happened twenty years ago. The men who murdered your family deserve to hang for their crimes but so do those who forced women and children out of their beds every time someone found coal or gold on Native land. Not all of those children made it, you know." Jewel's voice turned misty. "And not all the women and elderly. What if it were your little daughter or pregnant wife who didn't make it?"

"I don't know!" Wyatt cried, gripping his head with both hands. "I'm just very alone in the world, Miss Moreau—and I despise it. I just thought perhaps you'd understand, that's all."

Jewel stared, immobile, statuesque. "I understand all right," she said coldly, folding her hands under her shawl. "You're right. You aren't half the man your father was then, if that's what you consider a good use of your life. Revenge? Blood money?" She shook her head. "None of those will bring you peace. I expected so much more from you, Mr. Kelly."

"Sometimes the truth hurts, Miss Moreau," Wyatt whispered, staring out through the trees with hollow eyes.

Then he stalked back to the outhouse to gather up his things.

"I'll pack the tools on Samson, then, since your pony's loaded down," Wyatt called after Jewel as the snow blew harder, stinging his cheeks with tiny ice particles. He tromped through the snow and picked up the ax and spades, hoping he hadn't straddled the pony with too much weight. Bétee, Jewel called her—or something like that in Arapaho—was strong and sleek, but that much gold would weigh down any pack animal.

"Miss Moreau?"

Jewel didn't answer, and Wyatt turned, looking for her. He tied the tools to Samson's saddle and looked around uneasily. Samson reared suddenly, knocking snow off a spruce bough and into Wyatt's face. He whinnied, ears flicking.

"Whoa there. What was that all about, fella?" Wyatt patted Samson's graying head and swatted the snow from his face in irritation. "You mad at me, too? Or you just impatient for your oats?"

Samson's ears pricked, and he backed up several paces, stomping the snow-softened grass and straining at the lead.

Wyatt heard something. A rustling in the trees and a scuffling. The sound of a low whistle, like a magpie.

"Miss Moreau?" Wyatt loosened Samson's lead and then the pony's, letting them drop into the snow. If a wildcat was on the loose, he'd be a fool to leave his horses hobbled to a tree, utterly defenseless.

The underbrush crackled, and Wyatt whirled around, reaching for his rifle. *Nuts.* He'd left it at the outhouse, propped up against the side when he grabbed their tools. No self-respecting man would leave his rifle lying in the snow—especially not the burly Amos Kelly.

Samson backed up and whinnied again, a fearful sound, and Wyatt reached for his Colt. Wildcats proliferated in these parts; one of his neighbors killed one as big as an ox just a few weeks ago.

"Miss Moreau? Where have you gone?" Wyatt stalked through the falling snow, his footsteps carpeted and soundless. An eerie silence filled the gray sky, save the soft rustling of the wind in the firs and the great rushing sound they made in his ears, like a stormy ocean.

Without warning Jewel whirled around a tree, putting a finger to her lips. "Shh!" she whispered, her face white and startled. She ducked her head and flattened herself against the shaggy bark, not moving. "They've found us! Didn't you hear them?"

Then the world exploded. A blast of gunpowder, and a bullet whizzed past Wyatt, blasting the limb off a tree. Needles and snow whirled around him.

"Of all the. . ." Wyatt threw himself to the ground, pressing his face to the snow. Was Jewel trying to kill him after all, now that they'd found the gold?

Footsteps crunched through the underbrush.

When he opened his eyes, he saw Kirby Crowder standing over him, raising his musket to fire again.

Chapter 9

Wyatt rolled out of the way and scrambled to his feet, hands and knees muddied and smarting with snow. Nothing made sense; not the frantic loading of the musket, nor the man in a coonskin cap who lunged after him, barely missing his jacket collar. Two other shadows crunched through the trees, and someone fired a pistol behind him.

"Kirby Crowder?" Wyatt shouted, ducking behind a tree with Jewel as another blast shook the forest. Limbs rained around him, making his ears ring. The acrid odor of black powder hung in the woods over the soft scent of spruce and snow. "I thought the army hauled you off to the guardhouse for poaching."

"I busted out," Kirby drawled, calmly reloading. "And I came back for what I intended to do in the first place—but with reinforcements. Didn't expect to find you and that half-breed gal digging the place up. You're lookin' for ol' Pierre's gold, too, ain't ya?"

Wyatt halted as he scrambled for his Colt. *"You're lookin' for. . .Pierre's gold,"* Kirby had said. Did he not see them shove the gold in Jewel's pony's saddlebags?

"You know where the gold's hid. It's the second time I seen you down here snooping around, and it'll be your last."

"Get outta here, Kirby, or I'll shoot." Wyatt steadied his voice to keep his words from shaking as he cocked his Colt. "I don't wanna shoot you, but I will. You almost blew my head off."

"You? Shoot me?" Kirby's laughter echoed through the trees. "I'm shakin' in my boots, Wyatt. You can't even shoot a prairie dog. Now come out with your hands up and tell me where that gold's at, or I'll fill you both full of lead."

Wyatt spun around to Jewel. "How'd he know the prairie dog thing?" he whispered, humiliated. "I didn't tell a soul."

"What? Forget that." Jewel smacked him. "The barn," she whispered.

"It's our only hope. We're too far away to reach the horses, and they'll slaughter us out here in the open."

"How many guys are there?"

"I counted five. We're done for if we don't get to shelter—either from bullets or from freezing to death." Her teeth chattered, and Wyatt noticed a bluish sheen to her lips.

"See over there in the trees?" Jewel pointed. "Another one of Kirby's crew. They're surrounding us. We've got no choice but to move while the snow's the thickest. Cover me."

"What? Cover you?"

"Shoot, for goodness' sake!" Jewel pushed the barrel of his Colt toward the forest. "Distract them while I get to the barn, and I'll cover you while you run."

The forest curved to reveal a dilapidated barn behind the outhouse, and Jewel crawled backward on her knees. She slipped behind a shrub and then into a stand of aspens. Wyatt could barely see her; a wall of snow blew in from the north, making it almost impossible to open his eyes.

Wyatt watched her go, and a strange emptiness welled up in his chest. Jewel's strength somehow fortified him; when she was with him, she made him feel capable. Confident. Better than he was.

All he could do now was steady his shaking hands long enough to aim.

Wyatt blasted his revolver into the bushes then cocked and let the second bullet clink in the chamber. Two shots whizzed past him, and one grazed the skin of his shoulder, leaving a burned streak. Wyatt aimed, trying to see through ice-clouded glasses, and pulled the trigger. He heard a groan. A curse.

Had he really hit somebody? Wyatt lifted his head, surprised to see one of the men on the ground, holding his bleeding arm.

Well I'll be. Wyatt glanced down at his revolver in surprise.

"Wyatt Kelly, you little runt! I'll skin you alive for bustin' up my arm," a man's voice rang through the woods. "Come out now and I'll kill you quick-like. If not, you'll take whatever I decide to dish out—and I won't make it pretty."

Wyatt licked his lips and tried not to picture what the man had in mind, and instead scooted backward on his elbow and belly. He scooched to the side and fumbled in his pocket for more bullets and then hastily reloaded his Colt.

He'd just aimed through a patch of spruce limbs when somebody grabbed him roughly by the collar and threw him to the ground. Knocking the breath out of him.

Through a snowy haze Wyatt saw a musket butt raised to strike him. A hand slapped his revolver to the ground, and Wyatt clenched his eyes shut. Preparing himself for the blow and the bullet that would knock him senseless, into the arms of a God he'd only just begun to think about.

A rifle shot echoed against the trees, and Wyatt heard a yelp of pain. He opened his eyes in surprise to see the musket butt waver and fall. The man doubled over, leaning against a tree for support. Blood leaked through his shirt and coat, spattering in crimson drops on the white snow.

Wyatt gaped a few seconds, so shocking was the sight of another man's blood and the reality that he'd been granted another few seconds to live.

Run, you blockhead!

Sanity overcame his woozy senses, and Wyatt scrambled to his feet and darted into the snowstorm toward the barn.

"Did you really shoot that guy?" Wyatt leaned against the barn door with Jewel from the inside, panting hard. The whole structure had suffered years of neglect; wind whistled through open windows, and creaking shutters flapped open in the wind. "You're a very good shot. I'm. . .well, impressed."

"Of course I shot him." Jewel loaded her rifle again and pointed it through an empty knothole in the slats of the barn wall. "And I assure you, if I'd wanted to kill my husband this way, I could have at any moment."

Wyatt took a step back. "I believe you."

"But I didn't."

"I believe you again." Wyatt's own words surprised him. But he felt they were true, the same way hot coffee warmed his insides, shaking off the chill of winter.

"Let's barricade this place." Jewel set down her rifle and pulled an old plow against the door. "My only hope is that they'll run out of ammunition, if we can hold them off long enough."

"They'll try to bust inside by sheer force." Wyatt helped her push, sneezing as dust rose up in a fine cloud. "There are five of them, you know. Maybe more."

Jewel picked up a pitchfork and shoved it sideways across the door frame, into the latch. "Then we'll conserve our ammunition and pick them off one at a time. We can do this." Jewel met his gaze. "Do you believe me in that, too?"

"I want to." Wyatt's nose dripped with cold as he knelt down beside her, pushing the plow flush against the door with his shoulder.

"No. That's not good enough. Do you believe me?"

Wyatt shoved the plow harder in place and felt a surge of strength flow from his heart. "You know something? I do believe you, Miss Moreau. I do. I will. I choose to." He felt light suddenly, relieved—as if something heavy had fallen away.

"That's it." Jewel turned to him, her face strangely lit from the inside. Eyes sparkling like deep water. "You just said it."

"Said what?"

"What I've been trying to understand about the Bible. I don't know if I believe yet, but I'm willing to." She fingered the beaded necklace around her throat. "Therefore I say 'I do'—just like a wedding."

"A wedding, you say?" Wyatt's face was so close to hers that he felt her breath on his cheek, tickling his hair. Felt his knees melting, buckling.

"Neither the bride nor the groom know the full extent of their promise when they stand at the altar," she said softly. "But they say 'I do' anyway—without knowing all the answers. Because they know it's *right*."

Wyatt's heart pounded. Madmen were shooting at him outside, and flakes were coming down so hard that if he survived, he'd be snowed in in the barn without heat and frozen into a block of ice before morning.

And yet she'd hit on something—something big.

"It's even more than that. I'm willing to believe you because I *know* you," he whispered, his breath misting. "Because I know your character. Even if I don't understand all your reasons." He tipped his face down toward hers, so close their noses almost touched. "That's what faith is, isn't it?"

Jewel lifted her eyes to his in a deep, velvet expression that unnerved him, made his heart jump. She nodded wordlessly. The world seemed to hush, silent, and Wyatt couldn't seem to remember how to breathe. How to move his mouth.

Why was she looking at him that way? *That* way?

Almost as if she. . .

No. Wyatt forced himself to think over the loud hammering of his heart. A woman like Jewel wouldn't have anything to do with the likes of him, would she?

Shots rang out over the snow—and Wyatt jumped, reaching for his holster.

His empty holster. He stuck his hand in his pocket, incredulous, and shook it out. Then the other pocket.

Wyatt Kelly, you turkey! He slapped his forehead, recalling the man who'd grabbed him by the collar and knocked the revolver out of his hand. *You've done it again! You should have grabbed your gun—and his, too—and snatched up your rifle on the way to the barn.*

"You've lost your gun."

Wyatt jerked his head up like a frightened rabbit, hands stopping in his pockets in mid-search. "I'm sorry," he whispered miserably, straightening his glasses. "I'm no good. I told you that."

"No matter." Jewel reached for a heavy wagon tongue and slid it in front of the door, pushing a stack of wagon wheels with her hip. "God can save us if He wants to. He rolled back the Red Sea and rained fire from heaven on Sodom and Gomorrah."

"But why would He save me?" Wyatt's face contorted in another sneeze. "I'm nobody. I should have died there on that field with my father."

"No you shouldn't have." Jewel stood up to see him, nearly eye to eye. "God saved you, a defenseless child, just like He appeared to Hagar the slave girl. He has plans for your life, Wyatt. Good plans—not plans for revenge. Your father lived his life. Live yours. With justice and mercy." She grabbed a wooden hoe and thrust it into his empty hands. "God will help you live out your gifts if you give Him your life."

Wyatt's hands shook on the hoe. "I'll die anyway. I can't hold off five men."

"God held off thousands of Egyptian soldiers and chariots for a band of Israelites. And so what if you die? Do it with courage, like your father."

Wyatt took the hoe, barely seeing through his crooked and smudged glasses. His heart thumped in his throat. Before he could say another word, something moved from the corner of the barn. Wooden crates tumbled to the ground, and a wagon wheel rolled in an arc until it slid to a stop against an old bale of hay.

Wyatt jumped back, wielding the hoe, and Jewel leaped for the rifle. But not fast enough.

"Jean-François Boulé," Jewel gasped, shrinking back, pale as if she'd fainted. "What are you doing here?"

A bearded man with a scar across his cheek leaped from the jumble of crates and grabbed Jewel around the neck, shoving a pistol under her throat.

Chapter 10

Nice speech about faith, Miss Moreau. I didn't know you were a woman of such high morals." The man smiled, and Wyatt saw ice in his eyes as he bent her over double, wrestling the gun to her head. Wyatt raised the hoe with sweaty hands as she screamed.

"You so much as flinch and she's dead, Mr. Kelly," the man snarled in a heavy French accent. "Drop it and get your hands up right now, or I'll shoot!"

Wyatt hesitated, terrified of making a wrong decision, and Jean-François cocked the revolver. The metallic click echoed through the barren barn, and even Jewel halted, unmoving.

"Leave her alone," Wyatt growled, slowly dropping the hoe and putting his hands up. "Let her go."

"Why does it matter what I do with her?" asked Jean-François, slapping Jewel's hands away as she grabbed for her rifle. "She's a redskin, Wyatt. I should have killed her when I killed that fool husband of hers—but she was too slippery for me."

Wyatt flinched, sputtering for a response.

"Truth is, it's the letter from Pierre I want. Always has been. And I know she's got it." Jean stuck the pistol harder against Jewel's forehead. "I've been tracking her down for months, and thanks to those Crowder fellows, I've finally found her."

"Who cares about the letter?" Wyatt cried. "It'll make no sense to you anyway!"

Jean-François pulled Jewel upright, keeping the gun in place. "I'll make that decision, if you don't mind. I'm giving you exactly ten seconds to hand over the letter or tell me where the gold is, or I pull the trigger." He settled wild eyes on Wyatt. "And I'll slaughter every single person on that ranch to find it if I have to. Starting with your uncle." He narrowed his eyes into a scowl. "I know who you are, Kelly. I'll take that place apart board by board."

"The letter? Are you crazy? We already pulled the gold from the privy." Wyatt kept his hands up. "I swear. And then we packed it on her horse."

The gun wavered in Jean-François's hand, and a look of pure shock contorted his face. "You. . .you what?"

"We found the gold." Wyatt breathed too fast, light-headed, and tried to feel his feet on the floor. "He'd stashed it in the outhouse. It's all there; you can take it right off her pony. There were probably two hundred pounds of it."

Jean-François stood silent, frozen in place, eyes round as hotcakes. And then, before Wyatt could move, he began to shudder. A long, loud belly laugh, shaking his shoulders and ringing off the sides of the dilapidated old barn. Jean-François threw his head back and guffawed until he sniffled, stomping his boot as if in glee.

"What's. . .so funny?" Wyatt managed nervously, lowering his hands slightly.

"In the outhouse, you say?" Jean-François wheezed, wiping his eyes with his sleeve. "You're telling me Pierre left all his bounty in his doggone john?"

"That's right." Wyatt shrugged. "Go figure."

Jean-François laughed again, raking his sleeve across his mouth, and then leveled cool eyes at Wyatt. "I don't believe a word of it."

"I'm serious!" Wyatt's hands trembled, and sweat burned his forehead. "Ask Miss Moreau! She'll tell you. We hauled it all out and put in on her pony."

Jean-François swore in French. "You're a liar, Wyatt Kelly." He took a step forward, dragging Jewel with him. "Crazy Pierre didn't hide nothin' in no toilet, and there isn't a pony around here for miles. We've combed the place twice. We were wondering how you folks walked out here on foot in the middle of the snow."

"We didn't walk! We rode here. We tied our horses right over there." Wyatt pointed out the ruined window. "Right by the. . .wait a second." He wiped a smudge on his glasses and craned his neck. "By George. They're not there."

"No, they're not." Jean-François breathed through his teeth, leveling his pistol at Wyatt. "Are you tryin' to tell me two hundred pounds of gold sprouted legs and walked off?"

"I'm not lying!" Wyatt moved one hand just enough to push his glasses up on his sweaty nose. "We put them on her horse—a little Indian pony. She couldn't have gone that far."

Jean-François's eye twitched. "I've had enough. This thieving gal's gonna die for your stupidity—and who cares? These redskins have been a blight on our land since the day they started cutting into our fur trade. They're not fit to live."

And with that, he cocked the hammer of his revolver.

"The letter or the gold, in ten seconds. *Un*," Jean-François counted in a calm voice, his face deadly stone. "*Deux.*"

Think fast, Wyatt!

"If it's money you want, don't shoot!" Wyatt cried. "There's a reason I'm trying to protect the girl. She's worth a fortune."

Jean-François's head shot up. "What?"

"There's a bounty on her head back in Idaho. A big one." Wyatt felt the blood drain from his face. He was a traitor, a rat. He kept his gaze fixed on Jean-François, not daring to meet eyes with Jewel. "She's wanted for murder—the murder you committed—and if you turn her in, they'll reward you handsomely."

Wyatt heard Jewel's sharp intake of breath, but he didn't flinch. Didn't seem to hear.

Jean-François turned Jewel to him, tipping her face up in the fading light. He turned her head from side to side, and something seemed to register in his expression, like a candle flickering to life.

"Why, you're right," he whispered. "Miss Collette Moreau from Idaho. The black widow." He grinned, showing yellow teeth. "Are they really that anxious to hang her back home?"

"You wouldn't believe how much." Wyatt lowered his voice. "I heard it back when I was in Cody. Some wealthy folks lookin' for her who've got money to burn, I reckon. And they'll pay up nicely if you turn her in alive." Wyatt moved around to Jean-François's side, keeping his hands up. "I know everything about her. I can prove she did it. Why do you think I partnered up with her from the beginning? Let me go, and I'll go in with you fifty-fifty. Or since you're the one holding the gun, sixty-forty. Shoot, seventy-thirty."

"How about I just let you live?"

Wyatt slowly put his hands down. "Not exactly the deal I'd expected, but..." He shrugged, avoiding Jewel's dagger eyes. "I suppose that'll work. You give me your word? You won't shoot me?"

"Nah. Not now, anyway." Jean-François tucked his gun inside his belt and turned Jewel around, eyes gleaming. "You're right, Wyatt. They say she murdered her husband in cold blood." He grinned. "You sure you can prove it?"

"I've been reading legal books since I was six. I'll have that jury on our side in ten seconds or the deal's off."

Jean-François grinned like a hungry fox. "This is almost as good as finding the doggone gold."

"So you're gonna let me go, right, boss?"

Jean-François winked. "Now you're talkin'. Fact is, folks in Cody say you were askin' about her in the courthouse, and I saw you at the sheriff's office myself." He chuckled. "Boss, huh? Not bad, boy. Not bad."

Jewel's eyes narrowed, dark and accusatory.

Jean-François adjusted the gun in his belt. "Good thing you decided to tell the truth, Wyatt, because I don't take kindly to folks tellin' me stories. You can tell a lot about a man by what kinda yarns he spins, you know that?"

"Character." Wyatt shrugged. "Just like she was saying. Anyhow, they'll pay the bounty in gold bars. Not bad if you ask me."

Jean-François's smile deepened. "I like the sound of that." He pulled Jewel's arms roughly behind her back and nodded at Wyatt. "Gimme that loop of baling twine over there."

"Baling twine? She'll bust out of that in a minute." Wyatt picked up a strand of frayed twine and rubbed it between his fingers. "You need rope. Like this over here." He tore a long section of braided rope from the hayloft pulley. "Strong stuff. What kind of a bounty hunter are you anyway?"

And Wyatt slapped a thick coil in Jean-François's hand.

❦

Footsteps tramped across the ground toward the barn, and Wyatt staggered back, willing himself to keep calm. He'd traded Jewel; perhaps Jean-François really would call it a deal and let him go.

"You find any horses or gold, fellas?" Jean-François stuck his head toward the door as Kirby Crowder pushed it open. "Wyatt here says they found a mess of it in the privy." He chuckled. "What do you make of that?"

"The privy?" Kirby grunted. "I'll be a fool if ol' Pierre hid the stash in his john." He brushed snow off his coonskin cap. "And not a sign of a horse anywhere. No hoof tracks. Nothin'."

"Of course not!" Wyatt threw up his hands. "It's snowing, for pity's sake! The fresh snow will cover up the tracks in seconds."

Jean-François waved him away. "Take care of this scum. They haven't handed over the gold or the letter, and my patience is running out."

Wyatt's jaw moved, but words stuck in his throat. "But. . .you said I could live!" he whined, turning to Jean-François. "I gave you the girl, didn't I?"

"But you lied about the gold. There's no horse on this property, and nobody's cut open nothin' inside the outhouse. The men said so. It's a lie." He bent close to Wyatt. "Character, remember? I don't take kindly to lies. But at least I have you to thank for the bounty."

And he aimed his pistol at Wyatt and pulled the trigger.

Chapter 11

The inside of the barn roared in a blast of sound and brilliance. Something whammed Wyatt in the side, and he crumpled to the ground in a puff of smoke—hay falling everywhere. Pain leaking from his side.

Three more shots blasted the barn, and a piece of lumber fell from the ceiling, crashing down on Wyatt's leg. He lay there unmoving. Not daring to open his eyes.

"That's enough, Frenchy. Save your ammo, and grab the girl's rifle while you're at it. We're liable to run into the sheriff on the way outta here, or the army, and we need to be able to hold 'em off." Kirby's boots scuffed on the plank floor. "C'mon, redskin. They're waitin' on you in Idaho."

The last thing Wyatt heard was the sound of breaking glass, and he inhaled the sharp scent of smoke and kerosene. And then the solid latching of the door from the outside.

As the door closed behind Kirby's men, Wyatt opened his eyes enough to see it: a broken lantern in flames, licking at the rotten boards and dry straw.

Heat blazed against the side of Wyatt's face before he could raise himself off the floor. The boards and scattered hay lay sticky with bright red blood, but Wyatt felt his belly and his chest with dawning surprise. He could breathe. He blinked and felt around for his glasses. Why, he could even see—sort of—through the thick haze of smoke that quickly filled the barn.

He sat up in bewilderment, wondering how he, clumsy Wyatt Kelly, who couldn't shoot a prairie dog, had managed to stay alive at the hands of Jean-François Boulé. The bullet must have grazed him, opening up a wound without penetrating any organs.

Doc might need to sew him up with a few stitches, but by gravy, he was alive.

Flames roared up the side of the barn, and chunks of loose roofing tumbled, shattering on the barn floor. Wyatt pushed the boards off his legs and jumped to his feet, holding his bloody side.

He stumbled over old rakes and wagon parts and rushed to the door as another burning beam crashed down, splintering to bits where he'd been standing. Flames swelled up in a sudden rush, like an angry bull, igniting the dry walls and hay mounds.

Wyatt rammed against the door with his shoulder, lungs choking with smoke and heat, but the latch didn't give. The windows had been boarded over long ago, like darkened eyes.

The hoe. Wyatt grabbed it off the dirty floor and swung it at the boarded window. Again and again, hacking away at wood like Jewel had chopped the outhouse roof. And just as he gasped a lungful of burning air, the window splintered.

Snow—air—wind—and a rush of exhilarating freedom! Wyatt smashed the boards with his bare hands, bloodying his knuckles, and pushed his shoulders through the opening. He lurched forward and landed in a heap on the snowy ground, snowflakes tickling his sweat-stained face as he breathed in lungfuls of air.

Just as the side of the barn collapsed with a roar, taking the roof with it.

Wyatt scrambled away from the inferno, gasping. His clothes charred and blackened, and his hair wild. No hat and no glasses. He staggered to his feet, clutching his bleeding side, and lurched to a stop just inches from a bright object on the ground, half covered with fallen snow.

Jewel's beaded earring. A tiny feather dangled from it, crusted with snowflakes.

Wyatt paused, heart flailing in his chest, and snatched up the earring from the frozen grass. The men were gone; the woods stood silent. Snow fell all around him in lonesome gusts; tree branches rattled like empty arms. They'd taken Jewel with them, and he was too late.

As usual. Bungling everything into a gigantic mess.

What could he possibly do now? Wyatt rubbed his dirty, ash-stained face in despair, turning her earring over in his blood-streaked hand.

He could still see her there in the firelight bent over the Bible. Her long black hair pulled back into a braid, earrings sparkling. Those elegant Arapaho cheekbones and black eyes, and her long, elegant neck from her French mother.

And now she thought him a traitor, too. Wonderful. Why, she wouldn't trust him for a minute if he—by some sheer miracle—caught up with Kirby Crowder and his posse. He could probably bring the whole militia and she wouldn't listen to a word he said.

Still. He had to do something—anything.

A gust of wind blew a piece of burning barn wall so that it swayed and then toppled—landing in a smoldering heap next to Wyatt. He jumped back, catching his breath, and then limped his way through the snow toward the woods to look for the horses.

Samson was gone. Thank goodness for that, or Kirby's bunch probably would have stolen him—or worse, shot him on the spot. All the gunshots must have spooked him into the next county.

But he'd promised Samson his oats. Wyatt sighed, looking down at his bleeding shirt. He might do a lot of things wrong, but he kept his word.

He called for Samson, whistled. No answer but the shrieking of wind through spruce needles and the soft sound of falling flakes. The barn smoldered over his shoulder, smoke mixing with snow and choking the sky with black haze.

Too bad Bétee was gone, too—wandering among the forested hillsides and lonesome prairie with two hundred pounds of gold strapped to her back. If someone found her at all, before the mountain lions and wolves did, they'd swipe the gold for sure.

But neither of the horses could have gone that far. It made no sense. Perhaps the men were lying; maybe they'd divided the gold among themselves and kept the truth from Kirby?

Wyatt paused there in the icy wind, remembering the way Jewel called her at the ranch. A soft, high-pitched whistle, followed by a shorter whistle, birdlike—and a terse command in Arapaho.

He stood on tiptoe and whistled. Once, then twice. And blabbered something that sounded sort of like Jewel's command. He might have been quoting the Declaration of Independence for all he knew; at least he'd tried.

He cupped his hand around his ear and tried to hear over the wind. Pine limbs tossed; dry winter grasses rattled together. Wolves howled in the distance, their ghostly voices rising and falling.

Wyatt squared his shoulders and marched into the wind back toward the barn, head down. Hoping he could survive with heat from the fire and make it to daybreak but counting his fading chances like the gold nuggets that had slipped through his empty fingers.

⤙⤙

Something whinnied softly from the forest, over the roar of snapping barn planks and crackling flames. Wyatt whirled around, reaching for his empty holster by instinct.

"Bétee?" Wyatt wiped his nearsighted eyes to see better. "Is that you?"

A blur of white and brown nervously trotted through the underbrush, head down, and nuzzled Wyatt's side. Her hot breath tickled Wyatt's ear, and he laughed. He patted Bétee's side and scratched his ear, hugging the pony to his neck.

"Well, I'll be. The gold's still here, too." Wyatt patted her bulging saddlebags and nuzzled her neck. "You're the smartest one of all of us—you know that? What did you do, hide out in the thicket until it was all over?" He combed his finger through Bétee's silky mane and gathered up the loose reins. "You might have tried to save me, you know. I'm no good to you dead."

Wyatt tried to climb on bareback, the way Jewel always preferred to ride, and caught a glimpse of the beaded earring in his hand. The feather lifeless, fluttering in the wind.

Those knotheads in Idaho were going to hang an innocent girl, and he'd helped them do it. Wyatt shook his head. If anybody deserved to die, it was Jean-François and Kirby—not Jewel.

Why don't you ask God for a chance to stand up and be a man like your father? Jewel had said.

A line of horse tracks led from the barn and forest toward a sparsely wooded trail. Half obscured by freshly fallen snow.

"I've no light, Bétee. No gun. There's nothing I can do, even if there were ten of me." Wyatt climbed up awkwardly and swung himself over her slender back. She was smaller than Samson; lithe. "And I'd probably faint anyway." He wiped the blood from his face with a ragged sleeve. "But by George, we're going to try. Aren't we? Even if it is impossible."

Bétee whinnied and tossed her head.

Impossible. Impossible. Impossible.

The Red Sea parting. A childless old woman giving birth. Jewel leaning over the family Bible, listening to line after line of impossible stories.

Wyatt squinted and leaned forward, trying to make out the soft

87

indentation of horse tracks in the snow. He was blind as a mole and half frozen—nothing like the gallant Amos Kelly with burly muscles and fiery eyes.

"You are not your father," Uncle Hiram had said. So did everybody else. But he could die trying to be.

Wyatt pulled on the reins, urging Bétee into a trot.

Chapter 12

The trail curved through the woods, through gusting wind and blinding flakes. Snow had been falling wild and thick; Wyatt leaned down and squinted hard to measure—it came nearly to the top of Bétee's hooves.

"Faster," whispered Wyatt, urging her into a gallop. "They can't be that far."

Branches flew past him, slapping him in the face, and Wyatt saw stars. The only thing he could see, ironically, in crisp detail.

Up ahead, the road curved into an open plain, white with snow. Brooding clouds hung down over the land like a mist, obscuring the trees.

And as far as he could see in a nearsighted blur, nothing else. No horses, and no Jewel. Evening began to darken, a sullen blue.

"Bétee," Wyatt spoke sharply, firmly, "we've got to find Miss Moreau. Jewel. Do you hear me? She's in trouble, and I can't see worth a lick to catch up. I want you to go as fast as you can." He leaned forward. "Do you understand?"

Bétee tossed her head, nostrils flaring, and for a moment Wyatt felt like a fool, talking to an Indian pony that Jewel had bought for a few cents from an unscrupulous dealer. Uncle Hiram nearly went through the roof when she'd brought it home. "A waste of money, that idiot pony," he'd snapped. "That girl's got no more sense than a tree branch when it comes to buying horses."

He reached forward to grab the reins and pull her to a stop, to turn back toward the homestead—when suddenly the ground began to move. Shake. Ripple beneath him.

Wyatt's legs turned to rubber as he groped to grab hold of the reins. Stars and trees and snowflakes swirled in dizzying lines, faster and faster—so fast the horse's feet seemed to lose contact with the ground. He was flying, floating.

The velocity forced his head back, chin up, and Wyatt felt his lips flap in the wind as he struggled to hold the reins, nearly losing them

89

altogether. He groped, grasped, unable even to scream. "Stop," he croaked, his hair flying out like a madman and bottom sliding on Bétee's sleek rump. "Stop! You're going to kill me!"

Bétee didn't ease up. If anything, she flew faster—jostling Wyatt's bones and organs together in a miserable heap. He cried out as his wounded side throbbed, leaking fresh blood, but she didn't slow her pace.

Hills blurred, and snow crusted in Wyatt's hair and eyes. He choked, gasped, slid sideways. The reins slipped out of his frozen hands, and he jolted forward, grasping desperately for Bétee's mane. His fingers found her thick strands of silk and clung to them like a drowning man grasping at a floating plank.

The way the Plains Indians rode in all their glory across Nebraska and Wyoming, bareback and proud, mastering the buffalo and subduing the bear and the wolf. Until white settlers encroached on their land, making and breaking treaties. Replacing the mighty buffalo with the weak and sickly dairy cow and spreading diseases that nearly wiped out entire tribes.

His people had not been entirely hard-hearted; some sat in on war councils and traded fairly. But clashing civilizations always left someone in the lurch. Someone like Jewel, who—when it was all over—had no place to go.

Bétee leaped over a ridge like a deer, barely jostling Wyatt, and landed gracefully on all four feet, still running. She rounded the corner, snowcapped trees jutting into her path, her hooves pounding the ground and throwing up snow.

Bétee made one more giant leap, straining and puffing, and then lurched to a sudden stop.

Wyatt shouted—grasped vainly at Bétee's mane—and felt himself hurtling through space. He landed in an undignified heap, facedown in the snow, just inches from a blur that looked like Jean-François Boulé—who looked up from where he squatted, fixing a drooping saddlebag. The other horses jammed up behind him in a dead stop, rearing and snorting.

Jean-François let out a squawk and jumped out of the way.

"Wyatt Kelly?" he snarled, fumbling for his pistol and shouting in angry French. "What in heaven's name are you doing here?"

Wyatt jerked his face out of the snow and scrambled to his feet, attempting a clever reply. "Well, hey, boss." He tried to smile, his lips shaking, and held up Jewel's feathered earring—blabbing the first ignorant thing that came to mind. "You forgot something."

Muskets blasted all around him, exploding the snow into white fireballs, and Jewel screamed. Bétee reared. Wyatt lunged for Bétee's reins and pulled her to a stop, dodging whining bullets, and he ripped open the saddlebag with the tips of his fingers.

He tugged on the strap and slashed at the burlap, and out poured a rain of gold nuggets. Down into the snow, glittering in the half light of musket fire and Kirby Crowder's lantern.

For a moment utter stillness descended on the field—so still that Wyatt heard the almost inaudible clink of snowflakes hitting the buttons on his coat. Musket fire ceased. Jaws dropped, and one man slid from his horse as if in a stupor.

"The gold," Jean-François croaked. "You found it. You really found it."

Bétee backed up, snorting, and a rain of nuggets tinkled, like sifted wheat.

Wyatt hauled the saddlebags, still dripping gold, off Bétee's back and hurled them as far as he could. Which meant. . .oh, a good four feet away. They splayed in a snowbank with a smattery *splut*, facedown.

All the men leaped from their horses, shouting, and descended on the saddlebags with a flurry of boots and lantern light, knives and fists flailing. A noisy fray of grasping, hollering, and scooping up nuggets.

Jean-François pulled up fist after fist of gold, his openmouthed profile visible in the yellow glow of the lantern.

"We've hit pay dirt, boys!" Kirby exclaimed in shrill tones, digging through the snow. "We're rich!" He giggled gleefully, almost like a child. "I'll build a new cabin. Two new cabins! Buy the best horses. And thanks to Mr. Kelly, I've got a fine idea—I'll buy that Cheyenne land and open up a coal mine!"

Kirby let out a shriek of exhilaration, and Wyatt froze. *Oh no. Not the land. Not that.*

"Will you hurry up?" Jewel hissed from the horse, reaching out her boot and nudging Wyatt in the shoulder. "While they're still occupied with the gold?"

"Sorry. I just. . .sorry." Wyatt awkwardly pulled Jewel down off her horse, dropping her in the snow several times, and borrowed a knife from Kirby's saddlebag to clumsily slit her ropes. None of the men noticed; nobody even seemed to care.

"Thank you." Jewel coldly handed him the rope. "Now excuse me while I take Kirby's horse. He's the fastest of the lot; he'll get me back to Nebraska in a few days."

Wyatt's mouth dropped open. He swayed, reaching for Bétee's spotted rump to steady himself. "You're going…where? Back to Nebraska? But I thought…"

"What, that you could collect the bounty on me yourself?" Jewel snapped, jerking at a tangle of reins and leads. "Well, forget it."

Wyatt remembered—vaguely—how to talk. "You must be joking. Surely you don't think I'd follow you all way in the snow and nearly get myself shot—with my side already busted open—only to turn you in?" He glanced down at his bleeding side, which had leaked onto his pants. A few red-brown droplets stained his leather boots. "For pity's sake. I'm not going to turn you in. I told that fellow about the bounty to save your life."

"Save my life? They want to hang me in Idaho!"

"But he'd have shot you on the spot if I didn't think of something." Wyatt sneezed, sniffling as he stood there in the snow. "I'm telling you the truth."

"How am I supposed to know if I can trust you or not?" Jewel turned, her beaded necklace jingling.

"You said it yourself. Look at my character and see." Wyatt scrubbed a sleeve across his runny nose. "And here. I brought you your earring."

He held it out on his bloodstained palm.

Jewel swallowed, looking from his hand to his eyes. "You expect me to think this means something?" Her voice shook, and her words came out softer than he expected.

"Sure it does. It's your heritage. Your past. Part of who you are, even though you've changed and moved on. You're still Arapaho. You still carry your father's blood." He glanced over at the men digging in the snow. "And if you don't hurry up and get on your horse, it might be the earring you wear when they stand you on the gallows."

Jewel took the beaded feather and tucked it into her ear. "Thank you," she said softly.

Wyatt tried to reply, eyes fluttering, and sneezed twice. His boots and pants hung damp from snow; his teeth chattered. Smoke had stained his bloody shirt an ugly gray-black. He sneezed again, and Jewel took off her shawl and wrapped it around his shaking shoulders. Drawing him close and fitting the folds snug around his neck.

"You can't see a thing, can you?" Jewel said in a soft tone. "No matter.

I'll get you home. Bétee will lead the way." She bent down and picked up the severed rope on the ground and then looped it around the bridle of Kirby Crowder's solid brown mare, whispering softly in her velvety ear.

"Miss Moreau?" Wyatt tried not to sneeze again. "Pardon, but what on earth are you doing? We've got to get out of here!"

"Right. And let those guys follow us and cut our throats? No thanks." Jewel grunted as she tied the rope and patted Kirby's horse on the muzzle. "Hurry, will you? Give me the reins of that big stallion back there so I can tether her to my lead."

"By jingle," Wyatt whispered hoarsely. "You're right. None of Kirby's men are paying a lick of attention."

"It's either that or we shoot their horses. But I'd rather not."

Wyatt scrambled for the reins, tearing a revolver from one of the saddles and tucking it in his belt. Then a rifle, and finally a slender pistol. He shook his head at the melee: Jean-François scooping up fistfuls of nuggets, Kirby frantically scooping away snow with his hat and digging in the underbrush. Laughter and fumbling in the snow, curses and brawls.

"Now, Mr. Kelly!" said Jewel, chucking to the horses and pulling the lead. "Get up behind me, and hurry!"

Wyatt reached for her hand, coughing up something bloody, and she pulled him up behind her on Bétee's rump. She gave a sharp command, and Bétee surged forward—with all the other horses on the lead trudging along obediently behind her. All laden down with packs and rifles.

Wyatt craned his neck to see over his shoulder, not quite believing what he saw. A line of horses moving forward in a blur of snow, and Kirby's men oblivious. Shouting and pushing.

Well. For a second anyway.

"What in the Sam Hill do they think they're doing?" Kirby hollered suddenly, looking up from a crouch and jerking his pistol from his holster. "Son of a gun! They got our horses!"

"Uh-oh," Wyatt whispered, ducking. "Here it comes."

Bullets whizzed past them right and left, dropping tree limbs, and the horses reared and whinnied, nearly knocking Bétee over. Wyatt yelled and held on for dear life, feeling his teeth knock together. Jewel dug her heels into her pony's side, giving an urgent command in Arapaho and making a soft sound to the other horses. Soothing and guttural, reassuring. Bétee surged forward under a thicket of tree limbs, and the other horses trotted together, faster and faster.

Ducking into the woods and down a deserted trail, until the noise of gunshots and Kirby's men died into the sibilant whisper of wind and pines.

"We made it," Wyatt said, gasping for breath. "They'll never catch up with us now."

"Not on foot, they won't." Jewel glanced back over her shoulder. "I just hope we can make it back to the ranch before they figure out a way to the nearest town and find appropriate mounts."

"They'll be too busy with the gold to worry about us, won't they?" Wyatt shivered, clutching his elbow close to his throbbing side. "In any case, we ought to call for the sheriff and turn them all in."

Jewel turned slightly, her expression icy. "And you're sure you're not going to turn me in to the sheriff, Mr. Kelly? Tell me now so I can dump you off into the snow. Because I still have my doubts."

"Of course not. You know I wouldn't, or you'd have left me back there with Kirby Crowder."

"That was a clever speech then, that you gave to Jean-François. You really checked up on me in Cody?"

"I did. And I think you should turn yourself in."

"What?" Jewel whirled around.

A branch smacked Wyatt in the face, and he saw floating lights.

"Turn myself in? You must be joking, Mr. Kelly. Mr. Boulé said it himself—they'll hang me."

"Not if you tell them the truth." Wyatt scrubbed the snow off his face and wrapped his arms awkwardly around her as he slid sideways. "It's impossible for you to have killed your husband, you know. Besides, we heard Jean-François's confession."

"What makes you say it's impossible?"

"You were in Yellowstone National Park that entire week, serving as a paid scout for a group of botanists and soldiers in southwestern Montana." Wyatt sniffled from the cold. "After all, not everyone can speak both French and Arapaho with such dexterity, along with a fine understanding of Crow and Sioux—or navigate the mountains and rivers of Montana. So very similar to the terrain of Idaho."

Jewel gasped. "How did you know about that?"

"I've been thinking about that all the way over here from Pierre's place." Wyatt groaned in pain as Bétee bumped over a snowy ridge, dropping to a trot over a frozen stream. "I saw an article about the expedition in the courthouse in Cody, and the more I consider it, the more that description of the pretty young guide sounds exactly like you."

Jewel said nothing, just pulled the reins tighter.

"The article is accurately dated, you know. None of the members of the expedition would have trouble identifying you if you came forward." Wyatt sniffled. "Fact is, if you played your cards right, you could countersue your husband's relatives for slander, demand monetary reparations and your due pension as Mr. Moreau's widow, and swear out your own warrant for the arrest of Jean-François Boulé. After all, he killed your husband and attempted to murder you. I think if we reconstruct the crime scene and his shaky alibis, we could prove it."

Wyatt coughed; his throat throbbed from smoke and cold. "Besides, you couldn't swing the stovepipe that they say ended your husband's all-too-short life."

"I'm certain I could."

Jewel's loose hair fluttered in the wind, thick and wild, like a flock of gleaming crows. Wyatt wrapped a strand around his finger and brought it to his lips, feeling something akin to delirium.

"Doubtful. With all due respect." Wyatt leaned against her shoulder and shook his head. "Not with enough force to kill a man like Jean-François did—and I could prove that scientifically, by demonstrating fulcrums and velocity and borrowing the expertise of a good physician. Although," he lifted his eyebrows, "I'm sure you could do some serious damage if you wanted to."

"Thank you." Jewel clucked to Bétee and urged her through a clearing, looking up at the clouds as if to check for any letup in the snow.

Wyatt groaned, clutching his wounded side. He sneezed again, and Jewel turned. "You're sick already, aren't you?"

"Probably. And Samson's missing." He reached into his pocket and wiped his nose on a bandanna, shivering. His knees knocking against Bétee's furry side.

And before he could stop himself, his frozen knees and elbows gave way. He slumped sideways and sort of dripped off the horse, landing in a pitiful heap in the snow. Snowflakes sifting down through the pines and tickling his closed lashes.

Jewel called a sharp halt to her pony and hastily dismounted, falling to her knees beside Wyatt on the pine-needle-carpeted floor. Not much snow had fallen there; sweet scents of spruce and earth welled up in Wyatt's nostrils like heady perfume.

"Mr. Kelly." Jewel gently shook his shoulder. "Please get up. We're almost home. But if Mr. Crowder finds us here, he'll kill us immediately."

Wyatt groaned and rolled his head back and forth, too tired and sore to raise his neck off the ground. For a moment the thought of Kirby Crowder's gunshot sounded preferable to this horrible aching cold. The sharp wind and throbbing ache of his side.

"I can't leave you here." Jewel took his face in her hands. "Come. I'll help you up."

Wyatt blinked up at her, trying to juxtapose the two images: a black-haired brave raising the spear to kill his father, and an Arapaho girl lifting him, bleeding, off the frozen ground with compassionate hands. Life seemed to have reversed itself, leaving his head spinning, floating, as if under water.

"Why do you care what happens to me?" Wyatt raised himself up on one shoulder, clutching his bleeding side. "The gold's gone, you know. Our deal is done."

"Says who?" Jewel combed his red hair back from his forehead with tender fingers. "I never said I was your partner only for the gold."

"You mean. . ." Wyatt's eyes stretched open, and his tongue seemed to stick in his mouth. No woman had ever cared for him, so far as he knew. Not bumbling Wyatt Kelly with his plain face and halting speech. Not him.

"I mean I said yes to you," Jewel whispered. "To *you*. Don't you understand?"

Wyatt's heart beat fast, loud, as he reached for her.

Jewel tugged him up off the ground and helped him onto his knees then massaged his frozen shoulders until he felt warmth again. "You can do this." She spoke close to his ear, her voice deliriously sweet. "We're a team, Mr. Kelly. Partners. We share everything." She cupped his stubbly cheek in her hand. "You're not as alone as you think you are, you know. Perhaps you never have been."

Wyatt, you knothead. He tried to sit up, despising his own foolishness. Why, if he had saved a bit of gold, he might have had something to offer her—right here, on his knees—and beg her to stay at the ranch.

"I threw all the gold away," he croaked, letting her rub his cold hands in her warm ones. "I should have saved some of it for us. I could have—"

"Shh." Jewel pressed a finger to his lips. "Forget the gold."

"I could have filled my pockets before I threw that saddlebag away, and none of the men would have known the difference." He pressed shaky fingers to his temples. "Then I could have sent out a hundred men to find Samson and bring him home. I blundered that one, too, didn't I?" He reached out and rubbed a thumb across her smooth cheek, feeling his throat tighten and burn. "Why, I could have. . .could have. . ."

"Listen to me." Jewel spoke over the sound of the wind in the pines. "There's a good side to every mistake, Mr. Kelly. An excess of anything corrupts the soul, doesn't it? Take poor Mr. Crowder as an example. A year from now he'll be up to his neck in debt, with ten men at any given time ready to slit his throat over card games or liquor or property—and all the gold in the world wouldn't solve his problems."

"You're just saying that because I'm half frozen and you want to keep me alive." Wyatt let her pull him to his feet, his arm draped over her shoulder for support.

"Perhaps." Jewel led him forward, arm around his waist, and he heard her smile. "Is it working?"

Wyatt licked his chapped and split lower lip. "Maybe. Keep trying."

"You've no gold now to buy the Cheyenne land with. You can start over, Mr. Kelly. Free from revenge. No regrets."

Wyatt groaned. "No, but now Kirby has enough gold to do it. The sorry snake." He heaved a heavy sigh. "And it's my fault. It was a fool idea to begin with."

"Don't think about that now. Just hold on. We'll be home soon." Jewel eased him up onto Bétee's back, tucking the shawl tight around his shoulders. She slid on in front of him and pulled at the reins.

"But. . ." Wyatt thought hard, trying not to focus on his throbbing side as Bétee jolted down the rocky side of a creek. "I think there may be a way out of Kirby buying the land."

"How, if there are coal deposits?"

"The national park." Wyatt nodded. "That's it. There are also several rare species of wildlife and botanicals on the land; I think I can convince them to make it a nature preserve run by the Cheyenne. So long as they'll agree to work jointly with Yellowstone and comply with basic park regulations."

"With a lifted restriction on hunting, of course. Unless you want them to starve."

"Of course not. I think I can write up something so convincing that even Kirby Crowder and his gold won't do much good. Just give me a few days with some books, park regulations, and a local survey of wildlife and plants, and I'll convince them that it would be a great ecological disaster to sell the land or open a mine on it. You'll see."

Jewel actually smiled. "Why, Mr. Kelly—I'm surprised at you. You're going soft on me."

Wyatt scowled. "Well, keep it to yourself, will you?"

He gazed out through the white woods, feeling stabs of pain pulse through his side, and felt his mind drift far away—to a snow-crusted plain at the edge of the prairie. A row of rough wooden crosses that made a sob catch in his throat.

The warm tears that burned his eyes felt good—healing—and he didn't try to blink them back.

They were gone, but he would always remember.

Always.

Until the day he died, he'd be a brother. The lone survivor.

His father's son, remembering the feel of those burly arms around his neck in a tight embrace. For he, too, carried his father's blood.

And that would never, ever change.

◦◦◦

Jewel turned suddenly. "You know you still have a handful of gold nuggets, don't you? The ones you stuffed in your pocket there at the outhouse."

Wyatt's emotion-hard face suddenly melted into a look of joy as he scrambled for his pocket with freezing fingers. "By George," he murmured, fingering out a handful of nuggets. "You're right."

"You can buy a new horse with it." Jewel spoke gently. "I know how you'll miss Samson. He's been your favorite ever since I've worked at your uncle's ranch."

Wyatt dipped his head, glad the gloomy darkness hid the watery sheen of his eyes. "It'd be impossible for him to survive out here alone all night, wouldn't it?" His voice came low and mournful. "Not with wildcats and mountain lions. The cold and coyotes." He sniffled, trying to keep from blubbering. "As old as he is now. He's not as strong as the young horses, but I always thought he was fine." Wyatt scrubbed his face with his palm and said no more.

"Never mind." Jewel spoke gently. "I'm sure one of the local ranchers will find him and turn him in."

"There's nothing around here for miles, and you know it." Wyatt wiped a palm across his nose. "He's a good horse, but I don't think he could find his way back to the ranch in this snow—not at his age. He'll be so lost he couldn't find his own tail."

"Perhaps he'll hole up for the night, and we can look for him tomorrow."

"You know a hungry mountain lion won't let him live that long—if we're even able to get out tomorrow in the snow. He's got arthritis. It'd be a miracle if he's still alive now." Wyatt sighed.

"Well, doesn't that God of yours do miracles?"

"Not to fellows like me, probably." He sniffled in the cold. "I promised Samson his oats," he said, jabbing a finger at his chest. "I've never failed him yet. I might do a lot of things wrong, Miss Moreau, but I keep my word, and I. . .I. . ." He wanted to say "love that fool horse," but the words stuck in his throat.

"You're a good English teacher. Isn't that what you were going to say?" Jewel spoke quickly.

"Me? Naw."

"On the contrary. In fact, I think you might make a fine lawyer. I can teach you Arapaho, if you like, and French—and you could consider legal cases and question witnesses from all over the state of Wyoming. Or all over the West, if you like. You could be a Yellowstone legal specialist." Jewel brushed snow from her long hair. "In fact, your uncle has quite a few connections in the academic world, does he not? You could go to law school. You've certainly got enough gold in your pocket to give you a good start."

"Law school." Wyatt whispered the words as if hearing them for the first time. They were magic; they rolled over his tongue. Hanging in a shiny haze like the yellow lights of the ranch, visible over the next ridge. "Law school, you say?"

"There's a shortage of lawyers in the West, Mr. Kelly. You'd be in high demand."

"Law school," Wyatt repeated, his voice thin and husky. "And you'd. . . teach me languages? That is, of course, if you'd consider me." He swallowed hard, and his mouth felt dry at the thought of Jewel bending over the table, pointing out verbs. Her slender hands guiding his as he formed the unfamiliar letters with his pen. "My Arapaho pronunciation may be a bit garbled, but I'm sure I could learn with time. And. . .tutoring of course."

"Lots of tutoring." Jewel's voice took on a lush tone. Soft, like the sleek side of a wildcat. "And it would be a pleasure to teach you. But how do I know you're not feigning your Arapaho language deficiencies, Mr. Kelly? The same way I did?"

"You can't know."

Jewel chuckled softly, sounding like sleigh bells. "Well, I'm determined to find out."

Wyatt blinked back snowflakes. He was delirious, warm and lightheaded and cold at the same time.

"And your father would be proud of you, Mr. Kelly, if you don't mind me saying so."

"For what?"

"For everything you are, Mr. Kelly, and everything you will be. I'm sure of that."

Bétee slowed to a trot at the entrance to the ranch, her hooves kicking up snow in the fading twilight. Black sky curved over navy blue of snowfall, fresh and smooth on the hillsides like smoothly spread sugar. Wyatt blinked through the snowflakes at the bright front door, where his uncle stood holding out the lantern. A worried look pasted across his face.

And Samson waited obediently at the stable door, his sleek face turned toward Wyatt. Saddle empty and reins dragging. Neighing impatiently for his oats.

FINDING YESTERDAY

Dedication

To the late Dr. Gayle Price, my friend and English professor
who taught me so much about life, writing,
and the Lord. I miss you dearly.

Chapter 1

1937

D on't look now, but I saw somethin' you didn't." Frankie grinned, dumping his mud-caked boots in a pile and wiping a filthy sleeve across his forehead.

Justin looked up from scrubbing mud between his fingers, the sunlight pouring behind the Camp Fremont Civilian Conservation Corps barracks blinding him. "What'd you see? That bull moose that showed up over by the bridge?"

"Naw. Better." Frankie bobbed his eyebrows. "Girls. I saw 'em."

"Here? At the camp?"

"Sure thing. Two gals, and they say the redhead's a real dish. Word is they're over visitin' ol' Bruno Hodges. Lucky stiff."

Justin rolled his eyes and peeled off his dirty work shirt, which reeked of sweat and loamy mountain soil. The pungent, sulfurlike stench from geothermal mud hung in the nearby rivers, the air, even his hair, messy as it was. The CCC barber had whacked it off short when he showed up in Pinedale, Wyoming, a year and a half ago, but now it hung over his forehead, thick and shaggy. Not slicked back like the movie stars.

"Tommy Wills said one of them dolls is a looker. Swell, huh? Course after this long out in the sticks even the old broads start to look good. Know what I mean?" Frankie elbowed Justin in the ribs. "Man, I can't wait to get back to Ohio!"

I can't wait till you get back either, pal. Justin dug a clothespin out of his pocket and shook out his freshly washed CCC bandanna, securing it to the rusty piece of wire that served as a clothesline. After dozens of washings in hard water and ruthless army-issued soap, its crisp navy had faded to an unappealing moldy blue-gray.

Laundry aside, President Roosevelt's New Deal ideas were pretty good, Justin thought as he stuck the clothespin in his teeth. At least the CCC, anyway. Shipping hundreds of jobless guys out of the cities and into state parks to do construction and rebuilding might sound a bit nuts, but it worked. They got a paycheck sent back to their folks, and good, honest, hard work to keep them off the streets and out of crime.

And the parks got fixed to boot. Which worked especially well with the drought and dust storms hitting the prairies hard.

The army ran the camps, which served double duty in the event they ever needed recruits—what with the regimented formations and work groups, the morning calisthenics and uniforms. Thousands of guys, all ready to march off to the front with pickaxes, shovels, and bags of pine saplings in their hands.

"Well, I'll go back to Columbus as soon as I can get a real job of course," Frankie jabbered on. "This place is the pits! It's not worth the pay, puttin' up with all them mosquitoes and cold an' whatnot. Out in the crummy sticks, gettin' covered with mud!" Frankie waved brown-and-red-streaked arms for emphasis.

"I think it's swell." Justin straightened his bandanna to catch the breeze. "One of the best things to ever happen to me. All the fresh air and work. I'd stay here forever if they'd let me."

"Are you nuts, Fairbanks?" Frankie pretended to knock on Justin's head. "Hello? Anybody home?"

Justin raised an eyebrow. "Didn't you just get here?"

"Yeah. Five crummy weeks ago. The only reason I'm here is 'cause it sure beats hangin' around town with straw in my pockets, since everybody's outta work." Frankie kicked a grass tuft. "This Depression business stinks, ya know? The economy's s'posed to be comin' back real soon though—jobs and everything, too." His certainty seemed to falter as he tugged off a mud-caked boot. "That's what everybody says—things'll probably be back to normal by the end of the year. Don't ya think so?"

Justin slapped a mosquito. Picturing the line of hobos down by the rail yard at Cheyenne. Bone thin, their clothes wearing out in gaping patches. At least here at Camp Fremont, Justin had never gone hungry. Although some of the burned beans and slobbery boiled cabbage made him think going hungry once in a while might not be so bad.

"Anyhow, Ma's real proud I can finally send home a few bucks every month to help out." Frankie eyed Justin. "Who you sendin' yours to?"

Justin's throat tightened at the sound of the word *home*.

"My older sister Margaret gets my dough," Justin replied, not meeting Frankie's eyes as he picked up a wet shirt. "She takes care of Beanie."

"Beanie? What is he, a dog?"

"My younger brother Benjamin." Justin shook out the shirt. "We call him Beanie. He's a swell kid." He looked sidelong at Frankie, as if daring him to say even a syllable in jest. "The swellest kid I've ever seen."

"What about your folks?"

"No folks." Justin took another clothespin out of his mouth and secured the bandanna tighter as it slid off the line.

"Crummy. Sorry for ya." Frankie scrubbed his face with his dirty shirt, mud still smeared over his left ear. Trying to hide a pale blue oval as it fell out of his patched pocket, grabbing it out of the grass.

"I don't believe it." Justin spun around.

"Don't believe what?" One corner of Frankie's mouth turned up in a guilty smile as he dug for the handkerchief in his pocket and wrapped it around the eggs.

"Gimme that." Justin held out his hand, and Frankie reluctantly plopped the two speckled birds' eggs there.

"Got the nest in my other pocket. You want that, too?" Frankie scowled. "And some petrified wood and obsidian and stuff—but I ain't givin' ya that. You can go get your own, for all I care. Yellowstone might be the pits, but I'm takin' some souvenirs with me when I go. Least I can do to make up for all this time I'm wastin' planting stupid trees."

Justin shook his head in disgust, turning the eggs over in his hand. "You know you're not supposed to take anything, bonehead. Some of those birds are rare, and this is a public park. What's the matter with you?"

Frankie didn't answer, snatching up his green army surplus backpack and digging through it. A panicked look on his face. He dumped the bag upside down and dislodged a wooden geyser plaque that had been ripped from its base, some agate stones, and a couple of smashed crystals.

"Hey. I'm talkin' to you, Frankie!" Justin grabbed his arm. "You ain't supposed to take nothin' out of the park. You're a thief. Put everything back!"

"I ain't puttin' anything back." Frankie shook the backpack. Rock chips and broken cookies trickled onto the grass. "I swear I put it here."

"Put what here?"

"Aw. Nothin'." Frankie shook the pack again and tossed it on the grass with a shrug. "At least I got my agates." He held one up to the light. "Nuts, huh? I bet each a these'll fetch a nice bit a dough." He tossed a red agate like a coin. "But this ain't the best thing I found, by a long shot."

"It's people like you that destroy this place, you know?" Justin huffed, blood seething in his throat.

"Yeah, yeah." Frankie snatched the eggs out of Justin's hand. "Every wet sock says that and then goes and carves his name on the rocks when nobody's looking."

He wrapped the eggs in his handkerchief and stuffed it back in his pocket. "There's a place up in the ridge—the one where we built that trail—with a swell waterfall and a mess of blue flowers. I might go back and see if I can find me some more a these eggs."

"You do and I'll knock you in the jaw."

"You don't wanna tangle with me, Fairbanks. I'm givin' ya fair warning. Might find your bed short-sheeted, and who knows what else." Frankie rocked back carelessly on the balls of his feet. "Anyhow, before I leave here I'm gonna catch a mess of owls and stuff, too, and see if the pet shop'll give me a couple a bucks for 'em. You'd do the same if you had any sense."

Justin shook his head. "I don't know why you're even here, Frankie."

"Yeah, well, me neither. Hope I won't be much longer." Frankie curled his lip in derision. "Stuck in Roosevelt's rotten Tree Army, bungling my way through the mud." He stretched his back. "Say, you gonna go over to Hodges's an' take a look at them dames?"

"Like this?" Justin wiped a grimy hand against his once-white undershirt then lifted soiled pant legs to show even more soiled ankles. Toes caked with reddish-brown soil from hacking trailways and cutting clearings out of the moist earth. Filthy work, but ironically Justin felt cleansed.

"Naw, idiot! After we clean up." Frankie tossed his shirt hard, and Justin caught it at face level. He tossed it up and over a corner of the long, angular Civilian Conservation Corps barracks so it stuck there on the shingles. One dirty sleeve waving like a roughed-up surrender flag.

"Hey buddy! What'd ya go and do that for?" Frankie wailed, jumping vainly for the roof.

"Aw, quit your whining, baby." Justin rolled his eyes as Frankie stalked around, picking up branches. "You'd drive the longest-suffering preacher insane, you know that?" He would, too, with his constant nagging, like a skinny, buzzing mosquito. His shrill voice rang through the camp, tinny-pitched with an underdeveloped eighteen years of youth.

True, Justin could count off the same eighteen years plus one, but the gulf of life and hardship that stretched between them rendered Justin an old man. Why, even the CCC recruiters had written him down as twenty-one when he first stepped up to enlist, probably on account of his thick build and sour expression, unlike the fresh-faced young recruits. The burly sergeant had chuckled as he scratched out "twenty-one" to write "eighteen."

"C'mon, Fairbanks! Gimme my shirt! Why'd ya do it? Why'd ya do it?" Frankie continued to jump, waving that ridiculous twig at the roof. Hurling it as hard as he could, where it caught in the folds of his shirt and hung there, immobile.

Oh well. Justin's lips curled into a smile. At least now something would keep him busy for a while.

"You'd drive the longest-suffering preacher insane." Justin's words stung like an ant on his leg, and he was instantly sorry he'd said them. He knelt on the patchy grass and scrubbed at his boots, wishing he hadn't even thought of preachers. Just the sound of the word made bile rise in his stomach.

"Hey, gimme my shirt back!" Frankie tried to throw a sort of headlock around Justin's neck, but Justin flicked it off.

"I'm busy gettin' ready for formation."

"Busy? Oh yeah? So's your grandma," Frankie mocked, huffing. Blowing out his lower lip as Justin calmly sponged dirt off his jaw with a cloth, his fingers tracing the long line of his scar. He could still feel it—a wicked reminder of everything he wished he could forget.

"Say, where'd you get that scar from anyhow?" Frankie picked up a rock and tossed it at the roof. It rattled across shingles and bounced off, and two heads appeared in the window.

Justin threw the cloth next to the basin, pretending not to hear. Dropping to one knee and unlacing his dirty boots.

"Hey, bozo. I'm talkin' to you! Where'd you get that scar?"

"What scar?" Justin didn't look up, pulling out his laces with more force than necessary. "And you call me bozo again, and you'll be sorry."

Frankie spit out his breath. "Aw, whaddaya mean what scar? That big thing across your lip down to your chin. And that little line on your forehead under all that pretty hair." Frankie used a mocking tone, hunting for another rock. "What are you, Frankenstein or somethin'?" He nodded toward Justin's leg. "You got a stiff knee, too. I see you limpin' sometimes."

Justin didn't answer for a long while, scrubbing the mud-caked leather laces with a rough cloth.

"Don't wanna talk about it, huh? Musta been bad, all right. What, a bar fight? C'mon, Fairbanks! Spill it."

Justin sighed, throwing down his laces. "Look, Frankie. I . . . An accident, okay? It was an accident."

He tried to blot out the crunch of metal and glass. The screams. The stench of burning rubber and the strident car horn, stuck on, blaring into his leaden mind. The pain he should have felt but didn't as his blood leaked out, and his shaky hand wavering, reaching, reaching for another bottle. Alcohol reeking on his breath.

"That's all you're gonna tell me? Swell, Fairbanks. Thanks for nothin'."

Justin pressed his fingers to his muddy forehead. He could still hear the shocked whispers: *"Reverend Summers passed away?"* Windows had glowed with candlelight all over dark Berea, Kentucky, like ominous lightning flashes. *"What happened?"*

"I need my shirt! I need my shirt!" Frankie was complaining again, jumping vainly for the gutter and trying to crawl up. Cheeks flushed and arms flailing. Somebody stuck a walking stick out the window, waving it at the roof.

Justin put his hands on his hips and shook his head, unable to keep back a laugh somewhere between pity and derision.

And pity eventually won out.

"Hold your scrawny horses, Frankie. I'll get it." Justin unhooked a clothes wire and jabbed it up toward the shingles, catching the shirt neatly by the sleeve. He slid it toward the gutter and over the edge of the barracks building like a freshly snared cutthroat trout. Right into Frankie's upturned hands.

"Next time you do that, I'll pound you," Frankie snapped, not bothering to thank him.

Justin snorted. Frankie, pound somebody? Frankie White was a chigger. A little, annoying chigger who resorted to messing up people's beds before inspection and stealing their underwear. Slipping ice under the blankets.

Justin hooked the wire back in place and reached into the basin, cupping handfuls of water to his dirty face. Inhaling the same sharp sulfur-water stench that boiled up from geothermal pots with their layers of overlapping colors: unnaturally blue-green and cobalt, ringed with otherworldly yellow and copper-colored rock.

Like eyes of a giant peering up through the dusty, pine-studded earth. The acid in the pools was so strong it'd eat your boots off if you weren't careful.

Everything in Wyoming was like this—vast, strange, and wild—heart-thuddingly large and startling—like Justin had landed on an alien planet. He saw it all through curious eyes: enormous, snorting moose with heavy fans of upturned antlers. Geysers puffing up steam from cracked earth like freight trains. Snowdrifts in alpine meadows at the tops of the mountains, and big-shouldered buffalo in shaggy brown coats. Ice in the river flows.

A far cry from the simple farm roads of Kentucky.

The memory of red dirt and hickory leaves made Justin's eyes sting for a second, and he wiped his face with a cloth by the washtub. Leaving reflections of pine branches in shattered rings, like so many broken memories.

"Fairbanks!" Ernie Sadler jumped through the open barracks window. "Don't move!"

A noisy group had congregated around the washbasin, slapping each other with wet rags and telling jokes, and they fell apart as Justin and Ernie plowed through them, nearly upsetting the washbasin.

"What in the fool nonsense are you hollerin' about, Ernie?" Justin shouted, pushing Ernie away and trying to right himself. Nearly putting his socked foot right on top of a baby Rocky Mountain rattler, which slid through the grass like a slender brown twig.

Slithering away from Frankie White's upturned backpack.

Chapter 2

Justin whirled his leg out of the way and jumped back. Two guys saw the snake and yelled, knocking into one of the wooden sawhorses that held up the basin. The basin lurched and splashed, falling into a wet heap on the grass, sending the snake scurrying in the other direction.

A mountain rattler had enough venom to kill a human—and a baby carried exactly the same amount in a smaller package. One strike and Justin'd be on the ground, swelling and moaning in pain.

"Hit it! Hit it!" screamed Ernie, grabbing up the walking stick and whacking away at the grass. "Where's the machete?"

Tucker and Jenkins fled for the barracks, pants half on and water dripping from their faces. Stumbling over discarded boots and the wooden sawhorse that had held up the basin.

Tommy disappeared around the side of the barracks, shirtsleeve flapping off, and ran back wielding a garden hoe. Waving it in the direction of the snake. "Where'd it go? Lemme at it!"

"Cut it out!" Justin bellowed, trying to wrestle the hoe away from Tommy. "You're gonna scare it into striking! Just hush up and see if we can pick it up on the end of a stick."

"He's right." Ernie paused, panting, and sponged his sweaty forehead. "Shut your traps, everybody! Tommy, gimme the hoe. C'mon. Let's see if we can't get it outta here nice and quiet like."

⁓

Justin's head ached as he plodded back into the barracks, which smelled of pine, sweat, and dusty army blankets and cots. His pulse had slowed after he and Ernie managed to get the snake on the end of the hoe, coiled like an angry little doughnut, and tossed it in some bushes on the other side of a stream. It darted off into the rocks, forked tongue whipping in defiance.

Justin had marched all over three barracks buildings looking for Frankie, ready to wring his puny neck, and finally heard him in the lieutenant's office doing push-ups. Getting chewed out for some infraction while Lieutenant Lytle scratched out more demerits.

Man, that kid was trouble. Justin had stalked back to the barracks in stony silence, not sure if he should squeal to the others about Frankie and the snake or not. He wanted to, but they'd all jump him—probably fifty guys—and the little squirt wouldn't make it out of CCC camp with any teeth left.

"So you goin' over to Hodges's place, Fairbanks?" Ernie looked up eagerly from the cracked window glass he was using as a mirror. Slicking back his hair with a comb a little too eagerly, smoothing it to the side. It shined back, sleek with gel, like a sheen of river ice.

Obviously violent and excruciating death from a mountain rattler rated a distant second after women for Ernie.

"You, too? I thought only Frankie was losin' his mind over a bunch of gals."

"Don't kid yourself. I ain't seen this much excitement around here in weeks. Maybe months." Ernie bent closer to the window and patted his hair back. "You're comin' after formation, too, ain't ya?"

Justin gave a derisive snort as he shrugged on a clean olive drab shirt. Army issue, and scratchy around the collar. "Naw. I got better things to do."

"Not me. It's been six weeks since I've seen a gal, Fairbanks."

Frankie White swung through the door smelling like some horrid combination of cheap cologne and hair tonic, his chin bleeding from several shaving cuts. As if he still hadn't figured out how to use a razor blade. "Remember that rancher we worked for, fixin' fences or somethin' equally stupid?" he said, butting in on the conversation. "He had a doll or two, didn't he? I could swear I saw one back there in the kitchen."

"That was his wife, stupid." Justin threw his clean boot at Frankie, his jaw clenching in dark fury. "What's the matter with you? She was probably sixty years old."

"Swell. Thanks for ruinin' my dreams." Frankie tossed the boot back a little harder than necessary. "Told ya they all start to look good after too long out in the sticks."

"You're just nuts. All of you. Forget it, okay?" Justin sighed and massaged the bridge of his nose, wishing he could think of something—anything—else to talk about.

Frankie huddled next to Ernie at the window, smugly fixing his tie. "Fact is, I told Bruno you went to school with one of the dames and wanted to catch up on all the old biz." He winked. "You're from Kentucky, too, ain't ya, Fairbanks? 'Cause that's what I told 'em. They're comin' over to see ya right after formation."

"Who's from Kentucky? One of the girls?" Justin's fingers froze on his bootlaces.

Ernie and a scattered crowd gathered around the doorway while Frankie calmly straightened his tie—leaving them all in agonizing suspense.

Justin pushed his way through and grabbed Frankie by the collar. "I'm through with Kentucky, and I don't wanna see anybody from back there. Got it?"

"Don't worry. She wouldn't like you anyway, with your scar face and big ol' nose." Frankie grinned, too intoxicated by the power of superior knowledge to be intimidated. He shook Justin's hand away and brushed off his shirt, flicking bits of lint in Justin's direction.

Frankie leaned his elbow lazily against the doorjamb. Tie thrown back rakishly. "One of them gals is from Kentucky. Some small town out in the country I've never heard of. Sounds kinda like you, don't it?" He winked. "Have fun catchin' up."

~❧~

Justin pushed his way through the door and stormed off, not caring where he went. Except that it was far from Bruno Hodges's barracks—and from anyone who called Kentucky home.

Especially somebody from the country who might have heard of the accident. After all, word travels fast in small towns. He grimly ran a finger over the scar on his chin, knowing that once you're branded, it's for life. No matter where you go or what you try to do differently.

A scar on society that never quite heals.

Until now he'd managed to hide away in silence, giving his address only to Margaret with her word that she wouldn't tell a soul. And Margaret was a good woman. She'd given up schooling for Beanie; she wouldn't lie. Justin would stake his life on her integrity—the integrity that should have gone to Pop and himself but didn't.

Afternoon sunlight pooled on the sparkling aspen leaves, shivering like September-gold gems over slender white trunks. Slipping down over the lupine-studded fields and turning the grass to copper fire, stretching Justin's shadow a dusky blue.

In the distance loomed the jagged range of the Rocky Mountains— thick and defiant, reaching sharp, snowcapped peaks into the sky like pointed wolf fangs. They rippled across the horizon in glorious tints of rose and slate, the forests at their base already streaked through with yellow from early fall.

Those mountains had anchored Justin here in Wyoming, like the Bible verses he'd read by faint lantern light before bed, page after page. His heart soaking up new conviction and a new life beyond his past.

But now Justin kept going, striding faster and faster. Hands clenched into fists in his pockets. He left behind the housing barracks and mess hall and school—all long, wooden rectangles against the mountains and thick pine forest. The ubiquitous flagpole that snapped crisp stars and stripes into the cobalt Wyoming sky.

If he skipped camp now he'd get stuck on KP duty until the country ran out of potatoes. Weekend leave was allowed, although there wasn't much to see outside Pinedale—but weekday skips were off-limits. Although Justin could list twenty guys like Ernie and Frankie who sneaked out nearly every night for booze, and the extra push-ups and hours spent peeling onions didn't curb their desperate forays.

After all, what could the army do? This was the CCC, not the army. And as good as the president's New Deal plans were, they didn't cover all the loopholes.

Not long ago Justin would have been one of the ones slipping out after dark, glancing back over his shoulder as he hustled through the grass. Trading a pack of cards or a pocketknife for a bottle at some cheap bar in Pinedale.

And yet none of that sounded good anymore.

The memory of the burn did, as the bitter booze slid over his throat, and the haze and stupor of delightful forgetfulness. But the rest blurred into a discordant mess of vomit, headaches, lying, sneaking—and a life Justin wanted to flee as far from as Kentucky.

Justin lunged for the split-log fence that lined a thicket of lodgepole pines and Douglas firs and hoisted himself over the top, swinging over a leg. He dropped down on the other side into a patch of grass, nearly flattening the figure huddled on the other side of the fence.

A girl in a jacket and muted blue dress with a white collar crouched there against a scaly fir trunk in the shadows. She drew back and yelped in horror, circling her head with her arms.

Justin stumbled back with a cry of shock, sputtering a hundred apologies.

Until she turned up those piercing blue eyes—eyes that reminded Justin desperately of someone, somewhere. Someone he wanted to forget, to vanish from the farthest corners of his memory.

Lia Summers, daughter of the late Reverend Summers. From beautiful, aching Berea, Kentucky.

Chapter 3

For a second Justin felt his senses failing him—like the blank darkness that had hit him after he brawled with Pop years ago. The wooden plank he'd hurled at Justin smashing against the barn siding and catching him across the forehead.

In a single flash of blue from Lia's eyes, Justin could see it all again: Reverend Summers's crumpled '29 Buick. Lia's red face, streaked with tears and anger. Those same eyes, swollen and grief-crazed, as she tried to tear away and fight him. "I hate you!" she shouted, her tear-wet hair clinging to her cheek. Those words shuddering into his already quivering chest with powerful force. "I hate you!"

Until somebody drew her away. Patting her cheek and whispering into her ear.

The light glinted on something crushed tightly in her hand: her father's glasses. One orb empty, the glass shattered.

Nausea heaved in Justin's chest as he jerked away from Lia, tripping over a dead branch studded with pinecones.

The same way he used to run from Pop. Dagger-eyed, alcohol-reeking-breath Pop with the horse's whip and the leather razor strap. Secretly glad his defiance had caused Pop to come after him instead of Margaret or Beanie—but terrified to the point of nausea.

When Pop swore through slurred lips that he'd kill Mutt, Beanie's gentle old hound, Justin slipped out one night and hustled her away to a good-hearted farm family in the next county—and told heartbroken Beanie he'd found her dead in her sleep.

After that Justin slept by Beanie's bed on the floor, just in case Pop showed up with a shotgun.

The memories hit Justin so abruptly that he felt his throat close up, damming back a waterfall of memories.

It was too much, all of it—Lia and Kentucky and the past he thought he'd left behind. Choking him like Pop's fist while he shook Justin until his teeth rattled.

Justin stumbled over a shallow dip in the grass and a downed pine limb, catching himself on his palms in a mess of prickly pinecones. When he got to his feet, he wiped lines of dark blood across his olive pants.

Blood that reminded him of Reverend Summers. Glass shattered. Slumped shoulders. Those eyes blinking and a rivulet of blood trickling down the side of the reverend's gentle face.

Running. He was running again. Just like he'd always run from everything—from Pop, from Kentucky. From the police on that fatal day he'd plowed his father's battered, patched-up old Model T clunker into Reverend Summers's Buick in a drunken stupor, nearly taking out the side of Mickel's Grocery and old man Tither's mule.

At stinking fourteen years old, to boot—just a few days shy of fifteen. Justin was bigger than the other boys, with a huskier build and jutting chin, and the police thought he was a college kid at first. Until they wiped the blood from his face, and why, it was that young Fairbanks boy again—drunk as a sot.

What kind of jerk would leave Lia huddled there by herself? She was a girl, for goodness' sake. No matter what fool reason she had for showing up in Wyoming or hiding out under a bunch of silly pines. The least he could do was see if she was all right or point out how to get back to Hodges's bunk.

Maybe say "I'm sorry" and accept her hate.

That's what a good man would do anyway. If Justin could ever figure out how to be one.

Justin wiped his sleeve over his eyes and let out his breath, a shaft of afternoon sunlight warming his face as he abruptly turned back. Then he squared his shoulders and forced one foot in front of the other, making his way toward Lia through the whispering grass.

Lia got up off the ground, quickly brushing off her long skirt. A twisted handkerchief held to her mouth with one hand.

"Justin Fairbanks." She said his name with the cool enunciation of a judge, her face even paler than before, if that was possible. Lips tightly closed, her shoulders rising and falling slightly as if holding back agitated breath. Eyes narrowing ever so slightly either in recollection or disgust.

Justin swallowed the knot in his throat and stuck his hands awkwardly in his pockets, not knowing what to say. "So you found me," he finally managed, his words coming out awkward and stiff. Scrubbing the grass harshly with one boot.

Wind whispered through the fir needles overhead with the glorious, heady scent of pine. But now it smelled all wrong—pungent, painful. Too perfect for him to stand before the daughter of the man he'd killed, the last of the season's glass-blue gentians blooming around their feet.

When he dared to look up, Lia's face had paled even more, and she bent over, clutching the fence post with one hand. Shoulders shaking as she clamped the handkerchief over her mouth.

And then, to Justin's horror, Lia vomited in the bushes. Gasping and choking. Wiping her mouth as tears rolled down her cheeks.

Justin stood there stupidly, hands frozen in his pockets, and then took a hesitant step back. "Well, I'll see ya," he said, feeling like an idiot. "There's a doc here at the camp. I'll call him for you."

And he turned to head back to the barracks. Wishing the CCC had shipped him to Alaska instead of Wyoming and wondering if there was any way he could get a transfer. Like. . .maybe now.

Lia called something after him, and Justin tipped his head back briefly. "What?"

"Carsick," she gasped. "I'm horribly carsick."

Justin scratched his head, his eyes scrunching in bewilderment.

"You know, like from the motion of a car," she said with a bit more acid in her voice. "The roads are awful, all those ups and downs over the rocks, and Cynthia's uncle drives like he's. . ." She wiped her mouth with the handkerchief, her hand shaking. "Those new cars go so fast. Forty-five miles an hour is ridiculous." Lia's eyelids quivered shut. "We've been lost for five hours. Why do you think we just got here now?"

Justin realized she was waiting for him to respond. "Uh. . .what?" He let his hand rest on the top of his head.

"My friend Cynthia's been dying to see her cousin Bruno, so her aunt and uncle drove to Yellowstone while we were in Montana."

"Montana?" Was Lia delirious? Nothing she said made any sense.

"I'm finishing summer vacation with Cynthia's family before school starts," she said a bit indignantly, as if he were supposed to know. "They've got relatives in Bozeman. Didn't Bruno say we were coming?"

Justin blinked the haze from his eyes long enough to shake his head in bewilderment. "How should I know? I don't know Bruno Hodges any more than the man on the moon. Why, did. . .did you know I was here?" he asked, glancing up.

Lia looked away. "No." She said it flatly, almost coldly.

Her slender throat bobbed slightly as she swallowed, the breeze blowing her hair ever so slightly. Chin up. Eyes focused far away.

They stood in uncomfortable silence as the spruce branches whispered again, wafting those dizzying smells of sun-warmed conifer needles and damp earth. A mountain bluebird warbled its distinctive trilly whistle, summerlike and earnest, like all the words Justin wanted to say and couldn't.

His hands shook as he glanced at her, wondering if he'd been mistaken about who she was. Lia never stood out—a lot of girls looked like her.

But no, it was Lia Summers all right—probably nineteen or so now? Twenty, maybe? That dark hair that used to fall nearly to her waist, now cut and curled around her shoulders—styled sort of like the movie stars but longer, looser. The faintest touch of lipstick. Dark eyebrows and pale skin and blue, blue eyes.

To tell the truth, Lia had never been especially pretty. Her mouth was too big and her hair too fine, and she wore a perpetual baby face that always made her look about twelve years old. She stood like a beanpole, tallish and gangly.

But she had this. . .sparkle. A glow under her skin when she smiled. A confidence that bloomed pink in her cheeks when she shared about Jesus to the schoolkids—well spoken and unashamed.

Until that day he saw the light die in her eyes. She couldn't have been more than fifteen when her father passed away, and small for her age. A scrawny slip of a girl, her cheeks still chubby with youth.

Lia opened her mouth to speak, but before she could, she heaved again—coughing into her handkerchief.

Justin winced, trying not to look at the handkerchief, and then peeled off his CCC bandanna and handed it to her.

She hesitated, and then to Justin's astonishment, reached out and took it. Nodding her head in thanks before bending over double.

If Lia had come all the way from Bozeman by car, no wonder she was carsick.

"Do you want to. . .go see the doc?" Justin felt awkward again, finer points of conversation still eluding him. "He's over there in that building. I'll get him for ya."

Lia nodded, arms wrapped around her middle. "I told Cynthia I was going to the bathroom, but—" She broke off, her face too green for conversation.

"Crackers?"

She turned those blue eyes toward him again in question.

"Soda crackers. You know, the kind you eat with soup. My sister Margaret swore they helped her seasickness when she went out on the lake." Justin slapped his mouth shut, ashamed of his blabbering. Of course Lia knew Margaret was his sister. Everybody knew everybody in Berea, and they'd all gone to school together practically forever. Until Ma died first and then Pop, leaving nobody but Margaret and Justin to take care of Beanie.

And there's no way Lia would want anything to eat after retching up breakfast for hours. What a ridiculous thing to ask.

Lia was nodding again.

"The crackers? You mean you. . .you want them?" Justin's face brightened with inexplicable joy, like a flash of sunlight glancing off the Snake River.

"If you don't mind. I'll try anything."

Justin's heart leaped. For the first time in his life, he was going to do something right. True, it was just crackers—but if Lia had asked for an angry she-bear, Justin felt like he'd willingly chase one down and wrestle it for her.

"Wait here. Okay? I'll come back." Justin's breath came fast, giddy, as he backed away, and then he broke into a frantic run toward the barracks.

Chapter 4

Lia Summers. What were the odds? Justin moved ghostlike through the scattered crowds who were heading to the bathhouse, laughing, stopping by the PX for a Pepsi or a smoke before formation and then dinner. Somebody reached out to trip him as a joke, waving a hand in his face, but Justin didn't even look up. His eyes glazed, registering none of it.

Instead he saw the reverend's simple walnut table the day he'd invited Justin over for dinner years ago—the light of compassion in his eyes so pure and strong that Justin felt, in his clumsy Bible ignorance, that he'd pulled out a chair across from God Himself. Mrs. Summers and little Miriam passed the biscuits, and the reverend spooned extra strawberry jam on Justin's biscuit when he hesitated. Pushing him the whole glass jar.

"Take it home, son," he said with a wink, resting his hand gently on Justin's head. "I heard your father's fond of strawberries. And you're a good fellow. You'll do it for him, won't you?"

At the sound of the word *father*, Justin's stomach buckled. Just how much did the reverend know anyhow?

"Naw, I couldn't take something of yours, sir." Justin felt like he'd forgotten how to talk, dropping his knife as he tried to cut off the thinnest slice of butter possible. After all, with the drought and Pop's throwing the family money away on liquor, it had been ages since Justin had seen anything as beautiful as homemade jam. And made with white sugar! He tried not to look at it there in the cut-glass jar, quivering glorious red.

"Please, son. You'll do us a favor. Isn't that right, Lia?"

Justin glanced over at her as she sat straight in her chair, her face so refined and so confident—yet she'd refilled his glass three times without even waiting for thanks, never once making him ask. And not a second glance at his poorly bandaged hand or the ragged shirtsleeve he so desperately tried to hide in his lap.

All that pretty, curly hair of hers pulled back in a chocolate-brown ribbon, leaving tendrils on her cheek.

"Please, Papa. I'm sick of seeing strawberries after all those weeks of picking." Lia twirled a curl of her hair around her finger like a young schoolgirl, an action that caused Justin to stare for a second, although he didn't exactly know why. "Can't you give him the rest? I know we've got two more back in the kitchen, and I can't look at them another minute."

"Well of course, Lia." Reverend Summers crossed his arms over his chest, glints of fading light from the windows reflecting his warm smile. "Since it bothers you that much. If Justin will oblige us, that is."

Justin scratched his ear, embarrassed and tongue-tied. "I reckon, sir. If it'll. . .you know. Help."

"Thank you," Lia said to Justin in a soft voice, shooting him a shy and grateful smile over her plate. "How is your father, anyway? Someone said he wasn't well these days."

Justin searched her eyes, but he saw only innocence glimmering there. Lashes blinking, waiting. Politely folded hands. Mrs. Summers gently touched her arm, and Lia looked up, blank-eyed in surprise. Lips parted.

Before Justin could reply to Lia's question, dry-mouthed, Reverend Summers straightened his glasses and leaned forward quickly, making both their heads turn his way. "Lia," he said in a bold, bright tone, "have I ever told you about the time I pulled an alligator out of Yellowstone Lake?"

"What?" Lia laughed, letting the curl of hair slide off her finger. "That's impossible!"

"Why, no, not at all! Listen." And the reverend scooted his chair closer, raising his hands, orator-fashion, to begin the story.

⁂

When Justin came scrambling back across the rustling Wyoming grass, a chilly bottle tucked in his hand, Lia hadn't moved much. She huddled there on fragrant pine straw with her arms around her middle. With her arms like that, he noticed—for the first time—a barely visible row of stitching on the underarm seam of her pretty jacket that showed it had been mended. The material of the elbow was a bit threadbare, and her shoes—rounded toes with a slight heel he'd never seen Lia wear—had worn through the soles, revealing the cardboard patch she'd fitted into the bottom.

Even her white gloves, tossed carelessly on a clump of grass by her hat, had been mended along the seams multiple times, and a tiny hole showed in the index finger.

The Depression obviously hadn't been good to the Summers family. *Especially without a father.*

Justin swallowed hard and knelt next to Lia, setting down the bottle and popping open his battered tin of soda crackers.

"Here ya go." He shook a cracker into her hand, ashamed of his dirty fingernails and calloused hands. "See if it helps any. I called for the doc, but he's over on the ridge sewing up some idiot who practically whacked his leg off with a machete." Justin started to spill more lurid details then reminded himself that Lia was a girl. He had a hard time keeping a rein on his tongue after living with two-hundred-plus sweaty, grubby, out-of-work joes.

Lia nibbled the corner of a cracker without reply, twisting Justin's CCC bandanna in her free hand and swabbing her chin.

"I brought you a ginger ale, too. Here." He knocked the bottle cap against a fence post a couple of times until one fluted edge crumpled, releasing a curl of fizzy steam. He passed the bottle to her, glad he'd had a few cents to plunk down at the PX. Most of the guys went there so often to buy 7UPs, Clark Bars, and Lucky Strike cigarettes that the PX kept a running tab; the guy on duty just now didn't even know Justin's name.

Lia wiped her mouth and took a sip of ginger ale then scrubbed her swollen eyes with the back of her hand. Her gaze cool and almost stiff but at the same time so wounded that Justin wanted to kneel there in the grass and cry.

Neither spoke, and Justin cleared his throat awkwardly. He flipped the bottle top in his palm, trying to think of anything to say that didn't bring up raw wounds. "So, you must be about twenty now, huh?"

"Next month." Lia wiped her mouth and took another sip.

Justin scratched his head, squinting at a stand of sparkling aspens before speaking again. "You...uh...been to the Rockies before?"

"Never."

Another long pause. A bee hovered over a scarlet Indian paintbrush bloom, buzzing.

"You like hiking, then? Or Cynthia does?" Justin tried again.

"I don't know. I haven't really been much, and neither has she." Lia took another hesitant sip and wrapped her arm around her middle, looking so fragile there against the pine fence that Justin's heart twisted inside his chest.

She set the bottle down, her eyes meeting his in a brief flash of blue, and then smoothed a strand of windblown hair out of her eyes. Twisting a curl around her finger as she drank.

Justin stared, opening his mouth and closing it. "You still do that," he said, his words coming out a hoarse whisper.

"Do what?" She curled the strand again.

Justin couldn't speak for a second. Then made an awkward motion toward his head. "That. . .that thing with your hair. You used to do that." He dropped his eyes. "A long time ago."

Lia let the piece of hair slip off her finger as if embarrassed, a hint of a smile on her lips. "I was shy, I guess." She shrugged, smoothing her hair back.

He looked down in the grass, afraid to meet her gaze. Shy? Around him, even back then? Justin Fairbanks, son of the town drunk—all nerves and chunky build and not knowing how to properly hold a knife and fork?

"Listen," he said, trying not to look at the strand of hair Lia had wrapped around her finger, now blowing in a thin, frizzy coil against her cheek. He licked his lips, wondering if he should say it—if he *could* say it. His mouth felt like pine straw. But it needed to come out. He felt it there inside his breastbone, burning like acid. Begging to be released.

A milkweed pod floated by on the breeze, which felt suddenly chilly, smelling of sun-warmed fall and damp leaves.

"About your. . .your. . .dad. Your father." Justin licked his lips, feeling his palms perspire. He dropped the bottle top and fumbled in the grass for it with shaking fingers. "I'm sorry. Real sorry." He couldn't finish because his throat choked. Wondering what it might have been like to have kind Reverend Summers as a dad instead of drunken Pop. Those deep eyes and smile lines around his mouth. The gentle way he rested a hand on a head, as if in blessing.

And then to leave him in a church cemetery, Indian grass and wild violets covering over the raw wound in the ground.

Justin kept his burning face turned down, praying that Lia would say something. Anything.

But she didn't.

Out of the corner of his eye he saw the bottle freeze at her lips, and her position seemed to stiffen.

"Where did you say the doctor's office is?" Lia finally asked, drawing up her knees and reaching for the fence post to stand. Justin blinked back moisture, hoping with all his heart she hadn't seen his emotion. He rushed to help her up, humiliated and all nerves, and she seemed not to notice.

"I think I'll wait for him there." Her words carried a hint of frost, like the edge of chill on the warm September air.

Justin nodded miserably then gathered up her gloves and hat and gave them to her. Dropping one glove on the grass in his agony and stooping to dig for it.

She took them without touching his hand and kept her face turned away as she strode ahead of him toward the doc's quarters.

Chapter 5

Justin stared up at the long, rough planks of the barracks ceiling, which were barely visible in the moonless darkness. The wool army blankets on the Camp Fremont beds scratched like maddening fleas, but they kept Justin warm. Back in Kentucky he'd sometimes awakened with snow from the broken window in the folds of his threadbare quilt.

"Boy, that kitten is one hot tamale," whispered Frankie from the next bunk over, shaking Justin's bed with his foot. "You awake, Fairbanks?"

Justin kicked Frankie's leg away as hard as he could.

"I'll take that as a yes." Frankie flopped over on his side. "So, ya saw her? I looked all over for ya, but you'd split like a big yella banana. Missed everything. Man, what a dish," he sighed. "Too bad for you. She's a real peach, I'm tellin' ya."

Justin bristled. He hadn't seen Lia the past two days and hoped she was okay. But doggone if he was gonna go asking around for her after the way she'd stalked off. Not that he blamed her. Not one bit. But it was best if he left her alone. He'd said what he'd needed to say, and nothing remained but empty space.

Justin had worked as hard as he could, clearing brush and pounding nails for handrails, trying to forget. After evening formation and dinner in the mess hall, he'd taken his high school books over to the school building and studied by lamplight until bedtime. After all, life with Pop and weeks of delinquency hadn't exactly been conducive to higher learning. Soon as he finished his high school studies, he'd take some college classes for sure—and learn a trade to help his family.

"A real doll. Yessiree."

"Who are you talking about?" Justin asked in irritation. "Lia?"

Frankie sat halfway up in his bed. "Who?"

"Lia. Cynthia's friend." Justin blinked up at the ceiling again, trying to recall Lia's crazy story about driving from Bozeman. Wondering if it had really happened or if he'd dreamed the whole thing.

But the ice in her eyes before she walked away hurt too deeply to forget.

"If you're talkin' about that skinny dame, no thanks. She's as shapely as an empty potato sack and kinda sad-lookin' eyes. But Cynthia. Cynthiaaaa!" Frankie let out his breath like a dying man and flopped back down on the bed. "She's eighteen like me, but I told her I was twenty. You shoulda got a peek at 'er. That hair! That. . .that. . .angel face! She's the most gorgeous thing I've ever seen."

Frankie shook a finger in the air for emphasis. "I tell you what I'm gonna do." He pushed himself up on one elbow.

"You're gonna shut your trap, that's what," snapped Justin, not in the mood for Frankie White's love laments. "And besides, you said all that nonsense about the last five dames you saw. Including the farmer's wife."

"Aw, knock it off, goon. You ain't even heard what I'm gonna do." He settled his cheek on his palm, raising his voice over Ernie's sputtering snores. "Lucky for me, Bruno Hodges got himself all whacked to pieces with a machete so bad Doc had to practically stitch his leg back on. So who's gonna take 'em on their hike over to Fremont Lake instead? After all, this *is* Yellowstone." Frankie leaned forward. "And her uncle's a real famous photographer. He spent a whole day down at the falls takin' pictures."

"Whose uncle, Lia's?"

"No, dimwit!" Frankie socked him with his pillow, making Justin see starry spots. "Cynthia. Do you need me to write it down for ya? Forget about that other gal." He plopped the pillow down. "Anyhow, I'm gonna impress the socks off Cynthia's uncle. He'll never believe what I found up in the mountains."

"What, another crummy bird's nest?" Justin growled. He held back his fist from knocking Frankie White in the nose. If he lobbed that pillow at him again, he'd do it, too.

"Naw. Way better." Frankie's voice fell to a whisper. "You ever heard of the Thoen Stone?"

"The what?"

"The Thoen Stone. A message scribbled on a rock—somethin' about Ezra Kind and gold from the Black Hills and Indians hunting him. Some guys in South Dakota found the message back in the 1800s."

"What's this got to do with you?" Justin's hair prickled, not liking where Frankie's blabbering was going.

"Everything. I found a letter." He scooted closer, his eyes so wide and earnest in the dark that Justin's heart skipped a beat. "In an old jar. Down in a bunch of rocks along the riverbed at the start of that trail we were cuttin' last week."

"You shouldn'ta kept anything, Frankie. You shoulda turned it in to Lieutenant."

Frankie ignored him. "The letter's written by a Jeremiah Wilde, tellin' his cousin how the Sioux Indians killed a fella named Kirby Crowder— and took all his gold. He thinks it's the same gold that belonged to Ezra Kind, 'cause nobody ever found it—and because of the legends and stuff. Somethin' like two hundred pounds of nuggets. Do you believe it?"

"Not for a second."

"It's dated July 1893, and the paper's falling apart."

"Liar."

Frankie hesitated, and the bed creaked as he leaned forward. "Jeremiah Wilde said he thinks it's up on Gallatin ridge," he whispered. "Near that field full of bellflowers. Is my luck good or what? I made a copy of the map, and I'm gonna ask Cynthia's uncle about it. He'll know if it's real, won't he?"

Justin shoved him away. "Go away, Frankie. I'm going to sleep."

"Not me. I'm gonna lay here and dream about Cynthia. Think she'll date me if I find the gold? Say, why don't you come with us on our hike? You can. . .I dunno. Carry my canteen or something. Imitate bird calls." He chortled to himself, plopping down on the pillow and looping his arms under his head. "Too bad you're helpin' out the Green River crew tomorrow, eh, Fairbanks? And on a Saturday! Haulin' logs or some such nonsense? Ah well. Your loss."

"You leadin' a group? That's the dumbest thing I ever heard." Justin reached over to shove Ernie and stop the snoring.

"Well, say hi to Mr. Tour Guide. I'm now the official Yellowstone expert in residence. At least that's what I told Mr. Parker, Cynthia's uncle. What I don't know, I'll make up. Simple. And he won't care when I dig two hundred pounds of gold out of a cave somewhere."

"That's park property. You'd never get away with it."

"They don't have to know a thing."

Justin could almost see Frankie puff up his chest with pride, even in the dark. "Lieutenant gave me permission, so long as we stay on the lake trail," Frankie rattled on. "Said I needed an activity to exercise dependability—whatever that's supposed to mean. Don't matter to me so long as I get to be with Cynthia."

"Oh brother," Justin muttered.

Frankie's voice trailed off in a disgustingly soft sort of way. "She's never seen snow. Can you believe it? Grew up in Florida. I wish I could show her some."

"You're an idiot. They'd never make it past the first ridge."

"Yeah well, a fella can dream, right?"

"Sure. Right into a lightning storm. I can see it now. The weather around here changes in a minute, and what are you gonna do if you cross a moose or a bear? You'd wet your pants like you did last time."

"Real funny, Fairbanks." Frankie's voice hardened. "What are you, some kinda worrywart? Everything's gonna be great. Anyhow, Lieutenant said Charlie Pryde's supposed to come, too, since he's got some know-how with plants and stuff, but Charlie hates it here. Once we get outta Lieutenant's sight, he can take off and do whatever he wants, and I'll find that gold myself. You'll see." He stretched and let out a long yawn. "I'll handle things swell."

"You. Handle things swell." Justin massaged his closed eyes in disgust. "Those girls don't have a lick of hiking experience, Frankie. Better go easy on 'em. I know Lia wasn't feeling so hot when she got here."

"Well, she doesn't have to go then. Whatever. I'm just doin' this to score some marks with the lieutenant of course." Frankie's words held a smirk. "I gotta make up for all my demerits. Only person who's got more than me is Charlie, and he's probably gonna skip this ol' camp and hitch a ride back to New York. He's homesick somethin' terrible like the rest of us."

"Speak for yourself. I think this place is swell. And if your record's that bad, Frankie, you oughtta volunteer to help me at the spike camp tomorrow instead of fooling around with some gal and her folks you don't even know." Justin snorted and smooshed his pillow into a thick roll. "You and your ridiculous notions. Letters in a jar? Gold? I don't know how you get any work done at all, always lookin' for stuff."

"I don't, really."

Slacker. Justin shook his head and turned on his side away from Frankie. "Now shut up and let me get some sleep, or I'll shut you up."

Frankie lay still awhile, quiet, until Justin thought he'd fallen asleep. Then a muffled whisper. "She was looking for ya. That skinny gal."

Justin's arms and legs tensed, and his fingers clenched the wool blanket tighter. "What do you mean?"

"I dunno. Seemed like she was tryin' to find ya these past couple days, but you was hidin' out in a cave or somethin'. Who knows? Maybe she's sweet on ya." Frankie yawned. "But that Cynthia's somethin' else. She wears Emeraude perfume! Did you know that? It's pure heaven."

"What do you know about heaven?" Justin growled, his teeth gritted at Frankie's "sweet on ya" comment. "You don't even go to chapel, although you oughtta. I bet you five bucks somebody back home is prayin' for ya to pick up a Bible and get a lick of sense in that empty head of yours, but you've been blowin' 'em off for years, thinkin' you can handle things on your own. Well, you're a fool, Frankie. Life's a lot tougher than it looks."

He swallowed hard, thinking of Lia. Tracing the scar on his forehead with his fingers. "Don't wait so long like I did. It'll take me a lifetime to clean up my mess, if I ever can."

Frankie rattled on, not appearing to hear. "Cynthia smells like rose petals. And...and...orange peels." He waved his arms in the air and let his breath expire dramatically. "I'm in love, Fairbanks! Slap me. Am I dreaming?"

"Oh, I'll slap you all right. With pleasure."

And Frankie yelped to get out of the way.

Chapter 6

Justin had just speared a bite of flavorless hotcake in the noisy mess hall when someone tapped him on the shoulder. He jumped, nearly knocking over his coffee. Bad coffee, thick as tar and nearly too bitter to swallow.

When he turned around, there stood Lia Summers in a close-fitting yellow hat, patiently clearing her throat and hands folded neatly in front of her.

Two of the guys next to Justin looked up at her briefly, but their eyes wandered back to the pink-cheeked girl in the doorway, her daylily-orange hair fashionably curled under her hat. Laughing with someone on the other side of the doorway.

"Sorry to interrupt your breakfast, Justin." Lia looked around nervously. "I know you're in a hurry, but Lieutenant Lytle said I could speak to you. I've been trying to find you for two days."

Justin sat there like a startled mule deer, nodding senselessly.

"I just wanted to say thank you."

"For what?" Justin's fork dripped blackstrap molasses.

"For what you said."

Lia laced and unlaced her fingers, which shook in the dim light of early dawn. Head bowed. She'd wrapped a white scarf around her neck, over her yellow dress, making her look like an out-of-place daisy in a room full of navy-blue-clad guys. Most of them sullen at being awakened on a perfect, sun-clear Saturday for hours of hacking trails through the woods, "cribbing" the eroded banks of the river with logs chinked with stones, and clearing fallen trees by Green River spike camp. Heavy rains had downed a whole ridge, and about a quarter of Camp Fremont's boys were helping out, either voluntarily (like Justin, for extra pay) or for penance (like Ernie, on account of getting caught on one of his liquor runs).

Justin's hand clenched the fork so tightly the metal edge dug into his palm. "You mean what I said about...about your...?"

"Papa." Lia's eyes suddenly quivered with tears. "I loved him. Do you know that?" She looked over at him fiercely, wiping her cheek.

Justin sat there like an idiot for a second then abruptly scooted back his chair and headed over to a quieter corner, leaving a space for her to follow. Careful not to touch her.

"I know you loved him," he finally said, lowering his voice and softening it to a husky tone. He stared up at the log corners of the wall, hands stuck in his pockets. "And I meant what I said. I'm sorry as I can be. I was a fool, Lia. All the beatings, and Pop, and. . ." Justin looked away, shrugging his shoulders uncomfortably. "I sort of lost my mind, I guess. But I was still a fool."

"What beatings?" Lia looked irritated, wiping the corner of her eye with her fingers.

Justin started to laugh in disbelief then slowly closed his mouth. "You. . .you mean you didn't know? Your pa didn't tell you?"

"Tell me what?"

"About my family. Stuff at home." Justin shrugged, incredulous. "I thought everybody knew."

"If Papa knew anything, he didn't tell me. He never was one for gossip."

Chairs shuffled behind him, and Justin glanced over his shoulder, wishing he could step outside. But they'd shout the end of breakfast in a minute, and Justin would line up for the truck with fifty other denim-clad schmucks, off for another day's work.

Lia reached for a curl of her hair and twirled it nervously, looking away. The unexpected gesture sending a stab of pain through Justin's chest.

"I knew you drank though." Lia didn't meet his eyes. Her voice so soft over the mess hall noise that Justin had to bend closer to hear it.

"Course I drank. I wanted to forget everything. And what happened with your pa—with. . .your father—was an accident. A pure accident. I took Pop's car, loaded up with gin and whiskey, and didn't know where I was going. I couldn't see my hand in front of my face." He swallowed, crossing his arms tight over his chest. "I wish I'da died instead of your father, Lia. I swear."

She blinked faster, still twirling that curl of hair.

"Did ya think I downed all that booze because I liked it?" he said a little more harshly than he intended. "You never thought that maybe my life was rotten and I wished I could die, too, like my ma?"

She flinched. "I guess I'd never thought about why you drank, to tell the truth."

"Only that you hated me."

Her cheeks colored slightly. "Maybe."

Neither of them spoke for a few minutes, and Lia finally raised her head. Letting her curl of hair go and smoothing it back in place. "I know your father wasn't around much. Margaret said so once, and Papa, he. . ." She swallowed. "He knew your father wasn't well, exactly, but he never shared with me the specifics."

"Pop 'wasn't around much'? Margaret said that?" Justin threw his head back and stared up at the ceiling, not sure whether he should laugh or pound a table with his fist. That was Margaret all right, always trying to smooth things over and believe for the good. One of the best people he'd ever known.

And Reverend Summers, too. If he'd known the whole story about the rages and the beatings, at least he'd had the courtesy not to spill to everybody else.

"Why, isn't what Margaret said about your father true?" Lia looked up at him, her eyes looking even bluer against the buttercup yellow of her hat. "Maybe he worked a lot, or. . . ?"

"Well, he wasn't good and kind like your pa, to say the least. Which incident do you want me to tell you about—the time he beat me so senseless I didn't get up for a day and a half after I jumped on him for tryin' to hit my ma?"

Lia's face paled, and her fingers stopped on her hair in mid-curl.

Justin barely saw her. "Or the time he held us all at gunpoint for six hours, dead drunk, because he swore we'd swiped his whiskey stash? I finally took him out with a kitchen chair but not before he put two bullet holes in the wall by my head."

He gave a derisive snort. "Liquor makes you forget, Lia. Or it makes you think you will. But in the end it kicks your tail even harder than the memories. I know that now."

Over the dull noise of breakfast talk and clinking plates, Justin felt an awful silence, like a gaping hole.

And when he looked down again, Lia Summers was mopping a wet palm against her streaming eyes. Her throat shuddering with sobs.

Swell. First I make her throw up, and now I make her cry. Justin felt like banging his head against the log wall in frustration. Couldn't he remember to hold his tongue? Everything he did seemed to be wrong in some way or another—especially around a girl. Like he'd forgotten the manners his ma tried to teach him so many years ago.

And he didn't even have a handkerchief to offer. Not with these ugly work denims.

Justin sighed, awkwardly scratching the back of his neck. "Look. I'm sorry about everything, okay? I didn't mean to. . ."

Before he could step away, Lia reached out quickly and put a gloved hand on his arm. "It's okay. I just. . .didn't know." She wiped her face, sniffling. "There's a lot I didn't know back then either. About you, I guess, and about life and. . .forgiveness."

Justin's gaze fixed on Lia's soft fingers on his shirtsleeve. Warmth soaking through the harsh fabric.

"I forgive you, Justin." She steadied her breath and raised her chin. "I've wanted to say that for a long time, but I never saw you again. Not after you left town, and nobody knew where you went." She pulled off a glove and wiped her cheek. "Bruno told Cynthia there were some guys here from Kentucky, but I never imagined in a hundred years you'd be one of them."

Justin stared at his boots as she gently withdrew her hand. His jaw clenching as he imagined Lia dressed in black, standing by her father's rough pine coffin.

"And I want you to know that my family's all right, even without Papa. God's been good to us. He never forsakes His own, you know. No matter what the economy's like or how bad it gets." Her voice caught again, but she took a deep breath and kept going. "I miss Papa, but. . . Mama's remarried, to a doctor, and he's a good man."

Justin didn't move a muscle, ashamed to hear about Lia's life. The present colliding with the past, just like those two cars on that rainy night back in Berea. His eyes bored into the outline of his boots against the hard floor, and he felt heat rush to his face.

"My stepfather doesn't make much out in the country, but we do all right. He got me into Berea College, where you don't have to pay tuition, and I'm studying to be a teacher. It'll be a good job, and Miriam can go, too, when she's older." She puckered her brow. "And somebody's been sending a few dollars every month ever since Papa died, and it's saved us more times than I can count."

Justin froze. Cleared his throat. Blood pumped to his face so fast he could hardly breathe. Palms growing clammy with sweat.

"We don't have a clue who's sending it. Nobody we know has that kind of money to give away. The church helped out for a long time, of course, but after things got so bad with the Depression and Mama married again, the help dwindled down to a little trickle and then disappeared. But every month those extra dollars are always there—sometimes two, sometimes five or more—sure as the sunrise." Her eyes took on a tender light. "Like the manna God sent to the children of Israel in the desert, Mama says. We used it when the well ran dry and when a storm tore the roof off the end of the house. When Miriam got sick. It's been a blessing."

Justin realized he'd better say something—and quick. "Well," he said, suddenly absorbed in the worn button on his sleeve. Working one loose thread with his close-cut fingernail. "That's mighty fine."

Lia took a deep breath, and Justin thought she'd finished everything she'd come to say.

"But there's one more thing, Justin," she said, shifting her weight a bit nervously. "I want you to forgive me, too."

He jerked his head up in bewilderment, still surprised at the sound of his name in her quiet voice. "What?"

"For the things I said to you." Her lips trembled as she raised her eyes, reaching as if to twine her hair and then abruptly folding her hands together. "I was angry, but I shouldn't have said them. I've felt terrible for that for years. After all my own sins God's forgiven, how could I hate you?" Lia played with the finger of her glove. "I was wrong, too. And I'm asking you to forgive me."

An army officer gave a shout to line up at the door, and the room filled with stifled groans and scuffling boots. Last minute gobbles of coffee and clinking forks.

Every last word flew out of Justin's head like a startled loon on the lake. He swallowed in disbelief then turned over his shoulder and looked at the departing tables. "I've got to. . .to. . .work," he managed, nodding his head. Not trusting his voice to speak. "I'll see ya."

"We'll be back this way around lunchtime. Franklin says the lake's pretty close by."

"Franklin? You. . .you mean Frankie? Frankie White?" Justin could barely look at her, turning back from the bright doorway. Hating the way a patch of sunlight spilled across the right side of her hair, painting the dark walnut brown curls gold and copper.

"Cynthia's uncle brought his camera, and Franklin says the lake's beautiful." She dipped her head again, hiding her face. "And then we'll leave for the Grand Tetons after that. Her uncle's planning to take some photos over there before we head back to Bozeman."

"I'll be on the crew until this evening." Justin shoved his hands in his pockets. "So. . .I guess this is good-bye." He managed a smile. What else could he say? *"Tell your folks hi"*? *"Come visit"*? Naw. "Take care of yourself, Lia."

"I will. And Justin?" Lia looked up, that shaft of sunlight catching the bright blue in her eye. "You didn't say you'd forgive me."

Justin hesitated, his hand on the open door hinge. A breath of dewy sage and pine wafting in from the mountains.

"Of course I do." His words came out so soft he could barely hear them.

And something grateful passed through her eyes before he stepped through the doorway, slants of white-gold morning sun blinding him in all its exquisite, cloudless radiance.

⌀

It was almost quitting time when Justin looked up from the mess of logs and stones he was cribbing along Green River's eroded bank, mud already up to his knees, and saw an odd slant of sun. Hazy and mist-covered, with dark clouds boiling on the horizon.

An ominous wind picked up, skidding across the gushing river water like a skipping stone. Bending spiky river grasses and flattening the leaves of a downed cottonwood that three guys were trying to saw into pieces.

"That's some wind," said one of the guys from Green River spike camp, whom Justin knew only as "Little Joe." He scrunched up pale blue eyes at the clouds. "Smells like snow, if ya ask me."

"It ain't gonna snow, ya idiot." Lanky Ernie Sadler from Camp Fremont, grumpy at giving up his much sought-after leisure time for another Saturday covered with mud, ran a dirty hand through his hair.

Little Joe glared. "I'm tellin' ya. I smell it. I'm from Indiana, and I've seen plenty a snow."

Ernie faced him. "Well, I'm from Wisconsin, and I've seen enough of the white stuff to cover you three times standing up. And I'm sayin' it ain't gonna snow."

"Why don't ya both jest shut up and get to work?" bellowed a redhead, wiping his hands on his stained pants as Justin reached for a log. "Soon as we can get this done, we'll get outta here. Y'all can spend your Saturday in the river if you want, but I shore ain't."

Another wind whipped the grasses as Justin and Ernie pushed the log into place in the soggy riverbank, and a wall of clouds slid across the sun. Blotting out the golden glints that had danced across the ripples like diamond fire and bringing a gust of sudden and shocking cold. Out of the corner of his eye he saw two of the supervisors talking, shirt collars turned up in the wind. And something about Fremont Lake.

"Lieutenant says the storm's blowin' in somethin' fierce over there," said one of them, raising his voice over the wind. "Turned over a boat."

Justin froze, his hand still reaching for a river stone to jam between the logs. "What's he saying?" he asked the redhead, stepping over a muddy limb to hear better.

"Just gimme another rock, will ya?" he scowled.

"Listen, pal," barked Justin, deliberately kicking the log out of place. "I asked you what he said, and I meant it. Some of our crew's over on the lake, and while it may not mean nothin' to you, it sure does to me."

The redhead curled his hands into fists then took a step back when Little Joe and Ernie turned on him. "Then ask him yourself," he growled. "I'm jest tryin' to get my work done and make tracks outta this place. Get it?"

Justin threw down the stones he'd gathered and climbed up the bank. Just in time to hear Ernie call something over his shoulder. "What?" Justin tipped his head back.

"Cynthia's gone, if that's who you're worried about."

"Cynthia?"

"That good-lookin' dish who was over at the camp. When Sweeney came to bring over those new trucks, he said they'd left already. Their car's gone. Nice son-of-a-gun car, too—a '34 Ford in some fancy-schmancy color. Seen it? It's a doozy." Ernie tugged his cap back on in the wind. "Anyhow, they left a thank-you gift for Lieutenant when they left."

Justin wiped a muddy hand on his shirt, staring over the horizon at the line of snowcapped Rockies. The angular shapes fading slowly into a gray soup of clouds. First Fremont Peak disappeared then Gannet Peak. Wiping the smear of pine forest smooth, as if the mountains had never existed at all.

⁓

"It's awful quiet in here." Ernie stepped into his olive uniform pants back in the barracks, gooseflesh raising on his arms from the sudden chill. "Ya don't reckon Frankie actually went on the rest of their trip to the Tetons with 'em, do ya?"

"With Cynthia's folks? No way." Justin buttoned up his regulation shirt, the same requisite shade of olive drab. "Why, ain't he over in the rec hall? Tucker said he saw him."

"Nope. Charlie Pryde's gone, too. But that don't surprise me none. If I know Charlie, he's probably made a break for it. The kid's homesick like the dickens."

Justin's fingers froze on a button. "You don't s'pose Frankie . . ."

"S'pose he hooked up with Cynthia? Not a chance." Ernie's face crinkled. "She's too good for him. Girls can be awful funny though, when it comes to the fellas." He punched Justin's arm. "Hey, wasn't that other gal talkin' to ya in the mess this morning? What about her? She ain't much of a looker, but hey, I'd take whatever I could get around here."

Wind whistled around the corner of the log barracks, rattling the door and windows, and several guys rushed over to bolt the windows tighter.

An oily feeling like bad beer settled in Justin's stomach as he fixed the wind-ruffled sheets on his cot, smoothing them back to regulation wrinkleless bliss. His eyes darting over to Frankie's bed. One blanket askew and pillow dented slightly as if made in a haphazard hurry.

The bird's eggs. The treasure map in a jar.

Oh no, Frankie. Please tell me you got more sense than that. Justin suddenly whirled around to Frankie's cot, ripping the blankets and sheets apart in careless mayhem. Shaking the pillow out of its case.

"You lost your mind, Fairbanks?" Ernie looked up from sticking his socked foot in a boot. "He's gonna jump ya when he sees this mess."

"I'm lookin' for somethin'." Justin flung the bedding back in an ugly pile and threw open Frankie's olive drab footlocker at the foot of his bed. He pulled out Frankie's socks and underwear and tossed them in a pile, pausing only to check one sock when it thunked on the hard floor. Justin fished out shiny chunks of obsidian like polished black glass then hurled them down in disgust.

"It's gotta be here. I know he said he found a map in that jar. Wait a second." Justin jerked out a muddy clay jar and held it up to the light. A ragged paper edge stuck out from the closed top, dull yellow and torn on one corner. "The little creep was tellin' the truth. He's got a map all right."

He pulled out the paper and flattened it carefully, trying to read the faded ink in the dim light: *Waterfall. Ridge. Two miles.* A bunch of arrows and lines.

"I swear, that kid must have mush for brains." Justin slammed the trunk lid shut and stood up, stuffing the map in his pocket. "You comin', too, Ernie? I'm worried Frankie mighta got himself stuck up there on the peak somewhere. Maybe with the whole passel of 'em."

"Me? Let Frankie freeze his own tail off." Ernie pulled on his flattened military-style wool hat, emblazoned with the round CCC emblem on the front. "I got invited to some folks' for the weekend, and I ain't turning down good home cookin' for a dimwit like Frankie White." He straightened his hat in the glass. "Besides, I doubt the rest of 'em are still there. Cynthia's uncle was in some all-fired hurry to get to the Tetons, so they probably done left."

"What about you fellas? Tanner? Jenkins?" Justin put his hands on his hips, turning to two other guys who were lacing up their boots. "Don't ya wanna at least see if they're all right?"

"They're fine. Quit your worryin'. It's a little squall, nothin' more." Tanner shook his head. "And besides, I'm goin' to Jackson for the weekend. Already got my tickets."

Justin pushed a window open a crack and peered at the gray sky. "Lieutenant'll kill Frankie if somethin' happens."

"Let him." Ernie shrugged. "Frankie short-sheeted my bed a week ago, the little squirt. Got me put on KP duty. If Lieutenant don't kill him, I'll do it myself." He pointed at Justin. "And he's the one who put ice in your bed that time, too, Fairbanks. You oughtta let him squirm."

Justin didn't answer. He ran a hand through his hair, jaw clenching as he stared at the cloudy horizon. And then he turned and marched out into the cold wind, slamming the door behind him.

~~~

By the time Justin came to the end of the shortcut path to the lake, clouds had boiled in thicker, and bits of snow drifted on the blustery wind. Chilly darkness descended over the wooded slopes, turning their exuberant green into ominous gray.

For the first time in a year and a half, Justin had skipped evening formation, leaving behind the olive drabs for his fur-trimmed boots and itchy wool winter coat: a belted surplus cast-off from the Great War, too short and too tight around the collar. Cap and gloves and as much stuff as he could shove inside an old military pack before snowflakes began to whirl.

Justin held his cap on with one hand as the wind picked up, following the faded trail through clumps of sage that sloped down toward the lake. A canteen slung across his chest and dread weighing down his boots.

Over the rim of a grassy ridge he spotted a curve of dark water. Fremont Lake was famously cold and surprisingly deep; it stretched down six hundred feet in the middle. Its oblong, slightly bow-shaped shores stretched around the forested Wind River Mountains and up past the ponds the Fremont CCC guys had carved from among the pines. From one side of the lake Justin could see the faint outline of Gannett Peak through the clouds, its white, snowcapped lines appearing briefly like a mirage.

He fingered the paper in his pocket, pulling it out and holding it up to the dull gray glow. The wind tried to whip it from his fingers as he turned it sideways, trying to make out the rough, scrawled handwriting and drawings.

When Justin breathed out, turning his head to keep out the cold-smarting wind, his breath misted like smoky morning, frigid predawn December, back at the Kentucky farm.

"Frankie!" Justin cupped his hands around his mouth and hollered, but no answer came except the crush of pines and tinkling aspens, their branches roaring together with the next blast of wind. A shower of pale snowflakes sifted down through the tops of the pines, settling in a soft white line on tawny grass.

Justin shouted again and then marched through the empty shores and patches of trees to the closest road, hoping against logic that there'd be a motorist there—packing up from a picnic perhaps—and he'd beg a ride to the other side of the lake. To the slopes of the Wind River Mountains indicated in the map, if Justin could read the scrawls correctly.

As soon as he rounded the bend, lake spray spitting against his face, he saw it: a shiny 1934 Ford parked off to the side, its sleek surface spattered with droplets. Stray grasses whipped under the windshield wipers, and a thin crust of snow lay in the grooves of the long, burgundy-brown hood.

An ominous sensation rippled through Justin as he cupped his hands around the snow-beaded glass, praying with all his heart that he was wrong. It couldn't be. *Please, God, not the Parkers' car.*

Then Justin spotted it: Lia's pretty hat and white gloves there on the backseat, tucked over a spray of wildflowers. The little hole at the end of the index finger barely visible through the darkened glass.

For a split second Justin hesitated, backing away from the car and turning back toward the CCC camp. Wondering if there was still time to get the lieutenant and call for help—maybe send up a rescue crew.

But when a second gust of wind, stronger than the first, blew snow in his eyes so thick he could hardly see, Justin felt a panic pulse in his veins. He had to leave a note—beg for help—but how?

A message spelled in rocks on the dirt side of the road? No, that wouldn't work. Snow could pile up over his crooked words and obliterate them in a minute—not to mention all the time he'd waste hunting for rocks in the wind.

Justin rested both hands on his head, trying to keep his wool cap on. Then he tugged hard at the metal door handle. It didn't budge. He tried the other then grabbed a thick fallen limb and began to pound at the back passenger window in desperation. Harder, harder, splinters flying. Until finally the glass cracked like a sudden spiderweb, streaking the smooth glass.

Justin heaved the limb one last time, smashing through the glass and shielding his eyes from the shards. A chunk of glass collapsed in gleaming pieces, scattering the snow-crusted grass and smooth leather seat inside the Ford. Snow and leaves fluttered across the boxes and jackets in the backseat—everything packed for the trip to the Tetons.

Justin reached through the shattered window opening and dug through Lia's modest pale blue handbag, catching the side of his arm on a sharp shard of glass. Blood dripped onto the leather seat as he sorted through her hairpins and lipstick, and at last his fingers closed around a colored pencil.

A prayer of hope rose inside him like a shout, filling him with a strange calm. Organic and unexpected, like prayers and God-clinging had become a second skin in this short year and a half.

A far cry from the rebellious and heart-angry soul who'd plowed his car into Reverend Summers.

Justin drew out the pencil, scratching another gash on his forearm against the broken glass, and scrawled a note for help and a crude map on one of Lia's sheets of sketch paper. He anchored the note in place against the back window with handfuls of heavy stones, dug from the fragrant, sandy lake soil.

Justin wrapped his sleeve around the cuts on his arm, stanching the flow of blood, and lifted his eyes to the snow-filled sky. Bits of white flew faster and faster, shrouding all but the faintest lines of Gannett Peak.

He tossed the pencil and sketch pad back into the car, and something caught his eye: a bit of dusty fabric that made him do a double take. That familiar bleached blue with fraying edging.

His CCC bandanna, folded carefully around a framed photo of her father. His black-and-white smile so tender Justin felt he could almost reach out and touch it. Loopy words in dark ink lined the corner of the photo—a note to Lia?

Justin stood there a moment, shivering and holding his sleeve against his bleeding forearm. Whistling wind fluttered Lia's sketchbook pages and hairpins across the floorboard of the car, rattling the chocolate-brown ribbon on her hat. Sending it scudding across the seat and bending the brim.

Justin reached back through the broken glass and began gently tucking Lia's handbag, hat, and gloves under Cynthia's silk scarf along with her wilting flowers. But letting his palm linger just a second on the worn finger of Lia's white glove, he changed his mind and stuffed them both in his breast pocket.

Snow poured down in heavy gusts, spitting ice and laying white in the hollows of fallen limbs and thick pine branches as Justin broke into a run toward the ridge overlooking the lake. Frankie's map branched off from the trail the Fremont guys had started to clear-cut for a trail a few weeks ago, still closed off with a rough pine-log gate.

Frankie had really done it this time. Besides the snow, the wooded slopes beyond the gate hid wolves. Wolves normally tended to avoid humans, slipping through shadows in graceful silver whispers. But with all the new towns encroaching into what had once been wilderness, new roads hacked into dense stands of virgin timber, sometimes the wolves became desperate.

The mountain slopes also harbored grizzlies. One of which could tear a man to pieces in minutes.

Justin ran the length of the lake until he felt his legs and lungs would give out, his boots hanging heavy on his feet. Mile after mile, wind stinging his face in snowy blasts. He stumbled over downed branches and hidden ridges in the snowy grass. When he came to the gate, he paused just long enough to catch his breath—bending over double—and then hopped the gate and took off through the trail, its dense carpet of Ponderosa pine needles now damp with snow. Eerie quiet closed in around him as snow-painted pines and junipers towered around him, closing him in until he could no longer see the lake. Leaving nothing but an angry patch of gray sky brooding overhead through the wind-trembling limbs.

A gust of wind whistled past him, nearly knocking him over, and tugged at the leather strap of his backpack. Reminding him of the ribbon on Lia's hat, ruffling from wind through the broken car window. Snow dusting its brim.

The coiled brown ribbon like a curl of her hair twisted shyly around her finger.

And he pushed his way deeper into the forest.

Chapter 7

The rough trail wound upward through the woods, tracking so steeply at times that Justin had to crawl on his hands and knees over rocks and boulders, muddying his hands. White and yellow cinquefoil bloomed thickly along the trail in open spots, frozen in beads of sleet. Sagebrush and shrubs grew so thickly in several places that Justin could barely find the trail.

Dense stands of pines and Douglas firs closed around the trail, blotting out the meadow patches and making a gloomy canopy. Evening fell, a dusky coyote gray, and sleet came mixed in the snow in stinging squalls. Wind screamed through the pines and across the exposed rock ridges like an angry wildcat as Justin stopped to catch his breath.

He shouted again for Frankie but heard only the whistle of wind.

In the dim half light of an angry sky, Justin huddled in a space between two fir trees. He unfolded Frankie's map and held it tight as wind snatched at corners.

The script hooked and looped in fine black lines, as if written in quill pen, and a few spatters of ink dotted the margin. A corner of the yellow paper crumbled in his fingers, brittle thin. Justin turned the paper over, wondering for the first time if Frankie was right—and the letter was authentic.

Either way, Frankie was an idiot for leading a bunch of girls up into the mountains in September.

Justin stuffed the letter in his pocket and followed the trail up the side of the ridge, breaking off a thick pine limb in case a grizzly got a whiff of him—or his backpack. Not that it would do much good anyhow against five hundred pounds of angry bear.

Justin made his way around a bend by a raging stream, its banks white with rapids and snow-clogged mosses, and shouted until his voice felt hoarse. Exhausted and not sure where to go next. He leaned, shivering, against a sturdy whitebark pine to rest, praying that he wouldn't be too late—that God would hold off the snow and the bears, and help him find his way through the thick maze of darkening trunks and heavy fringes of silent pine.

Seeking the lost—is that not what Jesus Himself had done when He left behind the ninety-nine good souls for hard-hearted fellows like Justin? Calling out for the lost sheep in the storm, and giving His very life to bring it home, safely tucked under His nail-scarred hands?

Just like Reverend Summers, laying down His life for the likes of Justin Fairbanks.

For even if he had lived, Justin knew the reverend would have loved him. Would have forgiven him, even there, covered in blood and broken glass. Ever hoping, ever praying, for the light to shine on the dull walls of Justin's dark heart.

He could still see it: the reverend's last struggling breaths as his life bled out. The shock in his wide eyes, and the startled recognition as they came to rest on Justin's face while Justin stumbled toward him, lurching sideways in a drunken haze as he tried to pull open the reverend's smashed car door. The stuck car horn shrieking in strident fury.

Justin remembered the hot scald of tears that had poured down his senseless face as his alcohol-leaden mind tried to take it all in, blubbering nonsensical words. And the reverend lifted one trembling hand and rested it—in inconceivable gentleness—on Justin's bruised and bloody head.

And let it fall there, lifeless. Limp. The warmth bleeding out of his fingers in the stiff rainfall.

"You're a good fellow," he'd said to Justin that day across the table, heaping strawberry jam on his biscuit.

Justin had stumbled away from the reverend's battered Buick and crawled back into the steaming, glass-strewn wreck of his father's Model T in a sobbing mess, trying to rev the gas in a vain attempt to flee. To forget. To force open his swollen eyes and pretend the whole thing had never happened. He careened sideways into a storefront and heard the vicious tearing of metal. Crushing weight on his arms, his feet. His consciousness fading like a falling curtain.

Shouts. The scream of a police siren. Brilliant lights and blinding pain. . .

"Frankie!" Justin cupped his hands around his mouth and yelled again, praying with all his heart that he could find the reverend's daughter before it was too late.

Something rattled the leaves near the trail, breaking a branch. Justin stiffened and jerked his head up in the gloom, clenching his cold-stiff hands against the bracing gusts.

A noise like a voice and then silence.

And then he heard it over the wind: a crash of twisted underbrush. Snapping twigs and heavy footfalls, and the sound of tearing leaves. Faster, faster.

Justin raised his pine limb and whirled around, ready to beat off a coiled mountain lion or tooth-bared wolf. The shadow came faster than Justin could think—and he swung—almost whacking the daylights out of a shadowy figure.

"Don't shoot!" came a familiar whiny voice, shrill with terror. Cringing and cowering. Covering his head with skinny arms.

Justin did a double take, nearly dropping the branch. He reached out with one hand, grabbing the guy's shirt collar in a tight wad and jerking him closer. The last bit of remaining daylight falling, low and dark, on the thin lines of Frankie White's pale, terrified face.

Frankie's purple lips shuddered and stammered with cold.

"Frankie Stinkin' White," Justin hollered over the wind, rattling him back and forth. "Did you bring them up here? Where are they?"

And Frankie began to nod and bawl, pointing up through the woods.

Justin drew back his other arm in a clenched fist, ready to knock Frankie's teeth into the nearest clump of cinquefoils.

In the shadowy darkness under the pine branches and stormy sky, Justin caught a faint glint of muted light on Frankie's face. The terrified whites of his eyes, and tears streaking down his pale cheeks.

Justin's heart raced, adrenaline pounding, but for some inexplicable reason his fist wavered. His fingers loosened, and he slowly lowered his arm.

He gave Frankie a shove, releasing his collar. "I oughtta pound you to kingdom come!" he shouted over the blustery gusts, his fingers still curled tightly shut. Not entirely sure if he'd decided not to sock Frankie. "You outta your ever-lovin' mind? What in the name a goodness were you thinkin'?" He surveyed Frankie's dirty, stained summer shirt and trousers and his flimsy leather loafers. "And dressed like some sorta ballroom dance boy at that?"

Frankie didn't reply, his skinny shoulders shuddering with sobs.

"Answer me!" Justin grabbed his shoulders and shook him again. "Where are they?"

"I didn't know it was gonna snow," Frankie blubbered, wiping his face with dirty fingers. "Honest, I didn't."

"Course you didn't! You ain't been here long enough to know anything about Wyoming. You're a city boy!"

Justin's heart pulsed in an odd sort of pity at Frankie's dirty, torn shirt and muddy shoes. One pant leg wet from apparently misstepping in a creek or something—and the shoe squished when he moved. The sole had come loose on the other, which had obviously been re-glued several times and patched with cardboard.

"My ma's gonna kill me." Justin had to lean closer to make out Frankie's words through wimpish sniffles. "Lieutenant's gonna send me home, and we'll lose the house. We'll be on the streets." He doubled over, arms wrapped around himself as he shivered, gasping back sobs. "I know it's my fault. I'm such a stupidhead. My brothers and sis ain't gonna have nothin' to eat, and it's all my doin'. My brother's sick, too, and they can't pay for a doc without my paycheck."

Frankie moaned, burying his head in his arms. "I thought I could do this job okay, but I ain't. I'm gonna be back in Ohio again, doin' nothin' while my brother dies."

He sobbed again then abruptly kicked a tree in anger. Making him howl louder.

"Frankie." Justin grabbed his shoulder, trying to pull him away from the tree as he kicked again wildly and then tried to ram it headfirst. "Get a hold of yourself, for Pete's sake! Cut it out!"

"I can't face 'em!" Frankie's voice strained with tears. "I'm done for."

"Lieutenant ain't gonna send you home." Justin jerked him still.

"Oh yes he is! He said if I so much as screw up one step on this hike, he'd can my tail first thing in the mornin'. Charlie bailed like I thought he would, and once the rest of us got lost, I didn't know what to do."

Frankie tried to head-butt the tree again, letting out a roar of grief, and Justin grabbed him, wrestling him to a halt and slapping his cheeks. "Pull yourself together, fella!" He stuck his face close to Frankie's. "We've gotta get the others, and you're gonna help me. You know where you left 'em?"

"Sure. Under a ridge, sorta outta the snow. Although it's comin' down so hard in all directions that they might as well be in the North Pole."

Justin groaned. "What'd ya do, leave 'em there as bear bait?"

"Mr. Parker fell and hit his head on the rocks, and that other dame slipped on a ridge. I was a fool to bring 'em up here. I just wanted to show Cynthia. . ." Frankie's voice trailed off into another bawl. "So I decided it was better to go and get help than stick around and let us all freeze."

"Lia's hurt?" Justin bristled again. "If anything happens to that gal, Frankie, or her friends, I swear I'll. . ." He clenched his jaw. "You just better pray like the dickens that everybody's okay when we find 'em."

He shook the snow from his hair and started to pull Frankie toward the trail when he suddenly stopped, glancing up through the woods. "Say, if you were goin' to get help, then why'd you come this way and not toward the camp?" He pointed. "Camp's over that way. This trail leads down to the road, and it's a doggone lot farther away than the camp." He narrowed his eyes. "Were you runnin' out on 'em like that fool Charlie?"

Frankie flinched, blinking faster. "N—naw. I swear. I thought I'd. . .I'd flag down a car or somethin'."

"In this storm?" Justin narrowed his eyes. "There are shelters down at the ponds by the road. You knew that, didn't you? You could dry yourself off and weather out the storm then stick out your thumb and hitchhike back to Ohio. Vanished. Eaten by a mountain lion. Everybody'd think you're a martyr—a hero."

Frankie's eyes darted back and forth away from Justin. "What. . .what ponds? What are you talkin' about?" His Adam's apple bobbed nervously.

For a split second Justin felt like throwing Frankie White headfirst down the mountain. His gut churned, not sure what to believe. Justin stood there, hands on his hips, feeling his arms and shoulders clamp tight with anger.

And then he shoved Frankie back toward the mountain trail, nearly knocking him down. "Git on up there, Frankie, and show me where they are before I kick your tail to kingdom come."

Frankie trotted ahead through the snow-sodden underbrush, sniffling. "I'll show ya. I swear, I left 'em in the best place I could. They're gonna be all right."

"They'd better be." Justin started forward like a bull, steam practically snorting from his nostrils.

Then he jerked Frankie to a stop. "And gimme those doggone stupid shoes a yours."

"What?" Frankie wiped his tear-streaked cheek.

"Your shoes. Give 'em to me." Justin bent down and started to unlace his boots.

"You ain't gonna…" Frankie's eyes widened, and his breath shuddered. "Naw. I ain't takin' 'em off."

Justin shook a finger in Frankie's face, losing patience. "You get those fool things off in ten seconds or I'll pound you into next week, hear me?" he bellowed. "And quit stallin' 'cause we ain't got no time. And put this on. You're gonna catch pneumonia out here dressed like this." He shrugged off his backpack and threw his coat at Frankie. "Put it on. Now. You squeak so much as a word and I'll deck you flat out. And I ain't haulin' your sorry tail down the mountain. So hurry up."

Frankie hastily grabbed the coat and stuck his arms through, double time, not daring to protest as Justin tugged off his boots and threw them at Frankie.

Justin stuck his feet into Frankie's own cracked, river-sodden shoes. One broken sole flapping.

⁓⋄⁓

When they reached the top of the trail, snow poured down so hard they could barely see. The temperature had dropped, and a thick layer of icy white crust, beaded like glass pellets, coated the pine boughs and rocks.

Justin dug in his bag and pulled out an army surplus flashlight—cold, cylindrical metal—and flipped on the weak beam. His toes had grown numb stuffed into Frankie's too small, battered shoes, ice leaking through the broken sole. Wind cut through his wool shirt, stinging his arms and shoulders.

They mounted a rocky clearing, the boulders slippery with snow, and struggled through the jagged openings to a wide field. Low clouds boiled overhead in a soupy fog. Justin held on to a group of boulders with one hand and his hat and flashlight with the other arm, trying to keep his balance in the thickening storm—and slowly losing hope that he'd find the others alive.

"We came up here to pick bellflowers and look for the gold." Frankie sniffled back a runny nose, gusts nearly snatching the words out of his mouth. His lips were ringed with purple, and he shivered even under Justin's thick coat. "Cynthia's uncle said the letter might be real, and he thinks Jeremiah Wilde is a relative of some lawyer named Kelly—who swears he saw the gold with his own eyes."

"A lawyer." Justin's eyebrows made an angry line. "You believed a stinkin' lawyer? I wouldn't trust one farther than I could throw him."

"I dunno. It sounded legit." Frankie sniffled and wiped his nose with the back of his hand. "But we shouldn'ta come up here like this. I know it now."

Justin was too tired and cold to respond with an insult, although several raced to the surface of his cold-leaden brain. "Where'd you go from here?"

"Behind the falls." Frankie pointed a trembling finger. "Mr. Parker got some swell pictures, too, and we were about to head back when the storm started brewing. The rocks got slippery, and. . ." He swallowed hard, looking like he might cry again. "I left everybody under a ledge and sorta outta the snow. Over this way."

Frankie hobbled through the snowy meadow, Justin's heavy winter boots sticking in the white muck. He linked arms with Justin to brace himself against the heavy gusts.

Frankie said something in low tones, his face turned down as if ashamed, but the wind snatched it.

"Huh?" Justin maneuvered around a boulder, trying to keep the snow out of his pant legs and bare ankles. He'd stripped off his wool socks, too, to warm up Frankie's frozen feet. If he got frostbite, he'd let Frankie work to pay off his medical bills, the stinker.

"I said, 'How'd ya know about my ma?'" Frankie turned to him.

"What?" Justin screwed up his face, wiping sleet from his brow and eyes with the back of his wrist. "You lost your marbles, Frankie? I don't know the first thing about your ma."

"No, I mean what you said the other night in the barracks." His lip trembled. "About somebody back home prayin' for me."

A blast of wind hit hard, kicking up a wall of snow, and both boys turned to cover their faces. When Frankie got his breath back, shaking the snow from his hair and finding another solid step through the thick layer of white, he sniffled again. "My ma's real into all that God stuff, ya know. Says He's watchin' out for us, and all this crazy mess about Jesus dyin' on the cross."

His words tumbled over themselves, fast as snowflakes. "I don't believe a word of it. I mean, what's a good God gotta do with me, first of all, the biggest dunce you ever seen—and second, why'd He let my pa get some kinda crazy disease?" His voice choked with emotion. "I watched him die, Fairbanks. He was a good man. And now my brother's got the same thing. Docs say it's some kinda genetic thing, and ain't no cure. All of us outta work. No jobs, no nothin'. Life is rotten, you know? I say there's no God up there who'd let all this happen to us, and if there is, I sure don't want nothin' to do with Him. My ma's a fool." He drew in a shuddering breath. "But how'd you know she was prayin' for me? Tell me that."

"You watch your mouth about God." Justin boiled up, raising his voice over the howl of wind through the rocks. "And your ma, too. Show some respect for once in your life. Maybe your ma's right, and you're the one who's a fool. After all, your own way hasn't done ya so swell, has it?"

Frankie didn't answer, pushing his way between some crystallized ferns. His breath smoky in the downpour.

"Has it?" Justin rattled Frankie's shoulder, softening his voice just a touch.

"I reckon not." Frankie's words carried a note of despair, like the barren sky over a whitening field.

"And I don't know the first thing about your ma prayin' for you. I was just guessin', is all. Seems like so many folks out there are runnin' from the very thing that'll straighten out the mess they've made. Drinkin' themselves to death to forget, or laughin' to cover the pain. But that road'll kill ya." Justin blinked back snowflakes. "You'll hurt other people, too—just like I did."

He braced his arm against Frankie's shoulder as they came to a low ridge, stepping carefully to keep from turning an ankle. "It ain't too late to straighten your life out, Frankie. Go to chapel and listen to what the old man says. Read the Bible your ma's always talkin' about. Shoot, read mine if ya want. But do somethin' to get right with God. Before you mess up worse than ya already have."

Frankie didn't answer for a long time, bending against the wind and stepping carefully. When he did speak, his voice sounded choked again. "You're pretty swell, Fairbanks. Ya know that?"

Justin lifted his head but didn't reply. Thinking of Reverend Summers's battered hand resting on his head amid the wreckage. The eyes that held love and pain, bright as stars, until their life ebbed away. Leaving them in a horrible, cold stare. Lashes still half open.

"No I ain't," Justin grunted. "Ain't nothin' swell about me. All I've done with my life 'til now is screw things up. You don't got any idea the things I've done."

"Don't matter. You're still as swell as can be." Frankie sniffled. "I hope I can be. . .well, like you one day."

Justin felt his throat contort so tightly he could hardly breathe. A sudden rush of emotion stung his eyes, and for a second he couldn't see.

"Aw, knock it off, bonehead," he growled, turning away and blinking faster. "You're full of it."

And then he raised his hand to Frankie's head in an unexpected tender gesture, ruffling his windblown hair. Resting it there for a second as if in blessing.

⤜⤏

"Over here!" Frankie called, pointing to a snowy decline clogged with boulders. Half hidden between a thickly forested clump of pines. "I brought 'em down this way."

Frankie offered his arm, and Justin grasped it, nearly losing his footing on the slippery, snow-coated stones. "Is this where Mr. Parker fell?" he gasped, catching himself on a pine limb and hauling himself upright. Scrambling for footing on the spongy, frozen ground.

"Yeah. It's real rough. Steep, too."

Justin's pack shifted, and the flashlight slipped out of his hand, dropping and rolling between the rocks. He choked back one of the old curses that used to fly from his lips. He hopped two boulders and followed its faint beam down through a clump of ice-glassed ferns, where it finally wedged itself against a stone. Justin got down on his knees and strained to reach it, but his arm still came up short.

"I can't believe it," Justin snapped, slapping his thigh. "Of all the times to lose a light! I don't got another one, and that battery ain't gonna last long in the cold."

"Let me help," sniffled Frankie. "I'll get it for ya." He crawled around the other boulder and stuck his bony arm through, grunting with effort. He poked a stick through the crack, managing only to push the flashlight farther into the rocks.

Justin hollered at him to stop and finally threw down his pack in disgust. "We're sunk without that light, Frankie!" he bellowed, kneeling on the cold ground. "We gotta think of somethin'."

"A shovel?" Frankie blabbered through chattering lips.

Bone-tired and cold, soaked to the skin, Justin felt like decking Frankie again. "Something I got in the pack, genius."

He looked up at the cobalt sky, black trees framing a jagged circle over their heads. Gray flakes flitted across his vision and into his lashes as he tried to jog his brain to think, think.

"Pray," Justin finally said. "You'd better get down on your knees right now and pray that we can get that light, or we'll be stuck up here who knows how long. No tellin' when this snow's gonna stop."

"Me? Pray?" Frankie's voice came out hesitant and squeaky. "I ain't never really prayed before, but if ya think it'll do any good, I can try. What do I say? Do I need to cross myself or somethin'?"

"Just pray to God, Frankie." Justin felt desperate, his last hope shredding like the tiny filaments inside the metal flashlight tube. "Tell Him we need that light. I'm gonna pray, too, hear me?"

"I'll do it. I'll do it." Frankie affected a pious posture on one knee, hands folded together. Eyes closed, lips moving. "A'ight." He shifted back up to his feet and brushed off his muddy pants. "I told Him. Don't know as He's gonna answer me though. Most of the time I use Jesus' name it's for a swear word, and I don't reckon He likes that too much."

"Well, quit doin' it then." Justin felt his patience slip another notch. "And I don't care who He answers so long as we get that light."

Justin scooted around to the other side of the massive boulder and tried to heave it off, but it didn't budge. Its outline too dark to follow in murky nightfall. "Get up here and help me, will ya?"

Frankie scrambled up beside him, and they pushed at the rock, grunting and straining. Nothing moved, save a few clods of dirt and rock that clattered down the ridge.

"Not enough," Justin grunted, feeling blind as blackness settled, thick as tar. He had to blink to make sure his eyes were still seeing. The only light came from a dull overhead glow from the blustery sky, faintest gray, and the weak glimmer of light from the flashlight beam shadowed against leaves under the rocks.

When Justin moved a hand in front of his face, he saw nothing. He had no idea how big the boulder was, or how far it stretched to the other side.

"God, gimme that light," he pleaded under his breath, worried for the first time that he and Frankie might catch hypothermia before they could even get to the others. His feet were freezing in Frankie's flimsy shoes, and he couldn't seem to stop shivering. He'd lost most of the feeling in his fingers long ago, and when he tried to move a stone out of the way, he fumbled and dropped it down through the hole, clogging it even more.

"C'mon, Frankie. Help me." He put his back and shoulders into the boulder, grunting and shouting, and Frankie joined in on the other side.

"This ain't movin', Fairbanks! I can't even get my arms around it."

"Push, or I'll knock you in the jaw!"

And then Justin felt the boulder shift slightly. Rolling back just enough to wedge his hand in and nearly reach the light. His fingers stretched black shadows across the bumpy earth in the bright beam but still came up short.

"Here. Lemme try." Frankie squeezed in close.

"You?" Justin spoke without thinking, not pulling his arm out.

"Sure, why not? We prayed, didn't we? Hurry up, Fairbanks. You're freezing. Move it."

Justin hesitated then backed away from the crack. *Oh Jesus, have mercy,* he thought wryly, licking his stinging lips, which started to crack with cold.

Once, and nothing. Twice. Frankie dug sideways, straining, and suddenly Justin's eyes dazzled with light. The flashlight lay there in Frankie's upturned palm, gleaming red through cold fingers.

Justin hollered and slapped his shoulder then threw his arm around him in an awkward hug.

Just as an eerie shout rose through the trees, wispy and faraway as a coyote song.

Justin shushed Frankie. "You hear that?"

They held their breath as the sound came again through the soft silence of falling snow. The low creak of pines bending under the weight of sleet and ice.

A cry for help.

Justin snatched up his backpack and scrambled across the rocks, Frankie holding out the flashlight like the glow of a skinny lighthouse. Its weak beam bobbing across snow and boulders in a blessed golden circle.

Chapter 8

Frankie gestured through the trees, his cheeks red from cold in the flashlight's pale glow. They ducked under pine boughs, powder falling from the needles, and scrambled over boulders studded with frozen moss.

When Justin turned his head he heard a tremulous rushing—the musical roar of water over stones, and its echo against rock—which he figured must be the waterfall Frankie spoke of. On a cloudless day, with streams of blue bellflowers and a waterfall crashing in a thousand streams of crystal, it'd be a swell place for photos.

But now the rocks hung craggy and dark, slippery with wet snow. In the distance, Justin heard the wail of a bobcat—its eerie scream high and mournful, deceptively vulnerable.

He'd seen bobcats slink through the trees in the Kentucky forests like black velvet, rippling and disappearing and barely rustling leaves. A blink to check the eyes, and the shadow had vanished. But when one big she-cat tried to carry off their hound Mutt, who'd been guarding Beanie, it took both Justin and a hired farm hand to beat it off with rifle stocks and fence planks. And not before it took a sizeable chunk out of Mutt's flank and nearly killed her with jagged puncture wounds.

If that was a Kentucky bobcat, Justin couldn't imagine the size of one grown in the vast forests of the Rockies, raised on a diet of muscular pronghorn antelope and furry-eared mule deer.

"What if Mr. Parker's dead?" Frankie quivered, tucking his chin tighter into Justin's wool coat as he hugged himself to keep out the cold. "What if we're too late? I'll die, Fairbanks. I swear I will."

"Quit talkin' about dying. We're almost there." Justin's voice came out snappish, but his heart quivered a moment, too, wondering if an unconscious man, bleeding from a head injury, could make it long in this breath-snatching cold.

Justin cupped his hands around his mouth and hollered, pulling

Frankie to a standstill, and two women's voices called back. One sounding like Lia Summers. Making an unexpected tingle under Justin's freezing skin.

⁓⊱⁓

Frankie got turned around twice, poking in the wrong bushes and scooting around the wrong cliffs, but for once Justin couldn't blame him. Everything looked the same: black, shapeless, snow-covered. Clumps of pines mirrored themselves in dizzying spitefulness, now here, now there, and another across the rocks—so that even Justin couldn't remember which ones he'd just seen.

"They're here! They're here!" Frankie called in shrill, excited tones, throwing back a thick, snow-laden pine limb and ducking under. Motioning Justin to follow.

Justin ducked under in a spray of fine, sifting snow, following the bobbing circle of light, and caught his breath: four people huddled together against a rock cliff on a cone-strewn carpet of pine needles. Dense pine boughs arched over them, white-covered, forming a little cavelike enclave.

Well, well. For once Frankie had done something smart. The rocks and pines kept out the wind, and only a fine film of snow had scudded under the thick, fragrant mounds of evergreen needles.

The flashlight beam wavered across Cynthia, her cheeks tear-stained and face pink and white with cold and her bright red-gold hair rumpled in messy waves. Even crumpled and shivering, Justin had to admit she was a strikingly pretty girl. Mrs. Parker shivered, arms wrapped around her husband as if trying to soothe him, and Lia huddled next to Cynthia, whose knees were tucked up under her long skirt to keep her extremities warm.

Justin couldn't think of Cynthia though, or her beauty—but only of Lia. Memories of her sunshiny smile crowded in his head. Her yellow dress was muddy, stained from the hem up, and her right leg lay out straight. The ankle swollen in a bulge just over her shoe and her face drawn tight in pain. One hand tightly gripped her shin as if trying to squeeze out the ache.

"They're here, Fairbanks. All of 'em." Frankie stripped off Justin's coat in uncharacteristic gallantry, his excited blabbering rising over the other voices. He draped the coat around Mrs. Parker's shoulders, spreading the other half over Cynthia. "I reckon I believe in prayer now, huh?"

"I got crackers and some cheese." Justin dug into his pack. "Here.

Give 'em somethin' to eat and pass my canteen around. Y'all ain't been drinkin' melted snow, have ya? It'll freeze ya from the inside out."

"A little." Mrs. Parker reached out a trembling hand and squeezed Justin's arm in greeting, her face tight and pale. "He's been begging for water for hours. I don't know what to do—is he going to make it?"

Justin squeezed her hand back. "He'll make it, ma'am. He'll be fine. You'll see. We'll get him to the doc first thing in the morning, if this snow lets up."

Justin tried to size up their limitations: four freezing folks drinking melted snow and two injuries so far. Wet wood and blowing snow. A couple of crackers, some tinned butter and cheese, and a canteen of water. *Dear Lord.* He rubbed his face with his hand, groaning inwardly. Even the stiff, uncomfortable army cots and rubbery stewed tomatoes back at the camp seemed like heaven compared to this.

Mr. Parker lay against his wife's shoulder, a bloody cloth wrapped around his head. But his eyes fluttered open, and a faint smile curved his lips. "Oh thank God," he moaned, rocking slightly back and forth. "Thank God you're here. Frankie, oh Frankie—he brought help! I knew you would."

He reached out a waxy white arm to grip Frankie's hand, and Justin saw Frankie dip his head slightly as if in shame, eyelashes fluttering. "Don't thank me, sir," he mumbled. "I ain't done a thing to be proud of."

Before Frankie could lay clean his cowardice, Justin quickly knelt beside Mr. Parker. "He came as soon as he could, sir. I'm so sorry for your injury. I hate that you had to wait so long for help." Justin ripped open the backpack and pulled out a wool army blanket, pressing it around his shoulders.

"Yeah, and of all the rotten folks to find," Frankie joked sheepishly, sounding like he'd bawl any minute if he didn't lighten things up.

Justin punched Frankie lightly in the arm and reached for another blanket, crawling over to Lia's spot and draping it over her shoulders. She let go of Cynthia for a second, teeth chattering, her eyes dark in the dim half glow of the flashlight. Her hair hung wild and disheveled, wind-whipped curls hanging down in her face.

"You okay? Can I see that ankle?" Justin reached for Frankie's flashlight, not sure what he should do. Try to brace it, maybe, with some twigs and a bandanna, splintlike?

Without meaning to, he stroked Lia's hair out of her cold cheeks so he could see her face and how dilated her pupils were—if she could still speak or if the injury had sent her into shock.

And without warning Lia suddenly reached out her arms, wrapping them around his neck in a clumsy embrace. "You came," she whispered, her lips shivering so much that Justin could hardly make out her words.

He was struck speechless for a moment, frozen in place. Not sure whether to move or speak, or even breathe. He'd killed her father, for goodness' sake. What kind of scum would that make him here, now, to deserve or accept even an ounce of her affection?

"Of course I came," he finally said, holding her there for a warm second and then helping her back to Cynthia's side. Tucking the blanket around her neck as she closed her eyes.

"You must be Justin," said Cynthia through shivers, the contours of her pretty face pale in the faint halo of light. "Lia said you might come."

"She did?" He glanced over at Lia with a start, but she didn't seem to hear. "But I didn't. . ." He narrowed his eyes. "How'd you know who I am? We ain't met yet."

Cynthia shrugged. "Lia said you'd come for us and that you'd do anything to help." She tucked the blanket tighter around her shoulders. "So I guessed it must be you. She said you grew up together, and she always thought you had a wonderfully good heart."

Justin's eyes bulged. "She. . .she told you that?"

"And she said her father loved you."

He smoothed the edge of Lia's blanket in silence, the sudden lump in his throat choking out the words. Finally he tipped his head sideways. "She okay, Cynthia? She. . .uh. . .well, she don't look so good."

Cynthia huddled deeper under the blanket, tears glimmering in her dark eyes. "I don't know," she whispered. "She's awfully cold, and a couple of hours ago she started to talk nonsense. Something about her dad, and you, and. . .I don't know. It didn't make any sense to me." She pressed her pale lips together. "Do you think she's got hypothermia? We've been trying to keep warm, but it's freezing out here."

"Hey Frankie, pass me that canteen, will ya?" Justin poured a little water in the tin cup, his fingers shaking in an unexpected mess of nerves, then held it up to Lia's mouth to drink. Picturing her at the table with the jar of strawberry jam, her lashes dark and her manners humble and demure.

"C'mon, Lia. Drink a little water."

Lia sipped, water running down her chin as she shifted forward stiffly, drawing up her good leg. "I'll be fine. I just need to say good-bye first, and then we can go."

Huh? Justin narrowed his eyes and bent closer to hear. "What'd you say? We ain't goin' nowhere, at least not until this snow lets up."

She was delirious. She had to be.

"I knew you'd come," Lia murmured, turning her face toward Justin. A crack on her lips showing a faint red line of blood. Her eyelids closed, and the blanket slipped off one shoulder.

Justin knelt just close enough to draw the blanket back up under her chin, tucking her fine curls of messy hair out of the way. Brushing out some dried pine needles that had clung there, little bits of bleached red-brown among nearly black.

She needed lip balm for sure—Vaseline, or oil even—to keep her lips from cracking even more. He opened his backpack and flipped the top off the dented can of butter then smoothed his finger on the dull yellow surface. Running his moistened finger across Lia's cracked lower lip.

And as his breath stirred her hair, ever so gently, he leaned forward and touched his lips briefly and soundlessly to her forehead.

If Lia noticed, she never said a word. But Justin felt as if his heart would soar right through the pines, exploding into little flakes of white brilliance, raining down across the snow-swept slopes of the Wind River Range.

"We've gotta get a fire goin' before they all freeze to death," Justin said to Frankie under his breath, digging through his pack for the drab olive army-issue fire starter. It was made of rough cloth with a piece of flint, a steel striker, and a pile of fine, blond tinder that looked like horsehair. All cinched together with a leather cord.

"What are we gonna use for firewood? Everything out here's wet and frozen." Frankie was shivering again. And no wonder—the temperature must've fallen another twenty degrees. Their breath misted, and Justin could barely feel his fingers.

If he wasn't careful, he might shiver and drop the spark, wasting good tinder and ruining their shot at starting a fire.

"We'll look for dry wood, both of us, up next to the trunks and outta the snow," said Justin, wiping his damp hair out of his eyes with his sleeve. "You got your knife on ya?"

"Got it." Frankie patted his pocket. "Pine resin burns real well, too, and dead needles, if we can find some dry."

"Well, then, look for 'em. We'll shave the outer wood off the branches if we have to, to find somethin' dry, and make a big enough pile to last us all night. If that fire goes out, we'll have a doozy of a time startin' it again." He poked his head through the pine boughs, careful not to dislodge the snow.

Frankie sniffled back a runny nose. "The snow ain't that deep. We can dig down to the ground and start the fire right there in that open patch." He pointed toward a small pocket of open ground close to the campsite.

Justin bit his lip, twisting his head sideways to look up and make sure there was good clearance. They couldn't have smoke doubling back into their dry alcove, forcing them to move to a wetter, colder spot. "Looks good to me, I reckon. Not that I can be picky. And we need a lotta wood, hear? Not just a stick or two. Plus enough twigs to start a bundle—and it might take us awhile to gather in this mess. I don't got another coat or blanket. We're just gonna hafta keel over ot hypothermia gettin' it, or we'll all six freeze." He grimaced up at the blustery sky. "And we probably ain't gonna sleep. You with me?"

Frankie met his eyes for a second, their characteristic goofy look turning suddenly sober. "I'm with ya. Here. I'll hold the light."

"Don't drop it." Justin raised his eyebrows in a warning look. "C'mon now, and let's get 'em warmed up."

⁂

Frankie's eyes looked glassy as he wrapped the bandanna around the steaming cup handle, squatting by the sputtering fire. "Reckon we're all gonna make it, Fairbanks? Mr. Parker's hurt awful bad."

"We're gonna make it." Justin spoke with more courage than he felt, reaching out to take the cup. "We gotta. I ain't losin' another father like I did last time."

"Like your pop?" Frankie looked up in sympathy.

"No." Justin spoke so quietly that a gust of wind and crackle of flame nearly covered his words. He turned his eyes down into the steaming cup. "Like Lia's father."

"You mean. . . ?" Frankie cocked his head in confusion, scrunching up his nose.

Justin jerked his hand away as the hot metal handle burned through the bandanna. Its searing sting reminding him of crunching metal and squealing tires. The acrid scent of burning rubber.

He sucked on a burned thumb for a second, wishing Frankie would just shut up so he wouldn't have to spill the truth. But Frankie's mouth just hung there in a bewildered grimace.

"I killed her father, Frankie." Justin spoke in a near whisper. "It was an accident. I told ya you don't know nothin' about me. And you sure don't wanna be like me neither."

Justin got up and carried the steaming cup to Mr. Parker's side, leaving Frankie sitting at the fire, his head gawking over his shoulder. Snow falling between them in fine white bits, like a freshly billowed curtain.

⸻

Coyotes. Justin jerked his head up in a predawn gray, hearing the distant howls. Musical and ghostlike, eerie, seeping through the trees in mournful wails, yips, and barks. Falling and rising again, mingling together in shimmering chords.

Coyotes normally didn't bother anybody, but they, too, were unpredictable as wolves. They hid up in the peaks, driven back into lonely places by the ring of the hammer and blast of the shotgun.

Justin snapped himself upright, rubbing his face with a dirty hand. He must've dozed off against the knobby pine trunk, his fire-prodding stick limp in his hand. The flames had nearly disappeared, but the wood still smoked.

He forced his heavy eyelids open and crawled forward, tossing a branch into the fire and stirring the embers—poppy-orange under black coals, opening like a beautiful flower. He puffed on the ashes, shielding them from the wind and coaxing the glowing bits brighter and brighter. Feeding them twigs.

Lia slept against Cynthia's side, burrowed in the blankets, and even Mr. Parker began to rally a bit after cups of warm water. He'd propped himself up on an elbow and even asked about his camera, wondering if he'd smashed it to oblivion on the rocks.

Justin scooted back from the fire as smoke spread in choking puffs, listening to the coyote songs echo through the snowy pines. Wondering if the snow had let up enough for them to try and make it down the mountain.

He stood there between two spruce trees, shivering, arms crossed and hands pressed under his armpits to keep warm. His fingers, nose, and ears had survived the cold fine, but he still couldn't feel his toes—even after he'd peeled off Frankie's thin shoes and tried to warm his feet by the fire. An odd yellow-white color mottled his toes, never warming and never flushing rosy pink, which made his stomach lurch with fear.

Losing a couple of toes was nothing compared to losing a father like Reverend Summers. But if Justin could help it, he'd like to keep his toes just the same.

And during the cold-black hours of the night, it seemed that Justin had lost something else as well: the tendrils of trust he'd built with Frankie.

Frankie obeyed him wordlessly, helped build up the fire, and—to his credit—even stayed awake and on the patrol against wolves, bears, and wildcats that might be attracted by the smell of food or blood. Brandishing a hefty limb in both hands.

But he stood a cool distance away, head turned away and arms huddled. Twice Justin caught Frankie looking down at his own boots, laced there on Frankie's feet, and then up at Justin's face with a crushed look he couldn't decipher. But when his gaze met Justin's, it had skittered away like a nervous squirrel.

"Hey, here's your boots back," said Frankie, as if attempting a smile, bending down to unlace them. "I done had 'em longer than my fair share."

Justin scowled. "Keep 'em, Frankie."

"Naw. Really. I'm good now." And he stood on one foot, holding out a boot in the firelight.

Dawn broke with light, lacy flakes in dizzy spirals, floating like dandelion fluff on the wind.

Justin gathered limbs and branches, shaking off the snow, and stripped off the twigs and rough spots with his pocketknife. Forming a splint for Lia's ankle first and then a stretcher for Mr. Parker. He'd already divided it up in his head: Frankie and Justin would carry Mr. Parker, and Cynthia and Mrs. Parker could support Lia between them.

"You think we can head out?" Frankie spoke in that same guarded tone, looking at the fire.

"Well, I'm makin' a stretcher, ain't I?" Justin flared, tired of Frankie's childish silent treatment. "G'won and get one of the blankets so we can link the poles."

Frankie skittered off, and Justin hung his head in his hand, kneading his forehead. Wishing for a second he'd chosen Florida or Texas or somewhere warmer to join up with the CCC—and equally far away from Frankie White as Berea, Kentucky.

But he'd stopped running. This was life, and he'd have to live it. Have to face it. Just like Lia did—one day at a time, one step after the next. Giving God glory and gracefully bending under the weight of life's injustices.

Justin set down his pocketknife and rubbed the toe of his boot, surprised that the feeling in his toes hadn't returned yet. He'd been wearing his own boots for a couple of hours now, and he figured once they were good and cocooned inside leather, the blood would flow through the chilled flesh. Awakening the nerves with a stinging salute.

He flexed his foot. Doc at the camp would help him when they got back; there wasn't time to waste on worries now.

"We're all ready." Frankie appeared under the dark fringe of pine branch, shouldering Justin's pack. "All we gotta do is finish fixin' Mr. Parker's stretcher, and we can head out."

Justin nodded stonily and turned back to douse and dismantle the fire.

But Frankie just stood there, the wind blowing through his hair and ruffling his grimy CCC shirt.

"What?" Justin growled, whirling around. Throwing down the twig in his hand. "You wanna say somethin', Frankie? Just say it and quit lookin' at me like that."

Frankie didn't speak—just stood there blinking like a bullfrog. He stuffed one hand in his pocket and scuffed the snow with the end of his broken shoe. "It was an accident, wasn't it?" he finally said, looking up and meeting Justin's gaze. He sniffled and wiped his nose on his sleeve.

"What was an accident?"

"What happened with Lia's father." He dropped his voice, his breath coming out like smoke.

"Course it was an accident, you moron. You think I'd do somethin' like that on purpose?" Justin raised his voice instead of lowering it.

Frankie ducked his head, looking embarrassed. "Course ya wouldn't. I just thought. . .thought. . ." He bit his lips and pawed the snow again.

"Thought what?" Justin got up and faced Frankie, his blood boiling so hot he had to remind himself that there were ladies around. As much as he felt like knocking Frankie White through a bunch of cedars, now might not be the best time and place to do it.

"I dunno." Frankie shrugged. "I thought you were just full a talk and all about that God stuff and about mistakes you said you'd made." He met Justin's gaze. "I thought ya figured you knew it all and hadn't ever set foot in the real world. Shucks, like you were some kinda dandy or somethin'." His nose reddened, and he looked down. "I was the one who put ice in your bed to bring you down a peg. Know that?"

"I know." Justin snorted in disgust. "I shoulda strung you up for that."

Frankie blanched. "You mean you...you knew I did it?"

"Sure I did. Cook saw you steal the ice from the chest and told me five minutes after."

"Oh." Frankie swallowed and looked down.

"And that stupid mountain rattler. You put it in your pack, and it crawled off." Justin hugged himself in the cold. "I saw you lookin' for it that day when I took your bird eggs. You know you coulda killed me or Ernie or one of the guys?"

"I thought babies didn't have venom! It was this big!" Frankie gestured wildly with his fingers.

"Well they do, stupid!" Justin hollered, flaring up. Feeling that old itch to grab Frankie by the shirt collar and shake a lick of intelligence into him.

Frankie stuck his hands in his pockets and scrubbed his shoes in the snow. He finally looked up. "And...you still come up here after me?" he asked in a small voice. "Even after ya knew all that?"

"Sure I did. 'Cause you're an idiot." Justin picked up a twig and started whittling it again.

"Yeah. I reckon." Frankie gave a half grin. Then he drew himself up taller, the grin fading. "But no matter what you mighta done, Fairbanks, I still think you're swell." He sniffled again, and Justin wasn't sure if it was the cold or emotion. "Mighty swell."

Frankie's throat quivered. "Truth is, I ain't never done nothin' good for nobody else in my life. All I've done is make trouble. I didn't deserve to wear your boots, Fairbanks. You shoulda let me freeze."

"I might if you keep on talkin' like that." Justin clicked his knife shut and shoved it in his pocket, thinking of Reverend Summers.

Frankie's expression stayed sober. "I swear when I get back to camp I'm gonna try and straighten out my life. I'll even give my rocks and stuff back to the lieutenant."

"And the letter you found about the gold?" Justin glared.

"That, too. Honest Injun. I'll even read that Bible of yours if ya want."

"Well, you can start by helpin' me splint Lia's ankle, double time, or we might never get outta this ice hole."

Frankie grinned and gave a mock salute. "Yes sir! I'm on it."

⁓

Snow gusted as they mounted the rocky, boulder-clogged ledge, hauling Mr. Parker on a blanket trussed together with ropes and sticks to keep his back straight. They helped Lia up the slippery embankment, the wind screaming across the meadow and blowing snow.

Frankie paused, red-faced and panting, and pulled on Justin's arm as they climbed the last rocky flank that outcropped the meadow. "Say, ain't that where we dropped the light? It can't be, can it?"

"You mean where *I* dropped the light." Justin wiped his sleeve across his face. "And I dunno. Everything looks the same to me."

"No, I'm sure it's here. But. . .nah. There's no way."

Justin scowled in irritation, stretching his back for one final heave of Mr. Parker's stretcher, which they'd wedged between a clump of stones. Mr. Parker moaned, clutching his head.

"I don't really care, Frankie. We just gotta. . ." Justin broke off, staring down at the mass of stones. Trying to remember the cracks and grooves. "Hey, are those what's left of our boot tracks?"

Frankie straightened up in surprise. "So it *was* here! The flashlight fell down between those rocks, and then you grabbed in the hole there, but. . .but look at that big ol' boulder! There's no way we coulda moved that."

Justin ran his hand over the boulder, which stretched farther than he could reach both up and out. A heavy chunk of granite, solid, wedged back against a heavy pack of earth and stones. A white skiff of snow on top.

Justin's mouth hung open as he tried to replay the scene. He felt along the smooth and wrinkled stone, cold to the touch, where he'd gripped and pushed. It couldn't be. Could it? That piece of rock must weigh more than a freight train.

"That's it all right." Frankie's eyes bugged. "But how'd we do it? How'd we move that thing? You don't think it's because we. . ."

"Because we what?"

Frankie flushed. "I mean, I don't really believe in all that prayer mess, but we moved that rock somehow."

"Well," Justin shrugged, "you got some other explanation? Space aliens, maybe?"

Frankie laughed briefly, but his face stayed sober. "Dunno, Fairbanks. Maybe I'm gonna hafta think about all that God business again. 'Cause man, we sure needed that light." He wiped his wet nose on his sleeve. "I ain't gonna be no preacher though. Uh-uh."

Justin gazed up at the boulder. "I can't think of nothin' better to be, Frankie, than a preacher. I promise ya that."

Chapter 9

Justin guessed it must be noon from the brightness of the clouds and the rumbling in his stomach at the thought of the mess hall. Anything they plopped on a plate sounded good. Slimy boiled potatoes? Fine. Soggy leftover chicken? Dandy. It was food, and with the cold temperatures and physical exertion, he'd probably eat the plate and the table, too.

They'd struggled partway down the ridge, pausing only once to rest and build a fire when Mr. Parker began to shiver uncontrollably in the makeshift stretcher. Justin rested there, spent, while a weak fire sputtered. His wrists and back ached from gripping the sides of the rough pine stretcher, and he flexed his stiff fingers. All the blood seemed to have pooled there in one desperate attempt not to let Mr. Parker slide off the stretcher—leaving red gouges across his wrists and forearms.

Worst of all, Justin felt clumsy and off balance. His toes had no feeling, perhaps from the tight boots, and he wasn't as fleet and nimble as before. Several times he'd had to brace himself from falling, holding an arm against a shaggy pine trunk while he shouldered Mr. Parker's stretcher.

He'd just let his head sink into his bent knees when Lia whispered something next to him, her breath stirring his hair.

"What'd ya say?" He jerked his head up.

"It was you who sent it."

Justin turned to look at Lia as she knelt there next to him on a folded blanket over snow, her dress filthy and eyes swimming with tears. A frightening bewilderment creeping into his chest that—by George—he'd somehow made her cry again.

"Sent. . .sent what?" He ran a dirty hand through his hair, wondering if she was hallucinating again.

"The money every month." She winced as she shifted position to let her injured leg out straight, adjusting the flimsy splint and pulling the wool blanket tighter around her shoulders. "You're the one who's been sending it. I figured it out."

Justin dug his boot heels into the thin crust of snow to steady himself. "What makes you think that?" he finally asked, trying to keep his voice neutral. Reaching out to rub his hands in the glow of fire warmth and avoiding her gaze.

"Frankie said you're always signing up for extra work, taking jobs at local farms on the weekends, but you never buy anything—and still never have a nickel to your name." Lia ran a finger over her cracked lower lip, which had begun to heal slightly.

Justin's shoulders jumped in unexpected laughter. "That sounds like somethin' Frankie would say." He shook his head, picking uncomfortably at a blue-black fingernail he'd smashed with a hammer awhile back.

Lia leaned closer, fingering a strand of hair. "And every time the money comes in, we meet Margaret at the market. Like her money comes in around the same time ours does." She watched the fire, waving away smoke. "I thought I saw Beanie once, on the road from our house to yours, right after we found the money but I never knew for sure." She looked up at him. "Is it you, Justin?"

He picked at his thumb a few more minutes, his forehead creasing into a deep line. "I reckon that's why there's a fifth amendment in the Constitution, Lia," he finally said, keeping his eyes down. "Can you do me a favor and not ask me so many questions? No offense, but I'd really rather not talk about it. Please."

Lia seemed to understand, and she brushed her hair back with her fingers, nodding. A snowflake streaking past her face and another landing in her hair.

Justin hesitated then brushed the snowflake out of her messy curls. Then he wrapped his arms around his knees, suddenly shy. "As long as your folks are doin' all right, your mom and sis especially, then I'm happy. There's nothin' more to say."

"What did you do to your thumb?" She reached abruptly over his arm and ran her finger across the bruised thumbnail.

"Ah. Nothin'." Justin shrugged in embarrassment, suddenly self-conscious at the sensation of her tender touch, light as it might have been. "Nothin' that won't heal up in a month or two."

"It's funny how even the worst injuries eventually heal," she said in soft tones. "Even when we think they won't."

Justin caught his misty breath, raising his eyes to her. "But my thumb ain't. . .ain't the same as it used to be. Won't ever be again." He ran his hand over the lines on his jaw, heart thumping in his throat.

"We're all scarred, Justin. Every single one of us." Lia met his gaze. "And we won't be new until eternity. But we can choose to go on living or give up. God can give us a new life."

He didn't trust his voice to speak. Wondering, in a wild flail of his heartbeat, if she meant "us" as collective humanity or a different "us."

Whichever way Lia meant it, she didn't explain. She simply squeezed his wrist lightly and then withdrew her hand, pulling the blanket around her and turning back to the fire.

Leaning ever so slightly against the curve of his arm.

"Did you hear that, Fairbanks?" Frankie whirled around. "Is my brain playin' tricks on me, or was that somebody hollerin'?"

Justin skidded to a stop in the snowy ground, holding his breath. A noisy blue jay rattled a branch overhead, sifting down a shower of snow.

"I heard something, too." Mrs. Parker stopped, her arm tight around Lia's waist in support. She turned wire-rimmed glasses, frosty with condensation, toward the sound.

Justin glanced at the direction she'd looked—the trail—and felt his heart leap up in hope. "Holler, everybody!" He cupped his hands around his mouth.

And they all yelled together—even Mr. Parker—startling a flock of grosbeaks from a nearby tree. Wings flapped and snow tumbled. Spruce boughs quivered then slowly swayed to a stop.

And then: a chorus of shouts, echoing off snowy hillsides. Ringing against the rocky slopes of the mountain like the most beautiful sound Justin had ever heard.

The first person Justin saw when the rescue crew from Camp Fremont dug their way through boulders and snowdrifts was Ernie Sadler—a wool cap pulled over his head and an anxious look on his cold-red face.

"Good lands, Fairbanks!" Ernie yelled, nearly knocking Justin over with his pounding hug. "Boy, am I glad to see you!"

Guys swarmed around him with whoops and shouts, slapping hands. Three of them took Mr. Parker's stretcher, passing him a canteen of hot coffee.

Justin laughed and smacked him with his cap. "Not as glad as I am."

Ernie shook Justin's shoulder, his nose flushed with cold and eyes wild with excitement. "You scared the spit outta me! Why, you'd all be frozen as solid as penguins if we hadn't found that note on the Parkers' car."

"You found my note?"

"Sure I did. When you didn't show up at the mess for dinner Saturday I got kinda worried, and nobody saw ya all day today—or Frankie either. I called the other guys to check it out, and somebody said they'd spotted that snazzy Ford over by the lake." Ernie rubbed Justin's head. "I know you're dumb, Fairbanks, but I didn't know you were dumb enough to go up after Frankie by yourself in a freak blizzard!"

"Hey. I asked for help." Justin shivered as Ernie opened another canteen of coffee and pressed it, warm and steaming, into his hands.

Justin pushed away the canteen. "Naw. Give it to the gals. They've been up here longer than I have."

"There's plenty for everybody. Cook sent up sandwiches, too—pretty awful ones, mind you." Ernie broke off in a laugh, shaking his head as one of the men barked orders to the others. He pulled off Lia's twig splint and wrapped her ankle in a sturdy cotton bandage, and someone else opened wool blankets.

"Shucks, the whole camp's been in a tizzy since you guys disappeared," said Ernie as they headed back down the mountain, glancing up over the ridge at the sky. Probably worried about more snow. He paused to navigate his way down an icy rock formation, reaching out to help Cynthia. He needn't have; Cynthia already had three guys swarming around her like bees on honey.

Ernie spoke close to Justin's ear. "Tell you what. Soon as we get back to camp, I'm gonna knock Frankie White's lights out. The dummy." He snorted in disgust. "He's got it comin' to him, and ain't nobody gonna tell me otherwise." He turned to Justin in a low whisper. "You with me?"

Justin hesitated, glancing back over his shoulder at Frankie, who was helping Mrs. Parker down an incline. His arm wrapped protectively around her shoulders. Those silly loafers flapped open, showing threadbare socks.

"I think you oughtta go easy on him." Justin unscrewed the canteen and sipped hot coffee, burning his tongue. Warmth swirled inside him, delirious, and he almost forgot his next words. "Really. The poor kid's all shook up."

Ernie stopped dead still, and the two guys behind him almost knocked into him from behind. "You gotta be joking."

Justin shrugged and lifted the canteen again. "He's an all-right kid, Ernie. Just gets a little turned around sometimes, ya know? But I think he learned his lesson." His eyes softened, remembering his hand on the top of Frankie's head. "I think he's gonna straighten some things out."

Ernie stared at Justin. "You nuts? You got hypothermia or somethin'?" His eyes didn't smile.

"No, but Mr. Parker might have it. He couldn't stop shivering. And maybe Lia, too. You've gotta take care of her."

Lia. Justin's heart caught a bit, and he swiveled around to see her there as two men from the camp boosted her up in a makeshift seat. The color had returned to her cheeks as she sipped a canteen of hot coffee, the steam rising up in front of her face like a sheer wedding veil. Her downturned eyes lifting briefly to his.

"She'll be all right." Ernie slapped Justin's arm. He opened his mouth with a slight smile as if he wanted to make a joke and then thought better of it. "You'll be all right, too. Even that doggone Frankie White, if he lives through the night. I'm thinkin' ice in his bed though, at least. If he ain't seen enough of it since yesterday."

⁂

Faint snow dusted the ground at the entrance of the camp as the rescue party tromped back through the trees, sending up shouts of victory. Cheers echoed through the camp buildings and into the calm, gray evening—overcast but without the blustery wind that had tormented them up on the ridge.

Justin remembered the first time he'd seen Camp Fremont. He'd been a green recruit then, just off the train and mind spinning with heady independence and near intoxication of being far—farther than he'd ever imagined—from Berea, Kentucky.

He'd wanted to sink to his knees in reverence and give thanks to someone—God, perhaps—even all those months ago before he knew Him. Before he prayed for that same God to forgive his sins and change his life.

But now, here on a misty afternoon and all the lupines dark, the sparrows and juncos silent under scudding clouds, Justin felt like he'd never seen anything more beautiful. He wanted to weep at the sight of the flag on its flagpole, at the long log buildings that housed classrooms and bunks and horrible chow.

"Doc's waitin' for ya." Ernie pushed Justin ahead. "Anything you need, just tell me, and we'll bring it, okay? Soon as Doc checks ya out, Cook's got a hot meal waitin' for ya."

"What did he make?" Justin half closed his eyes, prodding his empty stomach to go a few minutes longer by imagining.

"Dunno. Reckon it's that rotten meat loaf like the rest of us had for lunch."

Meat loaf. The oily, grainy one with half-raw onions and skimpy on the salt. Baked as hard as a brick and with a funny burned aftertaste.

And for the first time Justin could remember on meat loaf day, his mouth watered in ravenous pleasure.

"Justin Fairbanks. You alive?" Lieutenant Lytle strode across the cold grass in his uniform toward the infirmary building, his craggy face a mixture of relief and rage.

"Yes sir." Justin drew himself up tall. Inside Doc was taking a look at Frankie, while two local doctors called in on emergency treated the others—namely, Mr. Parker. Justin had waited until the end to hear how they'd fared. After all, what did he really need Doc for? He was warm now, and his stomach would be filled shortly.

Why, if it weren't for some scratches and those numb toes, Justin hardly knew he'd crawled up a mountain in a storm.

"Then I want to talk to you. Immediately." The lieutenant gestured with his head toward his office, doing an immediate about-face and leaving Justin standing there. His shoulders rigid with what Justin guessed was rightful fury over having his explicit orders disobeyed—nearly resulting in the deaths of five people. Four of them guests, and three of them women.

Justin stuck his hands in his pockets and followed the lieutenant, dreading what would happen to Frankie White when he spilled the truth.

"Shut the door." The lieutenant didn't sit down. "It was Frankie, wasn't it?"

"Sorry?" Justin took his hands out of his pockets and put them behind his back, trying to keep his nervous fingers from fidgeting.

"This whole harebrained idea to go up in the middle of nowhere against my orders." The lieutenant pounded a fist on his upturned palm. "He had no right! That White kid's been a mistake since the beginning, and first thing tomorrow morning, he's out of here. You went after him, didn't you?"

Justin's mouth opened to speak, but the air inside the lieutenant's quarters suddenly felt stifling. Dry.

He closed his eyes, unable to see anything but Frankie's tears. "*My brothers and sis ain't gonna have nothin' to eat, and it's my fault,*" he'd said, trying to ram himself headfirst into a tree.

"How'd you know about his fool idea anyway?" Lieutenant demanded, his mustache twitching with anger.

"Sorry, sir?" Justin felt unable to breathe, the weight of the room about to collapse his lungs.

"I asked how you knew where White was going." His eyes burned black as coal, smoldering under a shock of dark hair. "You gonna answer me, or you gonna stand there all day? You've always been a good kid—the best of the bunch. But I'm in no mood for stammering." He pointed a finger in the direction of the infirmary. "If that man with the head injury dies, so help me, I'll have that kid court-martialed."

Justin heard the faint tick of a pocket watch from the lieutenant's desk as he took a deep breath and opened his mouth to speak.

Chapter 10

I t was my idea, sir."

Justin exhaled, feeling sweat break out on his palms and forehead, even in the drafty cool of the lieutenant's quarters. A low wind whined around the corner of the building, lonesome and mournful. The sound of loss and crushed hopes.

The lieutenant stood still, one hand raised as if in mid-sentence.

"Excuse me?" He leaned closer, dark eyes blinking incredulously. "What did you just say?"

Justin cleared his throat and strengthened his voice. "It was my idea, sir," he repeated crisply, so clear and sure that he even sounded convincing to himself. "Frankie said he was just going to stay by the lake, but I told him to go up to the ridge. I drew him a map and everything."

Justin's hand shook slightly as he pulled the battered paper from his pocket, holding it out. His face blazed with shame.

The lieutenant's mouth opened, his eyes round as river stones. "You?"

"Yes sir." Justin forced himself to raise his chin and meet the lieutenant's eyes.

Color pooled first in the lieutenant's flat cheeks then up to his forehead. "You?" he thundered again, louder this time. Reaching out and grabbing Justin by the collar, jerking his face close. "You told that White kid to disobey my orders?"

Bits of spittle spattered on Justin's face, and he struggled to swallow. "Yes sir."

The lieutenant stared at him, eye to eye, the red veins bulging around black pupils. Then he flung Justin away in disgust. "I don't believe it."

Justin kept his eyes down and calmly straightened his clothes. The same wool pants he'd had on since Saturday afternoon, snow-sodden and wrinkled. The lower inches shredded and muddy.

"Why would you do a thing like that?" The lieutenant eyed him fiercely. "You're one of the best in the camp. Maybe the best of all." He pounded out points with his index finger on his weathered palm. "You show up to work early and stay late. You've never missed formation, stayed out sick, or gone missing after the weekend. You're passing all your studies with high marks. Why, you've never even gotten a demerit. Fairbanks, this is ridiculous! I don't buy it." He swiped an arm through the air.

"It's true, sir." Justin forced himself to meet the lieutenant's eyes. "The whole thing was my idea. Frankie saved them all by hunkering down in an enclave by the rocks and building a shelter and starting a fire. They'd have died if it wasn't for Frankie."

The words stung like sharp sleet cutting into his skin, but Justin didn't lower his head.

"Why. . .why he wouldn't even accept my boots, sir." Justin gestured with his head. "Go see for yourself if his shoes ain't fallin' to pieces."

The lieutenant stared at him a second, jaw twitching, and jerked open the door. Letting in an icy gust of wind. Warmer than on the ridge but still chilling Justin enough that he had to stiffen his arms and back to keep from shivering.

Justin heard him stalk to the next door, rap on it, and then demand Frankie White's shoes from the infirmary. Then he stormed back into his quarters and took out a pipe, banging the tins as he shook out the tobacco. He smoked in angry silence while voices rattled outside, muffled by the thick log walls.

"Sir." A private rapped on the door and opened it, holding out a wooden crate with Frankie's shoes inside. The thin soles had split and broken, crusted with mud and snow. Dirty laces fraying.

The lieutenant stalked over and took the box, staring down without a word. Puffing stiffly on his pipe. Then he shoved the box on his desk and stalked over to the window, smoking in stony silence.

"Why'd you do it, Fairbanks?" He finally spoke, his words tense and brittle.

Justin swallowed, letting his pulse slow before speaking. "I'm in love with a girl, sir. I wanted to show her the falls."

The lieutenant snorted in disgust, shaking his head. Mumbling something under his breath that sounded like a curse. "What do you know about love anyway? How old are you, twenty-two? Twenty-three?"

Justin fixed his eyes on a pine knot in the wall in humiliation. "Nineteen, sir."

"Nineteen," spat the lieutenant, shooting him a laugh of derision.

"Barely outta high school. I bet you wouldn't know what love is if it kicked you in the pants. All you boys are alike, you know that? Mooning over the first female that bats her eyelashes at you and turning your brain to mush. I thought you were different." He turned his back again, staring out the window at the empty trees. "That dratted redhead. I never should have let her come into the camp, turning all my recruits into fools."

Justin's eyes flickered closed, grateful that Lieutenant Lytle hadn't singled out Lia. By some stroke of luck he'd protected her, as if wrapping her in a blanket. That was her way, all right. Plain and humble, without an ounce of ostentation. Maybe she wasn't so much to look at like some of the other gals, but her beauty was hidden inside—like crystals in a geode. Locked and closed for one man, who would delight in her quiet radiance and strength the rest of his life.

And whoever he was, Justin knew he'd be a lucky guy.

The lieutenant spun around. "So that's the kind of recruits I'm raising here, is it? Self-centered, ignorant imbeciles who lose their senses over a dame and put people's lives in danger?"

He eyed Justin angrily, puffs of fragrant smoke curling up to the log ceiling. "Do you know I was going to promote you, Fairbanks?"

The words caught him unawares, like a mountain lion pouncing soundlessly from behind. Knocking him to the ground.

"Sorry, sir?"

"I was going to promote you. You've stood out to all your leaders—they've all recommended you. I was going to make you assistant foreman. The papers are ready." He gestured to his desk. Then he shook his head bitterly, turning away. "But you're not ready yet. When I think of what you did, why, I oughtta..."

He stomped over to his desk and dropped down in his chair, massaging his hair with his hands. Then he grabbed up the papers that Justin assumed were his and tore them into shreds, emptying them all into the trash bin. Like little bits of hateful falling snow.

"If it weren't for your good record, I'd be puttin' you on the next train to wherever you're from. And if I catch you anywhere near that redhead, I just might do it. Understood?" He took out his pipe and tapped it on the desk. "But I promise you one thing—it'll be months before you see the outside of the kitchen again in your spare time. Maybe years. And I hope you love push-ups 'cause they're going to be your best friend. You can start by giving me a hundred right now. Count 'em off."

Justin got down on his knees, the stiff right one complaining, and pushed himself up on his boots and palms. Still not feeling anything in his toes.

"One," he grunted, pushing himself up and then down again, touching his nose to the pine floor. "Two. Three." The strain on his sore knee ached, and exhaustion strained at his weary back. He swore he could smell the food from the mess hall like a cloudy mirage.

"Louder, Fairbanks! I can't hear you!" barked the lieutenant, taking out a fountain pen to write something. Demerits, maybe? An order to put Justin on the roughest work crew at the camp or consign him to the kitchen for eternity?

"Four. Five."

And Justin squeezed his eyes shut, fixing his mind on the one thing that had brought him peace through all these painful years: an image of Jesus, arms outstretched on a bloody cross.

Taking Justin's sins and nailing them there for eternity.

Chapter 11

"Frostbite." Doctor Hollowford turned over Justin's foot with knowing fingers. "Yep. On both feet. See the yellowish tissue there?"

Justin leaned back on the white enamel examining chair, a groan slipping through his lips. His stomach and biceps screamed from endless push-ups, and the lukewarm meat loaf and boiled cabbage he'd downed in the mess hall had dissipated in five minutes. He'd dragged himself to the mess hall in disgrace, Lieutenant Lytle bellowing after him not to show his face in his quarters again.

"You're kidding. How bad is it?" Justin rubbed his weary face in both hands, ready to throw himself in his cot, bury his head under warm blankets, and sleep for the rest of the week.

At least someone had brought him a change of clothes, trading his dirty wool pants for clean khakis and warm socks. Ernie got him a clean coat and mittens from surplus, and now he just needed a warm bath and some shut-eye.

The doctor studied his feet a minute, turning the toes over in the light. "I've seen worse. But we need to get this flesh warmed up, or it could turn into gangrene." He glanced up at Justin. "Ain't gonna feel like a back rub, son. You ready for that?"

"I don't got much choice, do I, Doc?"

"Nope." Doctor Hollowford shot him a wry smile. "But you'll feel a lot better after we get some feeling back in these toes. They'll probably blister a bit, but if we get 'em thawed out, I hope you won't lose any tissue."

"You hope."

"That's what I said." He shot Justin a sympathetic glance.

Justin leaned back in the examining chair and rolled his head back and forth, wondering how he'd gotten in this mess in the first place.

"You're legal, ain't ya?"

"Sorry?"

"For me to pour you something stout. You gotta be older than twenty-one." The doc washed his hands in a basin, looking over his shoulder at Justin's hefty frame and angular face. "You drink, don't you, son?"

"Me?" Justin's mouth turned sticky.

"It'll help with the pain. I promise you that." The doctor dried his hands on a towel and reached for the cabinet handle where he kept his medicines. "I'll pour you a glass. It'll warm you up, too." He touched Justin's cheek and forehead. "No symptoms of hypothermia, but you've got some windburn on your face, and a little extra heat in your veins won't hurt. Can't have you catching pneumonia, can we?"

Justin shook his head, staring up at the log ceiling. "I'm nineteen, Doc."

"You?" The doctor hooted, his hand hesitating on the cabinet door. "What'd your ma feed you, lard and molasses?"

Justin's lips tipped in an unexpected smile. "I wish she had." He pressed his lips together at the thought of the warm burn of liquor oozing down his throat and forcefully turned his head away. "No drink. But thanks anyway."

Doctor Hollowford scrunched his brow inquisitively, tightening the loose knob on the cabinet. "No? You sure? It's for medicinal purposes. It's not like you're tipping bottles on the job. I'll write you a medical note if you need one."

"No." Justin spoke so loudly and firmly that the doctor turned around in surprise. "No thanks. I'll be fine."

"Well." Doctor Hollowford patted Justin's head like a fond father, reminding him for a brief instant of Reverend Summers. "Lie back then, and let's get those feet warmed up."

Justin gripped the sides of the chair as the doctor filled a basin with warm water, testing it several times with a thermometer. Then he rolled up Justin's pant legs and gently took his right foot in his hand.

"I still don't feel nothin'," said Justin as the doctor immersed his foot in the basin. Only the tops and soles of his feet felt warm, bathed in velvety liquid and gratefully free of snow-chilled shoes and boots.

"You will, son." The doctor lifted a sympathetic eyebrow. "You will."

⸙

Justin had a secret. When it came to pain, he was a wimp. A big wimp. Despite his tough exterior, he'd bawled like a baby that day he hammered his thumb. Once he was in the lavatory building and far from the other guys of course.

And when the excruciating electrical tingle coursed through his right foot, he jerked so hard he almost upset the basin. He splashed water all over the doctor and the lower row of cabinets. Doctor Hollowford had to yell and force his leg back in the basin—calling for somebody to come help hold Justin down.

Two army medical assistants rushed in, gripping him one on either side and pushing him back down in the chair. They held his leg in the basin while Justin alternately twisted, moaned, and sweated. They pinned down his left leg, too, as the pain began to tingle in almost unbearable bursts.

Through his agony he heard a knock at the door and a familiar voice that sounded too soft to be another doctor.

When he opened his wet lashes, there were Lia's eyes—looking down at him with a face of startling compassion. Pink lips pressed together, and her hair barely damp and combed.

He searched for words but found none. Except the cries that welled up from his lungs and throat—and the sudden regret that he hadn't accepted the doctor's glass of whiskey.

No. No. That was all wrong. He gritted his teeth against the pain, glad he'd said no. He'd say it again if he needed to, out loud, just to enjoy the breathless freedom of, for once in his life, giving orders from his head and not his flesh. Putting his foot down and charting his own stubborn course.

Justin felt warm fingers lace through his—soft fingers, smaller and so much finer than his—and somehow the pain seemed to ebb a bit. He gripped her hand tightly, hoping he wouldn't crush it, but she neither flinched nor pulled away.

The doctor pulled up a stool behind Lia, and she sat, pulling her long skirt and coat to the side with one hand. Never letting go of his hand or his gaze.

When Justin's tears ran down his cheeks in damp streaks, she wiped them with her palm.

~⁂~

The pain ebbed sometime after dark, the jolting, blinding bursts replaced by the dull ache of swollen flesh. Some needle pricks and a rush of something numb in his feet. The doctor and two medics worked side by side with shiny instruments, heads bent over Justin's feet. Probably removing the dead skin and flesh.

His toes had blistered, and when they'd finished cleaning the wounds, Doctor Hollowford wrapped them gently in gauze bandages. Moving carefully around sleeping Lia, her head resting on the edge of the examining chair where Justin lay.

He opened groggy eyes, dull with pain and throbbing muscles, and passed a hand over her head. Twining one of her soft curls between his fingers and bringing it briefly up to his lips.

The most beautiful color he'd ever seen, a black-brown of painful regret laid to rest.

When Justin awoke, he no longer lay on the examining chair. He had a hazy recollection of being moved, half carried and half walked, to a stiff infirmary cot in the back room—where he dreamed in fitful, exhausting spurts, hour after floating, convoluted hour. The bandages still circled his feet, stiff and immovable, and someone had covered him in an itchy wool army blanket. He blinked and yawned, gazing around at the empty cots and slats of light streaming through closed shutters.

Justin groaned, his body sore and toes aching, and sat up just enough to see Lia's empty stool in the sterile white examining room. "Doc?" he called, his voice sounding like a bullfrog's ragged croak.

He heard the squeak of shoes on the pine floor, and Doctor Hollowford poked his head in the door. "Well, well. Rise and shine. Although it's a little late for that." He wiped his stethoscope with a cloth. "How do those feet feel?"

"Like they've been stepped on by a moose." Justin rubbed his face. "Are all my toes still there?"

"For now." Doc smiled gently, lines crinkling at the corners of his eyes. "We'll have to see how the tissue responds, but I'm hopeful it'll heal up all right if it doesn't get infected. You'll have to use crutches for a while though, and stay off your feet a bit."

A stab rushed through Justin's chest as he pictured the work crews along the green woods, fresh morning sunshine slanting through the pines as he raised a hammer or reached out to grab a board. Doing something bigger, better, than he'd ever done with his life. Filling his lungs with fresh mountain air, his body ragged from sweaty exhaustion— and never happier.

"Where's Lia?" Justin glanced at the light through the window.

"Who?"

"The girl who was here." He rubbed his arm over his face, trying to jog his groggy memory. "She sat with me, didn't she?"

"Oh, that little gal." The doctor held up his stethoscope to the light, squinting. Wiping at another spot. "Your girlfriend, I reckon?"

Justin's heart missed a beat, lurching as if he'd lost his balance. "No. A friend." He felt his blood beat faster, warmer, at the very idea that he could call Lia Summers a friend. "A good friend. Where is she?"

"Dunno. She woke up when we moved you back here to sleep, and I haven't seen her today. The folks she's with are heading out though. Chad Parker suffered a pretty bad concussion, and I'm sending him to Jackson to get better help."

"Jackson?" Justin jerked upright. "Have they gone yet?"

The doctor glanced at his pocket watch. "Probably. It's a long drive."

"All of them?"

The doctor tipped his head at Justin. "I'm assuming so. Why?"

Justin started to get out of bed, trying to roll his injured, bandaged feet to the floor. Unrolling his pant legs and reaching for the next cot to brace himself.

"You nuts, boy? You don't even have crutches. Hold on and I'll help you. But you'll be on bed rest for a couple of days, and—" The doctor turned at a knock on the door and held up a finger. "Hold on. Let me get this, and I'll show you how to use the crutches."

Justin finished unrolling his pants, barely hearing the doctor, and dug on the nearby chair for his socks. He desperately needed a shower, a shave, and a toothbrush. A cup of steaming coffee after sleeping on the chilly cot and about three plates of the heartiest food Cook could dish out.

He'd just tried unsuccessfully to stuff his swollen, bandaged foot into a scratchy wool sock when Doctor Hollowford rapped at the door. "Justin?" He poked his graying head in. "Lieutenant Lytle's here to see you."

"The lieutenant?" Justin dropped the sock on the floor, his heart hammering. "What have I done now?"

The door opened, and in strode the lieutenant, all stars and buttons and badges. He slammed the door behind him, and sleek boots tapped across the hard floor in staccato beats. Justin could smell the crisp wool of his uniform mingled with the pungent scent of pipe tobacco.

"Sir?" Justin tried to scramble to his feet.

"For pity's sake, Fairbanks. Sit down." The lieutenant waved an arm and drew his black brows together in a look of irritation as he seated himself on a nearby cot. "Tell me something. I've been trying to figure this out since last night, and I'm hoping you can shed some light on my little quandary."

Justin drew back. "Shoot," he said. "Sir."

The lieutenant leaned forward, making the cot squeak. "Explain this." He jabbed a finger into his calloused palm. "If Frankie White refused to take your boots, then why do you have frostbitten toes and he doesn't?"

The room fell so silent that Justin heard a clock tick from the doctor's examining room behind the closed door.

"Fairbanks?" The lieutenant raised his voice so that Justin jerked upright.

"Sir?" Justin gulped. "I...uh..." He ran his hand over his stubbly jaw, blinking faster as he searched for words. "It's...sort of hard to explain."

The lieutenant studied him, motionless. Staring at him so intensely that Justin felt sweat bead on his forehead.

"I see," said the lieutenant finally, settling back on the cot and stroking his thick mustache. "I think I get it. You don't want to tell me Frankie did it, do you? Is that it?"

Justin swallowed nervously, his gaze bouncing down to the floor and back up.

The lieutenant narrowed his eyes at Justin. "I thought as much." He leaned back and massaged his close-shaved chin. "I've no idea *why*, mind you, but it's the only thing that makes sense to me. Do you agree?"

"Yes sir." Justin's brow furrowed in confusion. "I...I think so."

"Well then." The lieutenant stood. "Rest easy, Fairbanks. If there's one man in this camp I trust, it's you, boy. You must have your reasons." He moved, and a glint of light fell on his medals. "I'll reissue those orders for you to be moved up as supervisor, and we'll say no more about it this time."

He clapped Justin on the shoulder. "Take care of those feet, young man. Hear me? That's an order."

And he winked before stalking out of the room.

꧁꧂

Justin was still sitting there in a dumb stupor, wondering what had just happened, when Doc knocked on the door again. "By gravy, son, you've got another visitor. Who are you, Clark Gable?"

"Another visitor?" Justin knocked his pillow to the floor in surprise, reaching for it on the wood floor. It lay just out of reach, tormenting him. So many simple things would be difficult now—walking, moving, standing.

The door opened, and Lia edged in, one crutch under her arm. A fawn-colored hat on her head, nearly matching her brown tweed jacket. Her dress fell in a slim ivory pool, like the satin billow of Yellowstone Falls, and Justin thought he'd never seen anything more beautiful.

The doctor helped her to the cot opposite Justin, leaning her crutch against the wall, and she nodded her thanks. Barely seeming to notice when he slipped discreetly back into the examining room, leaving the door open a crack.

What should he say? Justin wanted to say everything, but nothing sounded right.

"You're still here?" he finally managed, running a hand over his scratchy jaw in embarrassment. Wishing to goodness the doc had let him get a shave and maybe a haircut before letting Lia see him like this.

"The Parkers are leaving now, but I had to tell you good-bye," said Lia, sitting down carefully on the cot where Lieutenant Lytle had been just minutes ago. She grimaced as she extended her splinted ankle. "And I wanted to say thank you."

"Thank you? To me?"

"Of course. You saved our lives. Cynthia pretty much hates Frankie's guts by now," she added with a laugh. "But I told her she can't hate him. She can't. It'll eat her from the inside." She dropped her head and picked at the hole in the index finger of her glove. "If she can let go of her hate and remember her own sins, then there's room to grow again." She pressed her lips together, their color redder than Justin remembered. "There's room to...to...well, love again."

Justin's heartbeat quickened, and he longed to reach out and press her to his chest. But he restrained himself, running his hand along a crease in the sheet. "I'm so sorry I hurt you, Lia." He forced his gaze up and into her eyes, determined to make her hear it. "I'm not the same person I used to be, but I can't bring your father back. I'll be sorry about that forever. As long as I live I'll never be able to right it for ya."

Tears glittered briefly in her eyes, and she managed a smile. "I'm not the same person I was either, Justin. I've grown a lot in four years. Everything's changed—my life, my family, the whole country with this Depression. I never imagined my life could change so much in a few short years. But...that's life. We never stop. We just go on, one day at a time, begging God for strength and mercy." She swallowed, tracing the edges of her glove. "And if my father were here, I know he'd forgive you and love you. The way he did back then."

Justin couldn't speak, the lump in his throat choking him.

"God's sovereign over death, Justin. You know that?" Lia raised her eyes to him. "He gave my father life, and He chose to take it away—like Job said in the Bible. And we bless His name no matter what."

She bit her lip, which had begun to heal. The spot of blood gone, and the dryness of dehydration exchanged for a satiny sheen. "God could have spared my father, but He didn't. And He didn't spare His own Son either. For you and for me."

Justin heard the clatter of dishes from the distant mess hall even through the thick infirmary walls. The rattle of truck wheels at the far end of the camp. In a few minutes they'd be calling for her, and she'd get in the car and disappear in a puff of gravel and dust.

All those years he'd wished time would speed forward to his death, and for the first time he suddenly wanted to jerk it to a stop. Suspending himself in this moment, this hush, forever. The color of her eyes like the shade of a country nightfall, crickets chirping in warm waves from the grass.

A horn honked outside, and Lia flinched. "That's for me."

Instead of speaking, Justin reached out and took Lia's hand, pressing her fingers to his lips. Trying to memorize her scent. Fresh like soap, simple and quiet. No boisterous perfumes or exotic fragrances. Just soap and cotton and something gentle he couldn't describe, like face powder or cold cream. She didn't pull her hand away.

"Come home, Justin," she whispered, her tears spilling over.

"What?" He could hardly breathe over the rush of emotion.

"Come home. To Kentucky." Lia let out her breath. "You're welcome there."

The words stunned him, jolting his brain more than the first twinges of numbed flesh warming in water. "Home?" he repeated stupidly, gently sandwiching her hand between his. Picturing what Margaret must look like after a year and a half—dear Margaret—and Beanie. How big Beanie must be now. Lanky and skinny like Frankie White but with shy eyes. Practically a teenager probably.

Justin had pictured that long dirt road that led to the farm a thousand times in his sleep, never once believing he'd see it again. The aching hole in his heart throbbed each time he remembered, trying to harden itself to force out the memories.

"I'd think about it," he said, more gruffly than he intended, "for you."

The horn blared again, and Lia jumped, turning to the window.

Justin wanted to pull her back, to tell her to forget the car and Jackson and stay. But that was nonsense. What would she do at a CCC camp of two hundred guys? And besides, Mr. Parker needed medical treatment, and fast. He'd suffered enough already.

Instead Justin kissed her fingertips one last time, trying to cling to their softness as long as possible. But he had to let her go. As he'd trusted God with his life, he'd trust Him with Lia as well. He slowly released her hand, letting one finger slip free at a time.

The cot squeaked as Lia stood up, careful not to jar her ankle, and she reached for her crutch. Justin wished he could help her—carry her even—but there he sat, a broken-up wretch who could do no more than watch her leave.

She leaned closer, catching him in a shy hug with her free arm. One side of her curls pressing against his cheek, intoxicating him with their fragrance. "I'll be waiting for you," she whispered, her voice close to his ear as she raised her head. And then she stood up, leaning on her crutch, and turned toward the door.

Justin couldn't say a word. Couldn't trust himself to speak.

The doc pushed the door open with a gentle squeak as she eased her way through the cots. "Lia Summers?" he said, holding the door wider. "They're calling for you."

"I'm sorry. I'm coming." Lia wiped her nose with a handkerchief and turned to slip through the door then stopped, digging for something in her pocket. "I almost forgot." She reached a cloth bundle toward Justin. "It's for you."

Justin strained to reach it, his fingers catching on a rectangle of familiar faded blue. The color of his CCC bandanna. Something hard and flat tucked inside.

When he unwrapped the rectangle, there it lay: Lia's precious photo of Reverend Summers. His smile wide and beaming, as if seeing straight into Justin's heart. And there in the corner, the note he'd written in black ink. A Bible verse. *For charity shall cover the multitude of sins.*

"I can't take this." Justin spoke in a whisper, holding it out.

"Please." Lia gently pushed it back. "I had fifteen years with him. My best memories are inside. I'll never forget him."

He blinked back tears. "Then take this." He offered his bandanna.

Lia reached out and took it, her fingers trembling. And instead of putting it in her pocket, she pressed it to her heart. Giving him one last glance over her shoulder as the doctor helped her through the door, offering his arm to lean on.

~·~

Justin watched the car until he could see it no more, leaning out the window of the infirmary. Dust rising up in a soft haze and burning his eyes the same way it had so many years ago when he counted the miles away from Kentucky.

And from Lia.

Never looking back.

AFTER THE ASHES

Dedication

To my father, Larry Rogers, who taught me to love the west.

Chapter 1

1988

"What? You're joking." Alicia forced her eyes open in the darkness of her bedroom, the dispatch guy's gravelly voice blaring into her ear from her pager. "What time is it, three in the morning?" She fumbled on her dented thrift-store nightstand for her clock radio.

"Yellowstone's burning out of control." Paco's voice came crisp and strident across the line. "We need the whole fire crew at the bus station in two hours, and we'll ship out to Albuquerque pronto. After that we've got a chartered flight to Jackson Hole. They want you guys there yesterday."

"*Caramba*," Alicia muttered as snatches of CBS news footage of blackened, smoldering hillsides flashed through her leaden brain. "Thanks, Paco. I'll be there."

She switched off the pager and sat there in a sleepy lethargy. *Call Carlita.* But before she could dial, the phone rang.

"Carlita?" She untangled the phone cord as she crawled out of bed. "You going, too?"

"To Yellowstone? Of course. They're calling out pretty much every firefighter in the country."

"How did I miss this?" Alicia ran a hand through her sleep-messy hair. "Is it really that bad?"

"Bad? It's torched. They're worried they might lose the whole park. Don't you watch the news?"

"While I'm rolling silverware at the restaurant." Alicia wiped sleep-teary eyes, stumbling over cheap pink jelly shoes and canvas Keds sneakers, and pulled the striped bedsheets up by rote. Her yard-sale pillowcases didn't match; one boasted a guitar with a British flag, and Care Bears slid across a rainbow on the other.

"I work 24/7, Carlita. I haven't watched *MacGyver* in a year. What's a TV? And my car radio's broken, too." Alicia held the phone under her chin as she tugged up the thin blanket. "But of course Yellowstone's torched. They don't put fires out in national parks, thanks to their famous 'let it burn' policy."

"It's big this time, Alicia. The place was as dry as a matchstick with the first fires burned, and now the smoke's showing up as far away as Oklahoma and Texas—and nothing's bringing it down. The Park Service shut down the park altogether except for authorized personnel."

"I had no idea. I figured it would burn itself out after a while."

"There are *eight thousand* firefighters on the ground there now—and it's still out of control. A week ago winds blew fire across a hundred and fifty thousand acres in a single day. If they don't put it out fast, there might not be any park left. It's that bad."

Alicia stood up quickly, nearly pulling the phone off the bedside table. "You mean it's threatening Old Faithful? I've always wanted to see Yellowstone." She untangled the cord and pushed the phone back in place. "One of my foster dads swore his grandfather's brother—a lieutenant in the army—had a treasure map of Gallatin Mountain that some kid found back in the '30s. Something about hidden gold. My foster dad thought it was the real thing, but it's not like you can take a shovel and dig up a national park."

"I don't know about any gold, but I can't guarantee Old Faithful will be left in a few more days."

Alicia coughed, trying to rid her throat of that sleepy film that made her voice croak like one of the frogs she sometimes found on her rickety balcony. "Well, all right, *amiga*. I'll be at the bus station in two hours, *bueno?*"

"See ya there."

Streetlights flickered in honey-colored sparkles through the thread-bare spots in her curtains as Alicia hung up the phone. *Two hours. Yeah. I can do that.* Her eyelids still felt heavy, but adrenaline coursed in tingling waves.

Alicia knew the firefighter drill by memory: pour instant Folgers coffee into her Star Wars mug, dig past rolled-ankle jeans, paint-splatter tops, and stirrup pants for her olive green denims and pull on her bulky yellow Nomex fire shirt. All of this she could do without opening her eyes, but then she needed light to pack her overnight bag and feed her fish.

Yes, fish. Serving on a fire crew didn't offer enough time for Alicia to deal with a dog or even a cat. After all, what kennel would open at God-forsaken hours of the early morning on twenty minutes' notice, even in downtown Santa Fe?

Thankfully, discount store betta fish could survive in Alicia's secondhand aquarium and chipped fish bowl for three weeks, so long as she remembered to slide the note and key under Mrs. Miklos's door on her way out.

Only once she'd forgotten. And even then, both bettas blinked insipidly at her from their tanks when she unlocked the door, her dingy red backpack slung over one shoulder and hair still reeking of smoke and dollar-store travel shampoo.

"Be good for Mrs. Miklos, okay?" Alicia shook some fish food into the top of the tank. "And I'll bring you a souvenir."

Right. A souvenir from Yellowstone. What, a snow globe or something? If the tourist lodge hadn't burst into flames, that is.

Alicia snapped the aquarium door shut and flipped on the lamp, squinting in the glare. Red Dog lace-up boots, since she couldn't afford the snazzy Whites? Check. Fire pack with the mandatory Fire Line Handbook? Ready to go. Hard hat? On a broken peg by the door.

She flipped on the radio to wake herself up and hummed along to Tiffany on the Spanish-language Santa Fe station as she sipped her coffee. A handful of Corn Pops straight from the box and that would have to be enough until crew breakfast.

The harsh bathroom light made Alicia's eyes water as she pulled her hair back in a ponytail. Her perm had grown out a long time ago, and her messy bangs left something to be desired—flat and lifeless—so a little finger-fluff and mist of Aqua Net hairspray in lieu of her ancient curling iron. Some ugly fake gold hoop earrings from K-Mart. A touch of eyeliner, maybe, but between her black eyelashes and her sleepless dark circles, she'd better go easy with the eye pencil.

Alicia nudged open the bathroom drawer—the one without a handle—and grabbed the tube of Crest then reached for her blue toothbrush. Grabbing her former boyfriend Miguel's old red one by mistake.

Miguel. She froze, remembering his slurred, drunken shouts as she'd shoved him out of the apartment, pushing the rickety dead bolt and chain shut and throwing herself against the door.

"I know you have it!" Miguel had hollered, his speech slurred.

"Where did you hide it?"

He'd pounded so loudly that Mrs. Miklos threatened to call the police, and when Miguel cursed her, Mr. Miklos stormed into the hallway with a sawed-off shotgun.

After that Miguel hadn't shown up again—at least publicly. But she'd seen his battered Ford pickup trailing her after she left her job at Little India restaurant, and after that she bought her first Smith & Wesson Model 36 and kept it zipped in her purse.

Alicia tossed Miguel's toothbrush forcefully in the trash. *Good riddance.*

Three thirty-six. Alicia glanced at the clock and strapped on her Coca-Cola coupon watch, her toothbrush dripping pale blue foam, and caught a glimpse of herself in the broken mirror, the bright yellow of her Nomex shirt making her tired eyes ache. *I look like a freaking canary. And a newbie at that.* She fixed her top button, wishing she had her old shirt back—the faded, salty-looking pale yellow one that had lost its hue to ruthless ash and smoke and harsh detergents. But at least it testified to her five years of fighting fires with the US Forest Service with the rest of her Mexican American crew. Or it had, until she ripped it nearly in half on an old, abandoned fence line in the woods near Los Alamos.

And fat. Ugh. Have I always been such a porker? Alicia turned sideways, smoothing her collar. Maybe working on the fire line would help her burn off some of the weight hanging on her hips.

Alicia rinsed out her toothbrush and strode out of the bathroom in disgust, flipping the flickering light off behind her. Just one more thing.

She scooted the old floor lamp out of the way and knelt by a patch of worn carpet, carefully peeling it up with the edge of a credit card to expose scuffed wooden boards. The crack between two boards lay in a thick and dusty line, slightly wider than the others, and she pried them apart.

It was there. Alicia passed her hand over the little glass jar she'd wedged in the opening, sagging in relief. If anything happened now, she was safe. Even Miguel wouldn't think to look here if he broke into her apartment.

Alicia pressed the boards back into place and smoothed the carpet then replaced the lamp and stood up. The sky outside the window had lightened, spreading gray-blue over the darkened streets. White and copper streetlights glowed back in pale spots.

Time to go. Alicia glanced at the digits on her watch and grabbed her red fire jacket. Her boots made a reassuring clomping sound on the carpet as she paused by the fish tank.

"Looks like this is it, fellas," she said, gathering up her keys and pack and giving the glass a fond pat. "Don't give Mrs. Miklos any trouble, you hear? I'll be back soon." She traced the glass with a bitten fingernail, suddenly sober. "And if I don't come back, you'll get along fine with Mrs. Miklos. Just remind her to buy Sparky brand fish food. That other stuff she buys smells like dead flies."

Alicia slid her arm through her backpack strap. "Come to think of it, it probably *is* dead flies. But don't tell her I said that."

She locked the door behind her, blowing a kiss over her shoulder.

"Sanchez." Jorge leaned across the seat as the line of firefighters snaked off the plane in the little Wyoming airport, grabbing their red fire packs from the overhead bins as they went. He winked and leaned closer, giving her a too-close glimpse of his stubbly, pockmarked cheek. "Why didn't you sit with me? I saved you a seat."

"Get lost." Alicia looked over his head to see if Carlita had emerged from the airplane lavatory.

"How'd you manage to get on this crew anyway, Sanchez? Convict labor?"

Alicia pulled off her headphones in annoyance. "Knock it off, Jorge. I've been fighting fires longer than you. And you're the one with the DUI on your record, not me." Dusty guitar chords from When in Rome's new song died as she switched off her Walkman—a cheerful, aching tune about love, ironic for how she'd felt dragging herself to a grungy bus station at five a.m.

But this was Wyoming, and everything felt different. Smelled different. She caught a whiff of fresh, pine-scented air from the tarmac as someone opened the cabin door to put down the ladder. The landscape beyond the plane window swelled in gentle, rolling curves, with dark pines jutting against sagebrush plains. Verdant, lush—so different from the parched adobe clays and cliffs of New Mexico.

Alicia looped her headphones around her neck as she bent to watch a white-tailed hawk glide and swoop in gentle spirals, eventually disappearing behind a splash of yellow wildflowers. Too bad she couldn't afford a camera.

"Aw, c'mon." Jorge winked, showing a gold tooth in the corner of his grin. "You never forget, do ya?"

"What?" Alicia looked up in annoyance, pushing her aviator sunglasses up on her hair. "No, I don't forget. Not when my so-called date gets pulled over for drunk driving. I told you you'd had too much tequila, but you wouldn't listen. I'm never getting in the car with you again."

"What do you mean 'so-called' date? It was a date. You said so."

"I said no such thing." Alicia ducked under the overhead bin. "You asked me to buy you a burger, and I did. And you lost all your senses after your bartender friend gave you all those free drinks. Never again, Jorge."

"Aw, come on, Sanchez. Gimme another chance." Jorge tried to grab Alicia's pack for her, but she pulled away and slid her arms through the straps without any help.

"There's nobody else to look at on the crew except Chava, and he looks like a rat," Jorge pleaded, putting his hands up. Several people behind him snickered. "Please? I won't drink tequila this time. I swear."

"Never."

"Why not? You're beautiful, and so am I." He cocked his greasy head. "A little skinny though. You lose weight?"

"Ha. Right." Alicia slipped her headphones back over her ears.

"No really. You're what, a size two now?" He tugged at the baggy edge of her Nomex shirt.

"Shut up." Alicia's voice turned cold, and she raised it loud enough for others to hear. "Those pickup lines didn't work last year, and they're certainly not going to work this time. Leave me alone, will you?"

Jorge ducked his head and moved closer to whisper in her ear. The warm mirth gone from his face, leaving cold black eyes. "I hear from Miguel that you're free again, although he swears he'll get you back." His coffee breath stirred her hair. "I'd watch out for that *burro* if I were you, eh? He wasn't too happy about you calling it splits."

"Hey." Alicia whirled around, nearly knocking Jorge over. "Leave Miguel out of this, okay?"

"*Calma*, calma." Jorge showed his gold tooth again. "I ain't sayin' nothin'. I just. . .thought you should know." He grinned, the smile not reaching his eyes. "You never know where that snake will show up next."

Alicia excused herself and pushed ahead of two firefighters to get away from Jorge. She ducked through the windy door and stepped onto the metal platform, wishing Jorge hadn't brought up Miguel. It had been what, a month now since she'd kicked him out? Three weeks? Her heart had been closed to him for far longer than that, but fear made her say yes to him time and time again.

"You'll be sorry, you fat idiota!*"* he'd shouted before knocking her into the blistered wallpaper, blood coursing between her eyes. *"I swear I'll kill you if you ever leave me. You hear me?"*

Wind whipped Alicia's hair out of its ponytail as she held on to the metal handrail, trying to leave Miguel and Santa Fe behind. She inched her way down the ladder and onto the wide tarmac, gazing up at a crystal blue Wyoming morning. At least here the sky seemed wide and endless and large enough to absorb all the heaviness in her heart. Free from the glimpses of Miguel's truck in the shadows or the memory of the scar on his thick chin.

Where on earth was Carlita? Alicia shielded her eyes to look back up the ladder and then felt someone bump her from the side.

"There you are," Alicia scolded, falling in step beside her. "What happened? You fall in?"

"You know those suction toilets. I caught my belt in one once, and it nearly pulled me under."

Alicia chuckled, keeping a wary eye out for Jorge. "So how's your little gal?"

"Trisha? She's a doll." Carlita untangled a chunk of salt-and-pepper hair from her backpack strap. "Gonna be eight next month. Can you believe it? Says the only thing she wants for her birthday is for me to come home safe." Her mouth twitched as if trying to quickly cover her emotions with a smile. "Here I am old enough to be a grandmother, and I still go to Girl Scouts and PTA meetings." She shook her head. "Who knew I'd be a mom again at my age? 'Oops.' That's my only explanation. But I wouldn't trade it for anything in the world."

"Old enough to be a grandmother? You are one, last I checked."

"Yeah." Carlita's eyes sparkled with pride. "It's not so bad."

"C'mon." Alicia rolled her eyes. "I hear you bragging all the way from Santa Fe. Anyway, *mamacita*, I brought Trisha one of those My Little Pony things. With the pink hair and braids and stuff." Alicia patted her backpack. "Not a Cabbage Patch doll like everybody wants now, but I hope she likes it anyway."

"You and your presents!" Carlita smacked Alicia. "If you don't quit that, you're gonna be flat broke. You probably already are. Now cut it out."

"Whatever. You know Trisha asks for it as soon as you get home."

"You make me look bad."

"Impossible. Trisha loves you more than life." The words *love* and *life* made her think, oddly, of Miguel. Of past arguments with him and other men who vanished like smoke when the going got tough. Alicia looked up at the sky, turning the subject away quickly. "Think the fire is as big as they say? I think I smell smoke, but it can't be from the fire. We're miles away."

"Dunno." Carlita rubbed her nose. "I smell it, too." She nodded through the crowd. "The crew boss said they've called in the military and still no signs of letting up."

Alicia imagined the lush fields of lupines and pink fireweed seared to a blackened crust. "Nah. No problem. We'll stomp the beast out in a day or two, if it's not already on its last legs—and we'll all pocket a nice chunk of hazard-duty pay."

"You can say that again. I don't know about you, but I'm going to that fancy resort in Taos when this is all over."

Alicia tried to guess how many Little India paychecks it would take to pay for a resort vacation anywhere. So far all the restaurant had done was pay her rent and leave her clothes smelling like curry and fry oil. "So what squad are you hoping for?"

"Mop-up. For sure. They don't pay me enough to risk my life on initial attack. Give me a rake or a hose lay any day."

"Wimp." Alicia wrinkled her nose playfully. "I hate mop-up. I'm all about initial attack."

"I know." Carlita's gray eyes turned sober. "I've seen you on the hotshot crew more times than I can count. You march right into the flanks of forest fires with nothing but a hand shovel and a bladder bag, and you never back off—even when they want to pull you off for smoke inhalation. You've been knocked out twice by dead snags."

"So? That's what fighting fires is all about." Alicia bristled slightly. "If I wanted a cushy job, I'd serve burgers at McDonald's. But I don't. I'm a firefighter."

"Right, but that's not what I meant." Carlita stuffed her hands in her pant pockets. "You're a great firefighter, but you fight too hard. You scared me last year when that big branch knocked you out—and you were arguing to go back on the front lines within the hour."

"So what?" Alicia walked faster, her breath coming in angry short spurts. "What's your point, Carlita?"

"Maybe nothing. But it just seems like you. . .I don't know. Don't value your life much."

Alicia stumbled over a bootlace and knelt briefly to tie it, whipping the laces tighter than necessary. "I don't value my life, huh?" She squinted up at Carlita with cool eyes.

"Don't take me wrong." Carlita put both palms up. "You're an amazing firefighter. My best crew partner. But you've got to be careful, too. Guard your life. It's not worth dying out there, you know?"

Alicia stuffed both hands in her pockets and walked beside Carlita, not speaking for a long time. Finally she gave a wry laugh. "Why?"

"Why what?" Carlita brushed her bangs out of her eyes.

"Why should I bother? I mean, what do I have to value in my so-called life, Carlita? A couple of betta fish?" Alicia kicked a spot in the concrete. "Look at you. You've got three kids and a new grandkid. I've got nothing."

"Mio Dios." Carlita looked up to heaven and crossed herself. "How can you say you've got nothing?"

Alicia scratched at an itchy seam on her sleeve, avoiding Carlita's eyes. "Life just doesn't work out for me. Trust me. If you had my life, you'd understand." She twisted her sleeve down over her wrist, hoping it covered the scars and burn marks.

"No I wouldn't." Carlita aimed a severe gaze at Alicia. "Life is always precious. The greatest gift of all. No matter who you have to share it with."

Alicia made a face. "C'mon. Let's talk about something else, okay?"

"You and your death wish," Carlita muttered. She eyed Alicia suspiciously. "You lost more weight, didn't you?"

"Good grief. Not you, too."

Carlita opened her mouth as if she'd like to say more then pressed lipstick-red lips together. "How about the scoop on Jorge then?" She managed a weak chuckle. "He's got the hots for ya, you know. And he's always fun to gossip about."

"Ha. Well." A corner of Alicia's mouth turned up. "Talking about Jorge and his issues ought to keep us busy for a while. The guy needs a psychiatrist."

"For sure. Well, then, there's always that Indian fella to jaw about, too. What's his name?"

"Who?" Alicia whipped her head around.

"You know who I'm talking about." Carlita's face turned smug. "That tall Iron Buffalo guy, or whatever his name is. From. . .Nevada? The engine captain."

"From Arizona. And his name is Thomas." Alicia's shoulders tightened. "What about him?"

"Thomas what? He's got one of those Indian names about a beaver or something. I forget what it is."

"Eagles, Carlita. Thomas Walks-with-Eagles." Her voice rose in irritation. "He's Apache."

"Walks-with-Eagles. Yeah, that's it. I knew his name had something to do with forest creatures. Anyway, I'm sure he'll be here." She smirked. "And with all your mechanics know-how, I bet you anything they'll put you on a truck crew with him."

"Thomas is a friend." Alicia pressed her lips together, and she stared up at a pale white moon in the blue sky. "Nothing more. And who cares if he's here? He's a firefighter. It's his job."

"Oh, you'll find each other. I'm no dummy. I've seen you talking to that guy on some of our fire details, *muchachita*. He's quite protective of you."

"Thomas is such a goon." Alicia chuckled, shaking her head. "He always gets the movie lines wrong. Every time. And he's hopelessly scatterbrained and eccentric and weird." She fell silent as Carlita fluttered a know-it-all look in her direction. "Whatever. I'm telling you, he's only a friend."

"Good thing because he isn't much to look at. If you don't mind me saying so."

Alicia stiffened as they headed between two rows of grounded small-engine planes on the tarmac. "I never said I liked Thomas. But he's a good guy." She tucked a strand of hair behind her ear. "A really good guy." She quickly cleared her throat. "So let's go back to gossiping about Jorge then, eh? I heard some stuff from María Teresa that could curl your hair."

"Tell me." Carlita leaned in closer. "I need another perm."

And before Alicia could spout off about Jorge's jail stint, the crew boss a few paces away let out a low whistle. "Check it out, folks!" he said, sweeping an arm toward the distant horizon. "There she is."

"There who is?" Alicia stretched her head around the nose of a yellow Cessna.

And there above the plain of wheat-colored grasses boiled an angry black-brown sky, billowing into the clear blue like ominous ink. Thicker and blacker than smoke from any fire she'd ever fought—including the double collision gas tanker wreck that had melted steel and burned for three days straight.

The entire crew halted as the mass of smoke quivered, mushrooming larger so that it covered the left slope of the plain.

Alicia nearly walked into Carlita's side as she gawked. "That?" she yelped, standing on tiptoe to see around the corner of the hangar. "That's our fire?"

"That's the tip of our fire," corrected the crew boss, worry lines creasing his tanned and fleshy brow. "Headquarters tells me they've made considerable progress this particular stretch."

The other firefighters began to walk again, talking in low tones, and Alicia tagged along behind Carlita. "What do you think of that?" she asked, eyes glued on the horizon.

Carlita shuddered and crossed herself in reply.

Chapter 2

Alicia Sanchez." Somebody tapped her arm from three heads back in the chow line at base camp. "I can't believe it. You're here, too?"

"Thomas?" Alicia searched for a bottle of plain water in the slushy Styrofoam cooler, pushing aside frosty cans of Coke and Tab. "So they're dragging you guys out of your beds in Arizona, too, huh?"

The makeshift tent at base camp inside Yellowstone housed lines of firefighters, all queued for lunch with paper plates. Outside the tarps, sun glimmered through a smoke-fogged haze—mingled now with scents of hamburgers and beanie-weenies. From the smells, Alicia might have thought herself at a Girl Scouts camp.

"Arizona's nothing, Alicia. They're pulling people from all over." Thomas reached over the half-filled plates to shake her hand. He'd cut his hair short, making his almond-shaped eyes and humpback nose stand out against clay-brown skin. "This thing's gonna be a bear, isn't it?"

Alicia reached for a napkin and spoke over the laughter and noisy thrum of conversation. "I've never seen anything like it. There've been some close calls with firefighters already, and one guy died outside the park."

Thomas shook his head, revealing a few threads of gray among the black. "It's scary stuff."

"Scary? Nah." Alicia turned back to the chow-line servers and shook her head no at the proffered corn.

"C'mon, Sanchez. I'm shaking in my boots. And you'd better be careful, hear me? I know how you are." Thomas picked up a shiny packet of Capri Sun fruit punch and tucked it under his arm as he accepted a paper plate. "So you still can't give it up, can you?"

"Give up what?" Alicia grimaced and gestured for the server to scoop off most of the beans on her plate, and she grabbed a paper cup of coffee. Tucking her water bottle under her arm.

"Fighting fires. I thought you wanted to go back to school or something. You told me you were saving money."

"Oh, that." Alicia shrugged, trying not to think of the hundreds of dollars she'd wasted on Miguel. Buying him drinks, giving him cash for the casinos—and extinguishing any hope she had of sending herself to night law school. *"I'll pay you back when I get paid,"* he'd promised. But the paycheck never came.

At least she'd managed to hide the most important thing from him—right there under his nose, concealed beneath a little patch of tatty carpet.

"So how about you?" Alicia avoided Thomas's question about school. "You gonna fight fires your whole life or what? Carlita tells me it's dangerous work." She bobbed her eyebrows. "She thinks you can't value your life much if you're nuts enough to like initial attack."

"She's probably right." Thomas shrugged and flashed a friendly, white-toothed smile at the server, ducking his head in thanks. "Which is why I'm smart enough to stay off the crew when I'm out for smoke inhalation." He poked her shoulder with a plastic spork. "Unlike some people."

"Don't you start. You forgot your nail clippers last time and were begging to use mine."

"Me, begging?" Thomas grinned, a clean, salt-of-the-earth smile that made Alicia feel faint joy stir inside her. "You're one to talk, always stealing my compass mirror to check your lipstick. You brought your own this time, didn't you?"

"Why should I? So long as I have yours, there's no need to weigh down my pack with mine."

"Ha." Thomas smiled again. "Lucky for you I brought two. One for you, one for me." He slipped a little wrapped package from his back pocket and twirled it between two fingers. "You can thank me later."

Alicia stared as Thomas tossed the package onto the corner of her tray. "You didn't. Those things cost fifty bucks apiece." The package looked too big for a compass though. "What else did you stick in here?"

"Be afraid. Be very afraid."

Alicia put her tray and coffee down and tore at the tape. "You wrapped this in a McDonald's hamburger wrapper, Thomas! Gross. Is that supposed to mean something?"

"That's what I found on the floor of my Jeep this morning when I showed up at the airport." He narrowed thick eyebrows. "Be glad I wrapped it at all."

Alicia pulled off the wrapper and made a show of wiping her hands on her napkin before reaching inside. There lay the compass, sure enough—he hadn't lied. And underneath it?

"Freeze-dried Sea-Monkeys?" She held up the plastic packet. "Are you serious?"

But Thomas had already turned, slapping hands across the chow line with a big African American guy from another crew.

Weirdo. Alicia smiled as she tucked the compass in her pocket. She marched through the rows of picnic tables, searching through the sea of yellow and olive green for a friendly face but wavered when she saw the back of Carlita's ponytail next to a pair of too-big triangle earrings. Earrings owned by hateful Melissa Ramirez of the second Albuquerque crew.

The last time she saw those trademark hot-pink plastic triangles they'd been on the dashboard of Miguel's car.

Alicia slipped behind a lanky fire captain, ignoring Jorge's leering grin from across the crowded mess area—and searched for an empty space. She eased into a metal folding chair by a discarded paper plate and Mello Yello can, then set down her tray and steaming coffee, rubbing her tired eyes and trying not to smudge her eyeliner. She unwrapped a plastic fork and reluctantly poked at her beans, wishing for a second she'd stayed home.

Alicia had always loved the thrill of smoke and flame, the adrenaline rush that pushed her into the heat with nothing more than a few government-issued tools. Sweat, ash, and the dull roar of falling trees clouded her eyes, making her feel half delirious with fatigue and odd exhilaration. Exhilaration that she, a no-name Mexican American who didn't even know her own parents' names, could help stomp the angriest inferno into sullen soot and embers—reducing the mighty giant to its knees.

But this time even she felt outmatched as she stared at the smoke boiling up from the distant trees. Thick and sinister, as if it could swallow her alive.

Perhaps if it did, things would work out better anyhow.

Alicia played with the plastic top on her water bottle with her short fingernail, wondering what it would feel like to wilt in the white-hot heat, gasping lungfuls of smoky air. Burning branches raining down like hailstones, the forest exploding around her.

At least she'd left things ready just in case.

"So you ditched me, huh?" A familiar voice rang next to her ear.

Alicia twisted around to look up at Thomas. "You again?" She smiled and pushed the dirty paper plate next to her out of his way, shaking the empty Mello Yello can. "You that desperate for a free soda?"

"You know me well."

Thomas pretended to reach for the can as he sat down, and Alicia whacked him with it. "You're such a goofball, you know that?"

"Yeah." He grinned, rubbing a brown hand over his face.

"Don't you have anybody else to sit with?" Alicia tried to keep her mouth straight as she tore off a tiny bit of her roll.

"Me? Not really." He unwrapped the plastic straw on his Capri Sun and punched it into the foil. "Nobody wants to hear about my French-speaking ferret or my rotten tomato collection. I dunno why."

Alicia stared. "A ferret. That speaks French."

"A cheap-o tape series I got at the library. Works like a charm. In fact, I'm gonna start paying him to give *me* lessons now." Thomas bowed his head in a quick, silent prayer and then unwrapped his napkin and plastic utensils. "And the rotten tomatoes are for the seeds. I swear. Something about the acid eating away the seed casings so they sprout better."

Thomas stuffed a big forkful of beanie-weenies in his mouth and closed his eyes. "Man, that's good stuff. What's the matter with you, Sanchez? Don't you eat?"

"Gross. No." Alicia sniffed the little piece of roll and grimaced before dropping it back on her plate. "Not on trips like these. Ugh." She pushed her plate away and reached for her bottle of mineral water.

"Are you kidding? It's a hot lunch. This is tons better than the premade MRE lunches we get out at the spike camp. Meals Ready to Eat." His lips turned up in a grin. "Or, better, Meals Refused by Ethiopians." He smeared butter on his roll and took a big bite. "After a few days on the fire line, even those Sea-Monkeys will start to look good."

Alicia spluttered her water in an unexpected laugh. "Do I dare ask if they're reconstituted the same way as our MREs?"

"Just add water." He shook a forkful of beanie-weenies. "So enjoy this while it lasts."

"No thanks." Alicia poked her roll with her plastic fork. "This looks like it fell out of last decade's army surplus. I'm not that hungry."

Thomas reached over his tray and picked up her roll. "What's wrong with it? It's bread. Not as good as my fry bread back home, but it's edible. I got an extra." He hovered his hand over her tray. "If you're not careful, I'll swipe yours, too."

Right. Alicia smiled, remembering how he'd voluntarily skipped lunch twice last year when the supply truck broke down—so the rest of the crew could eat. "Take my roll. I don't eat white flour anyway."

"Huh?" He cocked an eyebrow. "Not at all? A dinner roll never killed anybody." He shook it for emphasis: a shapeless round blob of pasty white.

"You're wrong." Alicia wrinkled her nose. "That stuff's terrible for you. Makes you fat."

"If you're worried about health, quit using that chemical-saturated Equal stuff." He nodded to her artificial sweetener packets. "It's creepy." Thomas narrowed black eyes at her. "Fat? Don't tell me you're on some crazy diet or something again. You're all skin and bones, Alicia."

"Please." She rolled her eyes. "Don't be so dramatic."

"I'm serious." The mirth fizzled for a minute, and he put the roll down and dug in his jacket pocket. "Here, then, if you're so all-fired hippie. Eat this." And he tossed her a package of whole-wheat peanut butter crackers. "Eat something, for goodness' sake, before you start sprouting Q-tips out your ears like that kid in *ET*."

Alicia blinked. "Elliot didn't put Q-tips in his ears. That was in *Better Off Dead*—the John Cusack film." She raised an eyebrow. "And that analogy made no sense anyway, regardless of which movie you're talking about."

"Aw, no." Thomas dug into his beans again with gusto. "You're wrong about the movies. It's right after the part where the creepy alien asks to phone home, and Elliot sticks his ears full of Q-tips. Haven't you seen it?"

"What? You're totally wrong." Alicia put down her water bottle. "You're getting the movies mixed up again, just like you always do. That was *Better Off Dead*. The movie where the kid on the bike keeps saying, 'I want my two dollars!'"

"You're making this up." Thomas wiped his mouth with a napkin. "I told you, that's *ET*, not *Better Off Dead*. I remember that kid on the bike riding through the mist. Think about it—after the Q-tips, they dress the alien in some kind of homemade pink New Wave frock for prom."

"No!" Alicia pounded the table. "That was Molly Ringwald in *Pretty in Pink*! Andie makes the dress and goes to prom with Duckie. Don't you remember anything you see in the theater?"

"You poor misguided soul." Thomas gave her a pitying look as he scooped up his beans. "You must have gone a few years between viewings. How old are you again? Forty-six?"

"Forty-six?" Alicia yelped, causing a wiry, white-haired crew boss to jerk his head in her direction. Thomas's shoulders shook with silent laughter. "I'm twenty-nine, you freak-o." She reached out and slugged his shoulder. "Not as old as you, you old goat."

"Try again, *chica*." Thomas winked as he bit into his roll. "Twenty-eight, baby."

"What?" Alicia's eyes bugged out. "You've got white hair! You're lying. You can't be twenty-eight."

"Blame bad genetics for my white hairs." Thomas reached into his vest pocket and tossed his driver's license on the table without flinching. "Read it and weep."

Alicia glared at him then sneaked a peek at the license. "Right. Like that thing's legit." She shoved it back across the table. "Where'd you get it, a Cracker Jack box?"

"Sore loser, aren't we?" Thomas stuck his license back in his vest pocket then leaned back in his chair and stretched in victory. "So what was that about an old goat? I'd like to hear it again, if you don't mind."

"Shut up." Alicia crossed her arms.

Thomas snickered and poked the packet of crackers across the table at her. "I win. Eat."

"I don't eat peanuts."

"What?" Thomas threw up his arms. "What do you eat, woman? *Frijoles*?"

"Beans? Don't be disgusting."

"You're Mexican, for Pete's sake." Thomas scowled.

"So? I hate all that stuff. It's full of carbs."

"Rice?"

"No."

"Rutabagas?"

"Be serious."

Thomas rubbed his forehead. "Come on. There must be something you like. Tell me. Your favorite food in the world." He lowered his voice as if telling a secret. "Your last meal. What would it be?"

Alicia studied him a second, thinking, then leaned across her tray. "I'm listening."

"Butter on Velvet Gold graham crackers." She shook one of her

Equal packets, avoiding his eyes. "My favorite foster mom used to make it. It sounds silly, I know. But when I'd had a rough day at school, she'd sit at the kitchen table with me and spread graham crackers with butter. They were wonderful. Crisp and sweet, with a little spread of creamy stuff across the top." Alicia tried to laugh. "Disgusting, right?"

"Not at all." Thomas's eyes sobered. "Velvet Gold graham crackers." He wrinkled his brow in thought. "I remember those. They stopped making them awhile back, didn't they?"

"Yeah." Alicia leaned her cheek in her hand. "Nabisco graham crackers aren't the same at all. I sent some letters to different baking companies trying to find Velvet Gold, but apparently it's defunct. I haven't tasted those graham crackers since I was nine."

Thomas ate in silence as if wondering whether or not to ask and then raised his head slightly. "So what happened to your foster mother?"

"Which one?" A flicker of irritation snatched at Alicia's dark brows.

"You had more than one?"

"Seven, last time I counted." Alicia's tone took on a harder edge. "And if you're talking about Mrs. Coffman, the one I ate graham crackers with, she died of a sudden heart attack at age fifty-two. Nobody knows why." She checked her watch and turned away from the table, scanning the mess tent. "So what time are we supposed to be out on the fire line?"

"I'm sorry." Thomas didn't move, except to raise his head.

"About?" She looked up as if annoyed.

"Mrs. Coffman. The graham crackers." Thomas poked the rest of his beanie-weenies with his fork and chewed thoughtfully. "And the seven foster mothers. That must have been rough to feel bounced between so many homes, especially when you were so young."

The scent of smoke hung in the air in a sudden, unmistakable breath, and Alicia's eyes felt warm. The way they did when bits of ash swirled on the horizon.

"You don't know the half of it." Alicia ran a hand through her ponytail in a harsh gesture. "But that's life, I guess, right?"

"Sort of, but..." Thomas put down his fork and nested his chin in his hand. "I knew you'd been through a lot." He sighed. "Tell me something. Were any of the foster mothers kind like Mrs. Coffman?"

"No," said Alicia crisply, dabbing a napkin at her lips and effectively ending the subject. "Not in the slightest. Now, where'd I put that compass mirror, or do I need to borrow yours again?"

"One last thing." Alicia reached out to stop Thomas as he gathered up his empty tray. "You never told me."

"Told you what?" He drained the last of his Capri Sun, and the foil packet made a slurping sound.

"What would you want to eat for your last meal?"

Thomas put his Capri Sun down and rattled it on the table while he thought. "I think I know."

"What?" Alicia balled up her napkin and pushed her mostly full plate away.

"Whatever would make you smile like you meant it." He winked and stood up then waved good-bye as he carried his plate to the trash.

Chapter 3

You've got your will written, don't you?" Carlita called over through the gloom.

Alicia jumped, blinking burning eyes into a pour of sweat from her hairline. Her mouth stammered as she scrambled for a reply. "What's that supposed to mean? It's not like people are going to be fighting over my betta fish."

She raised her voice over the roar of the fire and the shouts of the crew as they dug into the fragrant earth with fire rakes. The pines overhead still glowed bright green in the mid-afternoon sun, but just a few feet to the right they'd scorched like overdone marshmallows.

"I mean we're probably all gonna die out here." Carlita paused long enough to wipe sweat from her neck. "Either from scorched lungs or smoke inhalation. This fire's a monster! We've been chasing it for hours, and it's done nothing but pick up speed."

She put down her pulaski fire rake and tied a dusty purple bandanna around her forehead—making her look like a fiftyish female Rambo. Thick, murky smoke boiled in from the huge swath of burned forest, and glimmers of orange still licked at a blackened stump.

"Speak for yourself. I'm not dying out here." Alicia coughed into her bandanna. "Maybe not, but I'm so mad at the Park Service I could spit." Carlita shook her head in disgust. "If they'd put this thing out earlier, we wouldn't be in this mess. Look at it!" She swept a filthy, ash-stained arm at the blackened stretch of forest. Rippling heat waves made the whole scene look hazy, as if Alicia were seeing underwater.

"It's not all their fault. This is the driest summer on record, and all this timber just waiting to burst into flame. We'll put it out if it takes all week. Besides, I've seen worse."

"You're a liar." Carlita didn't even look up. "You've never seen worse than this."

"Maybe." Alicia hid a smile.

"Maybe nothing. If this is what hell looks like, count me out."

"I don't believe in hell." Alicia stomped on a piece of ash that floated in on a warm gust. "Life is hell. That's my theory."

"And when you die you go to heaven? Right. Like that makes any more sense than us digging the daylights out of a strip of land that's just going to go up in smoke in an hour anyway." Carlita made a face. "So anyway, you got your wish."

"My what?" Alicia coughed and wiped her gloves on her ash-stained pants before gripping her fire rake. In a few minutes the whole line of firefighters would dig a single swipe into the soil with their fire rakes, in perfect succession, one after another. A step forward and another swipe— digging trenches into the furnace and whittling away at its mighty power.

"Your wish." Carlita nodded her head behind them.

Alicia twisted around to see through the thick cloak of gray-black smoke. And there, barely visible through the gloom, came a glint of Forest Service sea green: Thomas's fire truck rumbling through a distant dirt road. It disappeared behind a charred cottonwood, one of the dead branches still glowing with flame.

"Give me a break, Carlita." Alicia turned back, sponging her face with the back of her glove. "I told you I don't like him like that. Really. Why don't you give it up?" She watched as the last crew member down the line swung his fire rake, and then she stepped forward with the others. "I don't care if he's here. He's just a friend."

"What?" Carlita spun around. "I was talking about them assigning us initial attack. Your wish. Remember?" She glared. "What were *you* talking about?"

Alicia nearly dropped her fire rake. "Oh," she mumbled, feeling her face color with embarrassment. "Sorry. I misunderstood you."

Carlita didn't respond, stomping soot and soil from her boots as the crew boss shouted at them to put their backs into it. A wall of heat hit Alicia from the side with unexpected force, and hoses hissed as crew members rushed to keep the fire from spreading.

"Really. I'm sorry." Alicia wiped the sweat drops tickling the side of her face with a dusty bandanna, keeping an eye on the fire line. Ghostly orange flames flickered through the gloom, and she instinctively covered her head as a crash of falling timber reverberated through the woods. "I just thought you meant something else."

"Or *somebody* else," Carlita muttered, gripping her fire rake to raise on cue. "I tell you what, for somebody who doesn't like that Thomas fellow, you sure spend a lot of time thinking about him."

Alicia avoided her eyes, trying to swallow the grit that lodged in her throat. "It's not that I'm thinking about him exactly. But he's. . .I don't know. Different." She coughed into her bandanna, and then softened her tone. "He seems to really care how I am, you know? And he keeps his eyes above my neckline, unlike half the guys on this crew."

"Whew. Yeah." Carlita laughed as she raised her fire rake and scooped deep into fresh brown soil.

Through the charred trees Alicia saw a faraway quiver of bright flame, and a swell of heat made sweat prickle on her neck. Distant trees roared and snapped.

The blaze was big all right—maybe even bigger than they were saying. And if the wind picked up from the wrong angle and caught them at the flank, they were toast. Literally.

Carlita groaned with effort as she tore out a clump of earth and stones with her fire rake, and Alicia raised hers with ash-dusty gloves.

"In all the years I've known Thomas, he's never once tried to sleep with me—or even ask me out." Alicia let out a grunt as she heaved her fire rake into the hard soil, making a soft thud as she tore open the earth. "I don't know what to make of him."

She dug the heavy blade out of the ground, turning over a fresh section of fragrant earth. Wishing she could turn her own life inside out and start over—or if it would even be worth the effort to try.

Carlita put her head down, red-faced, and mopped sweat from her forehead with the edge of her bandanna. "I don't want to ask this the wrong way," she said in hesitant tones, raising her eyes to Alicia. "But Thomas isn't. . .you know. Gay. Is he?"

"What? No." Alicia bristled, whirling around. "Why would you even ask something like that?"

"Dunno. Just wondering. You said he never asked you out or flirted with you, and with that new disease going around, you can't be too careful." Carlita shrugged. "I've never seen him hang out with the chicks."

"That doesn't mean anything!" Alicia snapped. "He's been engaged twice, for your information. To *women*. One dumped him for some good-looking banker, and the other married her childhood sweetheart instead." She shook her head in disgust. "Stupid girls."

"He tell you all this?"

"No. Some of the other guys on the crew."

"Oh." Carlita smoothed her hair back into a ponytail and coughed into her bandanna. "Well, what's wrong with him? Why doesn't he ask you out?" She reached over and nudged Alicia with her elbow. "Or better, why don't you ask him out? This is the '80s, you know. You don't always have to be so old-fashioned."

"I'm not old-fashioned." Alicia pulled away. "But I can't ask him out. I just. . .can't." She stepped forward with the other crew members, feeling like one in a line of trained monkeys. "He's one of those Bible freaks. You know. Went to Bible college. Reading the scriptures and praying for people."

She kept her eyes on the line of firefighters. "I just can't get into it myself. I sure admire people who believe something as much as he does. But. . ." She messed with the grip tape on the end of her fire rake. "I'm not going to ask him out."

"Hmph. What is he, some kind of freaky cult leader?"

"Nah. One of those regular old 'born-again' people, whatever that's supposed to mean." She squinted over at Carlita. "Do you believe in God? Or Jesus, as Thomas always talks about?"

"Sure I do." Carlita's eyes turned sober. "With all my heart. I used to go to Mass only at Christmas and Easter, but the older I get, the more I feel like there's gotta be more than that." She pressed dry lips together. "I'm. . .actually thinking of joining a Bible study."

"A Bible study? You?"

"Why not? I might as well learn about what I'm supposed to believe, right?"

"Wow." Alicia blew out her breath. "I didn't know you were so thick with religion."

"How about you?" Carlita kept her eyes on the row of firefighters, gripping her fire rake with both hands as they plunged and dug.

"What about me?"

"Do you believe in God?"

Alicia scrunched her eyebrows. "God? I don't know, Carlita. Probably not."

"Shouldn't you decide?"

Alicia waited for Carlita to swing then hacked her fire rake into the soil. "If I believe in God or not? No." She strained her back and shoulders with effort, digging her fire rake in deep and scooping up soil and rocks.

"Why should I? If He exists, He certainly hasn't done a good job of taking care of me. That's all I'm saying."

"You're saying a lot more than that, *muchacha.*"

"Look." Alicia stood up straight and banged her fire rake into the ground to shake off the dirt. "If you're so all-fired about God, why don't *you* ask Thomas out?" she flared. "You'd be a perfect match."

"I'm old enough to be his mother," Carlita growled. "And besides that, I'm married. Remember?" She pulled off her glove, revealing a carved wooden ring that didn't heat against the skin like metal. "Or did you think I'd ditched Simón already?"

"Oh yeah," Alicia said meekly, cringing in embarrassment. "I forgot. Six months, right?"

"Ten." Carlita's face twisted with anger. "Seems like you forget a lot of things, Alicia Sanchez. Maybe God's been looking out for you a lot longer than you realize. That Mrs. Coffman woman you've mentioned before. Wasn't she some sort of Christian?"

"Nope. An atheist." Alicia faced Carlita with a triumphant smile, her sweaty hair hanging out of her ponytail and around her ears. "Gotcha."

"You got me on nothing. It's even more amazing." Carlita raised a hand toward the ash-choked sky. "God used a woman that didn't even believe in Him to carry out His will of cradling your heart and giving you your dearest childhood memories. Ever think of that?" She stuck her face closer, almost bumping noses with Alicia. "God," she began, her voice fierce, "is far more concerned about you than you give Him credit for." She straightened up. "That's what I think. And it would do you good to consider that before you throw your life away."

Alicia jumped, so startled she dropped her fire rake. "What are you talking about? Who said I'm throwing my life away?" She groped for the rake on the leaf-strewn ground.

"You don't fool me." Carlita shot her a severe look. "I don't know where that empty look in your eyes came from, but I don't like it." She glared. "And if it takes God to fix your problems, so be it. I should have brought you to Mass a long time ago."

"Right. In Latin," Alicia mumbled.

"So get a Bible in English or Spanish," Carlita snapped back. "Simón used to be a sorry druggie, you know that? I divorced him ten years ago. But since he's got all this religion, he's changed." Her eyes softened as she traced her wooden ring with her gloved hand. "I wouldn't trade him for anybody now. He's not perfect, but he's trying. He's a good man. Maybe some religion would do you good, too."

"Maybe it wouldn't." Alicia lifted her chin.

"Well, what you're doing now sure isn't helping. You got a better idea?"

Alicia turned her fire-scorched face away, not sure what to say.

Chapter 4

Well, wonders never cease. I think I've fixed something for a change." Alicia dropped the hood down on the ancient Forest Service fire truck, its engine chugging weakly. Chris and Duncan, two firefighters from one of the Wyoming crews, recoiled the hoses on the other side of the truck after yet another breakdown. The reason this time? A radiator leak, compounded by a devilishly stubborn hood prop and too slippery gears. "Methuselah," they called the fire truck—after years of breakdowns, repairs, and long-distance runs that had racked up more than two hundred thousand miles in ugly wear and tear.

In fact, Methuselah had been headed for the scrap bin when the head engine captain got an urgent call from Yellowstone begging for trucks.

Alicia tossed the toolbox behind the truck seat and shut the door, her mind an exhausted muddle of flames, shouts, acrid smoke, and cold showers before a few hours of shallow sleep. Then up again at dawn, and the whole thing all over again. Those beautiful fields blackened, trees splintered and fallen like brittle Pick Up Sticks. Dead deer and elk stranded in Yellowstone River.

"So you believe in Jesus, huh?" Alicia wiped her grease-stained palms on her grimy, ash-blackened pants. Even her nails, clipped short as they were, had taken on a grayish sheen under her bubblegum-pink nail polish.

Thomas, who was squatting on the ground over an empty radiator fluid canister, looked up at her with a wrinkled brow. If he grew his hair out longer and maybe stuck a feather in it, Alicia could picture him sitting next to a fire in buckskins, roasting a deer over a spit.

"Me? Of course I believe in Jesus." Thomas raised his voice over the rattling drone of the engine, and the image fled. "You know I do." He cocked his head. "But where in the world did that come from?"

Alicia didn't answer, scrubbing a clump of charred soil from the

214

bottom of her boot. Smoke rose up from the distant hillside like spilled ink, boiling into the already hazy sky.

"Why do you ask?" Thomas dumped the empty canister in the back of the truck.

"No reason." Alicia crossed her arms stiffly. "I just wonder sometimes… why. You seem to be a rational guy. Why do you let religion hold you back?"

Thomas froze there in mid-bend, reaching down to tie his bootlace. He blinked then stood up slowly, coming up to face her with a tender look in his eyes.

"What?" She put her hands on her hips in irritation.

"Nothing." Thomas looked away meekly. "You just seem so…angry."

"Angry?" Alicia waved a hand in front of her face as the rickety engine belched exhaust. "Why wouldn't I be angry? God's never been there for me, if He does exist." She kicked the side of Methuselah's back tire, which was appropriately leaking air.

"Of course He exists. He's always been with you." Thomas bit his lips. "You might not have seen it, but He was. I don't know all you've been through, but I just wish. . ." He broke off with a sigh.

"Wish what?"

Thomas studied her a moment, holding her gaze. "I just wish I could show you somehow—in a way you could understand."

"Ha." Alicia spat out a bitter laugh. "Good luck with that. I don't buy any religious sob stories about a God who loves me." She shook a finger at him. "And you of all people. Shouldn't you be following whatever your ancestors worshipped rather than some imported white man's god?"

"Whoa, Nelly." Thomas took a step back and raised his palms as if afraid she'd belt him. "Don't call out the firing squad just yet."

"Sorry." Alicia managed a smile. "But you know I'm right. Why won't you just admit it?"

"Right?" Thomas chuckled, and his eyes glinted like black water. "I'm afraid that depends on who you ask. For starters, almost nobody's pure-blooded Apache anymore. My grandmother was white. My mom had blue eyes." He shrugged. "So whose ancestors am I supposed to follow? My white grandmother's or my Apache grandfather's? Or my French-Seminole stepfather's?" He scratched his fingers through thick hair. "It's not as easy as you think, Alicia."

"At any rate, I'd choose one of those fire-breathing gods rather than hear people harp about how much the God of the Bible loves me." Alicia turned quickly. "No offense, Thomas. I just don't believe it."

"But He does." Thomas touched her arm lightly. "He died for you. The Bible compares Him to a shepherd who left ninety-nine so-called righteous people to seek the one lost sheep—and then He gave His life for you. Can't you even try to picture it?"

Alicia slapped a mosquito on her shirtsleeve and rubbed her arm in disgust. "Gave up His life for me?" She looked up with a scowl. "Please. I know several people who'd like to see me dead. But there isn't a soul alive who'd give their life for me." She held a finger up to his face in defiance. "Not one. When push comes to shove, everybody looks out for number one. Every single time."

Thomas shook his head sorrowfully and opened his mouth as if to speak, but the sudden and unexpected backward lurch of the truck startled them both.

As if in slow motion, Alicia watched Methuselah roll right over the triangular chock against the back tire and reverse toward a cliff of thick Ponderosa pines, the engine bleating pitifully like a sick goat.

"Get out of the way!" Alicia screamed, lunging for the truck door. "She popped out of gear again!"

Thomas nearly tackled Duncan, shoving him to the side as Methuselah sped past in a cloud of gray dust.

"Oh my word." Chris jumped out of the truck's path. "That thing's gonna go over the cliff!"

"Watch out!" Thomas sprinted after the truck with Alicia on his heels, cupping his hands around his mouth. "Get everybody out of the way!"

Duncan and Chris fanned out over the hillside, stumbling over pine limbs and shouting out warnings while Thomas tried unsuccessfully to grab the door handle. The truck picked up speed on the decline, bumping over a boulder and shooting between two pines on a downhill slant toward the cliff.

Down below the steep drop-off lay a rolling green valley of deserted hills, the thick patches of pine forest interspersed with smooth green meadow.

"It's too late." Thomas grabbed Alicia's arm as she dove for the side of the truck—Methuselah careening toward the ravine, kicking up stones and soil.

"Oh no it's not." Alicia pulled herself free and snatched at the door handle, jerked it open. One of her boots dragged along the ground, banging against roots and boulders as she tried twice to pull herself up into the cab.

As the truck roared through a patch of clearing, Alicia gave a final hefty push against the door frame and shoved her head inside then hauled herself up and into the cab. Ducking just as a cottonwood limb raked across the window, snapping off the side-view mirror like a pesky fly.

Alicia's cheek banged against the door glass, knocking her teeth together as the truck bumped over a boulder and cracked her forehead against the windshield. The rearview mirror flap fell open and whacked her in the face as she fumbled for the gearshift. Windshield wipers scraped the glass, swishing against thick pine boughs.

She heard Duncan shout, saw Chris through a spot of clearing cupping his hands around his mouth.

Alicia found the wobbly gearshift and tried to shove it into DRIVE—just as she felt the back tire give. Dropping down with a sickening thunk. She let go of the steering wheel and smashed the jammed gearshift with both hands, shouting as it popped into gear, and poked her heavy boot around on the floorboard in search of the gas pedal. The engine revved, and she heard the wheels spin—screaming against the crumbly forest soil and the weight of a truck already on its downhill slide over the cliff.

The landscape lurched upward with a bump as the rear right tire gave way, slamming her against the door and giving her an eerie glimpse of tufted tree tops against smoke-gray clouds.

"C'mon, Methuselah, you old horse! Drive!" Alicia punched the gas pedal to the floor, pinning it with all her weight and spinning the wheel.

Out of the corner of her eye, Alicia saw a blurred Thomas racing toward her at an unnatural angle, his face ashen—screaming. His black hair disheveled. "Are you crazy?" he was shouting before the scrape of boulders and limbs under the truck roared in her ears.

Alicia felt the truck turn, saw tree branches pass across the windshield. Spaces of sky glimmered through the pine needles like sparkling gray stars, oddly still and silent amid the crunch of grinding earth against the undercarriage.

A bang, and the truck seemed to settle. She felt her hand reaching for the gearshift.

Something warm trickled down her forehead. Alicia blinked, letting her foot off the gas as her vision seemed to cloud over. Hazy and smokelike, until she could no longer see the steering wheel.

Chapter 5

Alicia Sanchez. For goodness' sake." Thomas's voice came out somewhere between a growl and a whisper of relief. "You sprained your wrist, you know that? And you're all banged up. A badly bruised rib and two stitches on that cut on your cheek."

"Thomas?" Alicia opened one eye, but the other one felt stuck together. She reached up to touch it, but her wrist had been wrapped in something stiff. An IV bag dripped into a tube taped to the crook of her elbow.

Her eyelid fluttered as she tried to see, taking in the tiny hospital room and small window. A fly buzzed against the dull fluorescent light, and Alicia tried to follow it with her gaze. Everything looked grainy, weak.

"And that eye." Thomas looked furious as he crossed his arms, his expression darker than Alicia had ever seen him. Jaw clenching. "That thing's gonna swell up royally."

"Is the truck okay?" Alicia patted gingerly at a patch over her eye. Her cheekbone throbbed, and her rib cage hurt when she breathed.

"The truck? Yeah, sure. Methuselah's fine—the old rattler." The corner of his mouth tipped up as if trying to smile, but his face looked too pale and stiff for mirth. "I don't know how you did it, Alicia, but you hung on to that cliff like a mountain goat." His mouth wobbled, dry-lipped. "Another inch or two and. . ."

Thomas rubbed his forehead as if in bewilderment. A smear of engine grease still blackened the side of his stubbly chin.

Alicia pushed herself up on one elbow. "But I saved her, right?"

"Saved her?" Thomas's eyes popped open, and he began to pace angrily. "You could have killed yourself! I told you to let it go. It's Methuselah, Alicia! A rusty old bolt box on her last legs. So long as nobody was in the way, she wasn't worth risking your life over."

"But I saved the truck. Right?"

218

"Yes, but. . ." Thomas sputtered, stretching his arms out. "Why? What on earth got into you?"

Alicia felt her mouth twist into a sour frown. "What do you mean? The truck was about to go over the cliff, and I stopped it."

Thomas stuck his face closer to hers, his voice harsh. "You could have killed yourself. Did you think of that?"

"I did what needed to be done." Alicia attempted a shrug, but it hurt too badly.

Two angry lines creased between his eyes. "Why? Why would you risk your life for. . .for Methuselah?" He banged a fist into his palm. "There was nobody in the way. She was headed for the scrap heap. Why?"

"Why not?" Alicia stuck her chin out.

Thomas looked at her a moment, speechless. His mouth partially open. "Doesn't your life mean anything to you?"

"Not much. Why should it?" She wiped a bit of blood from the corner of her mouth, swallowing the metallic taste. "And what's it to you anyway? I was just doing my job."

"Why should it matter? Because. . .because. . .it just does!" Thomas sputtered again, waving his arms. "God made you, Alicia! He loves you. I. . .well, I admire you a lot, you know that? You're an amazing firefighter and an amazing friend. Your life is priceless."

He paced the room in silence for a minute, his shoes squeaking on the tile floor. "I don't know why you gamble with your life as if it means nothing to you, but no broken-up old truck is worth dying over. Don't you understand?"

Alicia stiffened at his tone, her eyebrows coolly arched. "No," she finally said, turning away from him and fixing her gaze out the window. "I don't."

Thomas stared at her. "What?"

"I just don't get it. Your whole 'life is priceless' speech." Alicia's eyes were icy. "You're making a big deal out of nothing."

"Nothing?" Thomas poked his head down to her level. "You think throwing your life away is nothing?"

"So what? That's my business. What's it to you anyway?" She drew her knees up and wrapped her arm stiffly around them.

Thomas stared at her as if in disbelief, shaking his head. "You really mean that," he finally whispered, his eyebrows peaking in a hollow sort of sadness.

"Of course I do."

"What if you'd died out there?" Tears glistened in Thomas's eyes as he stabbed a finger toward the window.

"What if I did?" Alicia spoke through clenched teeth. "You'd have one less person to drive the fire truck. You'd find another one—and another friend—in no time. I'm not as irreplaceable as you think. I've had twenty-nine years to figure that out." She nodded stiffly toward the door, feeling inexplicably cold. "Now give me a rest, will you?"

She sank back on the pillow and fingered her bandages. "When am I back on the fire line? And don't tell me to take a day off or something equally stupid."

Thomas didn't move.

"The doctor said your blood sugar was extremely low." He spoke in nearly a whisper, nodding toward the IV pole. "You're more than twenty pounds underweight, and she needed to give you intravenous dextrose. Have you been eating anything at all?"

"What?" Alicia jerked up straight. "He told you that? That's confidential, Thomas." Her voice burned. "How dare he tell you my personal information."

Thomas took a step back. "*She* told me, Alicia. Your doctor's a woman. And I'm so sorry about the breach of confidentiality. But you were on my watch, and somebody needed to know since you'd blacked out—either from hunger or a blow to the head or both. I was in charge of the crew, so she told me." He rubbed his face in his hands. "Forgive me. I just. . .want to see you whole. Healthy. It's like. . .I'm losing you."

Fat idiota. Alicia turned her face away, remembering Miguel's curses. "Leave me alone, Thomas."

She saw his face fall by tiniest degrees, the moisture in his eyes intensifying until his eyes burned red, as if stung by smoke.

Instead of turning to the door, Thomas walked quietly over to her bedside and stood there a second. Then he reached down and smoothed her bangs out of her eyes.

"The Lord loves you, Alicia," he whispered hoarsely. "You're precious to Him. And to others."

"I'm not precious." Alicia spoke through her teeth. "I've meant nothing to anybody as long as I can remember. I've lived a life you can't even begin to imagine."

"Try me."

"I've done drugs. I ran away from home. I've been in rehab for alcohol more times than I can count." Alicia counted them off on her fingers. "I've sold myself on the streets to have money to eat." Tears swelled in her eyes. "Once one of my foster fathers beat me so badly I had to have reconstructive surgery." She rolled up her sleeve to show an arm riddled with scars and scratches. "I cut myself for years."

Thomas's eyes watered. "You've told me some of this before, Alicia. I'm not dumb. I know you've suffered a lot—for things that weren't your fault. And made some bad choices because of it. But I've never condemned you."

Alicia paused, running her fingers over the IV tape. "I'll never be one of your squeaky-clean Bible-college girls with the long dresses and big Bibles. Hear me?" She glared. "Go ahead and tell me I'm precious now."

Thomas's lips tightened, but he didn't change his expression. "You *are* precious," he whispered. "No matter what you say."

He touched two fingers to his lips and then to her forehead.

And then he turned and walked out of the hospital room, his footsteps clomping mournfully down the empty corridor.

Alicia reached up to press the CALL button. As she shifted her arm, several Forest Service firefighters strode past her doorway, their faces streaked with ash. One moaned while he held his arm.

Someone paused, and a familiar face flashed in the doorway. Stepping back just as two orderlies rolled an empty gurney past her room, its wheels squeaking.

"Miguel?" she gasped, raising herself up on one arm. "What are you doing here?"

Chapter 6

Miguel? That's impossible." Carlita scrubbed her wet hair with a towel and stared at Alicia's reflection in the chipped mirror. Base camp shower facilities weren't much to brag about, but at least they offered indoor plumbing. On the other side of the showers, several women had even plugged in a few curling irons and hair dryers.

"Miguel's a thousand miles from here." Carlita pulled the towel off her neck and dug in her makeup bag for an Avon blush compact. *Pink Lemonade*, Alicia read sideways on the label.

"I'm telling you, I saw him." Alicia pulled her toothbrush from her mouth to speak. "He started to walk into my room, but then he disappeared." She tore off a brown paper towel and wiped Crest foam off her chin, trying to hide her shaking hands. "I asked the nurse to look for him, but nobody'd seen him but me. He had that scar on his jaw."

She gestured at her chin with her pinkie, catching a glimpse of her face in the glass: pale and tight. The swelling had gone down from her escapade in Methuselah, but the bruises and cuts on the side of her face bloomed bright and scabby.

"I'm sure it was him. He blended right in with the rest of the guys— wearing Forest Service firefighter clothes and everything. Yellow shirt and green pants. The whole bit."

Carlita raised an eyebrow above moisture-frosted glasses. "Miguel. In Forest Service clothes."

"I know it sounds crazy, but I'd know that face anywhere. I've been with him two stinking years."

"Alicia." Carlita put her blush brush down. "I know Miguel's threatened you, but do you really think he'd come all the way to Wyoming and mingle with a bunch of firefighters in a hospital? Miguel might be foolhardy, like you, but he's not stupid."

"I'm not foolhardy." Alicia scowled and turned on the faucet, eliciting a spray of cloudy, metallic-scented water that reeked of iron. "But I'm telling you. He's dangerous. He swore if I left him, he'd. . .he'd. . ." She broke off and rinsed her toothbrush in silence, shaking off the droplets.

"He'd what?"

"Aw, he's just full of talk." Alicia tried to put the toothbrush in her yellow plastic holder and fumbled, dropping one of the pieces. "Why should I believe anything that jerk says?"

Carlita knelt and picked up the plastic tube, not taking her eyes off Alicia. "What did he say?"

Alicia picked at her chipped nail polish, inhaling a whiff of Aqua Net hairspray from the other end of the bathroom. Someone jingled bracelets, and the sound echoed against the dank tile and concrete walls.

Carlita waited for two other women to pass, both of them laughing at some shared joke, and then raised herself up to Alicia's eye level. Hands on her hips and dark eyes spitting fire. "So help me, Alicia Sanchez, you'd better tell me the truth right now."

"Fine." Alicia spat out a breath. "He said he'd. . .kill me." She took the plastic tube from Carlita and stuffed her toothbrush inside, clicking it closed. "I don't believe him really, but it gives me the creeps. Miguel can be pretty rough."

A faucet dripped on the nearby sink, leaving a rusty orange stain down the old porcelain.

"Alicia." Carlita sighed and rested a palm on Alicia's shoulder. "That man's evil. You can't trust him."

"I know that." Alicia zipped her zebra-striped travel bag closed, tugging hard at the stuck zipper. "And he's vengeful, too. But I didn't think he'd try to come all the way here." She leaned both hands on the sink and stared down at the rusty drain, raising one hand to scratch through her damp hair. "Do you really think it was him? Or am I losing it?"

"For pity's sake, Alicia. I wish you'd told me sooner that Miguel threatened you. He can't be here in Wyoming, but he might be waiting for you when you get back. When Miguel gets his mind set on something, he'll never back down. Hear me? Watch yourself." She let out a heavy breath. "Isn't he wanted for something?"

"Yeah." Alicia massaged the back of her neck. For three days she'd reeked of ash and smoke, and it felt good to smell of freesia body wash and pale green Prell shampoo. "Robbery and attempted murder. He says he didn't do it, but I've heard him slip enough times to believe he did."

"Do you have a restraining order? Anything?"

"No."

Carlita scowled, pretending to smack Alicia. "What's the matter with you?"

"He said he'd kill me if he heard I was even thinking of it. And with as many friends as he has down at the jail, I knew better than to try and slip anything past him. If he didn't do it, one of them would." She played with a strand of wet hair. "And he kept saying he'd change. He'd be different. He'd be better. But..."

Carlita shook her head, the white-gray chunks in her hair standing out starkly against the black as she dug in her bag for Avon perfume. "You need help, Alicia. I never knew it was this bad." She blew out an angry breath and spritzed perfume on both wrists. "Maybe you should get a transfer or something. Move away from Santa Fe. From New Mexico, even."

"Wait a second." Alicia whirled around, not appearing to hear. "If Miguel's wanted, he wouldn't show up in a crowd of Feds, would he? And in a hospital?" She chewed on a broken nail. "I mean, he'd be surrounded by hundreds of Park Service and Forest Service employees, not to mention all the local police and firefighters. Anybody could identify him."

"And he'd have to give his name and ID to come into the park and hospital, too. Which again, if he's wanted, he'd never do. And," she lifted one finger, "Melissa Ramirez told me herself Miguel was in Juarez last week, and I called my cousin from a pay phone last night to confirm. He says Miguel's there."

"What? Why in the world would you call your cousin about Miguel?"

"Because Jorge said a few things that bugged me. But he's a liar. Just like I always said."

"So Miguel's in...Juarez?"

"Yep. Staying at some seedy place in the red-light district. Exactly as I suspected." Carlita dumped the perfume back in her bag.

A couple of laughing women pushed open the heavy bathroom door, still clad in their ash-stained pants and shirts, heading for the showers.

Alicia slung her travel bag over her shoulder as she faced Carlita. "So you think I'm seeing things?"

"People? Yes. You're stressed." Carlita waved at one of the women and combed her wet hair in silence until she and Alicia were alone again. "My cousin runs a hotel there in Juarez, a gambling place, and he'd know if Miguel was in town."

"Oh." Alicia let out a breath of relief. "Then I'm okay."

"No." Carlita took a step forward, sticking a pointed index finger at Alicia's nose. "You're not okay." Her nostrils flared. "I've worked with you for five years now, and I can tell you're in trouble." She stuck her face close to Alicia. "You came to my wedding. I made you Trisha's godmother."

Alicia's breath seemed to go out. "I love that girl, Carlita," she whispered. "I'd do anything for her." Glimpses of little dark-haired Trisha flashed through her mind. The day she'd worn pigtails for the first time, so tender and childlike, Alicia had bawled in Carlita's bathroom.

"I know you love her. She adores you. But I feel every day like I'm losing you."

Alicia drew back, speechless. "Losing me? That's. . .that's what Thomas said," she blurted. "And it's absurd. What's the matter with the two of you? Are you in cahoots or something?"

"Look at you." Carlita ignored Alicia and tugged on her baggy sweatshirt sleeve. "You've lost so much weight I don't recognize you. You never eat, and you bite my head off every time I mention it." She shook her head sadly. "I think you need help."

"What?" Alicia jerked her sleeve away, heat pinking her cheeks.

"I mean it." Carlita took a threatening step forward. "If you won't talk to me about it, talk to somebody." She waved an arm in frustration. "Talk to that Thomas guy, for goodness' sake."

"Thomas?" gasped Alicia angrily, backing away from the sink. "What does he have to do with anything?"

"He's a friend. And when you're having a hard time, that's what you need more than anything—a friend. Thomas listens to you. He's protective of you. And I hear from the engine crew that he moped around all day after they took you to the hospital." She pointed to her heart. "I'm always here for you, too. You know that. But maybe Thomas can break through that thick skin of yours and convince you of what I can't—that you're worth fighting for."

Chapter 7

H i, could I speak to Thomas Walks-with-Eagles, please? He's the engine captain." Alicia spoke quietly into the camp pay phone, her breath making a chilly mist. She'd put her meager change together and walked to the far end of camp, early morning shadows and dampness painting the trees deep gray.

"Hold on a sec." Somebody spoke in muffled tones on the other end of the phone and Alicia waited. Leaning against the cold wooden phone booth and staring at the coiled metal phone cord.

Her unbandaged hand circled a paper cup of steaming black coffee as she vainly tried to ward off the predawn chill. Even her down vest didn't warm her like she'd hoped. Mornings in the Rockies were legendary: crisp and crackling cold even in the summer, stars shimmering like diamonds and giving way to a sky of splintered stained glass. Pines edged in blue and silver.

"Thomas speaking. May I help you?" Thomas's voice crackled into the phone receiver—a dead giveaway of wind where his crew was packing up to head for breakfast. He sounded crisp and professional, and for a second the knot in Alicia's stomach tightened.

"Hello?" Thomas spoke again.

"Hi. It's…Alicia." She cleared her throat, setting her coffee cup down on the stand next to the phone. "Alicia Sanchez," she added awkwardly, in case Thomas didn't recognize her.

Thomas didn't reply, and she silently banged her head against the wooden phone booth. Of course Thomas knew who she was. As if he'd forget their five years of banter back and forth. Their "Top Ten Horrible Forest Service Lunches" contest and goofy paper-clip awards. The gear he left in her locker as a surprise when she packed up, and the miracle peanut butter brownies she'd once made him in a skillet over a sputtering campfire.

"Alicia?" Thomas's voice lost its professional edge, and he sounded almost sad. "Hey."

"Hey."

She stood there a moment, not sure what to say. A gust of breeze blew her hair, bringing with it the sharp stench of ash and burned wood. A harsh smell that made her want to cover her mouth and nose.

"Listen. Thomas." Alicia watched the steam curl up from her coffee cup in pale spirals. "I just. . .well, I wanted to tell you I'm sorry." The cold made her nose run, and she dug in her pocket for a Kleenex. "I shouldn't have talked to you like that in the hospital."

The line fell so silent that Alicia heard the slam of a truck door from her camp through the pines. Some guys laughing about Wayne Gretzky and hockey player trades.

"Thomas?"

"I'm here." He sounded choked up.

"Well, I'm sorry." She scrubbed her heel in the dirt, indignant about having to say it twice.

"I heard you. Thanks." The words came tenderly. "And I understand. You've been through. . .well, a lot, to say the least."

"No, you don't understand." Alicia's voice turned cold. "You say you do, but you don't. Everybody says that. But you haven't lived my life."

"And you haven't lived mine," Thomas countered, his voice rising a touch. "I never claimed to understand what you went through, Alicia, but I do understand you."

"What?"

"I've been where you are before. Grieving. Hurt. Angry. Wanting to live, but at the same time feeling that I just couldn't take it anymore. That life was too difficult, and I'd never be able to get out of the mess I'd made of things."

Alicia stayed silent, sipping her coffee. "So what was the answer for you?" she asked, trying to keep the bile out of her voice. "Jesus?"

"But there's one area where you've gone even beyond me." Thomas spoke again, seemingly ignoring her question. "I don't think you even want to live anymore. I see it in your eyes."

Alicia drew back from the phone, keeping the receiver pressed to her ear. A flock of Canada geese soared overhead, their wings making black lines against the gray sky. Their calls rang loud and throaty, echoing against the distant pines, and a shaft of sunlight suddenly pierced through the gloom with a radiant golden glow.

All around her the forest shined, alive with dewdrops and a sudden stunning, sparkling brilliance. A scatter of gauzy milkweed pods floated by on the breeze like miniature dancers. Spinning in slow, dizzy circles.

"Alicia?"

She turned back to the phone.

"Listen. I've got something I'd. . .well, like to say to you. When you have time to sit down with me and talk."

Alicia's heart skipped a beat. She felt light-headed, staring out at the sun-striped pines. All the lime green needles and scaly bark shags stood out in sharp contrast, as if she'd finally figured something out.

What if. . . ? Alicia pressed a shaking hand to her forehead, wondering how she could've been so dense. After all these years, all those pranks and birthday cards and jokes? She'd never thought of Thomas as anything but a friend—and he'd never even broached the subject. But what if. . . ?

Alicia picked at her nails in astonishment as a sudden rush of thoughts poured into her mind. Thomas? Thomas Walks-with-Eagles? She'd figured he wouldn't want a scarred-up girl like herself. And that Christians only liked and married Christians. But maybe she'd been wrong.

In a weird way, she and Thomas made. . .sense.

Perfect sense. His clean laughter and bright smile coupled with her pain-dark eyes and acerbic wit. The way he'd held a jacket over her head in the rain. The funny notes she'd tucked in his lunch box.

She could learn the Bible, too, couldn't she? For his sake?

Alicia traced her reflection in the shiny metal of the phone booth, wondering how she could have missed it all these years.

For a split second Alicia felt like digging into her backpack and making a rudimentary elementary school note on a sheet of notebook paper: "Do you like me? Yes or no. Circle one."

"Alicia? Did you hear me?"

"I did." She twirled the phone cord again, suddenly self-conscious about her hollow cheeks and windblown hair. "And I'd like to say something to you, too. If you don't mind."

"Of course I don't mind."

Alicia closed her eyes and listened to the velvety timbre of his voice, so comforting and so familiar. Like an old pair of socks, well worn into softness. Socks pulled tight on cold feet so that the blood begins to flow again, to heat again.

Thomas hesitated as if he wanted to say more and then finally spoke again. "Would you consider telling me what's been eating at you these days?" He paused. "Please?"

"I guess so." Alicia ran her fingers nervously across her ragged nails. "I'm on mop-up all day today and probably tomorrow, too. I hate mop-up," she muttered. "It's for wimps and crews with no experience."

"Maybe, but it's necessary. This fire isn't burning out like we'd hoped. If anything, it's worse."

"That can't be true. We've been on it for three days now with every crew we can get."

"I know, but it is." Thomas sighed, a short, clipped sound. "It's bad, Alicia. Be careful out there, okay?"

Alicia didn't answer.

"And listen, I'd be mad, too, if my doctor shared my confidential health information with anybody," Thomas added in a lighter tone. "My spleen acts up from time to time, you know. It's embarrassing."

Alicia gave a shocked laugh then clapped her hand over her mouth. "Sorry. I didn't mean to laugh if that was. . .you know. For real."

"My spleen? Yeah. It's real. But my knee is artificial. I messed it up skiing."

"Skiing?" She spoke haltingly, not sure whether or not Thomas was joking—and if it was appropriate to laugh. "I didn't know you ski. Where do you go, Colorado?"

"Ha. That would mean that I *ski*—present tense. I went once when I was nineteen, fell down the side of the cliff, and tore my knee up something awful. Haven't hit the slopes since."

"Like Lane trying to ski the K 12 in *Better Off Dead*."

"Exactly. You got the movies right this time. Except it was that Andie chick, not Lane."

Alicia clapped a hand over her mouth to stifle her laughter.

An awkward silence fell over the line, and the distant whine of coyotes hovered in the cobalt blue sky just beyond the campground. Yipping and howling, calling out across the morning in tremulous layers as if gathering voices for a ghostly cantata.

She'd heard the coyotes before, lots of times: in the sun-parched deserts of Chihuahua and Jornada del Muerto. Each time she'd stood still, breathless, like an outside listener of secret songs. Joy songs and triumph songs, each alive with frosty morning and brilliant moon, with silver-beige fur and bright eyes.

But this morning the coyote wails chilled her. Alicia turned, phone still to her ear, and tried to follow the sound, but she saw nothing past the lights of camp but smoke and forest, all buried in layers of gray.

Alicia pulled her vest tighter and jingled the change in her pocket nervously. "Well, they'll be packing up soon. I guess I'll see you around, chief." *Chief. Native American.* She smacked her forehead. "I didn't mean that as a joke. Like I was making fun of you."

Wait, was Thomas *laughing*? Alicia glared into the phone.

"That's pretty good," he chuckled. "But since my family lineage is mostly drunks and delinquents, being chief is probably out of the question. I'll tell the leaders of the Yavapai-Apache Nation that you put in a good word for me though."

"Very funny." Alicia put her bandaged hand on her hip. "So where does the Walks-with-Eagles come in, since we're on the topic? Is that really your last name?"

Thomas's laughter died.

"Sorry." She put her hand up. "I didn't mean to pry."

"Oh no. It's actually a great story. And you're right—it is my last name. But it was given to me. Chosen."

"You mean given only to you?" Alicia's mind reeled through the multiple family names bequeathed on Mexican children. For her, Sanchez was only one of three. But it wasn't chosen, and it wasn't unique to herself. Probably one out of every three Mexicans had a similar last name.

"Yes. It's my name, and mine only." Thomas fell strangely silent.

"Okay." Alicia twisted her head around to check her watch. "Well, I've got to head out." She scuffed a fingernail on a scratch on the phone booth. "And let's talk. But I'm warning you. My confessions won't be pretty."

Warning. Someone stepped on a pine branch in the shadows behind her, making a sharp snap in the morning calm. Alicia whirled around. Coyotes howled again in the distance, making goose bumps bristle on her arms.

A man stepped through the pines on the other side of the pay phone, his black eyes narrowing into spiteful slits.

"It doesn't need to be pretty, Alicia." Thomas spoke soberly into the phone. "It needs to be real. We all have problems, and God helps us get through them." He paused. "He loves you, you know that?"

But Alicia stood motionless, her mouth still partially open.

"Alicia?" Thomas's voice rang into the phone again.

"I saw him again," she whispered, her breath curling up in a puff of mist.

"Saw. . .who?"

Alicia whirled around, but the man disappeared. "I saw him. I could swear it." She stood on tiptoe. "Where'd he go? I'm not crazy."

"Alicia? Talk to me." Thomas's voice turned sharp. "And I never said you were crazy."

"It's Miguel. My old boyfriend." Alicia spoke in a whisper. "He was standing right over there."

"That hot-tempered jerk you told me about last time?"

"That's him." Alicia's hands shook as she stretched as far as the cord reached, trying to see. "Carlita said he can't be here, but. . .I saw him, Thomas. I know I did."

"I'll be over in five minutes." And Thomas hung up, leaving a harsh dial tone ringing in her ear.

Chapter 8

I must be losing my mind." Alicia heaved her shovel up and rained a pile of dry soil on a flaming stump, watching the orange flickers die. "I saw him again this morning, Carlita. I'm sure of it."

"Who, Miguel?" Carlita grunted. She raised her ax and hacked at a patch of burning roots.

"I know, I know. It's impossible." Alicia scooped up another shovelful as the rest of the Mexican American crew hosed down still-burning limbs and stumps. Most of the swelling had gone down in her wrist, and she could still lean on the strength of her right arm.

"But either I saw him, or my eyes are playing tricks on me. Thomas came over to the camp with a couple of guys, but nobody could find him." Alicia shook her bangs out of her eyes. "I don't know what to think."

"I think you're stressed." Carlita leveled her eyes at Alicia. "I don't know what's been going on with you, but when you get back to Santa Fe, you need a rest. Come with us to Taos. I'm serious. I'll pay." She banged the shovel on its side to knock off the dirt. "Simón will understand."

"Carlita." Alicia reached out and squeezed her arm through the thick Nomex sleeve. "I can't go to Taos. But you're sweet."

"Why not? You can. It'll knock you out of this funk you're in."

All around Alicia the lush forest had been gutted: blackened, singed. An open canopy of leafless trees where shade used to fall thick over wildflowers. Ruined trunks and spindly branches splayed at hideous angles like skeleton fingers.

On initial attack she'd stood on the "green side," hugging the fire line and walking through unburned timber. But now she stood on the other side, covered with ash, trying desperately to keep the fire that had roared through from flaring back up.

Alicia wiped her sweaty face, feeling as if she'd stepped into a sickly cathedral of broken, lifeless branches. All reaching vainly for the smoke-scarred heavens.

Just down the ridge the Apache crew worked tirelessly in the blazing August sun, shouting in words Alicia couldn't understand without the accompanying translations. She had watched them as they filed past her on the dirt road to the spike camp, most of them dark like Thomas, with the same black hair and almond-shaped eyes. But Thomas was right about Apache mixed ancestry. Two of the guys sported blond ponytails, and one woman had the clearest hazel-green eyes Alicia had ever seen.

Thomas was out with the fire truck, certainly, but being close to people he called his own made her feel comforted somehow. Safe, even. As if she could somehow catch his heart from their elegant cheekbones and lilting, guttural speech, mingled with English.

"You'll have to hold my place a minute, *compadre*." Alicia leaned her shovel against a blackened tree. "Nature calls." She nodded her head toward the line of distant green Porta-Potties.

"Gross." Carlita made a face. "I just hold it. You're gonna use one of those?"

"What choice do I have? I'll be back in a second."

Alicia mucked her way past fellow hosers and shovelers through the ash, which sank nearly up to her ankles in scattered drifts. All along the way the trees had been scorched to velvet black. Smoke curled up from still-hot limbs.

The Porta-Potties stood in a stalwart line, shoulder to shoulder. As soon as she swung open the creaking door, holding her nose, she heard the rumble of a familiar fire truck in the distance. She turned, hand still clamped over her face, and glimpsed Methuselah's scratched and battered side glinting in faint sunlight.

Thomas blinked his light at her—light, singular, as the right headlight had been bashed out—and Alicia stuck out her thumb like a hitchhiker.

"Well, well, well. Just in time." Thomas eased to a stop beside her.

"Just in time for what?" Alicia shielded her eyes, one hand on her hip.

"I got you something." Thomas dug on the seat and shook a brown paper package. "It just came in."

"For me?" Alicia called out in surprise over the rattling engine as Thomas downshifted into neutral.

"Yep. I think you'll like it." He waved his hand. "C'mon. I'm off duty."

Alicia ran a finger over Methuselah's dusty side, which sported several nasty dents and scratches. Someone had slapped a new coat of poorly matched primer over one side, smoothing out the worst of the damage. "Hey, she doesn't look so bad for practically sailing over a cliff," she said, wiping the dust off her hand. "A little beat up, but she'll make it."

"Too bad you didn't let her go." Thomas rolled the squeaky window down with hard hand cranks. "Then I wouldn't be bringing her in for the fourth time this morning."

"What is it this time?" Alicia stuck her hands in her pockets and looked up at him in his battered John Deere baseball cap. "And you look like a redneck in that hat."

"What are you talking about? I *am* a redneck. I farm, remember? Doesn't that qualify me?" Thomas held up a clipboard. "And about the truck—I've got a list of her new problems. Don't even get me started."

He tipped his head toward the row of Porta-Potties. "On the other hand, it means I get to save you from a fate worse than death. You weren't actually going to go in there, were you? I've heard horror stories about people who never came out." He tipped his head. "You ever seen a wolf spider? I hear the one they got in the *Guinness Book of World Records* came from inside a Porta-Potty. No joke."

"Okay, okay. I'm getting in." Alicia crossed over to the passenger's side and tugged at the stuck door. "You didn't wrap my package in a hamburger wrapper this time, did you?"

The door hinges stuck tight. Thomas heaved on it with his free arm, and it finally popped open, banging her square in the cheek.

"Oh my word. Alicia? You okay?" Thomas cut the engine and jumped out of the truck, trotting over to her in his boots and yellow-and-green uniform.

"I'm fine, chief." Alicia tried to laugh as she wiped a smear of blood from her cheek with her sleeve. "Another bruise will just complete my collection."

Thomas dug in the rusty glove compartment for a first-aid kit and, finding nothing, grabbed a handful of Taco Bell napkins from the console. "You're gonna swell up big-time." He reached back inside the truck and grabbed his water bottle. He squirted some on the napkins and pried her fingers off.

Alicia blinked as he held the moist napkins there, easing the initial stinging and swelling. "I'm fine, you know," she mumbled, feeling color creep into her cheeks. "You don't need to baby me."

"Maybe somebody should." Thomas spoke almost as if angry, but his face remained relaxed. His dark lashes just inches from hers. "You certainly don't know how to do it yourself."

He reached for the door handle and took her elbow, helping her up into the torn leather seat. "C'mon. You can use the restroom at the station. It's just up the road about three miles."

Alicia moved his regulation yellow hard hat to the dash and buckled herself in with her free hand, still holding the napkin to her cheek as the truck grumbled reluctantly to life. Pines slipped by the windows in various shades of green, ending abruptly with pockets of horrible emptiness, pockmarked with scorched patches and lone, burned tree trunks like skinny snaggleteeth.

He had just turned a curve when the engine abruptly shuddered and died. Smoke poured out from under the hood, and Thomas lurched to the side of the road, wrenching the wheel hard. The truck bumped over a couple of jagged stones and fallen limbs and rolled to a stop in a patch of tall, yellow goatsbeard blooms.

Alicia braced herself against the dashboard as the truck gave one mighty sputter and then died. Leaving nothing but an angry gurgling from the engine.

Thomas, in an unusual burst of emotion, yanked off his baseball cap and smacked the steering wheel with it. His nostrils flaring.

And Alicia threw her head back and laughed like she hadn't in a long, long time.

⁓

When nature called, Alicia answered in the bushes. Hoping she hadn't grabbed a poison ivy leaf by mistake.

"So what's in my package?" She swung up in the truck seat and slammed the door behind her. "It is for me, isn't it?"

"Go ahead. Open it."

Alicia shook the rectangular package, and it made a noisy shifting sound. "More Sea-Monkeys? You shouldn't have."

Thomas turned sideways in his seat like a giddy schoolboy. "Hurry up and open it, or I will."

"Hold your horses, chief." Alicia pulled her pocketknife from her belt clip and sliced the tape. "Or should I call you chief wannabe?"

"Very funny." Thomas reached out to rip some of the tape. "You're taking too long."

Alicia tore at the paper and slid out a box. She felt herself seize up.

Hand still frozen on the paper, mouth partially open. Her heart seemed to fall through the rusty floorboard of the truck.

"Velvet Gold graham crackers," she whispered, her voice scratchy with emotion. "You found them." She lifted the box out of the paper, handling it gently as if afraid it would break. "How did you do it, Thomas? Where did you find them?"

"My secret." He winked.

"No secrets." She punched his arm, her eyes stinging with tears. "Tell me the truth. Where did you find them?"

"I called a friend of mine, and he tracked down a vintage bakery in Connecticut that just went out of business. He bought the last two boxes for me and overnighted them here." Thomas smoothed the box. "I just hope they're not broken."

Alicia looked up as if in a daze.

"But you need something to complete the set." He reached under the seat and pulled out a lunch box. "See? I brought two knives." He held them up: two plastic jobs from the mess hall.

"For butter?" Alicia's eyes welled.

Thomas pretended to bow, looping his finger from his nose. And he reached down and pulled a fresh tub of butter from his lunch box, placing it, still cool, into her upturned hand.

⁂

"How's your cheek?" Thomas moistened another napkin and handed it to her.

Alicia brushed graham cracker crumbs from her lips, still smiling, and touched the cut gingerly. "Don't worry. I'm used to getting beat up." She shrugged. "No biggie."

Thomas froze.

"What?" Alicia drew back, shaking the graham crackers back into their plastic sleeve and closing the cardboard box flaps. "Why are you looking at me like that?"

Before he could reply, a zooming rumble sounded in the distance, and another Forest Service fire truck appeared around the bend. Light from a break in the clouds gleamed across its smooth finish.

Thomas laid on the horn, which gave a weak and sickly squawk, and the other fire truck pulled up in a cloud of dust.

"Tommy, Tommy. You're broken down *again*?" Duncan poked his head out the driver's side window.

"What do you think? This is Methuselah we're talking about." Thomas leaned through the open window. "Can you send us a tow? Please? It's like the fourth time today."

"Sorry we didn't take your call. Everybody's out. The fire's spread over to Canyon, and it's bad. They're about to lose a whole new section of the park. Spray helicopters are overrunning the place, and nothing's taking the blaze down." Duncan shifted back into DRIVE, and the engine roared. "I'll radio you in, but it's gonna be awhile before anybody has time to send a tow." He slapped the side of the truck. "Hang tight, okay?"

And he thundered off down the road in a cloud of dust and ash.

To Alicia's surprise, Thomas spoke not another word. He just stared out the cracked windshield, the muscle in his jaw clenching. A gust of breeze blew dust up in a cloud from the parched road like a dirt devil, making dry leaves spin.

"What?" Alicia leaned forward to catch his eye. "You're upset about the truck or something?"

"Huh?" Thomas turned, not seeming to see her. Cloud shadows moved slowly in the distance, like a slowly creeping cat.

"What's the matter?"

"The matter?" Thomas gave a weak laugh, avoiding her eyes. "I'll just be a second. I'll see if I can get this old thing working again." And he swung out of the side of the truck, banging the door behind him.

⁓

"So you think this is the end of the road for Methuselah?" Alicia patted the dented dashboard. She'd crawled out of the truck and dug around under the hood with Thomas, toolbox laying open by their feet, but nothing did the trick. She eventually threw all the wrenches, battery testers, belts, and hoses back in the toolbox and crawled up in the cab, grease-spattered and ready to take a nap. Wondering, with reluctance, if she should try to hike back the several miles to spike camp.

"Methuselah? Who knows." Thomas slumped back in the seat and rocked his head back, still strangely quiet. "This thing never gives up. And Uncle Sam keeps throwing wrenches and air filters at her. You know what?" He sat up straight, looking so indignant that Alicia covered another laugh with her hand. "How much do you wanna bet that when we get back to the station they'll make me fix her up again?"

The truck tipped as air gushed out of the front tire again, and Thomas's clipboard slid across the seat. Alicia chuckled. "There's no way they'll make you fix her up now. She's headed for the scrap heap."

"You're on." He held out his hand. "A buck says they do."

"Any day."

Alicia reached out and shook his hand, surprised at how beautiful his fingers looked wrapped around hers. A slightly darker shade of toffee brown, with smooth pink nails and palms. Warm and large boned, with thick knuckles.

When she looked over at him, Thomas still hadn't pulled away.

"What did you mean by that?"

"Mean by what?" Alicia's pulse pounded, trying to tear her eyes away from the image of their two hands together there on the truck seat.

"That you're used to getting beat up." He brushed her hair back from the cut with his thumb. "I've been thinking about it ever since you said it. Were you talking about the day you got banged up in the truck?"

Alicia pulled back, startled. "Used to getting beat up? I didn't say that."

"Yes you did. You said, 'No biggie. I'm used to it.'" Thomas leaned closer, his dark eyes boring into her. "What did you mean by that?"

Alicia's mouth went cotton dry, and her tongue stuck to the roof of her mouth.

A vein in Thomas's throat beat wildly, in fitful shivers. His eyes lay dark like black velvet, almost too beautiful to look at.

"I think I know what you meant." His words came out husky, almost in a whisper. "And it kills me. Why do you let people treat you like that? You're beautiful. You're smart. You're. . .you're amazing. Why?"

Something tickled in the pit of Alicia's stomach, like speeding over a hill too fast, and she started to disentangle her fingers. Keeping her face turned down so he wouldn't see the flush mounting in her cheeks.

Except she felt Thomas pulling her—ever so slightly—toward him.

When she raised her head, his face gazed back at her with twin looks of desire and terror. Flushed and white at the same time, teenager-like. Beneath her palm, she felt his fingers moisten with sweat.

He's going to kiss me. Alicia tried to think, tried to turn her mind to anything but the startled rush that tingled through her veins.

Chapter 9

Before Alicia could react or spit out a single word, Thomas pulled back. He let her hand go, turning abruptly away to the driver's side window. He squeezed his eyes closed and rubbed a fist on his forehead.

"What?" Alicia blurted, her mouth falling open. "What did I do?"

"Do?" Thomas's eyes popped open with a wounded look. "Alicia, you didn't do anything. I'm so sorry." He took a deep breath and closed his eyes again. "Forgive me. Please. I was. . .terribly out of line."

Alicia's eyebrows shot up, and she decided to keep her mouth shut.

Thomas rubbed his hand across his face, messing up his hair. "I'm sorry. Really. I had no right to do that." He slapped his John Deere cap back on his head and fumbled for the gearshift.

The color drained from his face, and he turned the key in the ignition, pressing vainly on the gas. Methuselah gave a spiteful sputter and died again, leaving only metallic clicks when Thomas turned the key again.

"I'm not even going to bother with the two-way anymore. Nobody answers. I'm so sorry." Thomas shook his head. When he put his hands back on the wheel, his fingers trembled.

"Thomas." She spoke deliberately and carefully, pressing her nervous lips together. "Why. . .are you so sorry?"

"Because." He swallowed, keeping his eyes averted. "It's not right. You're not. . .ready. I'm sorry."

"Ready for what?" Alicia's heart beat loud in her throat. She crossed her arms stiffly across her chest, trying not to think of the fifty-dollar compass Thomas had bought her, all wrapped in a hamburger paper. For all his generosity, she knew he didn't earn much more than she did.

"Me." Thomas turned to her with a look so raw that Alicia drew back involuntarily.

She opened her mouth and closed it, feeling irritability creep up her neck. "Doubting Thomas," she should call him for his naive hesitancy and caution. It even sounded biblical, too.

"What makes you think I'm not ready?" Alicia turned toward him with a squeak of the seat.

"Alicia." Thomas's eyelids fluttered as he closed them. "I know you. You're a beautiful woman. One of my best friends. And you're. . .broken inside. I can feel it."

Unexpected tears stung Alicia's eyes, and her look hardened. "So that means I'm not good enough for you?"

"What?" Thomas jerked his head around to look at her. "No. Of course not. But it's not right. You're not ready. You're not. . .healed. To me it's on the same level as taking advantage of you, if you see what I'm trying to say."

"No. I don't see." Alicia tucked her arms tighter, crossing a leg rigidly away from him.

Thomas raised his hands helplessly as if groping for words. "It's my fault. Ever since I met you, I've liked you. I thought it was platonic, but maybe I've liked you more than I should." He curved his fingers into a fist and raised it up to his mouth as he thought. "I've just wanted to see you well. Healthy. Whole. Happy. You're special to me, Alicia. More special than you know."

Alicia sat there, not having a clue what to say. Dried Sea-Monkeys and French-speaking ferrets jolted into her mind, making her want to laugh inappropriately.

"So that's it?" she asked, attempting to steady her voice. "I'm your charity case now?"

Even as she said it, Alicia felt herself wince. Thomas might have a million flaws, but he'd never once treated her or his crewmates as anything but equals. Equals with humble preference, even.

"No." Thomas's voice came out as a hoarse whisper, and he covered his face with both hands. "Never. I can't believe you'd think that."

Alicia let out an angry sigh, turning away from him and gazing out over the windswept grasses. Behind her, the road curved, desolate, into endless forest.

"Okay. That's not what I meant," she muttered. "But I don't get your whole 'you're not ready' speech. Why don't you ask me if I'm ready?" She turned her head in his direction. "Maybe my answer would surprise you."

"But there's one more thing." Thomas met her gaze soberly, even tenderly. "I can't forsake my God."

It took a second for the words to register, and Alicia's eyes bugged out. "Huh? What in the world is that supposed to mean?"

"It means that as much as I care for you, I can't pair up with someone who doesn't love Jesus as much as I do." He let out a long, shuddering breath. "The Bible says that. It's called being 'unequally yoked.' Have you read it?" Thomas turned to her, the rims of his eyes red.

Alicia shook her head no, speechless.

"It's like. . .two cows plowing." Thomas gestured awkwardly with his hands. "They have this wooden thing across them. A yoke. If they're not matched, one goes one way, and the other goes the other way. They never get anything accomplished because they're. . .well, unequally yoked."

He stuffed his hands miserably in his vest pockets. "For a split second I forgot that, Alicia. Please forgive me." He drew in a shaky breath. "But after what God's done for me, I owe Him my life. I have to wait for Him to pair me with someone who loves Him, too."

"And if He doesn't?" Alicia spat, angry color burning her face. Wondering if Thomas, and not her, was the crazy one, blabbering away about plowing at a time like this. Cows? Yokes? Was he out of his mind?

"If He doesn't choose someone for me who loves Him, I'll stay single and serve Him that way." Thomas kept his voice even, low and husky. "I haven't always been called Thomas Walks-with-Eagles, you know. I used to be called Thomas Two-Fires."

Alicia heard angry blood racing past her ears, thrumming with hurt and disappointment.

"I dropped out of school when I was twelve and spent my time on the reservation drinking, gambling, and shooting mailboxes. I was an arsonist, Alicia. I set fire to empty buildings and fields, watching behind rocks and laughing as the fire crews scrambled to put out the blaze." He swallowed deliberately, looking out the window. "Only one time, one of the buildings wasn't empty."

Even in her haze of anger, Alicia gasped.

"I killed an old man. A homeless guy sleeping inside an old barn I torched with gasoline." Thomas squeezed his eyes shut. "I saw them pull him out and put him on a stretcher. They tried to save him, but he was too far gone."

Thomas blinked faster, and he stayed silent a minute. "I saw him writhe in pain, his body covered with burns." Emotion choked his voice. "He struggled to breathe, and then he just. . .stopped. Like my grandfather in the hospital. Only this time it was my fault."

Thomas traced the steering wheel with his fingers. "The police swore out a warrant for my arrest, but federal law only goes so far on the reservation. The tribal council declared me innocent, even though everybody knew I'd done it. They said the old man was a public nuisance anyway—a drunkard and a fighter." He hung his head. "But I saw him try to breathe. I saw his clothes burned black, all the way to his flesh. And it was my fault. I killed a man."

Alicia sat unmoving, unable to tear her eyes from Thomas's face. Carlita was right: He wasn't much to look at, per se. He wasn't handsome. His nose was too big, and dark brows protruded over deep-set eyes. But as he sat there against a shaft of sunlight, holding back tears, his chiseled face and high cheekbones looked, for a moment, more beautiful than she'd ever seen on a man.

Sunlight gleamed on his shiny, sand-pink lower lip as he opened his mouth to speak again. "I ran away. I stayed for months on top of a cliff, in a little lean-to shelter I made out of sticks, barely eating. I wanted to die, to return to the earth like some of the old men of my tribe claimed we did—and complete the spirit's circle of life. And I prayed." He stared out over the whispering fields. "Day after day, I prayed for the spirits to forgive me. I named all the gods I knew—the gods of water and sun and harvest. When nothing happened, I prayed to the God who hung on the cross—the white man's God I'd seen in a painting once in a book on my grandmother's bookshelf. And still nothing happened."

Thomas chewed on his lip a minute, and the bright shine disappeared. "And then one windy day a man came to me, climbing up the mountain. Over boulders and rocks, knocking off rattlesnakes with a hiking stick. I figured he'd come from town to arrest me, so I went out to meet him, with my clothes all tattered and my hair matted. To turn myself in. But you know what he said?" Thomas turned to her with eyes wide and earnest.

"What?"

"That I needed Jesus." Thomas reached into his vest pocket. "He gave me this: a little Gideon New Testament. He said he was a traveling preacher, and God had sent him to tell me He loved me."

Thomas flipped the pages of the little Bible with his thumb. "And that was it. He shook my hand and climbed back down the mountain, and I never saw him again. I thought maybe he was crazy, but he didn't look crazy—so I read. Day after day, by firelight, by sunlight. I read it through fifteen times in two weeks." He rocked back in the seat, his face calm. "And that's how I came to know about Jesus. I gave my life to Him. I washed my hair and cut it and cleaned myself in the stream, and I went back down the mountain to my relatives' house."

"And?" Alicia looked up hesitantly.

Thomas smiled. "They didn't recognize me at first, after all the weight I'd lost. They said my eyes were clear and bright, and the haunted look had fled from my face." He chuckled. "They thought I'd been smoking peyote."

Thomas shifted in his seat. "I asked them to take me to the library to find the rest of the Bible because I knew there had to be more. And there was. The entire Old Testament. I devoured it, like a man who hadn't tasted food in months. And that's when they changed my name. They said I walked as a man with my head in the clouds."

"A compliment?" Alicia asked hesitantly.

"Sort of, but not really." Thomas shrugged. "Nobody really knew what to make of it."

A puff of wind scratched lonely grasses against Methuselah's metal side, and something dripped under the hood.

"So you gave your life to firefighting to pay for the old man's death." Alicia drew one knee up on the truck seat and hugged it.

"Not to pay for it, because that would be impossible." Thomas took off his baseball cap and ran his hand through his hair. "No one can pay for a life. But I can take what was once a setback and turn it into a blessing. Because of Jesus, I can fight fires instead of setting them, and I can save lives instead of taking them. And that's what I plan to do for the rest of my life."

Alicia turned to look at him. "That's noble, Thomas. But I still don't understand why we can't. . .be together. What's wrong with that?" She twisted her fingers together, dropping her gaze. "We don't have to get married or anything. We can just. . .be together. Sort of."

"Be together?" Thomas sighed, stretching out an arm across the seat. "It doesn't work like that. A love relationship is like. . .fire. It flares up when you least expect it, and before you know it, it's out of control." He swallowed, keeping his eyes down. Color flushed his cheeks and nose. "And then you're left with. . .with this." He swept his arm toward a stand of blackened pines, their naked branches hanging helplessly askew.

Alicia stared at the scorched clearing, her jaw tensing with anger.

"I can't do that to you." Thomas shook his head. "Or to God. I'm sorry."

"Why, Thomas?" Alicia's eyes blazed. "Why can't you just love me?" She clenched her fingers tighter under her folded arms. "You could be a blessing to me, just like you said about that man you killed."

He waited a long time to answer, scuffing his short fingernail against a scratch in the steering wheel. "You don't understand. I can't be with you because I *do* love you." Thomas's eyes pleaded. "You need to be whole first—through Jesus. Otherwise you'll always lean on me to heal you. And as much as I'd try, I could never do it."

He lifted his eyes to hers, so dark she couldn't see where his brown irises and pupils separated. "I can't save you, Alicia. I'm only a man." He lifted a hand hesitantly and touched the edge of her shirtsleeve with one finger. "You need someone far greater than me to fix what's hurting."

Alicia sat there in silence, feeling an icy slash through her heart, as if he'd opened his Thermos and thrown his stale morning coffee at her.

"What do you suggest?" Her eyes narrowed into cold slits.

"Read this." He pushed a weatherworn New Testament across the seat toward her. "And call my sister."

"Your sister?" Alicia yelped, jerking her head up in bewilderment.

"She helps run a Christian shelter for battered women in Montana. They deal with anorexia, bulimia, even cutting. They could help you." He pulled his wallet out of his back pocket and thumbed through it, taking out a white business card. "Here. Her number's on here."

Alicia sat there, stunned. Her eyes wide with dawning realization. She didn't reach out to take the card, so he set it hesitantly into her open palm.

"I'd do anything to get you there, Alicia. I'll pay for you to go. I'll find someone to take care of your apartment while you're gone." Thomas gripped the steering wheel until his knuckles showed.

Alicia stuffed the stupid card into her vest pocket, crinkling the corner. "Why would you need somebody to take care of my apartment?" Alicia raised her voice, fresh anger coursing through her.

Thomas blinked. "Why, your fish of course. Don't you have two betta fish?"

Her fish. Thomas had remembered her fish.

Alicia choked back a sob, groping for the door handle with one hand and pushing herself across the seat with the other.

"Alicia?" Thomas leaned after her. "Where are you going?"

Alicia didn't answer. She kicked at the stuck door with her boot and threw herself out of the truck with so much force that she stumbled on the cool ridge of grasses.

"Alicia!" Thomas scooted hastily toward the passenger's side door as if he might jump out. "Don't do this. Please."

She whirled around, furious, and slammed the door shut with all her might—right in his horrified face. And then she stalked off across the field, not once looking back.

Chapter 10

Alicia stomped through the field toward a thicket of still-green pines, the truck fading behind her. Long, prickly grasses slashed at her ash-stained olive denims, catching at her bootlaces with burs and thorns like ugly memories, refusing to release her.

She stormed through a cluster of pines, their branches strong and thick against the sky, and broke into a run. Dodging limbs and brambles, the sound of her heaving breaths loud in her ears. Alicia heard the frantic flutter of wings as she tore through the brush—gray owls and ruffled grouse frightened from their nests among the leaves—but she didn't stop. She needed to be far from Thomas—far from Wyoming—far from everyone and everywhere.

When her side cramped painfully, Alicia finally paused, leaning against a pine trunk and bending over double to catch her breath.

The forest stood still around her, peaceful. She sank to her knees in the rich, pine-scented soil, breathing in the sweet scent of fresh, unburned earth and stones. She inhaled, eyes closed, and felt the stress and anger slip off her shoulders like a too-heavy pack.

Forget work today. Alicia sniffled, rubbing her eyes with her fingers. She'd use the compass Thomas gave her to get back to base camp and check in sick for the next day or two. Maybe she'd even go home.

The forest seemed quiet suddenly—too quiet—like the silence before an owl pounces on a mouse.

Wings flapped from somewhere in the distance, and Alicia turned her head sharply. Silence settled again, leaving nothing but the rustle of leaves.

An eerie bird call, throaty and throbbing. Like a warning.

Something dropped from a tree just beyond her, rattling the leaves. Hitting the ground with a soft thump. In the clearing between two trees, Alicia saw a fern quiver, its lace-green leaves shuddering against a sapling.

Alicia started to scramble to her feet, heart pounding in her throat, but she wasn't fast enough.

In a liquid second a yellow Nomex-clad arm had thrown itself around her throat, dragging her back down to her knees. A cold knife blade gouged painfully into her throbbing neck.

Alicia tried to scream, tried to twist herself around to see her attacker. And there on his wrist—the gang tattoo he'd carved years ago.

Miguel.

So you thought you could ditch me." Miguel dragged Alicia up by her hair, pressing the knife harder against her throat. He moved his eyes close to hers—bloodshot and angry, clouded by a haze of anger and drugs. "Lucky for me, I got friends everywhere."

Jorge. Alicia flinched, remembering the gleam of his gold tooth.

"I told you I'd kill you. You didn't believe me." He pulled her face closer. "I've been tracking you for weeks. Do you know how much I had to pay for these silly clothes?" He nodded to the Forest Service regulation olive pants and yellow shirt. "You're not worth it. You're washed up. Nobody would ever want you." Miguel jerked her hair, making her cry out. "But nobody kicks me out. Hear me?"

Miguel moved, tugging her across the dirt, and Alicia noted—with horror—a holster bulging under the edge of his shirt. "You need me, Alicia. You're nothing without me." His voice twisted from anger to a husky growl, almost pleading in its sickly sweet tone. "Who else would come all this way to find you? To bring you back? Because you know I'm the only one for you."

He twisted her against a tree, banging her head against the rough bark so hard she cried out. "If only you didn't make me drink so much. Didn't make me have to hunt you down. It's your fault, you know. You make me do it."

Wind flapped at the trees, bringing the scent of smoke, and Alicia's mind reeled, hazy, to angry nights in Santa Fe. The sound of his blows and the stench of alcohol on his breath.

"I'm sorry, Miguel," she'd pleaded, tears and blood streaming down her face. *"You're right. I'll do better. I promise."*

The horrible wrench of push-pull, the loving and hating him at the same time. The fear of him leaving, and the longing for him to disappear.

And somehow she was never, ever good enough. It was always her fault.

Endless days stretched out, dull and lifeless, like fading daylight through a rotten corridor with no way out. Even the woods around her began to stink of smoke, the familiar stench of burning timber—as if everything, eventually, went up in flames.

"Say it." Miguel hissed like a grass snake, pushing his face into hers. She could feel the hard knob of his gold earring, the stubble on his chin. "Say you're sorry. Say it's your fault before I kill you."

Alicia's mouth wobbled, tear streaked.

The old darkness seemed to choke her, tugging at her from the corners of her mind. The gutter of her broken heart, and the alcohol and drugs that drowned her pain. It should have worked—should have evened out—but instead she felt like the ground was tilted downward. Always slipping, always sliding a few inches farther from herself.

Until she no longer cared.

"I'll kill you," Miguel hissed. "You don't deserve to live."

Alicia opened her mouth to say the words she'd always spoken: *You're right. I'm so sorry. It's all my fault.* The old habits came easily, almost comforting, and the familiar downward slide eased the ache. If she closed her heart tight, she felt almost nothing.

"I know what you're planning to do. You bought a life insurance policy and named that Trisha kid benefactor of all of it." Miguel cursed her in Spanish, wiping his sweaty forehead with his sleeve. "I don't know where you hid it, but I'll tear apart your apartment piece by piece until I find it."

He shook her by the neck until she cried out in pain. "How could you be so selfish? After all I have done to put up with you?" Miguel gripped her face hard with one hand, still holding the knife to her throat. "I don't know why I love you. You're not worth it."

Love.

The word slapped her in the face so sharply that she barely felt Miguel strike her. Barely felt the blood trickle down the side of her face. It was the way he said it—the twisted sickness in his eyes as he spat out the word.

"Greater love hath no man than this, that a man lay down his life for his friends."

The words seemed to materialize out of nowhere, and Alicia wasn't sure exactly where she'd heard them. A snatch of a radio sermon somewhere over the years? A sentence from a televangelist while she switched channels?

"The Lord loves you, Alicia," Thomas had whispered. *"You're precious to Him. And to others."*

As soon as she remembered Thomas, something crackled the distant underbrush. A voice, and a rustle of branches.

"Alicia?" Thomas called, his voice faraway. "Where'd you go?"

For an instant Miguel turned his face away from her, his lips curving tight around his lips. "There he is. That half-breed *idiota* that's been coming on to you. I saw you in his truck, and he came to your hospital room. I'll kill him." He shook Alicia so fiercely her teeth rattled. "And then I'll deal with you."

Miguel whistled through his teeth, clamping a hand over Alicia's mouth so she couldn't scream.

"Alicia?" The crunching in the leaves stopped.

Miguel whistled again, lowering the knife into his belt sheath and reaching quietly for the pistol in his holster.

Thomas's footsteps crunched in the leaves, closer this time.

Miguel clicked the safety off and aimed for the bushes. Holding it deadly still with an accuracy that chilled Alicia to her core.

"Call for him," he whispered, not turning his eyes from Thomas's direction. "Or I'll shoot you, too."

Finger by stealthy finger, Miguel released her mouth.

Alicia's heart pounded in her throat like Indian drums, louder and louder.

Thomas's footsteps snapped on fallen twigs, so close she could see the glint of red and yellow from his shirt and fire pack through the limbs. The barely audible click of the hammer as Miguel cocked the pistol, coolly composed, with his thumb.

And Alicia opened her mouth to cry out.

Chapter 11

Watch out, Thomas! He's got a gun!" Alicia screamed and ducked her head as the gun went off, knocking against Miguel's arm as it exploded in her ear.

She felt Miguel knock her to the ground and a heavy thud as his boots kicked her in the head. Stars glittered together like tree branches, doubled and blurry, as she heard Miguel cock the gun at her. A glimmer of steel aimed at her face.

Thomas shouted—Alicia screamed—tried to twist free—Miguel crumpled as Thomas lunged for him—Miguel's arm came up—and an another blast. A kick in the leg.

At first Alicia felt nothing but the thud of impact on her shin. She inhaled the sharp scent of gunpowder and wood smoke, heard leaves falling around her like rain. A branch twirled down from a pine tree, landing in a green tuft by her knee.

Until she saw blood leak from her leg where Miguel had kicked it.

Kicked it?

No. He'd shot her.

Alicia clawed her way off the root-knotted ground, her wounded leg trembling, as Thomas and Miguel twisted in a death match, both shouting and grunting in a smoke-filled haze. She hugged the tree next to her with all her might, the shaggy bark digging into her cheek, and pulled herself to her knees.

Miguel was bigger than Thomas, and his muscles bulged under his torn Nomex fire shirt. He lunged—punched—cursed.

"Stay back, Alicia!" Thomas shouted, his face bloody, as Alicia crawled closer. "Go for help!"

Miguel paused just long enough to swipe for her arm, barely missing. He cursed and tried to steady his pistol, aiming it at Thomas's head. Thomas swung at him, catching his wrist with his teeth and trying to yank the gun away.

250

The knife.

Alicia crawled back a pace or two, leaves and soil cutting into the palms of her hands, and then lunged for Miguel's belt, ripping the knife from its leather sheath.

He turned, forgetting Thomas for a second, and tackled her to the ground, knocking the wind out of her. Her hair twisted around her mouth and face as he wrapped both hands around her throat in a death grip.

Alicia prayed with all her might and wiggled one hand partially free, plunging the knife into Miguel's heavy, muscle-hard stomach.

Miguel screamed—a horrible sound in Alicia's ear—just as Thomas grabbed up a thick limb, ready to swing. Miguel loosened his grip on her throat, rolling slightly to the side, and Alicia slid out from under his powerful shoulder.

As if in slow motion, Miguel raised the gun at Thomas, pushing himself up on one arm. But it was too late. Thomas's limb was in full swing, and it caught him square in the wrist, hitting it hard. The gun wobbled in Miguel's fingers as he groped to regain his grip, yelling curses, but a second blow sent it tumbling to the ground. They fought for it in the leaves, shouting, and Alicia grabbed up the fallen limb and swung it hard at Miguel's head.

It clipped him in the back of the skull, and he faltered and fell.

Thomas tore the limb from her hands and hit Miguel again, harder, opening up a gash on the side of his head.

He pushed Alicia back as Miguel finally staggered, still on his knees, and dropped to the ground.

"My word." Thomas gasped, his chest heaving. Leaves clung to his wild hair, and sweat poured down his forehead. "That's one big dude. Where in the world did you meet him?"

"Never mind." Alicia sat still, trying to catch her breath. "He's not dead, is he?"

"No. We probably just knocked him out for a minute or two." Thomas dug in his pack for a length of chain and manhandled Miguel against a tree, wrapping the chain as tight as it would go and snapping it with a padlock. "This is as good as I can do. But it might give us time to get out of here."

He wrapped Miguel's big arms around the tree, and Alicia held them together as Thomas looped a length of neon pink flagging tape around his wrists.

"He'll hate you for using pink," Alicia whispered as Thomas dropped the roll of flagging tape in his fire pack. "He's Latino, you know. The whole macho thing."

"He'll hate me anyway." Thomas helped her to her feet, snatching his two-way radio out of his pocket. "And he'll probably come to any second, so let's get out of here."

Alicia's leg had begun to throb, blood leaking through her denims, and she limped through the woods on Thomas's arm. Thomas pressed the button on his two-way radio, giving directions rapid-fire and begging for help.

"Why did you come after me?" Alicia paused, bending over double to catch her breath.

"The woods are on fire." Thomas brushed a thick cluster of vines out of the way. "It's gone nuts, and it's heading this way. Headquarters called back on my two-way just after you walked off."

"Miguel's gonna be fried if he stays tied to that tree." Alicia bit back a smirk, her eyes stinging from thicker smoke.

"They'll get him. They're on their way." Thomas stopped suddenly, swiveling his head back and forth. "Wait a second. Didn't they say the fire was coming from the east? I think the wind's changed to the southwest. Do you feel it?"

Alicia stood still, listening to leaves rustle all around her. Strands of hair blew across her battered face, tickling her nose.

"You're right." Alicia reached for her compass. "We've got to get out of here."

Thomas didn't answer, his eyes fixed on something on the horizon.

"What is it?" Alicia shook his arm frantically. "Is Miguel coming back?"

Before Thomas could reply, she saw it: a wall of orange licking at the trees. Black smoke boiled up through the forest floor, so thick she could barely see, and a wall of heat hit her with full force. Heat shimmers melted her vision, and she dropped to the ground, her sense of direction momentarily lost in the shuddering roar.

Chapter 12

"Get up, Alicia!" Thomas tugged her to her feet, tearing a bandanna from her pocket and slapping it over her mouth. "Don't you dare stop!"

The thicket crackled with lightning-fast shadows and shuddering underbrush as deer sailed away from the fire, white tails up. Slender feet so fast they seemed not to touch the ground. Bellowing moose and sleek antelope tore through the underbrush. The branches overhead snapped with squirrels, and the sky filled with clouds of birds. Flapping and soaring, cracking twigs as they soared from the treetops.

"Hello?" Thomas shouted into his radio, steering Alicia in the other direction and breaking into a run. "Lawrence? This is Thomas. Do you read me?"

No one answered, and Thomas tugged her along by the arm, punching the CALL button furiously.

"Where is everybody? Why don't they answer?" Alicia hollered through the bandanna, glancing back over her shoulder at the darkened woods, so thick with gloom she could barely see. Limbs whacked her in the face, making her see sparkles. "They answered a few minutes ago. Try again!"

"I am trying!" Thomas paused, out of breath, just long enough to dig through his fire pack for a signal flare. He knelt, hands shaking, and lit the end with a match. He pushed Alicia out of the way, and she ducked her head as the flare went off. A brilliant white light, searing so bright it hurt her eyes. Up through the tops of the trees.

An earthshaking *boom*, and cherry-red sparks rained down.

"They'll find us." Alicia crawled to her feet, her wounded leg still leaking blood, and forced herself forward. A wall of hot wind blew, gusting leaves and ash in her mouth and throat. She dropped to her knees, choking for breath, and lost her grip on Thomas's arm.

She couldn't see—couldn't even fumble for her compass without letting go of the bandanna over her mouth. She reached for the zipper on her fire pack and tugged it open, dumping half the contents on the ground. She pawed through them, and a heavy wind poured up from the fire, blowing leaves and limbs. Through a stinging blast of ash she saw the glint of silver—her fireproof silver cover blanket. She lunged for it, but another breath of hot wind kicked up a cloud of leaves. Covering everything with a jagged layer of branches and debris.

Heat blasted Alicia so strongly she could hardly think, and her skin sweated fiercely under her shirt and pants. The material clung to her, hot and sticky, sweltering. Alicia clawed at her collar, gasping, trying to let in a bit of air.

In a blinding flash she saw herself in Thomas's truck, leaning toward him ever so slightly, her pulse beating in her throat.

What if he'd kissed her? What if she'd kissed him back, and then. . . ?

How would she feel standing alone at the tarmac for the trip home, ashamed and abandoned, left by yet another selfish man? The last in a long, long line.

Another second, and anything could have happened. Maybe Thomas wasn't so foolish after all.

"The wind's spreading everything!" Thomas shouted as darkness thickened, so heavy and greaselike that Alicia barely saw the sky. He tugged her to her feet as another blast nearly knocked them to the ground, and she clutched the dusty bandanna to her mouth.

"Come on, Alicia! I'll carry you if I have to." Thomas pushed her ahead.

"Wait." She tugged him to a stop, choking as a fresh cloud of ash rose up from the fire. "You go ahead. I'm holding you back. I'll catch up."

"Don't be ridiculous." Thomas glared. "We're going together. What kind of friend leaves his teammate?"

"Go, Thomas!" She angrily jerked her arm free. "I'm not pulling you down with me. I've done that long enough. Don't you get it?"

"I'm not leaving!" Thomas shouted over the roar of snapping limbs, yanking her toward him and putting his face close to hers. "I'm choosing to stay. You're my friend, Alicia. And I never leave friends."

The land sloped slightly downward, and he yanked her with him, coming through a thick tangle of pine limbs that scratched at her face. "This way," he panted as wind tore at his hair. "Fire runs uphill. Let's hope it's passed through here already."

"I feel it behind me." Alicia gave a spasm of coughs. "There's got to be a break in here somewhere."

"The wind's too strong." Thomas strained to see his compass in the gloom, flipping on a feeble flashlight. "I can't tell which direction it's coming from anymore. Can you?"

Alicia didn't reply. As if in slow motion, she watched as a huge pine tree to her right suddenly ignited in a burst of orange flame. The fire spread to a cluster of vines, which hissed and popped, and breathed a fiery wall across a patch of dried leaves. To the left, a burning branch sizzled and snapped, crashing to the ground and igniting a puddle of flame.

"We're too late," Alicia whispered, taking a step backward.

"No we're not," Thomas shouted in her ear, pushing her forward to a more sheltered spot. "You're going to go on from here, you hear me?" He shook her, knocking her teeth together. "You're going to turn your life around and marry a man who loves you. A man who loves God. You're going to be okay."

"What? Are you crazy?" Alicia shouted, twisting around to see him there in the gloom, and froze, unable to tear her eyes from the searing, golden spots of flame. Like watching stars appear in the evening sky, one glimmer after another, the woods around her seemed to glow. A branch here, a leaf there, until everything swam with ghostly flickering light. Heat rippled, waterlike, merging into shimmering walls.

A burning branch fell on Thomas's arm, and she screamed, knocking it off with her sleeve. Glowing bits of ash cascaded around her like falling stars.

She felt her knees buckle. Her lungs and skin burned with heat and smoke.

Falling, falling—burning limbs and leaves streaked like comets as the limbs overhead burst into flame. When she closed her burning eyes, she saw glowing spots and lines, like after seeing fireworks.

"Thomas?" Alicia cried out, groping for his arm in the darkness.

"I'm here!" Thomas called back. "Hold still, will you?"

She spun around, and Thomas slapped something blanketlike around her. Something silver. She swung at him, trying to tear it off.

"Don't you dare!" Alicia screamed, pummeling him with all her might. "Get your fire blanket off me!" Tears leaked from her eyes from the ash and smoke, and she tried to rip his fingers away through burning smears of light.

"Alicia!" Thomas shouted. "Watch out!"

A huge pine, alive with leaping ripples of fire, suddenly splintered. It swayed, and Alicia saw a blinding wall of flame teetering toward them. "Get your blanket off me!" she screamed, trying to free herself. "Or I'll hit you! I swear!"

Alicia screamed as a heavy weight hit her hard, knocking her to the ground. She felt something wrap over her, thick and heavy. Covering her face from the blinding blast.

She tried to turn, roll, push it off her, but her arms and legs were pinned there, motionless.

Then the woods exploded, blinding light leaking under the edges of her consciousness. The world rained fire. Heat blinded her, hot enough to melt her clothes.

Alicia imagined herself glowing white, searing her shape into the scorched earth.

A rumble of earth and stones raining onto her face, and smoke so thick and scalding it hurt to breathe.

And Alicia saw no more.

Chapter 13

Alicia. Oh *mio* Dios." Someone sobbed. *"Mio Jésus."*

Alicia opened one groggy eye, wincing at the blue-white light. She scrunched her eyes closed, her head throbbing. A plastic tube wrenched the inside of her nose, and it hurt to breathe. Everything hurt. She lay back against the clean sheets in exhaustion, trying to summon the courage to breathe again.

"Thomas?" Alicia slowly raised her head, fumbling for his arm. "Thomas, where are you?"

A dark shape materialized beside her bed, and Alicia blinked. One eye felt stuck shut, swollen. "Carlita?"

"Oh *mio Pastor*," Carlita moaned through her sobs, gripping Alicia's hand so tight it smarted. Alicia grunted and tried to pull her hand away.

"You're alive. I could kiss you. I will kiss you." Carlita brushed Alicia's hair back from her cheek and planted it with a tender smooch. "I thought you were dead. I've been in agony for hours." She blinked swollen, red eyes. "They couldn't find you. Nobody could find you. Thank God you're okay."

Carlita wept aloud, openmouthed, hugging her middle with her free hand.

Alicia's head felt groggy, smoke-filled. The rustle of sheets against her skin sounded like snapping flames.

"What happened?" Alicia tugged urgently on Carlita's hand. "Where am I?"

"We don't know what happened." Carlita sponged her streaming face and nose. "You'll have to put the pieces together for us, but by the time they found you, you'd inhaled so much smoke they thought you wouldn't make it. But a few hours ago you began to come around. I prayed for you." Carlita pointed at her chest. "I prayed for you, Alicia—nonstop. My lips hurt. I never prayed before. Not really."

Carlita looked haggard, her hair hanging around her face in dampened streaks.

257

"The soles of your boots melted. They had to hack limbs and brush for an hour to get that tree off you." Her voice broke, and she let out a gasp. "Trisha's called here twenty times. She's inconsolable."

"Tree? What tree?" Alicia ran a hand over her face, remembering the burst of brilliance. The thud of her body against the hot ground.

Alicia reached for her fire pack by instinct and couldn't move her arm. Tubes pulled at her skin.

"Carlita." Alicia jerked upright in bed with a groan. "Where's Thomas?"

Carlita didn't answer, sponging her nose again. Head turned down.

"Carlita?" Alicia screamed, jerking her legs over and trying to get up. "Where is he?"

Monitors beeped and alarms went off, but Alicia didn't stop. She jerked the silver pole with her, tubes and all, and tried to force her way out of bed.

Carlita rushed at her, wrestling her back to the bed and shouting for help. Two nurses pulled Alicia back to the bed, trying to calm her with gentle words. She swung at one, and Carlita gripped her face in both hands, speaking sharply in Spanish.

Something burned in her IV tube—cool and calming—and her veins rushed with softness. Light as cotton. Floating, like smoke clouds rolling across the pines. Alicia's muscles relaxed against the starched white sheets, and she felt the ceiling shimmer and ripple. Transparent, light as air.

Carlita's tear-streaked face hovered near her, patting her cheek.

"Where's Thomas?" Alicia's lips felt rubbery, and she couldn't make them work right.

Carlita didn't answer. She took a deep breath and slowly, sadly, shook her head no. Back and forth. Tears shining on her face like sunlight on a stream. She bowed her head and crossed herself.

The last thing Alicia remembered was the sound of her own screams. Her body racked with sobs.

~ॐ~

"They found him on top of you, holding you under that fire blanket." Carlita wept. "He saved you, Alicia. That fire blanket was his. It had his name on it. They found yours about half a mile away, under a pile of ash."

Alicia turned her face away. *Please, God. Let me die.*

She couldn't speak, only shudder with sobs.

"He left all of his effects in your name. His gear, everything." Carlita gasped into a Kleenex. "His note said you lose all your stuff anyway, so you'd have some extras."

Alicia laughed and sobbed, rocking back and forth.

"One thing on his person survived," whispered Carlita. "In his vest pocket, and nobody knows how. It's for you. It's got. . .his name on the cover."

She held out a cardboard box, and Alicia tried to see through tear-swollen lashes.

Cover? The cover of what?

Before she reached hesitantly into the box, Alicia knew what it was. "His New Testament," she whispered, her voice gravelly from too much smoke.

She lifted it carefully, cradling the fragile pages. The cover had singed, blackened on one corner.

"And one other thing." Carlita sniffled, scrubbing at her nose with a tissue. "Do you have any idea why this stuff was in his truck?"

She lifted it out.

Alicia stared, her vision tear-smeared.

A box of Velvet Gold graham crackers and a container of butter.

Thomas's last meal.

"Whatever would make you smile like you meant it," he'd said.

And he got his wish.

Alicia snatched the graham cracker box from Carlita and hugged it to her chest, bawling like a wounded deer.

Chapter 14

S o you're gonna stay in Santa Fe for good?" Carlita walked through the boarding gate a protective few inches away, both thumbs looped through the straps of her JanSport backpack. Two pins glittered from the back pocket: "It's always a Manic Monday," read one, and "Firefighters Take the Heat," boasted the other.

Three weeks had passed, and Alicia was due another haircut. She smoothed her ragged ponytail, more grateful than words that Carlita stayed near her, coming back in three trips. The news of Thomas's funeral, the agony and skin grafts, the stitches and empty hospital walls. Without Carlita, she didn't know how she'd have made it.

The park lost nearly eight hundred thousand acres to fire before rains and cool autumn weather finally put out the fire. It would take years to recover. Decades.

Alicia could blink now, clear-eyed, but if she thought about it long enough she'd burst into tears.

"Nah. I'll go back home just long enough to pack up my stuff." Alicia looped her headphones over her shoulders. The Cure crooned a British-flavored song about heaven on the overhead system, right on the heels of Belinda Carlisle and the Pet Shop Boys. A TV advertisement for California Raisins glimmered side by side with a rerun of *The Cosby Show*.

"You're not going back to Santa Fe?" Carlita crossed her arms, popping watermelon Bubblicious over the TV laugh track. "Why, what are you gonna do?" She leaned closer. "No more death wishes, right?"

"No." Alicia looked numbly away, watching through the large glass window as a small Embraer jet eased into the gate. Her heart still felt ruined, shattered forever, but reading the pages of Thomas's Bible in her hospital bed eased the pain into a dull ache. In her sleep she heard the verses whispering, calling to her, in a voice she imagined Jesus might have.

The Cure's melancholy guitar chords died, and Starship belted out a peppy tune with too-happy lyrics, and for a moment Alicia hated Starship. The hum of crowds in the terminal around her, the laughter. How dare anyone laugh when Thomas's work boots lay empty and silent, never to be worn again?

She'd tucked his battered hard hat into her checked suitcase, still lettered with his name in sloppy, faded black Sharpie marker. But it might be awhile before she found the courage to pull open the suitcase zipper. If she ever did.

"Well, what are you going to do then?" Uneasiness creased Carlita's gently lined forehead. She'd curled her bangs to a pretty fluff, and geometric earrings clinked. "You know they're not going to hold Miguel for long. Impersonating a federal employee is one thing. But you can't prove he jumped or threatened you because it's just your word against his. You've got no other witnesses."

Of course not. Because Thomas was dead.

Alicia choked back an unexpected sob, and Carlita seemed to realize her gaffe in a horrible instant.

"I'm sorry," Carlita whispered, hugging her tight. "I didn't mean it. Forgive me, *amor*." Her voice swelled with tears.

Travelers streamed around them like water around a fallen log. Never stopping, only turning a curious head to glance.

"It's okay." Alicia looped an arm around Carlita's shoulders and wiped her eyes with her free hand. "I know what you mean. I won't be safe forever." She dug for the now customary Kleenex in the pocket of her stonewashed jeans.

She walked toward the boarding gate, arm still around Carlita. "But I'm not scared of Miguel anymore. I think I know what I'm going to do."

"What?" Carlita raised a wary eyebrow over tear-red eyes. "Move in with us? Good, because that's the only way I'll let you have any sleep at night. Otherwise I'll be calling you every minute of the day and night, so help me."

"I believe you." Alicia laughed weakly. "But I've got another plan."

"It better be good." Carlita glared.

"I think I'm going to Montana." Alicia fingered the business card in her flowered jean jacket pocket. "There's a place that might be able to. . . well, help me." She licked her dry lips, which Carlita insisted she paint coral pink. *A Burst of Color*, the Avon label read on the lipstick tube.

Which is exactly what Carlita said she needed.

"Montana?" Carlita's eyebrows shot up, and she didn't bother to lower her voice. "Are you nuts?"

"Nah." Alicia shrugged, embarrassed. She lifted a finger to her lips. "But keep it down, will you? I don't want one of Miguel's cohorts hearing me." She scowled. "And so help me, if I ever meet Jorge again, I'll kick him so hard he won't get up for a week."

"You and me both. So what's with Montana?"

Alicia hesitated then reached under her strappy K-Mart purse and dug the business card from her pocket. She plopped it in Carlita's hand. "It's a ranch. A Christian place. Thomas's sister helps run it, and he said they work with women who've been abused. And. . .so forth." She turned away, too emotional to meet Carlita's eyes. "I think maybe it could help me. I called her already, and. . .she seemed really nice. I think I'll go."

"How are you gonna pay for it?"

Alicia shrugged, picturing the little jar hidden under her living room carpet. Her precious life insurance policy. All she had to do now was cash it in, and she'd be good to go.

"I've got a little stash," she mumbled, not daring to look at Carlita. "I'll be okay. Maybe I'll even have enough to start over again somewhere far from Miguel. Get a job in a different city."

Carlita stayed silent a long time, reading the business card. Flipping it over and reading the back then flipping it over again.

Finally she stuck it back in Alicia's hand. "You know what? I think you're right." She put an arm around Alicia's shoulders and patted her. "On one condition."

"What's that?"

"That you accept visitors named Carlita and Trisha any time they want to see you." She raised an eyebrow in warning. "Because believe me, we'll take that place apart brick by brick if you don't."

Alicia laughed and nodded, tucking her arm through Carlita's as they headed toward the sunlit gate.

KAMIKAZE

Dedication

To Mr. Kenji Miwa of Saitama, Japan,
and one of my great heroes of the faith.
Thank you for serving our Lord so faithfully all these years.

Chapter 1

2012

This way, everybody. Hands on the rails, please, and watch your step." Jersey Peterson's hiking boots clomped down the wooden boardwalk over Yellowstone's misty, muddy-colored water, which billowed sulfur-scented steam. "This water's only two degrees below boiling—which means the bubbles don't come from heat but from escaping gases in underground vents. Can anybody guess how many similar geothermal features we have in the park?"

Jersey leaned closer to the group to hear the answers. "Two?" She smiled at the kid, who stared back in a smirky grin. "Sorry. We've already seen six in the past half hour. And no, don't. . .no. No gum on the railings. Could you pick that up, please?"

Brat Boy didn't respond, shrugging his shoulders and snickering, and his parents didn't seem to notice. Dad pecked away at his iPhone, and Mom chuckled with another woman over some shared joke.

Jersey peeled the label off her water bottle and used it like a napkin, scraping off the neon pink bubblegum and folding the wad into her pale green uniform pocket.

"Anybody else? How many hot springs and geysers?" Jersey asked. "And remember, the Upper Geyser Basin has more geothermal features than the entire Yellowstone Park or anywhere else in the world." She pointed to a woman in the back. "A thousand? You're pretty close. More than ten thousand. We don't even know for sure how many."

Three teens huddled in a bunch, giggling, whispering, and sharing an iPod bud. Heads together, not hearing a word Jersey said.

Oh no. "Sir?" Jersey called, louder this time. "With the camera? Please don't lean between the railings—it's dangerous. People have died here in Yellowstone's hot springs. Not only are they full of acid but. . . sir? Sir!" She marched back through the group and faced him. "Please. Nikons don't function well when dropped into scalding water. Believe me, I've seen enough people try it that I'm thinking of selling camera insurance."

The others tittered as the guy snapped three more rapid-fire shots then slowly retracted his camera and torso. Coolly wiping his lens and avoiding her eyes as if she'd never spoken.

Argh. Did anybody listen anymore? Jersey walked back to the front of the group, trying not to think of the ignorant mom who'd wanted a picture of her child with a bear—so she set him in the middle of a field in grizzly territory with an open jar of honey. Jersey's colleague Nelson had saved the child that time—storming through the field in his truck and hazing the approaching she-bear with rubber bullets. He'd given the mom a tongue-lashing and called the police and social services, and still Jersey had to hold herself from taking a punch at the woman across the ranger station table as she coolly lit up a cigarette, blowing smoke in Nelson's face.

Or what about the Chinese tour bus that unloaded sixty sardine-packed hikers who made a collective trash pile to attract wild animals and then climbed on top of the bus to watch? You'd think the two bison who rocked the bus back and forth might have created some healthy fear, but the following day (after the group had been ordered to leave the park) Jersey picked up seven of them for slipping through boardwalk railings and onto thin snowdrifts covering boiling mud pits to take pictures. About to fall through the ice and cook themselves alive in front of other tourists—and destroying fragile mineral deposits in the process.

At the moment, Jersey wondered which would've been worse.

The plaid-wearing redneck who shot two mule deer and tried to exit the park with them stuffed inside his camper? Been there, done that. The drunk college students who left their campsite a mess of broken beer bottles, vomit, and toilet paper—and tried unsuccessfully to burn a broken metal lawn chair in their campfire? Yup. The French hiker who dug up ginseng roots and got caught when Nelson found his stupid "fresh, hours-old, ginseng roots from Yellowstone" post on the Internet? Mmm-hmm.

Jersey motioned the group ahead. "Everybody remembers Old Faithful, right? Well, even Old Faithful isn't as precise as you think, and its timing has changed quite a bit in recent years. Any ideas what can make a shift that big?"

"Dinosaurs?" quipped the bubblegum boy in a sarcastic tone.

One of the teens poked his head up from the iPod. "Dinosaurs? Who saw a dinosaur?"

His sidekick, who sported the shortest shorts Jersey had ever seen, laughed and shrugged long, sleek hair over her shoulder. She popped a bubble, hand on her hip, sunlight glinting off fancy oversized sunglasses. "Can we hurry up?" she whined, checking her watch. "I'm starving. Who cares about this stuff?"

"What was the question again?" Bubblegum Kid's dad asked with a hint of irritation. "Something about dinosaurs?" His cell phone rang a shrill and annoying jingle, and everybody turned while he proceeded to laugh over football stats with his buddy, so loudly that people across the geothermal pits on a different boardwalk turned to stare.

"No dinosaurs." Jersey held back a sigh, speaking over a noisy criticism of the Packers' defense. "It's okay. I was just saying that Old Faithful's accuracy is subject to earthquakes that affect rock layers— changing temperatures or causing more gases to escape."

Teen Girl snapped another loud bubble. "I know somebody who's got the same problem," she said, elbowing her friend in the side. "Escaping gases."

"Hey, no writing on the rails!" Jersey jumped forward. The same kid. *Again.* "Could I have some help, please, Mom?"

He jumped forward, scribbled on her hand in green ink, and then threw the marker cap into the mud pit. Grabbing for the other half of the marker to throw it in, too.

"No, no! Don't do that!" Jersey searched for the brat's parents, but they'd walked forward, leaning over the railings. "These are fragile environmental ecosystems, and when that plastic melts from acid and heat, it's going to. . .wait, what are you doing?" She straightened up. "An X-ACTO knife?"

Jersey walked up the boardwalk and tapped the kid's mother on the shoulder. "Sorry, could you take the knife from your son, please? No knives."

"What?" Brat Boy's curvy mom finally looked up from her lengthy, lowered-voice conversation with the miniskirted bottle blond. Appraising Jersey's shapeless, light green park ranger's uniform and brimmed hat with a nose scrunch of open distain. "What's he done now?"

"The knife." Jersey tried to pull him away from the rail, where he'd begun to carve in silent defiance. "Please."

His mom pushed herself off the railing and took a few steps toward him. She sighed and held out her palm, showing the undersides of long, red acrylic nails and a little too much cleavage. "Give it, Parker. Now."

"Naw. I don't wanna." He continued carving and swiping at Jersey with the other hand.

"I swear this boy's gonna wear me out. Doesn't do a thing I say." Mom turned back to her blond buddy, apparently giving up the chase. "It's the age, I guess. That's what everybody says. His teacher wants to put him on Ritalin—thinks he's got ADHD or something fancy like that— but I think he's upset by new school rules. They've gotta wear uniforms, which, if you ask me, is borderline child abuse."

Jersey reached for her walkie-talkie to call for another ranger's help when something hit her square in the forehead. Something sharp, like tiny folded paper.

The folded wad of gum wrappers fell to the boardwalk, slipping between two slats and into the bubbling mud pit. Bobbing away on a roiling tide.

The teen girl with the short shorts buried her head in her friend's arm, shoulders shaking with silent laughter.

A headache pulsed in Jersey's head as she ended the tour and waved good-bye, trying to keep her smile pleasant. After all, park rangering had been a dream come true—the first thing in Jersey's life that truly clicked. Once she'd inhaled Yellowstone's dewy morning air, tinged with earth and pine and lupine sweetness, she'd never regretted it. Yellowstone lay in the rugged heart of the Rockies like an iridescent jewel: shimmering in snows and showers and vaulting peaks and a shocking froth of flowers.

A far cry from the smoggy Chicago skyscrapers of Jersey's past.

But lately people didn't seem to. . .notice. To care. Traipsing over thousand-year-old petrified wood without a glance and littering it with empty Aquafina water bottles and Diet Coke cans.

Maybe she was too hard on them. Jersey lifted her head to the pines, catching a bit of breeze from the mountains against her sweaty face. Not so long ago she'd been clueless, too—sitting around a campfire in a sort of wide-eyed wonder, like gazing at her first love.

Only Yellowstone didn't break hearts like he did. Leaving her to pick up the pieces and fend for herself.

Jersey pushed open the door to the ranger's station, catching a glimpse of herself in the glass: pale green hat sporting the iconic National Park Service patch, messy red-gold hair pulled back in a knot, badges glinting. Blue eyes starting to show the lines of thirty-three years, the last six of which she'd spent in the Wyoming sun and harsh winter wind.

"Morning." Nelson breezed past her on his way out, his brown ponytail tucked under his hat. A cup of coffee steaming in one hand. "You doing the Old Faithful tour after this? Heard there's a big group."

"Right after lunch." Jersey nodded. "But first I've got to do that funding report for Don. He'll have my head if it's not finished this week. Not that I have anything good to say in it anyway, with all our funding down." She let out a sigh. "We're all gonna have to pan for gold or something."

"Gold. Right." Nelson chuckled. "Well, good luck with any reports. Computer's down again this morning."

"Again? Are you kidding?"

"Sorry. Preet from the tech place is on vacation until next week."

"But it's urgent, Nelson! Really. Don'll flip! Maybe even write me up—depending on what kind of mood he's in."

"Know any magicians?"

Jersey groaned.

"Well, then, good luck." Nelson winked and blew on his coffee, waving over his shoulder as the door fell shut behind him. Blotting out the golden, sunshiny morning with the dull glow of artificial light.

"Mornin', Rodney." Jersey patted the taxidermied cougar by the wooden counter. "You're looking crabby today. What'd you do, stay up all night taking our computer down?"

Rodney showed pointy fangs in a permanent scowl.

"So you're not talking, huh? Well." She passed a wall of brochures that campers usually took and left littered all over the campsites. "That figures."

Jersey gave an exaggerated salute to Phyllis, one of the other rangers. She stopped by the coffee machine and poured a cup of horrible black stuff, which she doctored up with an unhealthy dose of sugar and artificially flavored vanilla creamer.

She was still mixing the powdery muck with her plastic stirrer (yes, park rangers resorted to plastic if it was cheaper than wood down at the closest Albertsons grocery) and started into the back office. Then as quick as she'd come, she jerked back out, leaning up against the side of the door. Hoping he hadn't noticed her.

"Is he in there again?" Jersey wrinkled up her nose at Phyllis in a whisper, nodding with her head toward the office.

"Who, that Japanese researcher guy?" Phyllis whispered back.

"Yeah. From Caltech, right? What's his name again?"

"Taki? Taco? Don't ask me. Researchers give me the creeps. He's probably a CIA plant, you know? Looking for drugs or something."

"Taka. That's his name." Jersey glanced through the crack in the door. "I don't want to be rude, but he's. . .weird. He bugs me."

"Tell me about it. He wears bedroom slippers to work, and he never smiles."

"Never."

"Those researchers all think they're better than everybody else," Phyllis muttered. "I knew one who went around with a pocket dictionary so he could correct everybody's grammar. Beastly little jerk. This guy carries one, too. I've seen it."

"No, I'm pretty sure his is a pocket translator. You know. To type in the Japanese words and get the English version."

"Well, he drinks weird stuff. Look at him." Phyllis pulled Jersey over to peek through the crack in the door. "What is that, tea? He carries it in a Thermos, and he packs little compartmented lunch boxes with perfectly trimmed carrots in the shape of flowers and stuff. Strange if you ask me."

Jersey shook her coffee cup. Frothy, lumpy, creamer-laden coffee quivered back, reminding her of the geothermal mud pits. "Then again, we're not really one to talk about drinking weird stuff, eh?"

"Good point." Phyllis smiled. "What's he doing, research on moose or something?"

"Elk, I think. Something about population patterns after the reintroduction of wolves and the big fire back in '88." Jersey sipped her coffee. "At least that's what Nelson said. But then again, never trust Nelson. He told me five years ago that you were only staying for the summer. And look at you now." She poked Phyllis's arm. "You're practically a tour exhibit."

"Old Faithful?"

"Nah. I was thinking of a different one."

"If you say Porkchop Geyser, I swear I'll slash your tires."

Jersey chuckled. "Snort Geyser—or maybe Spasm. Remember that birthday party at Nelson's? I think that Coke came out your nose."

Phyllis snickered. "Poor guy had carpet stains for weeks." She nodded toward the back office. "Well, I wouldn't worry about ol' what's-his-name. I'm sure he'll be gone in a few weeks."

Jersey sighed and shook her coffee cup, tapping the stirrer. "Probably. But it's not his tea drinking habits that bother me. It's. . .a lot of things. For starters, every time I turn around he's asking me for something. To ride out to the lake to put down some equipment. To go here and go there. To let him borrow my phone or take him out to the wilderness station." She raised her hands. "It drives me bats! I've got a job to do, and I sure don't get paid extra for ferrying researchers around."

"Snobby researchers that don't know how to use a normal two-syllable word. And I'm still not convinced he doesn't carry a pocket dictionary."

"Well." Jersey tossed her coffee stirrer in the trash. "I've got to get that report done, or I'm in trouble. The computer's really down?"

"Yep. Dead as the possum I scraped off the road this morning." Phyllis jerked a thumb in the direction of the office. "I hear that computer was here before Don, and it takes up more space than the truck. What a dinosaur!"

"Don't talk about dinosaurs." Jersey's headache throbbed again as she remembered her rowdy tour group. She swallowed the rest of her coffee and tossed the cup.

"Whatever, Jersey. But as long as that computer's still running, Uncle Sam won't spring for another one."

"Believe me, I can make it quit running. If that's what they want." Jersey picked up a taxidermied squirrel mounted on a slender log and pretended to swing it like a baseball bat.

Right as Taka Shimamori abruptly stepped through the door—the end of the log catching him square in the chest. His sheaf of papers spilling everywhere, glasses flying off. Dislodging the squirrel and sending it hurtling into the copier.

Chapter 2

I'm so sorry!" Jersey gasped, not sure whether to rush to help Taka or pick up the injured squirrel, which bonked off the copier and landed in a pitiful heap on the short gray carpet.

Phyllis shrieked and promptly backed into the coffeepot, knocking it sideways with her hip. Spilling coffee down the side of the maple cabinet—where they'd wedged the coffeemaker and a stash of supposedly recycled paper cups, plus an ancient jar of sugar that ants periodically invaded.

While Phyllis ran for a wad of paper towels, Jersey dropped to her knees and scooped up Taka's files, not daring to look him in the eyes. "I'm terribly sorry. I didn't know you were coming through the door just now. I'm. . .I'm an oaf. Forgive me."

Taka's face remained the same mask of sober, emotionless blank, but he blinked faster. Something like an embarrassed laugh choking out of his mouth as he avoided her eyes, reaching for some printouts. "It's okay. Please. Don't worry."

Jersey scrambled around on the carpet for his trendy rectangular-rimmed glasses, the style of young businessmen and artists, and then handed them back in humiliation. "Here. They're not broken, are they?"

"They're still usable, I'm sure."

Was he laughing at her? Jersey narrowed her eyes at him in contemplation then reached for another printout. "What is this, your research?"

"Yes. My initial analysis of elk migration patterns and factors affecting movement in the park area." Taka reached out to point, his pale fingers trembling slightly. The faintest Japanese accent clipping his syllables. "This one shows herd numbers following the 1988 fire, which disturbed breeding and feeding grounds, along with other more recent ecological dynamics of concern. Particularly the reintroduction of *Canis lupus*."

"Wow." Jersey bobbed her head like a lizard as if she understood. "Um...sure."

Wait a second. *Canis lupus.* Wolves. Aha! "You're talking about wolves, right?" she asked, relieved to have decrypted some of Taka's blabber. "So how are the numbers?"

Taka handed her a paper. "Overall the population has reduced due to predation but also because of a fear-based behavioral reaction. The elk are declining, with more and more frequency, to venture deep into thickets due to fear of attack in areas of very low visibility." He straightened his glasses. "Incidentally, *Populus tremula, Salix bebbiana,* and other new-growth vegetation species have increased, which is good for park biodiversity."

"Oh." Jersey felt as intelligent as the taxidermied squirrel. "So... that's good, right?"

"Not exactly." Taka ran a hand through his black hair. "You see, the recent long-term declines in elk recruitment has been across the board, which means that several potential biological factors are having a definite impact on population dynamics."

Riiiight. Exactly what I was going to say. Jersey handed him the rest of his papers and started to get up, annoyed at his show-offy gibberish, then noticed the broken squirrel lying by the copier. Its frozen arms in perpetual mid-run where they'd popped off the log.

"Oh no," she groaned, scrambling over and scooping it up off the floor. Its tail had broken off in a furry heap. "Don will kill me! He loves this squirrel."

She turned over the stiff body, its beady eyes glinting, and tried unsuccessfully to fit the tail back in place. She pictured Don scowling under thick gray eyebrows, writing a nasty note in her file.

"Superglue?" Jersey shrugged. She tugged off her hat with her free hand and scratched her hair, wondering if there were an emergency taxidermy hotline.

Taka peered at the squirrel tail. "No, you need something like... hmm. A polyepoxide, maybe? Something with a thermosetting polymer to bind the epoxide and polyamine to the surface of the material. But not too viscous that it'll soil the surrounding fibers."

Jersey stared.

"What do you call it...epoxy?"

"Oh." She narrowed her eyes in irritation. "Well, I don't think we've got anything beyond your basic Elmers."

"I can try to fix it."

Jersey turned to Taka in mounting exasperation. "You really think you know something about squirrels?" She shook the stiff, brushlike tail. "Long-dead squirrels?"

He bowed slightly and held out his palm.

"Fine." Jersey reluctantly handed over the pieces. "But don't mess it up any worse than it is, okay? Don raised this thing from a little ball of fluff, and he bawled like a baby when it got thumped in the head by a speeding car. Seriously. I think he had to spend some time in rehab to deal with the grief and. . . What are you doing?"

Taka didn't reply, rooting around on the walls and pulling down corners of Wyoming and Yellowstone Park maps.

"Hey, hey—what are you doing?" Jersey jumped up to press the maps back in place. Mentally kicking herself for giving a nerdy researcher Don's prized squirrel.

Taka scraped a bit of putty from the corner of a Yellowstone Falls poster and rolled it into a ball. He took a plastic coffee stirrer from the cup near Phyllis's shoulder, where she crouched, furiously scrubbing coffee from the carpet.

Jersey stood over Taka, hands on her hips, as he sat down at the table. Poking around inside the body of the squirrel. He broke off the coffee stirrer and fitted it inside then calmly produced a mini sewing kit from his backpack—the kind with needles and tiny thread spools—and began to thread a needle.

"You carry a sewing kit?" Jersey tipped an eyebrow upward.

"Glue?" Taka glanced up at her without taking her bait.

"Umm. . .let me check the supply closet." Jersey squeaked open the closet door and sorted through several boxes of flyers, markers, and scissors, and finally found it: a battered old bottle of Elmers wood glue, the orange cap crusted with repeated drenchings of yellowish stuff. Wondering where in the world Caltech got oddballs like Taka Shimamori.

"You think it's gonna work?" She held out the bottle to Taka.

He adjusted his glasses and took the glue without looking up. Giving her a curt nod.

Jersey rolled her eyes, but she stayed by the table, peering over his shoulder as he fitted together some kind of structure on the inside, holding it together with putty. Then he threaded together the two squirrel pieces, stitching carefully through the hard skin along the broken edge. Dabbing on glue with the end of the coffee stirrer.

Taka pressed the pieces together and reached for the log. He glued on the four feet, one at a time.

And then—voilà. Good as new.

"It's a flying squirrel after all, no?" Taka chuckled. The first time Jersey had seen him smile.

"Yeah, it is, actually." Jersey surveyed his work then spun around in surprise. "Hey, did you just make a joke? That was pretty good."

Taka shrugged as if embarrassed. He set the squirrel on the far end of the table and then silently reached for his Thermos and poured a cup of briny-looking brown stuff. He sipped it as he lifted a stack of papers, a bird's nest, a cluster of prickly nuts, and a shiny plastic pencil case decorated with smiling onions and pale blue Japanese *kanji* characters.

"Ah. There it is." He reached for a rogue mechanical pencil. "That's what I was looking for." And Taka settled down to work as if nothing had ever happened.

"Thanks. The squirrel looks…amazing." Jersey put it back in its place on the shelf and tipped her head sideways. "You wouldn't know I broke the tail." She turned back to Taka, who was busy making notes in a notebook, comparing something from a computer printout. "Where'd you learn to sew?"

"Sorry?" Taka peered at her through his glasses, hand pausing on the mug. Condensation frosting on the outside. Meaning Taka probably kept some kind of cold herbal stuff inside his Thermos instead of the ubiquitous green tea most Japanese carried around.

Jersey hoped one of those spiny nuts wasn't an ingredient. Or, heaven forbid, whatever came out of that bird's nest either.

"Sewing," she repeated. "Where'd you learn sewing? You know. With the needle and thread." Jersey imitated stitching. "Who taught you?"

A flicker of irritation flashed through his dark eyes. "I know what sewing is."

Jersey stepped back, involuntarily facing her palms outward. "Sorry. Just asking."

Taka still seemed reticent, so she turned back to the closet to replace the glue. "I'll just…put this away and be out of your hair. Thanks for the help."

She retreated to the closet and took her time wiping the cap and replacing the glue, making a face in the darkness. Weird. That's what Taka was.

Taka said something, so softly Jersey had to stop shuffling boxes to try to hear him.

"Sorry?" She leaned away from the baskets of scissors for kids' nature crafts.

"My mother," said Taka, clearing his throat. Tapping his papers together, upright, in a perfect stack. "She was a seamstress. A very good one."

And he dropped his papers back on the desk and began to work again, only briefly lifting his dark eyes to meet hers. So quickly that Jersey wondered if she'd blinked or actually seen it.

Was, he'd said. *"My mother* was *a seamstress."*

Jersey twisted her wooden T-shaped pendant around her neck as she studied him. "Well." She softened her tone. "Your mother taught you well."

And she slid the glue back and closed the closet door.

⁓⁂⁓

Jersey was on her knees under the computer trying to find the main power switch, when her walkie-talkie in her belt clip crackled, making her jump. She banged her head against the underside of the computer desk so hard that Taka dropped his mechanical pencil from across the room.

She groaned, rubbing the tender spot on her head, and reached for her walkie-talkie.

"Jersey?" Nelson's voice came over the connection, harsh and staticky. "Sorry to interrupt, but I need your help. We've got a bear incident on our hands."

Jersey depressed the button. "You're kidding."

"Nope. Wish I was. Phyllis will have to take over your tour after lunch. But I need you here for backup. A guy's been mauled, and his wife's hysterical. She saw the bear charge and fled to get help, so we're not even sure if he's alive. The emergency crew's here, ambulance on its way, but I need you to talk to reporters and field questions."

"I'm on my way."

Jersey crawled out from under the computer and nearly knocked down Phyllis, who was bent over the copier changing paper. "Sorry. Bear attack over by the lake."

She hurried through the room rapid-fire, grabbing up her keys, wallet, and cell phone and throwing them all in her backpack. Taka watched her, his pencil poised over paper.

Jersey looked up, shoving a first-aid kit in her pack and trying to zip it closed, struggling with the stuck zipper on one side. "You. . .need something, Taka?"

"No. Sorry." He jumped as if embarrassed, fidgeting with his pencil. "Actually, yes. You're headed to the lake?"

"On an emergency call." Jersey didn't look up, shaking her bag and pulling at the zipper. "Why?"

Taka hesitated then reached over and pulled out the tangled strands of fabric from the zipper with the tip of his pencil. Smoothly zipping it closed and pushing it back across the table to her. "Would you mind maybe. . .well, giving me a ride?"

"To the lake?" Jersey stammered, turning her bag over in amazement. "And. . .thanks. You fixed it. This thing always jams."

"If I won't be in the way. I've got some equipment to set up, some herds to count. I'll probably spend the rest of the day there."

Jersey slung her bag over her shoulder, pressing her lips together as she tried to figure him out. "Aren't you with Caltech on some important grant? And don't they. . .well, pay for your transportation?"

Slight color rose in Taka's pale cheeks. "My car's in the shop. But it's okay. I'll see if someone else can take me later."

Wonderful. Make me the bad guy. Jersey sighed and shook her head. "It's okay, Taka. If you go right now, I'll take you. But I can't wait, and I can't promise to bring you back."

"No problem. I'm ready." Taka slapped his laptop closed and grabbed up his papers, plus two giant duffle bags of stuff. He threw the prickly nuts in a laptop bag pocket and stuffed the bird's nest carefully in the breast pocket of his ugly yellow Lacoste shirt. "Can I carry something for you?"

Jersey stared as he reached for a third duffle, slinging it over his shoulder. "Maybe I should ask you the same thing."

"Sorry. Lot of gear. If it's too much, I can stay behind."

Jersey tried not to look at the bird's nest fibers sticking out of his shirt pocket. Probably housing all manner of lice and bird droppings. "It's okay. Just throw your things in the back of the truck."

Jersey strode across gravel to the white ranger's truck and tossed Taka's duffles in the backseat, Taka trotting after her.

"You sure carry a lot of stuff." She pulled on her sunglasses and stepped up into the driver's seat.

"I know. Blood sampling kits, listening station setups for remote monitoring, bands, recording equipment." Taka jumped in beside her, wedging two bags around his feet. Two bags that, from the gingerly way he handled them, probably cradled something fragile. Beakers of frogs floating in formaldehyde, perhaps?

Jersey forced her eyes away. "All that stuff for monitoring elk?"

"I monitor a few songbirds and butterflies, too. But mainly elk. Yes."

Jersey threw the truck into Reverse, looking briefly over her shoulder to back out. "I figure a researcher like you would drive a pretty cool car, even if it's in the shop." Jersey glanced over at him as she checked the road for other vehicles. "Don't you? Wait—let me guess." Lacoste shirt. Caltech. "A Prius." Her tone sounded smug in her ears.

"A 1992 Honda Civic. I bought it as an undergrad from my roommate."

No wonder it was in the shop. Jersey let out her breath, sorry she'd been snappish with Taka. Especially when her eyes landed on the backpack zipper he'd so patiently fixed.

"Wow. Your car's older than mine, and that's pretty hard to beat." Jersey's hands circled the steering wheel nervously as she tried to think of something to say.

"People aren't always what you think, you know," Taka said quietly, shifting the bags around his feet.

Jersey shot him a wry smile, her eyes fixed on the rearview mirror. "I used to think that," she replied, shifting into a faster gear. "But I'm wiser now."

The white ranger's truck bumped over a blur of rough-paved roads, past stands of lush summer pines that stood dark against the verdant green of open meadows. A glimmer of river sparkled in the distance, making a shiny slice through colorful spikes of lupines and sunflowers.

Exactly the change of scenery from the windswept skyscrapers of Chicago that had enchanted Jersey on her first trip to Wyoming years ago. She'd come for an interview for an accounting job in Billings that hadn't panned out, and instead of heading straight back to Chicago, she stopped by Yellowstone National Park to see the falls.

There she'd stood in gawking awe, wind whipping her coppery hair and face soaked with waterfall mist—and for the first time in her life,

Jersey knew exactly what she wanted to do.

"So, Taka, you're from Japan?" Jersey tried to make conversation, taking one hand off the steering wheel to fiddle with the cranky air-conditioning system.

"Fukushima."

"Oh." Jersey drove in uncomfortable silence, not sure if she should ask about the nuclear disaster following the tsunami or not. "Is your family okay?"

Taka pressed his lips together. "Yes. Healthwise, anyway."

"Good. I. . .uh. . .heard about it in the news awhile back." Jersey winced as she spoke. "Such a terrible thing to happen. I couldn't even watch most of the news footage."

Taka played with the strap on one of his camera cases. "It'll take us years to recover. And some people never will entirely." He glanced at an area with sparse trees. "Sort of like the Yellowstone fires from 1988. The park has never been the same."

"You're right about that." Jersey flexed her hands on the steering wheel, not sure what to say. Taka's left hand showed no wedding ring, and his face remained as unperturbed as ever: a pale mask with dark brown almond shaped eyes under black-rimmed glasses. And the faintest bit of stubble along his jaw from where he'd missed shaving—the first hint of anything human—no, vulnerable—about Taka that Jersey had seen so far.

"So. . .what's Fukushima like?" She accelerated the truck around a curve, and a spatter of bright sunlight through the trees surprised her, falling warm on the side of her face.

"Beautiful. Snow in the winter and cherry blossoms in the spring. White peaches so soft the juice runs down your chin." He shot her a hint of a smile. "How about you? You must be from. . .let me guess. New Jersey."

"You didn't." Jersey lowered her sunglasses to scowl at him. "No. It's just my name. Although I get that a lot. And I'm not from Wyoming either, so don't bother asking."

"I know. Chicago, right?"

Jersey's head jutted back in surprise. "How'd you know that? I didn't tell you."

"Well, for starters, the Bears mug you keep on your desk. And you put celery salt on hot dogs."

"Doesn't everybody?"

He grimaced. "No."

"Oh." Jersey shrugged. *Show-off researcher.* She glanced over at Taka, who looked like a college kid in his jeans and lace-up Converse sneakers—all of which clashed with his preppy button-up shirt. "I bet my name would be a pain to write in Japanese, wouldn't it?"

"You'd have to use *katakana* characters for foreign words."

"Right."

Taka raised his eyebrows. "You know about katakana?"

Jersey jumped and quickly waved a hand. "Oh, I just see Japanese tourists with their pocket dictionaries, all trying to pronounce geyser names in some kind of Japanese characters. Making shapes on their hands with their fingers." She traced an imaginary circle on her own palm while still gripping the steering wheel. When she looked up, Taka was already doing it.

He laughed out loud—the first time she'd seen it.

"I'm thinking how to write your name in katakana." He wrinkled his brow. "Jersey. Jaa-zee. Maybe?" He narrowed his eyes, tracing shapes on his palm. "That's a tough one."

"Told you." Jersey glanced over. "Does your name mean something?"

"Tall and honorable." Taka made the invisible marks for the kanji on his palm. "Unfortunately, I'm. . .well, not really either one."

He said it so soberly, with those nerdy glasses, that Jersey choked back a horrified laugh with her fist. Willing herself to keep her mouth shut. She eased the truck to a lower gear as two grazing bison appeared in the field, backed by a serrated line of slate blue, snowcapped mountains— and quickly changed the subject.

"Check out those bulls." She pointed. "Big ones, huh?"

Taka leaned toward the window. "Did you know Yellowstone bison retain the memory of migratory routes? I wonder if modern technological advancements might be hindering their breeding patterns to an extent that their rates of reproduction are low—which might, in fact, portend the creation of new migratory routes?"

He rubbed his chin, seemingly oblivious to Jersey's presence. "Then again, geneticists are finding out that many bison are not actually true bison but are instead bison-cow hybrids—so any testing of my hypotheses would be weakened."

I. Am. So. Sorry. I. Asked. "So you're a biologist?" Jersey shifted again in her seat, speaking through her teeth. The ranger truck whizzed past a red Mustang pulled to the side of the road, camera lenses sticking out of the windows in the direction of the bison. Jersey wished for a second she could pull over and toss Taka and his duffles in their backseat.

"I'm not a biologist exactly. I started out in geology. I'm a biochemist who specialized in Macropodidae, initially, and I acquired my doctorate in Australia. But more recently I've been participating in a research group studying causes of animal migratory routes and patterns, such as magnetic fields and climate change." Taka adjusted his glasses. "My field study is in terrestrial animal migration using light-stable isotopes. It's not the cutting-edge thing anymore, but combined with protein-folding results and some interesting DNA markers unique to the genus, I'm coming up with some new theories."

Maybe I should just stop talking. "Ah. You're going to be a professor." Jersey's voice sounded sarcastic in her ears.

"Possibly."

"Well, while you're here doing. . .well, whatever it is you're doing, maybe you can help us watch for poachers because the numbers have spiked recently. Especially elk, for the antlers, but black bear, too. Animal parts draw big bucks on the Chinese medicine black market. And there's simply no way we can patrol every inch of the park."

"You're against hunting?"

"Not at all—when it's done legally and during the proper season. But the animals here in the park are somewhat tame, even the ones that forage in the wild—and they're easier targets." Jersey swallowed hard. "Poachers prey on the little ones or those that trust humans, or worse, they whack the head off for a trophy and leave the meat to rot. It ticks me off big-time."

Jersey stared out the window at the mountains, shaking her head. "People aren't what they used to be, you know?"

"On the contrary." Taka cleared his throat. "I'd say that people haven't changed much. They've always been more or less the same."

"You mean you believe that people are basically good at heart, with a few crotchety flaws?" Jersey gave a wry laugh. "I used to believe that, too. But I sure don't now."

"Oh no. I meant that people have always been sinful. We've just developed different ways of covering it up through the years."

Jersey glanced in the rearview mirror then over at Taka in surprise. "Sinful? That doesn't sound very Buddhist. I thought you Japanese were supposed to be Buddhist, or maybe Shinto or something."

" 'Supposed to be'?" Taka seemed to bristle, though his words stayed soft. "We Japanese, as you put it, are individuals. We have a right to believe whatever we think is correct, just like you do. A majority of Japanese may claim some sort of Buddhist belief, yes, but that doesn't mean we all do, or we all should."

Jersey lifted her hands off the steering wheel in disbelief, not prepared for such a gushing philosophical lecture. Instantly regretting that she'd allowed Taka to ride along—*the opinionated jerk.* "Whoa. Sorry. I didn't mean it like that. I just. . .assumed."

"Assumptions are what build walls." Taka turned his eyes in her direction. "I prefer to get to know a person first and then draw conclusions."

Jersey's jaw clenched as she punched the gearshift into a higher gear. "What are you, then? Muslim?" she snipped, keeping her eyes straight ahead.

"I'm a Christian. One of Japan's less-than-one-percent, oddball Christians."

Well, you sure got the oddball part right. Jersey glanced over at his profile, keeping back any comments of surprise. Although she had to admit—even she hadn't seen that one coming.

"You?" Taka glanced at her.

Before she could respond, her cell phone jingled from her backpack on the floorboard. She reached for it clumsily, still holding the steering wheel with one hand. The truck bumped over a bad patch of paving as she dug at the zipper.

"May I?" Taka reached for the backpack.

"No. I'm fine." Jersey waved him away then thought better of it. She could see the photo in the *Jackson Hole News and Guide*: her ranger truck plowed into a bank of wild sunflowers, a dead mule deer sticking out from under the back wheel.

"Okay. Yes. Thanks."

Taka unzipped her backpack and found her cell phone. His long, slim fingers brushed hers as he placed it in her open palm.

"Mom?" Jersey put the phone to her ear in bewilderment and switched on the hazard lights, slowing the truck and pulling over to the shoulder. "Is that. . .you? It can't be." She pulled the phone away and stared at the number in surprise.

Jersey put the phone back to her ear and shifted to NEUTRAL, frowning. "The connection's bad, Mom. Where are you? Is everything okay?" She pushed the volume up. "We've got to talk fast because I'm on the way to. . . Sorry. I can't hear anything. I'll call you back in a few minutes, okay? Hold on."

Jersey pulled back into the road and felt Taka staring at her. "What?" She kept her eyes on the road.

"Nothing. You just seemed surprised that she called."

"Well, I am." Jersey handed him her silent cell phone. "We haven't spoken much in what, two years?"

Taka raised his eyebrows in an expression of surprise, which he quickly tried to cover.

Jersey scowled. "What, you think we American families have it all together?"

"No, I just. . .well, two years is a long time. And you seem like such a nice person."

"Excuse me?" Jersey whipped her head around long enough to freeze him with a cold stare. "You think whatever's happened between my mom and me is my fault? What, weren't you just saying something about assumptions?"

She coolly shifted to the next gear.

Taka leaned forward abruptly, digging in one of his bags for a pair of binoculars. "*Cervus elaphus*," he said, taking off his glasses and craning his neck for a closer look.

This researcher and his dratted lingo. "Elk?" Jersey looked up in irritation. "You're talking about elk?"

"Over there." Taka pointed. "Just around the bend, next to that large *Populus deltoides*. See there?"

Jersey pressed a hand to her forehead in irritation. "Sorry if this sounds rude, Taka, but could you please speak English? I do know a thing or two about trees, but most of the time I prefer to leave my Latin back where it belongs—in a dusty book in the classroom." She glanced at her backpack. "And if you don't mind, I've got to call my mom back as soon as we stop. She sounded upset, like something's wrong."

"I'm sorry. I actually don't know the English tree names as well." Taka swallowed. "Maybe. . .cottonwood? Is that right?"

"Ah. Cottonwood. That one I know. But I don't see what's the big deal over an elk, no matter what tree he's under. The park is full of them."

"No, Jersey. This one has an arrow sticking out of his side." He twisted the binocular lens to see better. "I can't be seeing right. But. . .it's what it looks like to me. He's trying to get up." Taka winced and sucked in his breath through his teeth. "Ouch. That's got to hurt."

"What?" Jersey tore off her sunglasses and squinted in the bright sun. "An arrow? Hunting isn't allowed in the park!" She jerked the truck to the side of the road, momentarily forgetting about Nelson's bear call.

"I'm sure of it. You can see if you back up a bit." Taka handed her the binoculars.

Jersey put the truck in REVERSE and craned her neck to see. "Shorty runs the grounds out this way. It couldn't be him, could it?"

"I don't know." Taka shrugged. "He did look a bit small for a full adult male *Cervus elaphus*, now that you mention it." He cocked his head. "Did you ever think that *Cervus elaphus* means literally 'deer deer'? You'd think they'd come up with a less redundant specimen label."

Jersey's jaw dropped at Taka's random bit of information while an elk lay possibly injured. If he spouted one more of his silly Latin-isms, she might shoot an arrow through him, too.

"I hope it's not Shorty." Jersey eased the truck to a stop and took the binoculars. "He's been a favorite around here for years. Survived brucellosis as a calf, although nobody quite knows how, and has a broken right rack."

"The right rack, you say?" Taka stretched out his lips in a grimace. "Oh."

"What? What's the rack on this one look like?" Her heart beat loud in her throat as she lifted the binoculars, twisting the lens to focus. "I don't know how you can see anything with these."

"Here." Taka leaned over to adjust, his breath tickling the sweaty strands of hair around her ear.

"Oh. There. Now I can see the trees, and—hold on." Jersey fiddled with the lens again. "Shorty's a bit too tame around people, but until today everyone's treated him well. I just hope some poacher didn't. . ."

She let out a cry, nearly dropping the binoculars.

Chapter 3

I can't believe it." Jersey thrust the binoculars back at Taka and scrambled for her seat belt. "Not Shorty. Why would somebody do that?" Her breath came fast and angry, almost tearful, as she thought of Shorty's bearded grin, as if posing for tourists' pictures. He'd chomp dandelions along the lake in cheerful bliss, unflinchingly close to curious passersby, pausing only to flick an ear at an errant fly.

"Do you have a good camera on you? Because I've got to document this." She scrolled through the veterinarian numbers on her phone while she tugged the truck door open.

"Maybe. Let me see." He unzipped one bag, digging through it, and then zipped it up and started on the second.

"You're taking too long." Jersey reached over him and stuck her hand in one of the pockets. She immediately let out a shriek as her fingers brushed against something nauseatingly cold and fuzzy, like a rotten Fukushima peach.

She jerked her hand out. "Gross! What on earth do you have in there?" she shouted, wiping her fingers on the seat.

"Oh. Sorry." Taka's head bobbed in apology as he looked up. "That's my *bryophyta* collection. I've found a good sample of *Leucobryum albidum*, which resembles a pincushion, and—"

Jersey scrubbed her palm against the seat again for good measure and shuddered then covered her face with her free hand. "Forget the moss, okay? Just. . .forget it. Shorty's injured. I'll proceed without photos."

"He's alive though." Taka reached for the truck handle and cracked it open, wincing at the mournful bellow that came, strained in agony, across the grass. "I can see him there still trying to get up. You think he can make it with an arrow stuck in his side?"

"Hey, you're the zoologist," snapped Jersey, stalking across the field in the sun.

"Biochemist." Taka scooted out of the truck and grabbed the camera from his third duffle.

"Whatever difference that's supposed to make."

"Higher paycheck." Taka bobbed his eyebrows.

Jersey's shoulders jumped with an unexpected snort of laughter, punching in the phone number to call the nearest vet.

Jersey's back ached as she took off her ranger's hat outside the vet clinic and ran a hand through her messy hair, tugging at the knot at the base of her neck. She reached into her pocket for her keys and then nearly jumped when Taka stood up from an outside bench, holding out an earthenware mug.

"What? You're still here?" Jersey dropped her hands down from her hair. "I thought you'd gone with Phyllis hours ago. She said she'd pick you up."

"No need. I wanted to hear how Shorty's surgery went."

"Really?" Jersey hesitated a second then sank down on the bench next to Taka and accepted the cool mug. "I don't know. They were able to remove the arrow, but he's injured pretty badly. The arrow punctured his liver and intestines, and he's lost a lot of blood. There's no telling how much more internal damage he's suffered."

"I'm sorry to hear that." Taka adjusted his glasses, which glinted back at her in the dim parking lot like glowing goggle eyes. "It seems that you have a special affinity for this animal, no?"

"If you mean that I like Shorty a lot, yes, I do." She lifted the cup to her lips. "What is this anyway?" she asked warily, sniffing the earthy, wheat-scented liquid.

"*Mugicha.* Japanese barley tea." Taka produced another mug and poured himself a cup then drank in silence.

"It doesn't have moss in it, does it?"

"Sorry?"

Jersey raised her eyes to the starry sky. "Forget it. I'd just better not find spiders floating on top or anything."

Taka didn't reply, and Jersey hesitantly took a sip. Tasting something crisp and cold, surprisingly refreshing. She drank quietly, wondering what else she could possibly talk about that wouldn't produce (1) Latin names, (2) long-winded, pompous discussions with scientific jargon, or (3) strange revelations in pockets of duffle bags.

"You know something?" Taka looked up abruptly.

Jersey braced herself. "What?" Her fingers tightened on the mug. "And the tea's good, by the way."

"Thanks. Well, did you know most species of plants have two sets of chromosomes in their vegetative cells, which makes them diploid? But by amazing contrast, bryophytes have only a single set of chromosomes—which makes them haploid." He put his cup down and lightly pounded his open palm with a fist for emphasis. "Yet there are periods in the bryophyte life cycle when they actually do possess a double set of paired chromosomes, but this happens only during the sporophyte stage. Isn't that amazing?"

Jersey was vaguely aware of her open mouth. The mug frozen halfway to her lips and a sudden longing to smack Taka again with a taxidermied squirrel.

"You know what?" she finally managed, setting the mug down coolly on the wooden bench. "I've. . .I've got to go. I'll see you tomorrow." *Or not, if I'm lucky.*

Taka didn't seem to hear. "You must have a supremely satisfying job, Jersey. I envy you."

"Excuse me?" Jersey sputtered, nearly upsetting her mug. "You what?"

"I envy you." Taka faced her. "Normally I spend so much of my time in laboratories and inside closed walls, reading books and researching biochemistry. But you." He nodded in her direction. "You're free. You spend your days outdoors and *really live life.* I admire that."

All of Jersey's planned "go-read-a-dictionary" speech died in her throat. "Taka, you can't mean that."

"About you living life? I certainly do. People talk about it all the time, but few people actually have the courage to do what you do. It's amazing. Just as amazing as. . .well, bryophyte life cycles and chromosomes."

Was he mocking her? Or—in his own warped way—trying to give her a compliment—albeit a compliment of the absolute oddest kind?

"You must be joking. I feel about as free as a caged bear." Jersey gestured to her weary face. "Look at me. I'm covered in blood from a poached animal, and I'm powerless to stop it. Almost nobody listens to the information on the tours anymore. I had to pull an X-ACTO knife away from a kid today, Taka. Two weeks ago I watched them pull the mangled body of a lost hiker—what was left of it, anyway—from the side of a mountain. He didn't check in at the ranger station, didn't bring extra clothes, and had carried—I kid you not—a Bic lighter, a wad of drugs, and a bag of banana chips in his backpack. No bear spray. Not even a compass."

She raised an arm. "The computer's down again, which means Don's going to be mad at me because I can't finish my report, and. . ." She flung up her arms, not wanting to add that she was "carting a weirdo researcher around the park" to her spoken litany. "My mom. I haven't even called my mom back—all because of an elk."

"But it's not about an elk at all," Taka added hesitantly. "It seems like it's more about people for you."

"You know what?" Jersey slapped her knee. "You're exactly right. People. People who could care less about rules and even less about nature. Every day I go out there ready to risk my neck catching guys who bow-hunt animals like Shorty, who do nothing more than eat dandelions." Jersey didn't take a breath. "I've spent an entire month getting ready for a volunteer work crew from Oregon to come do construction work next week, and they bailed on me half an hour ago."

"You're serious?"

"Fifteen people. They were supposed to build fences and repair one of the ranger stations out by the lake, pave trails and walkways—stuff we've been waiting for and needing for years. But they sent me a text message saying they'd decided to lobby against Wall Street instead."

Jersey tightened her hands, remembering how she'd had to scrub elk blood from her phone before picking it up to read the text message. "So instead of actually coming out here and doing something that needs to be done, they're going to stand in lines chanting inane messages about corporate evil and lobbing broken bottles at police officers. Way to go helping with conservation and protecting the parks, guys."

Taka sat there in silence, not even bothering to retort.

"We had everything ready. The building materials and showers fixed for them to use and everything. But"—Jersey flung her hands up—"I should have known. This isn't the first time a volunteer group has stood us up, and it probably won't be the last. We don't have enough funding to fix the boardwalks and put up fences to protect the geothermal features. And that's what I've got to tell Don in my report: that we're sunk. Basically. Without repairs, some of the lesser known geysers are going to disappear forever. We can't hold back the downhill process anymore."

Jersey spat out a sigh. "People simply don't see the parks as something worthy of preservation—or if they do, they always think somebody else will do it. But they forget that we are the 'somebody else.' " Her voice trailed off. "And I don't think I'm going to stay around and watch the wilderness die a slow death."

A battered station wagon buzzed up the road in front of the vet clinic, and a whiff of cloying, pungent-smelling antiseptic tickled Jersey's nose on the breeze.

Taka was staring at something. Tipping his head ever so slightly to see past Jersey's head.

"What?"

"Leucanthemum vulgare."

Jersey turned, feeling her hands curl into fists.

"Oxeye daisies." He gestured toward a sloppy planting of flowers in a spread of faded bark mulch. "They're classified as noxious weeds in Wyoming."

She relaxed her hands, meeting Taka's dark eyes for a second. "Yes." The breath seemed to go out of her. "You noticed."

"Certainly. In Australia in 1907, one single variety of venomous weed killed seven hundred bovine livestock animals. *Leucanthemum vulgare* grows aggressively, multiplies rapidly without natural controls such as native herbivores or soil chemistry, and adversely affects native habitats and croplands. Noxious weeds are injurious to humans, native fauna, and livestock through contact or ingestion or both."

Jersey sat back on the bench and crossed her arms. "Well said, Mr. Encyclopedia."

"But somebody planted these on purpose."

"Exactly." She raised a finger. "Because nobody cares. They're pretty, right? So what's the harm in a couple of daisies?" She gestured over the parking lot. "But the seeds have probably already spread across the road. Maybe already up to that ridgeline. And no matter how many times I say that oxeye daisies are threatening native species and killing beneficial insects and competing with native cereals and grains, nobody listens. Exactly the way nobody listens when I say to stay out of the geyser pits or not to hunt in the park—or that we need funding for maintenance and repairs. Natural features don't fix themselves. And I'm tired."

Taka turned his tea mug around. "But somebody needs to tell people, Jersey. That's your job."

"Forget it." Jersey sighed and bent over, resting her head in her hands. "I've got my thirty-days' notice all typed up," she said quietly, hoping nobody from the ranger's office could hear. "I've found a job back in Chicago—a good job—and I think my time here is done."

Taka spilled his tea. Right down the front of his shirt. "You mean you're going to leave the Park Service? For what?"

"A normal eight-to-five job."

"At what, a company?" He sponged his shirt with a cloth handkerchief from his jacket pocket.

Jersey didn't answer right away, dragging the side of her hiking boot against the concrete sidewalk. "At a cell phone company, okay?" Her words came out harsher than she meant. "It's a good job. I'd make somewhat close to the amount I do here after six years on the job."

"But you'll pay more than double in rent."

"So what?" Hot anger flushed her cheeks. "What does it matter to you if I leave anyway?"

Taka looked up at the stars briefly then turned calmly to face her. "Are you sure that's what you want, Jersey?"

His question hung in the air like a whiff of SUV exhaust from the main road—lingering after the dust settled. A soft wind blew, scuttling a Burger King wrapper across the sidewalk. "Everybody thinks being a park ranger is such a glamorous job, but it's not." She crossed her arms. "It's demanding. It's frustrating. And frankly, much of the time it's unappreciated."

She tipped her head sideways to scratch her head, which felt itchy under her hair and that ranger hat. "Don't get me wrong. I love my work, and I don't do it for thanks. But if it's not making a difference, then why bother? I could get ten hours of sun on my face by feeding people through turnstiles at an amusement park—and a lot less stress."

"Of course you're making a difference." Taka folded his handkerchief and blotted some more.

Jersey paused, momentarily distracted by the idea of a grown man who carried a cloth handkerchief. Most men she knew, like Nelson, either used (1) a battered KFC napkin from the car dash or (2) his sleeve.

"My work makes a difference to who, Taka? The few retired hikers who volunteer to come pick up trash? Or the kids who really get excited about butterflies and deer and want to go into conservation or wildlife studies?" Her eyes softened. "Possibly. But I'm not so sure anymore. Most of the time I'm just confirming what they already know. I'm not teaching them anything new."

A Schwan's delivery truck rumbled along the shrubby road in front of the vet clinic, its headlights splashing bright artificial light through the patch of oxeye daisies.

Taka finished his tea then sighed and started to gather up his Thermos. "Still," he said softly, his movements echoing on the hard wooden bench. "I think it means something that you still tell people the truth."

Jersey sipped the last of her tea and handed him back his mug. "Maybe."

"No," said Taka sternly, not smiling. "Not maybe. There's nothing greater in life than to speak the truth with your whole being—your whole life—as if nothing else ever really mattered. Because it doesn't."

He leaned forward, his eyes as black as the scoop of obsidian sky overhead. "Living out God's truth is the most beautiful thing in the world, Jersey. Art beyond comparison. The only thing that ever lasts."

Jersey sat there, frozen, staring at a crack in the sidewalk. And as if in slow motion, Taka reached into his pocket and pulled out a mechanical pencil with a too-long syringe of spiny lead. He twirled the end on a long, loose strand of Jersey's hair that had escaped its messy bun, and it twinkled in shadowy copper strands.

"Did you ever think that one day this hair will lose its pigment?"

"What?" Jersey snatched her hair back. "And give me that pencil, too, before you poke somebody." She grabbed it, wishing he'd brought his ridiculous onion pencil case. "And what does my hair have to do with anything?"

"We're finite." Taka's voice came out raspy, so quiet she had to lean forward to hear it. "Our days are numbered. You should wear your hair down." He snatched his pencil back and stuck it defiantly in his pocket, right next to the bird's nest. "It's beautiful. It's part of your truth—part of who you are. You should take pride in who you are and what you do and celebrate it—celebrate your Creator—with every single breath. That's what I do. And I'll do it for the rest of my life—no matter what anybody else thinks."

And with that, Taka got up and ran a hand through his thick hair, making it stand up in garish black spikes. Glasses askew. And he walked a few paces away, staring up at the moon with a face full of pure wonder, as if he'd never seen it before.

Chapter 4

Hiya, Jersey. You awake?" Phyllis's anxious voice chirped into Jersey's cell phone as she struggled to force her eyes open. A stream of sunlight poured across the foot of her bed in a lumpy rectangular shape, creating a halo around the caramel-blond hairs of her cat Gordon's belly.

"Phyllis?" Jersey rubbed her face and sat halfway up in bed, careful not to kick Gordon as she rooted around for a clock on her bedside table. 8:10. Not an ungodly hour compared to the four-thirties and five o'clocks she usually pulled. "Shorty didn't die, did he?"

"Huh? No. Not that I'm aware. The only reason the vet called the ranger station was to tell us that they found one of 'our' researchers asleep on the front bench when they unlocked this morning and to ask if he was all right."

"Taka." Jersey slapped her forehead and let her palm drag down her face. "Something is seriously wrong with that guy. I'm not kidding."

"Did you know he rides a unicycle? Nelson found out that one from a friend of his at Caltech."

"I'm not surprised."

"And he used to foster kids through social services, too. I wasn't expecting that."

"Me either." Jersey grimaced. "Would you trust your kid with a man who rides unicycles and sleeps on benches?"

Phyllis laughed, but it sounded thin. "Well, anyway, are you still going this morning?"

"Going?" Jersey stared at the clock with bleary eyes, trying to register what the numbers were saying. "Going where? To pick up Taka? No. Let him get his own ride home—the weirdo. Maybe we should drop off a unicycle at the vet's."

Phyllis paused again. "No, Jersey. To church where that good-lookin' pastor speaks. You said you were going today."

"Church?" Jersey sat up straight, running a hand through her mass of wild hair as the awareness sank in. "Right. Of course—it's Sunday. Hold on a second. Why, are you coming, too, Phyllis?"

She didn't answer, and Jersey heard faint shuffling on the other side. Phyllis's muted voice as she spoke to someone in the background.

"Hey, if you want to come, I'll pick you up." Jersey swung both feet over the bed and wiggled her toes in the rug. "No problem. So long as my front door opens of course. It's been giving me fits again. I had to use the kitchen window for a solid week until the repair guy finally showed up."

The line stayed silent, and Jersey tentatively took it as a yes. Which was usually how Phyllis went about her sporadic church visits—not quite daring to mouth the request herself out loud.

"I'll be there in half an hour. If you're not out on the porch, I'm telling Don you agreed to do my report for me."

"What? No way!" Phyllis shrieked. "If you think I'm going to sit in front of that broken computer and hack away at some ridiculous piece of rubbish that isn't worth the—"

Jersey clicked the phone off in the middle of Phyllis's harangue, as she always did. Smirking to Gordon. "You lazy stinker." She rubbed his ears. "If somebody paid me a buck for every hour you sleep, I'd be a millionaire. And then I wouldn't have to do funding reports for Don or anyone else."

Gordon gave a toothy grin in reply, reminding her of Shorty, and yawned—showing the corrugated pink roof of his mouth and pointy little teeth that left marks in leather mice, plastic bottle tabs flicked across the kitchen floor, and an old sandal of Jersey's that now defied recognition.

Jersey dragged herself to the kitchen for coffee then through a warm shower of hard, sulfur-scented water, which her ten-dollar-a-trim hairstylist swore did a number on her hair.

Her hair. Jersey ran a hand through it, staring at her reflection in the mirror and remembering Taka's words in the shadows outside the vet clinic, the moon pouring down pale on her gingery strands.

He was correct about one thing—she was losing pigment all right. Right there—a long silver-white one glinting in the overhead light. And there, another one. And two more. How had she never noticed these? Or had she even bothered to stop and check after she pulled off her ranger hat in the evening, scalp and armpits sweaty from hiking through mud pits?

Jersey dug in her bathroom cabinet drawer for some tweezers and plucked out the gray. Then she fluffed her long hair with her fingers and noticed—for maybe the first time—a dull haze of broken fuzz along the back of her hair where she tied it back in its knot. She leaned forward, studying her reflection, and then rooted through messy bottles and cleaning products under her cabinet. Searching for the sample packet of repair serum her hairdresser had scolded her to use like. . .oh, eight months ago.

She scrubbed the serum through her hair, inhaling its lavender-y sweetness, and dug through her closet for something to wear to church. Her hands stopped on the ubiquitous baggy gray sweatshirt she usually lived in on weekends.

But as she pulled it out of the closet, it felt. . .wrong. Like cheating.

Instead Jersey rinsed out her hair and sprayed on an ancient conditioning spray, another stylist freebie, and stood in front of her closet again. Instead of the sweatshirt, she found herself tugging on a pair of nice jeans (that is, the ends weren't completely ragged). What else? A camel-colored button-up shirt that made a foil for her gingery hair—split ends and all. A coppery woven blazer since the sky looked a bit cool.

Yep. That did the trick. Jersey turned in front of the mirror, surprisingly self-conscious at the play of colors and tailored shapes that suited her tall figure. She wasn't a whale, exactly, but she wasn't a toothpick either. Somewhere in the vague "thirties" definition of average, which included a bit of spread and slide from a once-tight abdomen and slim hips.

But still. That was her truth anyway: Jersey Peterson, thirty-three. And yet still a woman under all those split ends and masculine-shaped ranger's digs.

She should probably look through her drawer for that coral pink lipstick, or at least some earrings, but the ranchers who frequented her little white clapboard church in their muddy boots wouldn't care one way or the other.

And yet. What if they did, or what if they didn't? This was her life, and as Taka said, she should live it to the full.

Jersey found the lipstick and tucked a simple New Mexican turquoise oval into each ear, gritting her teeth as she pushed the gold earring back through nearly closed holes in her earlobes. After all, how long had it been since she'd worn earrings? That '80s party Phyllis held at her house two years ago and those oversized, neon yellow bangles?

Jersey caught a glimpse of herself in the bedroom mirror as she pushed the top drawer closed: cheeks flushed and eyes bright. Her hair loose and glossy.

As if she were celebrating.

⁓

Jersey slammed her kitchen window shut and slid into her ancient Volkswagon—still boxy from mid-'90s design. It sported an extra feature that was worth every penny: automatically heated front seats. A godsend in the snowy winter months.

Phyllis's house lay just twelve minutes away—around a couple of bends, through some rich pastureland, and over a bumpy railroad track. The church though, took an extra twenty-five to reach—following a lonely ribbon of road that stretched endlessly through rolling Wyoming prairie. Power transformers, the only interruption of a perfectly vast horizon, lined up into the hazy distance like skeletal gingerbread men.

Jersey pulled up at the little white clapboard building in a thin forest of pines, distinctive only as a church by its silent pointed white steeple, and parked in a patch of dusty gravel. Phyllis got out beside her and shut the door, its sharp sound echoing across the grove of pines to the double outhouse.

"You okay, Phyllis?" Jersey paused on her way up the simple concrete front steps, just past the low metal bar where ranchers wiped their muddy boots before entering the church. "You just seem. . .upset today."

"Nah. Everything's fine." Phyllis gave a weak smile and patted Jersey's shoulder. "I'm just worried about Shorty."

"You, too, huh?" Jersey's gaze lingered on the side of Phyllis's short, curly 'do a minute longer, sizing her up.

"Yeah. Poor thing. Wait'll I get my hands on whoever did that." Phyllis avoided her eyes, twirling a fake pearl pendant. She flipped a strand of Jersey's hair a little too brightly. "And what about you, all dolled up. Look at that hair. I haven't seen you wear it down since. . .well, have I ever? What's the occasion?"

"Occasion? No occasion." Jersey touched her turquoise earring nervously. "Just trying to live out my truth. As Taka puts it."

"What truth?" Phyllis paused, halfway into the shadowy interior.

One shaft of light made the liquid blue-gray of her eyes stand out behind her glasses.

"That God lives." Jersey's words leaped unexpectedly from her mouth, surprising even herself. "And He lives in me."

Phyllis froze, and eyelashes, pale in the sunlight, blinked rapidly. "Hmph," she said. Sounding like Don when she'd turned in her last funding report.

Jersey pushed open the church door with a loud groan of weathered timbers, barnlike, and slipped into the hushed sanctuary. This was it—a sanctuary. No Sunday school rooms, no foyer. Not even a bathroom. Just a few rows of rough pine benches, a wooden altar table with a Bible, a podium, and a wooden cross made of old barn planks nailed to the back wall.

The simplicity of the place enchanted her—no, fed her. After all the clutter of job decisions and disappointments, the simple pine boards spoke security. Strength. Endurance. No ornaments, no fancy trappings. A God who came near, without fanfare, and humbled Himself to birth in a manger for animal feed.

A God who loved ranchers that wiped manure off their boots before entering His sanctuary and park rangers who crawled out kitchen windows on their way to church.

"That's the pastor, isn't it?" Phyllis whispered.

Jersey turned, wondering why everyone whispered. It must be the reverent hush, the sacred silence that spread out under the pines and beneath the rough wooden cross.

"Oh yeah. That's Pastor Jeff." Jersey reached out to shake his hand—a ruddy hand, calloused. A hand to match a tall and brawny frame, weather-lined face, and black eyes. Despite his name, Pastor Jeff Cox was Shoshone—and a plumber by trade.

"I told you he's good-lookin'," Phyllis whispered when he passed.

"Shh." Jersey scowled, smacking Phyllis's beige-pants-clad knee. "He's married, and so are you."

"Well, you aren't. What about that Mackenzie fella?"

"What?" Jersey gasped in horror. "Cut it out," she whispered fiercely. "He's twice my age!"

"No, he isn't. He's. . ." Phyllis paused, hand on her chin. "Okay. So maybe he is. But that doesn't mean anything. Sixty's not so old if you think about it." She poked Jersey's arm. "That is if Nelson doesn't walk into a wall when he sees you tomorrow, with your hair all down and all."

"Phyllis! We're in church. Quit!" Jersey hissed, putting a finger to her lips. "At least try to think about spiritual things, will you? Otherwise I'll drop you off by yourself at that giant First Baptist downtown next week with nothing but a Bible and a Bundt cake—and you know those ladies will put you right to work."

Phyllis pretended to zip her lips, affecting an exaggerated posture of horror.

⁓⁂⁓

The church had emptied, except for Pastor Jeff standing just outside the door, waiting to lock up with a plain padlock and chain. After all, what was there inside to steal? A couple of hymnbooks? But the church had been defaced once by a band of vandals, and only after that came the chain and then, reluctantly, the padlock.

Phyllis still sat there on the pew, staring down at her lap. Twisting her purse strap between shaking fingers.

"Phyllis," Jersey tentatively poked her arm, "what's wrong?"

Phyllis didn't answer. She just twisted the purse strap until Jersey thought it would pop off the metal hinge.

"What, the sermon?" Jersey ran a hand over her forehead, trying to understand. Some verses about God's amazing power to change lives, and the simple testimony of a rancher who prayed for salvation just minutes before he planned to turn an old cattle pistol on his head. "Or the music? Sorry. I know I can't sing, but I didn't know it was that bad."

Phyllis chuckled, but her eyes filled with tears. She looked away, face crumpling, and then buried her head in her hands. Shoulders shaking.

Out of the corner of her eye, Jersey could see Pastor Jeff lean inside the building, his face lined with worry and compassion, and then he lowered his forehead into a wrinkled hand. Eyes closed and free arm raised slightly toward Phyllis, lips moving in silent prayer.

"Phyllis?" Jersey tucked a tentative arm around Phyllis's shoulders, not sure what to say or do. Bungling butterfingers that she was some-times. "What's going on? I was kidding about the First Baptist thing, you know."

Phyllis sniffled and dug in her purse for a tissue, taking off her glasses. "I dreamed about her again," she finally managed through sob-tight breaths.

Jersey leaned closer to hear better. "Dreamed about who, Phyllis?"

Phyllis's face contorted again, and Jersey had to hold her breath to understand the words. "About...about my daughter. I saw her last night."

Jersey's mouth opened for the words to fly out, and at the last minute, she smacked her lips together. *Phyllis doesn't have a daughter.*

She had two sons—one fifteen and one seventeen. Both rosy brown boys with laughing eyes and black curly hair like their dad.

"Before I married Terrance," Phyllis whispered through a voice choked with grief. "I was nineteen years old. Mother said I was too young and Terrance was no good for me." She covered her face in white-knuckled hands. "And I believed her."

The bench creaked slightly as Phyllis rocked back and forth like the swaying pine boughs outside the window, painfully brilliant in a shaft of summer sun. "The nurses told me she wouldn't...feel a thing. That she wouldn't know...wouldn't..." She groaned, bending over double at the waist.

Jersey sat there like a chunk of granite, stupid, her eyes tear-glassed. Staring. Then she shook herself awake and hugged Phyllis tighter, letting their heads press together.

"It's okay, Phyllis," she whispered, tears streaking down her cheeks. "We all make mistakes. You were nineteen. What could you have known about life back then?"

Phyllis didn't answer, the graying threads in her caramel-colored hair standing out in ashen tones. "She'd be twenty-three years old, you know that?" She raised a wet face and turned pale eyes to Jersey. "A college graduate by now. Beautiful. Taller than me, probably, and eyes just like Terrance."

"Just about everybody's taller than you, Phyllis," Jersey said lightly, hoping she didn't sound flippant.

To her relief, Phyllis gave a brief smile before her face clouded again with fresh grief. "But I'll never know, and neither will she. Because I never gave her a chance."

Jersey swallowed hard, her heart beating in her throat as she searched for the words to say. To tell her own tale of agony—that began—and ended—much the same as Phyllis's but with a slightly different wrench of pain between the two.

"Phyllis, I know some of what you're talking about," Jersey whispered, forcing her tremors down her throat. "That's what my mom was calling about. I finally talked to her, and it wasn't pretty."

Phyllis didn't seem to hear. She pressed a trembling tissue to her eyes, rocking back and forth. "I took her life, her future. Everything. The nurses said she wasn't alive, really—that she was little more than a blob of tissue. But I felt her kick me. Here." She pressed tear-wet fingers across her abdomen. "She wanted to live, Jersey. Her heart was beating strong on the monitors. So strong I could almost feel its pounding in my own blood."

Without warning she looked up at Jersey with red, bleary eyes. "You've never done something like that, have you?"

Jersey's mouth went cotton-dry, and she thought she'd vomit. "No," she finally whispered, hugging herself with her free arm to keep from trembling. Hating herself for not being able to relate in just the way that would comfort Phyllis. "Not exactly."

Phyllis's eyelids fell closed. "I knew it."

"But I know what it feels like to lose a child." Jersey's lips felt so stiff she could hardly move them. "Don't assume that my life is any squeakier clean than yours. We've all done things we're sorry for."

Jersey saw, out of the corner of her eye, Pastor Jeff ease silently to a kneeling position in prayer, his hand covering his eyes. A gentle breeze made the pine walls around them groan lightly as if lifting up compassionate voices in sympathy, and a flutter of pine needles tickled the window glass.

"They told me my life would be better." Phyllis's voice came so soft and crushed that Jersey could barely hear. "But she *was* my life. I didn't know that then. And I still dream about her—even all these years later. The smell of the antiseptic. The hard table, and the nurse's cold hand squeezing mine. The frightened flutter in my belly, and the kick of her feet." She wheezed. "She knew, Jersey. I'm sure of it. And until the day I die, I'll never live down what I've done."

"Phyllis." Jersey's whisper seemed to echo against the hushed walls of the chapel. "God forgives."

She didn't reply, so Jersey laced her arm through hers. Drawing out a fresh tissue and wiping Phyllis's cheek. "God forgives. Do you believe me?"

Phyllis's shoulders jumped slightly as she shook her head. "God. My mother told me I'd go to hell for what I'd done."

Jersey winced. "For. . .for. . . ?"

"For getting pregnant before marriage. She called me all kinds of names. My dad threatened to beat me within an inch of my life. He told our church congregation I was a sinner, headed straight for hell, and I wasn't fit to set foot inside a church so long as I lived." Her breath contorted, pale eyelids fluttering closed. "I guess he's right, but I felt safe here for some reason." Her hand squeezed Jersey's. "Like maybe I could make it all right again somehow. But the dreams keep coming. Maybe that's my penance—God's way of punishing me when I dared to think I could go on with my life instead of paying for what I've done."

Jersey blinked, horrified. "But you said they wanted you to have the... operation." She licked her lips nervously, afraid to say the word *abortion* out loud. So harsh and raw it sounded.

"Sure they did. They said I ruined their ministry, and since my child was conceived in sin anyway and with a man of...well, a different race, the best thing I could do was finish the mess I'd started."

Jersey's mouth fell open despite her best efforts, and she took a deep breath and said a prayer for wisdom. Sense. Anything to keep from mangling what she wanted to say.

"Phyllis, your daughter didn't ruin your parents' ministry. And two wrongs certainly don't make a right, no matter what they told you." Her fingers gently massaged Phyllis's shoulder, and she wished she could draw out the ache like one drew out rattlesnake venom. "We all make mistakes. But God didn't see your daughter's life as a mistake. She was His creation. His joy. He loved her. And He loves her still." Jersey bit her lip as it wobbled. "Your parents called you a sinner, but they're forgetting that we're all sinners. Every one of us who's ever lived—except Jesus Himself."

Phyllis sniffled, playing with the tissue in her hand.

"What about Terrance's race? What about it? What about yours?" Jersey felt angry bile rise in her chest. "The Bible says nothing about marrying someone of a different race—only a different religion. If you think about it, we're all descended from the same Adam and Eve. Race is a human label—not a genetic one. Why, if you ask geneticists, most of them say there's actually no such thing as race anyway, since so many of the conditions are completely subjective. With the exception of a few familial markers, human DNA is all basically the same. We're the ones who like to build walls of assumption and slap labels on people."

Jersey stopped, sounding a bit like nerdy Taka. "Anyway, people don't go to hell for having abortions."

Phyllis raised her head. "No?"

"No way." Jersey stroked her fingers through a curl of Phyllis's hair.

"The Bible says people go to hell for one reason only: rejecting God's Son Jesus. Nothing more. Everything else He forgives entirely."

Phyllis sponged her face and twisted the limp tissue in her hands. "You said something a minute ago," she finally said, meeting Jersey's eyes. "You said God loves my daughter *still*. What did you mean by that?"

Jersey leaned back to look at her. "I mean she's alive, Phyllis. With Jesus. Where all people go who haven't rejected Him. Being loved by Him every moment."

Phyllis threw her head back and stared up at the peaked pine ceiling, tears streaming down her cheeks. "I don't believe that. There's no way that's possible."

"It is true." Jersey leaned forward, unafraid. "And if you believe in Him when you die, you'll see her again."

Phyllis covered her mouth with the crumpled tissue and wept into it, openmouthed.

"Come." Jersey started to her feet with a sudden burst of boldness. "Come pray with me. There at the altar, under the cross." She held out her hand. "I'll go with you."

"Not there. Not near the cross." Phyllis sobbed. "I couldn't."

"Yes you can. And you will. Come." Jersey offered her hand again. "Don't be afraid. He's not here to judge you but to save you. He loves you. He died for you. You'll see."

Phyllis hesitated, blotting her cheeks, and then got to her feet. Making her way shakily out of the narrow row of pews with Jersey. Up to the front of the church, boards creaking under their feet. A shaft of sunlight flickered fringes of pine along the glass. They got down on their knees by the altar, the faded wooden cross gazing down at them with outstretched arms.

"Why then, Jersey, is God sending me these dreams?" Phyllis whispered as she knelt there, her tears making dark circles on the pine floor. "Why doesn't He take them away if He loves me so much?"

Jersey wrapped her arm around Phyllis's shoulders, searching her tear-streaked face. "Maybe," she said softly, "God's trying to bring you to a place of peace. Did you ever think of that?" She glanced up at the cross. "To show you that He hasn't forgotten your precious daughter, and He hasn't forgotten you either. That He wants to do more than seal up the matter and never talk about it again. He wants to bring you healing. And more than that—life."

"Life." Phyllis's eyes blinked closed.

"Yes, life. Life and truth. New life with Him. I'm not the best example, maybe, but I know what it is to live again." And she bowed her head to pray.

Chapter 5

The first thing Nelson did was spill coffee all down the front of his shirt. He blinked down at Jersey like he'd seen a ghost.

"You'd better clean that up," said Phyllis from across the room. "This is the second time this week we've scrubbed coffee out of the carpet, and I'm not doing it again."

Nelson didn't move except to sponge his chin and dripping cup. "You're wearing perfume, Jersey."

"Yeah? So?"

"You never wear perfume. I thought you hated the stuff."

Jersey tucked a strand of hair behind her ear self-consciously. "Not all of it. I just had to find one I like. This one's a little more. . .natural. Less french poodle and more Off! Deep Woods." She shook a finger. "Which, by the way, I'm convinced actually attracts more mosquitoes than it repels."

"Your hair." A single drop of amber-brown dripped from the bottom of Nelson's mug. "You've never worn it like that."

"Like what?" Jersey averted her eyes. Since she couldn't roll on the floor and play dead like a possum, she could at least play dumb. It worked for other mammals; why not her?

Nelson's Adam's apple bobbed as he swallowed. "Sort of. . .down. Like. . .like that." He seemed to remember his coffee mug and shifted it to the other hand, shaking his coffee-wet fingers. "It's so long."

Out of the corner of her eye, she saw Phyllis shoot her a look. A smirky sort of "See? I told you so" look.

Jersey rolled her eyes, wondering if she'd been out of her mind to follow Taka's silly "live the truth" nonsense. Regardless, she didn't owe Nelson or anyone else an explanation. To be perfectly honest, the swish of her hair and the glint of earrings had made a surprising impression on even Jersey herself. She felt bold and confident. Radiant, even.

Who knows? Maybe next Sunday she'd do the unthinkable and wear heels to church.

Wait a second. Jersey craned her head over the bookshelf and gawked at the computer—which glowed back a cheerful blue screen. "What is this?" She marched over to the computer desk and stood there, hands on her hips. "The computer's working? Who fixed it? I thought Preet was on vacation."

"Don't look at me." Nelson seemed to jerk out of his stupor and fumble for a napkin, sponging the front of his ranger's shirt. He scrubbed at it in frustration and, when the beige circle didn't flinch, muttered some choice words under his breath and stomped back to the bathroom.

"Nope. Not me either." Phyllis shook her head, sipping a paper cup of coffee and staining the rim pinky-red with lipstick. "I don't do computers. But when I hit the power strip this morning by accident, it turned on."

Jersey grabbed the mouse and clicked and then let out a gasp as the start-up tones chimed. An image of a sunny field and then pretty little icons spilled across the cactus wallpaper. "The Internet works. It's never worked—except the first week we signed up with that new plan."

"Rodney?" She poked her head around the corner of the desk to see the stuffed cougar. "Did you fix it?"

Nelson tore a paper towel from the bathroom and poked his head out the open door. "Shh. I think he's shy about parading his technological prowess in public."

"His secret's safe with me."

Phyllis chuckled, taking another swig of her coffee. "Hey, what about that researcher guy? What's his name? Turk? Tack? I keep forgetting."

"Taka?" Jersey's hand froze on the mouse. "You think he did this?"

"Not him." Nelson grimaced and shut the bathroom door behind him. "That guy's a weirdo. Unless he did some kind of Chinese voodoo magic on it or something."

"He's Japanese, not Chinese." Jersey typed. "And I'm pretty sure Taka doesn't do voodoo."

"He had some weird stuff in that mug the other day. I'm just saying."

"Well, Taka couldn't have done it. He spent the night at the vet's office Saturday night, and Stacy over at the lake station said he checked in there early Sunday morning to do research. He's been there ever since."

"Well. The computer fairy then?" Nelson crossed his arms, shooting Jersey a cool look she couldn't interpret. "Since you know so much about Taka's whereabouts?"

"What?" Jersey spun around to face him. "What's that supposed to mean?"

"Whatever you think it means." Nelson eyed her coolly. "I guess you'll want to take that big tour group with Stacy then, since Taka's over there?"

Jersey slammed down the mouse and stood up, her eyes coming right to the bridge of Nelson's perfectly shaped, sun-browned nose. Tipping her hat back to see his eyes. "If you've got some notion about me and this researcher, forget it," she snapped. "He sleeps on vet benches, Nelson! He studies insect legs with decomposed hairs! And I can't stand people from. . .never mind." She threw up her hands. "Besides, what's it to you?"

Jersey was instantly aware of the quiet in the room and the unnatural hum of the computer. Phyllis must have slipped out to the front counter, silent as a muskrat slipping under a watery log.

Nelson crossed his arms stiffly over his chest, his brown ponytail curling down his back. "Maybe I'm wrong. But sometime I thought you and I might. . .you know. I thought you felt the same way."

Jersey's eyes popped, and she felt heat flood her face. "Nelson." She stuck her hands in her pockets, suddenly shy. "I had no idea. Why didn't you say something?"

Nelson seemed to draw himself up taller and stiffer. "Well, I am saying something."

Oh. My. Jersey stepped back, feeling woozy from lack of air. She reached awkwardly over Nelson and pushed open the sticky back window, wishing she'd tied her hair back up on her neck as she usually did. She tugged it over her shoulder, feeling the earring back snag on a strand. *Stupid earrings.*

"So?" Nelson turned, his hazel eyes blinking in an almost hard look. "Aren't you going to say anything?"

"Nelson. You're way younger than me." Jersey stuck her sweaty palms in her pockets.

"Oh. Like two years makes so much difference." He rolled unsmiling eyes.

"Three."

"Whatever."

Jersey put her hands on her forehead, feeling color slide up her face in red patches. "I. . .I don't know what to say. I think. . ."

Something crackled loud against Jersey's hip. She jumped, startled, and then reached for her walkie-talkie. "Sorry, Nelson. Gotta take this."

Nelson blew out his breath in irritation and turned his back while she depressed the button, tapping the toe of his boot.

"Jersey, this is Taka." Something sank in Jersey's stomach like too-greasy hash browns from that awful diner in Jackson Hole, and she looked up to find Nelson glaring at her. Color mounting in his cheeks.

"Go ahead, Taka." She turned slightly away from Nelson, keeping the volume loud and clear.

"I think I've got your poacher."

"You what?" Jersey shouted, and both Phyllis and Nelson whipped their heads around.

"I do a lot of tracking in remote places, and I spotted a white van parked way back in the woods. They had bows and arrows stacked everywhere. Guns. The works. And they seemed to be digging, using a metal detector."

"What, like for buried treasure?" Jersey spat, her heart pounding. "Did you call the police?"

"I got their license plate number through my binoculars and just called it in to the nearest ranger's station. They're on their way. They're. . ."

Jersey heard a muffling sound and a rush of staticky wind. "Taka? What's happening?" she hollered.

"The Park Service truck just showed up. Oh, look at this. The guys are running."

Phyllis and Nelson gathered around, heads together, as if listening to a football play-by-play over the radio. "What's going on? Tell us!" Jersey grabbed at her hat with her free hand.

"And. . .that's one down. The ranger got him. Make that two down. No, three. And they've got handcuffs. Wonder if it's the same people who shot Shorty." More wind, and Jersey leaned forward, straining to hear. "Local police is here, too. Good." Taka let out a sigh.

Jersey went limp, and she dropped into the computer chair. "Well done, Taka. Thanks."

She started to press off the walkie-talkie and then lifted it to her mouth. "Let me ask you something, Taka. Did you fix our computer?"

"Sorry?"

"Our computer. It's working."

"Huh. Funny. I thought it was on its last legs."

Jersey's heart pounded. "You didn't answer my question, techie."

"The police are here, Jersey. I've got to go." Static crackled. "And I'm not a techie. Google would laugh in my face if I showed them my fledgling computer programs."

~❦~

No sooner had Jersey pressed the OFF button than the office phone rang. Phyllis rushed to answer, and Jersey watched as her face morphed into a mask of gratitude then open-eyed shock. She scratched her head, screwing up her forehead.

"Gold, you say? You must be kidding."

Phyllis nodded and "uh-huh"ed on the phone, turning sideways while she talked and running a hand through her curly hair. "Well, I've never heard of any Jeremiah Wilde, or what did you say the lawyer's name was?—Wyatt Kelly?—to save my life. Sounds like a bunch of hooey to me." She shrugged. "But anyway, thanks for the message, Stacy. Seems like our researcher hit a home run."

Phyllis bobbed eyebrows at Jersey, and she looked away, face flaming.

"The poachers were after elk," said Phyllis, hanging up the phone. "And bison. They found two headless elk along the trail, like somebody had just hacked off the heads for trophies. The police are taking them into custody now. But here's the weirdest thing: They claim they were looking for gold."

"Gold? Ridiculous." Nelson wrinkled up his forehead with a look of derision.

"Yeah. A mother lode of it from the 1800s. Something about an old message called the Thoen Stone."

"Never heard of it." Nelson crossed his arms, still grumpy. Shooting dagger-eyed glances at Jersey.

"The Thoen Stone. Stacy says it's on display in Deadwood, South Dakota. I'd never heard of it either." Phyllis tipped her head. "Did you know that more drivers hit deer in South Dakota than in any other state?"

"You're a fountain of knowledge, Phyllis." Jersey swiveled around in the computer chair and tapped into the keyboard, scrolling through row after row of Internet sites. It felt sinfully easily, as if something were wrong. The computer had never worked without a healthy dose of help center calls, restarting, wire-untangling, kicking, and foaming at the mouth. "Look here, guys. The Thoen Stone."

Phyllis leaned over her shoulder, and Nelson craned his neck to see from where he stood.

Jersey skimmed the text. "So...two brothers found the message back in 1887, carved into a slab of sandstone. 'Come to these hills in 1833—seven of us,'" Jersey read off the screen. "'All dead but me, Ezra Kind. Got all the gold we could carry. Our ponies all got by the Indians. I have lost my gun and nothing to eat and—Indians hunting me.'"

Nelson marched forward and peered at the computer, not making eye contact with Jersey. "Wait a second. I have heard of this," he said. "Didn't they think the Indians took the gold and some settlers got it back a few years later?"

"The Sioux got it in the end." Jersey typed rapidly, opening zillions of tabs. "I remember this, too. The gold changed hands a bunch of times, and a guy named Kirby Crowder ended up with it somehow. The Sioux killed him and then reburied the gold, saying it was sacred."

"So that's what those poachers were after?" Phyllis raised an eyebrow. "Black Hills gold?"

Jersey typed faster, her mind spinning with wild images. She grabbed the mouse and clicked through a row of pages, feeling something shaky ripple in her stomach. "What did you say that other guy's name was? When you were talking on the phone?"

"Who, the Wyatt fellow?"

"No. The other one. Started with a *J*."

"Jeremiah Wilde. I've heard his name before. Why?"

Jersey opened a new page and skimmed the lines of text. "He used to work here as a park ranger in the early 1900s. I've seen his name on some of our history stuff. Maybe even a photo."

"What do you mean he worked here?" Nelson regarded her coldly.

"At Yellowstone. I remember his name because the fire back in '88 unearthed a bunch of artifacts that had been covered over by soil—lost, thrown away, whatever—and his name was on something."

Phyllis suddenly gasped. "The jar."

Jersey and Nelson turned.

"A firefighter in '88 found a jar with a note inside. They debated the authenticity of it for years—and I guess it got tabled when nobody could decide. The map didn't make any sense either, and it didn't lead to any gold."

"Jeremiah Wilde." Jersey's eyes glowed. "They put all his stuff in the museum, didn't they?"

"Some of his log books and diaries and things. I think I've seen them."

Nelson stuck his hands in his pockets. "He left a bunch of numbers in the last few pages that nobody can figure out. Most people think it's a mathematical game he was playing or some accounting that he didn't label."

Jersey typed some more, and she bent close to see a blurry photo in the museum archives. She clicked and zoomed closer, whispering the strange numbers to herself and shaking her head. "I don't get it." She scrolled down the page. "He died in 1903 when Theodore Roosevelt dedicated the park. And. . .that's it."

She turned back to the page and jotted down some numbers.

Nelson eyed her. "What, you're really going to try to figure this out?" He gave a snort of derisive laughter. His pride probably still injured.

"Maybe." Jersey shot him a frosty gaze.

Before Nelson could reply, the fax machine on the nearby counter jerked to life, buzzing and beeping—and then unceremoniously spit a sheet of paper into Phyllis's lap.

Phyllis jerked it up and read through the lines, her brow crinkling. "What the flip is this?" Phyllis turned the fax printout over. "I didn't invite them. Did you, Jersey?"

"Invite who?" Jersey reached for the paper, eyes still on the Thoen Stone website. "What are you talking about?"

"Living Hope Church of Pasadena," Phyllis read, following the line of type with her finger. "Something about a volunteer group. Just about everything else is in Greek or whatever crazy language this is."

"What?" Jersey yelped, grabbing the sheet. "Why in the world is this in Japanese?" She flipped the sheet over in disbelief, trying to match the English words and make sense of the fax. "I didn't contact them!"

" 'We are thankful for your kind invitation and would be happy to serve the National Park Service through volunteer work at Yellowstone Lake's ranger station, including road paving, fence building, and construction,' " Phyllis read aloud. " 'We will arrive on July eighth by bus at approximately six p.m.' "

"July eighth? That's tomorrow!" Jersey hollered.

"Isn't that the day the Oregon group was supposed to come?"

"Yes, but. . .but I didn't contact anybody for a replacement!" Jersey's voice rose to shrill tones as she flipped the fax over again. "There must be some mistake. Who in the world invited somebody from Pasadena?" She shook the paper. "Who are these people?"

As if in mockery, the fax began to move again. Churning and grinding. Vomiting curled sheets of printed paper.

Phyllis gingerly reached over and picked up the first sheet.

"Masao Fujimori, age sixty-five—and a bio," she read, her eyes as round as prairie dog holes. "Keiko Morisaku, age sixty-one." She shuffled to the next page. "Hiroshige Nakagawa, age eighty-three."

"Eighty-three?" Phyllis and Jersey yelped together.

"What? You're making this up." Nelson, still huffy, crossed behind them in angry strides and snatched the paper out of Phyllis's hand. "There's no way a bunch of geriatrics are going to do construction at the lake station. That's hard work."

The fax spit out another sheet, and Jersey grabbed it. "Kenji Sakamoto, age seventy-two." A photo of a bald man with a stiff smile. "Previous work experience: doctorate in literature, college professor."

"There's got to be some mistake." Jersey sorted through the stack as the fax machine continued to churn. "There's no way they'd be able to handle construction."

Phyllis thought a moment, leafing through the pages. "Pasadena. Isn't that where Caltech is?"

Something cold washed over Jersey like lake water filling up a leaky canoe. "Oh no. Tell me Taka didn't do this."

Christian. Japanese. Pasadena.

"Oh nooooo," Jersey groaned, covering her face with the sheaf of papers. "It must be Taka! I told him the Oregon group canceled, and maybe he wanted to. . .I don't know. Help us or something. But this is terrible!" She tossed the pages on the counter in frustration. "Having eighty-three-year-olds is going to be worse than no volunteers at all, you know that?"

Gold. Eighty-three-year-olds. Taka. It was too much, like a wild swirl of hailstones.

"I'm doing guided wilderness backpacking for the next three days." Nelson's jaw tightened stubbornly. "And I'm not canceling."

"Don't look at me." Phyllis shrugged. "My vacation time starts tomorrow. Terrance and I are going to Utah. Stacy's covering for me—remember?"

"Utah?" Jersey grabbed her head in both hands. "Come on, Phyllis! You can go to Utah anytime. Please."

"No way! Terrance's niece is getting married. We've already bought the tickets." Phyllis raised her arms helplessly. "Besides, I don't think this Japanese group is really coming. This was probably just Taka's brilliant idea to help you out."

"And what if they do come? I can't take them, Phyllis." Jersey squeezed her eyes closed. "I know it sounds horrible, but I. . ." She let out a tight breath. "I don't do Japanese people."

Phyllis's eyes bugged. "Excuse me?"

"I just don't. Trust me, okay? I have my reasons."

"Jersey." Phyllis put her hands on her hips and leaned forward, lowering her voice to a whisper. "What about all that race business you told me about yesterday?" She glared. "Were you making that up, too? Just to make me feel better?"

"Of course I wasn't making it up! It's true, and I meant every word. It's just. . ." She sighed. "Forget it."

"Jersey, you're the only one who's free. You were supposed to do the Oregon group anyway." Nelson ignored their private conversation and pulled on his sunglasses with sullen, jerky movements. "So have at it. Or let Taka do it, since he caused all this ruckus in the first place. But I'm not being responsible for a bunch of eighty-year-olds having heart attacks. Got it?"

"Hey." Jersey threw down the papers and marched over to Nelson, anger climbing up her neck. "Is that what this is about? Something you think that's happening between Taka and me? Well, it's not. And you didn't even give me a chance to tell you what I think about. . .well, you and me."

"Don't bother. I know what you're going to say anyway."

"How can you possibly say that?"

"Simple, Jersey." Nelson tipped his sunglasses down and met her gaze with a blazing, wounded look like she'd seen in Shorty's eyes. "If you'd wanted to say yes, you would have."

And Nelson dropped his sunglasses back over his eyes, banging the front door closed behind him.

Chapter 6

Jersey saw the line into the ranger's station door before she even parked the truck: an orderly queue of Asian seniors in fishing caps and sandals, carrying backpacks and bandanna-flagged walking sticks. Bedrolls tucked neatly under their arms. She jumped out of the truck and slammed the door, and instantly thirteen Japanese faces turned to her.

Jersey panicked, coming to a halt in the gravel. Keys still swinging in her hands.

She should wave. Say hi. Something.

Instead, every word fled like a mouse from an owl. She lurched past them into the cool interior of the ranger's station, cold sweat prickling under her hair and the back of her neck.

"Jersey! There you are." Stacy looked up from the guidebook she was stamping for the elderly man at the front of the line. "They've been waiting for you. Zack can help you take the boat across the lake, but he can't stay with them." She shot up an eyebrow quizzically. "You're taking the whole group?"

"Me? Um. . ." Jersey tried not to watch as the whole line of people turned from her to Stacy and back again. Whispering.

"Bathroom," Jersey said apologetically, darting out of the room.

Bathroom. Right. Jersey strode down the hall in a sort of blind panic, coming to a closed door and rattling the handle.

"Jersey?" Stacy poked her head around the corner, her chocolate-brown skin shining in the dim overhead light. "That's the supply closet. Bathroom's down that way. Remember?"

"Oh. Right." Jersey backed up, not quite sure where she was headed. She fumbled her way to the bathroom, knocking over a roll of toilet paper stacked on the back of the toilet. She leaned there against the back of the door, wishing fiercely that she could swap places with Phyllis for the week. She'd shake hands with wedding guests she didn't know, listen to

312

a lame band cover love songs from Air Supply, and put up with Utah's cholla cacti and bad drivers if she had to. Anything but this.

"Jersey?" Stacy rapped hesitantly at the door.

"I'm coming." Jersey jumped, grabbing a paper towel and wiping her sweaty forehead. "Sorry."

She swung the door open, practically knocking over petite Stacy.

"You okay?" Stacy looked up worriedly, putting a hand on Jersey's cheek. "You sick or something? You look terrible."

"Sorry," said Jersey again, leaning back in the bathroom to toss her paper towel in the trash. "I'm fine. It's just that. . ." She glanced out at the long line of Japanese volunteers, wondering how to put it all into words. "Did you know Jell-O's the official snack food of Utah?" she heard herself say instead.

"Huh?" Stacy's eyes bugged. "You're sick—or you've been visiting Phyllis's random trivia sites."

"They've probably never been to Yellowstone before, have they?" Jersey chewed her nails.

Stacy shook her head again. "I don't think so." She lowered her voice to a whisper. "I don't think most of them have even been camping."

My word. Jersey lowered her forehead into her hand and grimaced. "Fine. I'll do it. Okay? I'll take them." She shook a finger at Stacy. "But you'd better leave a note for Taka and tell him where we are and that he's in big trouble when I find him." She pushed her hat brim back and squared her shoulders. "Their English is good though?"

Stacy tipped her head in sympathy. "Hope you brought a dictionary."

"Wait a second. No. Don't they live here in the US? This should be an English-speaking group, right?"

Stacy lowered her voice to a whisper. "Not for some of the older generation. I mean, they can communicate basically, but English isn't their first language. They still carry on most of their lives in Japanese." She smiled. "Good luck, Jersey." And she patted Jersey's arm as she brushed past.

⁓

"Hello," Jersey said to the group, giving a hesitant half wave, half bow.

"Jersey Peterson?" asked the man in the fishing hat at the front of the line, holding up a crisply folded sheet of paper.

"*Hai.* Yes." Jersey felt silly throwing out her few Japanese words in a thick American-English accent. All nasal and open vowels. "I'm Jersey, and I'll be helping you while you're here at Yellowstone." She bit her lip and stood on tiptoe to see the end of the line, hoping she wouldn't offend them with her next question. "How many of you are. . .well, fluent in English?"

She needn't have asked. The man in the front grunted something in Japanese, and five people hesitantly raised their hands. He repeated his sentence through a series of whispers, one person to another, and two of the three lowered their hand.

Great. Three people who speak English fluently, maybe, and what am I supposed to do?

"Hold on a second." Jersey gave a bright smile and dialed Taka from the office phone, listening to it ring and endlessly ring. Not even voice mail.

Jersey let out a breath of exasperation and banged down the phone then forced herself to turn and face the group. "Well," she said, raising her arms helplessly. "Welcome to Yellowstone."

The man repeated her comment, and smiles broke down the line of people one by one. And like an oddly polite "wave" at a football game, they all bent in unison. A polite bow, heads tucked. Tipping the tops of their sun visors and baseball caps toward her in respect.

Jersey blinked in astonishment and gave a weak bow in return.

"Jersey," said the man at the front of the line again with a grin, gripping her hand between his two strong, sun-spotted ones and giving it a firm, hard shake. "Thank you. I'm Masao Fujimori. We heard you needed help, and so we're here. As soon as we got the word. Show us what we can do."

"You brought tents?" Jersey braced herself for their response. Some volunteer groups had come with nothing more than umbrellas, expecting the Hyatt Regency once they stepped off the bus.

All down the line a murmur of whispers and nodding. They raised backpacks rattling with tent stakes, and the line parted so Jersey could see a pile of colorful Gore-Tex bundles piled against the far wall. Coleman lanterns and sleeping bags and shiny new camping stoves. Snazzier stuff than most campers brought in, and all lashed together in perfect little geometric stacks.

Well. Huh. Taka must have sent a detailed list. Jersey shifted her weight to the other foot. "Water and food? Because we don't really have any way to provide meals." Another common volunteer mistake.

Man-in-the-Front gestured toward the window. "It's all boxed up in the bear-safe locker. Enough for five days. Maybe six."

"For everybody?"

"Hai." He tipped his head in another bow. "All ready to go. I'm on cook crew for lunch. Wanna join us?"

Huh. Well. "We'll see how the day goes." Jersey ran her hand through her hair, trying to think of any other stupid questions she ought to ask before she hauled them all onto the boat and across Lake Yellowstone.

"No food in the tents, right? No toothpaste. Not even a bottle of water. We're going into bear country. Are you ready for that?"

"Hai." He drummed his fingers on the desk as if in boredom and checked his watch. "Anything else?"

Jersey stared at him then straightened her hat and pointed to the door. "Well, come on then," she said with a burst of boldness. "Let's go to the lake."

Chapter 7

The distant dock shimmered in Yellowstone Lake under a thick stand of green pines, and Jersey watched as they pulled close to the land. A thin stretch of sand extended along the endless shore until it curved out of sight, and back in the dense woods she could spot a corner of the dilapidated old ranger's cabin. Nothing else, as far as she turned in all directions.

Zack maneuvered the boat close enough so that Jersey could jump to the dock and help passengers down one at a time and then help haul the food locker and bear-safe storage Dumpsters to the dock. They passed the bags and gear assembly style, and then Jersey jerked a thumb toward the cabin. "This is us, folks. Let's go. We'll set up your tents over here and start making lunch."

"We've got rotating duty schedules." Masao crossed his arms over his chest. "Cook duty and clean-up duty for every meal while we're here. Everyone else can do prep work for our first job."

"Tomorrow, right? You'll probably want to rest a bit before we get started."

"Rest?" Masao laughed and put his hands on his shoulders. "We've been sitting on a plane for hours and then a tour bus. The last thing we want to do is rest."

Wow. The last college group Jersey had worked with hadn't gotten their tents and gear set up until nearly nightfall. "Okay then. Let's clear the grounds of twigs and branches to prepare for tomorrow's work."

Masao nodded and barked a translation.

Jersey led the way off the dock and onto a patch of green grass, and then she gave a mock bow. "Welcome to the Lake Yellowstone Hilton."

An ancient wooden shutter that had been hanging by a rusted hinge suddenly crashed and fell into a tangle of old weeds, as if on cue.

To her surprise, the whole group chuckled and dug into their backpacks, snapping photos with their thousand-dollar Fuji and Sony cameras.

The first thing Jersey heard when she turned over in her sleeping bag at dawn was the sharp sound of shouts. Rhythmic shouts, punctuated by short grunts.

Bears? She rolled out of her sleeping bag, still in her thick flannel pajamas and long woven underwear, and dug frantically for her canister of bear spray. She jerked the zipper of her tent down and poked her head out.

And as soon as she did, her mouth dropped. There in the clearing by the cabin stood all thirteen volunteers in orderly rows—already dressed in hiking clothes and boots. Stretching their arms and leaning side to side first then over at the waist in cadenced beats.

Of course. Morning calisthenics. The kind millions of Japanese practiced at Toyota shops and via the daily national news channel NIIK.

Jersey felt like an idiot as she zipped her tent closed and felt around for clothes in her backpack. After all, the sun wasn't even up yet. Her back ached, and the muscles in her arms throbbed from hours of heavy work. Yes, work. No trash pickup or litter crews—not that rangers didn't bend over backward in grateful appreciation for those.

But these Japanese people.

Jersey fought the urge to flop back down in her sleeping bag from sheer exhaustion. Not only had they prepared a scrumptious lunch of Japanese noodles and vegetables, complete with hot green tea, but they'd picked the entire grounds clean of pinecones and branches in. . .oh, less than two hours.

For the remainder of the day Jersey had jumped ahead of them from task to task: tearing out a heavy log horse fence, leveling a patch of uneven ground in backbreaking wheelbarrows, and stripping all the rotting wood trim from the old cabin.

Jersey had dozed off around the campfire.

"I'm a ski instructor," one of the sixty-something women had said in a chipper voice as she poured Jersey another cup of steaming green tea. "Too bad it isn't ski season in Wyoming."

And now they stood with their arms up, shouting the calls for group calisthenics before the sun had even risen through the pines.

Before Jersey could pull on her jeans, she heard the rattle of dishes and food lockers, and the scent of propane wafted across the pine-scented air. They were already making breakfast—and Ranger Jersey wasn't even out of bed yet.

Jersey groaned and covered her head with her pillow, determined to throttle Taka next time she saw him.

❧

She needn't have worried. Just before noon on the third day he sauntered over in hiking gear, piled to the brim with bags of research stuff. A tin cup dangled from his backpack, and he'd wrapped a bandanna around his sweaty forehead.

Jersey was up to her knees in dirt and sawdust, helping two of the volunteers saw an enormous pine trunk into a flat surface for a table, when she spotted him coming up the wooden trail.

"Well, well, well." She wiped her dirty hands smugly against her pants and strode over. "More research?"

"No, I'm here to help. Didn't you get my e-mail?"

"What e-mail?"

"You sent me the numbers you copied from Jeremiah Wilde's logbook, and I wrote you back."

"Wait a second." Jersey stared at Taka then at the lake. "How did you get here? Did you walk?" She shielded her eyes but saw no boat.

"Sure. Following the elk routes." He took off his glasses and wiped them. "So how's it going?"

"Going?" Jersey repeated, not sure how to answer his question. "Taka, they're machines. I've run out of building supplies twice. I'm not even sure we have enough work for them." She leaned back against a tree, letting the breeze cool her sweaty neck. "I'll tell you one thing. It's sure changed my perception of what senior groups can do."

"Why, you didn't think they were capable?" Taka squatted down and picked at something on a piece of pine bark with his fingernail.

"Of course not. It's just. . .wow. They're amazing." She tucked her hair back up in its bun. Which, by the way, she'd actually braided neatly first—rather than stuffing it in its usual messy knot with strands flying everywhere.

Taka must have seen it because his eyes traveled briefly to the nape of her neck with a quick flicker of approval before darting back to the tree bark. He lifted the shaggy chunk ever so carefully and then dug for a magnifying glass. "Look. *Dendroctonus ponderosae* larvae."

"Gross. No." Jersey wrinkled her nose and stepped away. "Well, thanks anyway for inviting this group. We really needed this work done, you know."

"I know." Taka poked his eye close to the magnifying glass. "Although I guess Japanese volunteers weren't your first pick, huh?"

"Excuse me?"

"I hear through the grapevine that you weren't crazy about dealing with a Japanese tour group. Why, do we send you bad tourists?" He looked up briefly.

"No, Taka. It's not that." She sighed and squatted down on her heels next to him.

"Then what is it?" He scraped at the bark again with a blade of grass.

"You want to know?"

"Yes." He put the magnifying glass down and faced her.

"Fine." She crossed her arms. "My grandfather was a POW during World War II, and he almost didn't make it." Her eyes filled with tears as she looked away. "You should have seen him when he returned. A skeleton. Sunken eyes and torture wounds." She snapped a pine needle between her fingers. "My family says he was never the same after that."

Taka studied her a moment with gentle eyes. "I'm sorry," he finally said, folding up his magnifying glass and dropping it back in his bag. A cool breeze from the lake rustled his hair, making it fall in his eyes. "I'm truly very sorry, Jersey."

He plucked at some blades of grass. "I remember when I first understood about the war. Years ago." He let out his breath and sat in quiet silence a long while as if remembering. "My grandfather used to build model planes with me back in Fukushima. Very good ones. I loved to help him."

"Hence your knowledge of taxidermied squirrel repair." A light came on. "Like airplane models."

"Exactly. I asked my grandfather about the war. About the planes we were building. Japanese war planes." Taka swallowed. A mosquito floated through the air, ghostlike, and he barely moved to swat it away. " 'Japan didn't really do that, did they?' " I asked him. " 'We didn't really try to take over the nations of the world one by one, did we? It's a lie. I don't believe we would do something so evil as that.' "

Taka shifted on the grass, his face still downturned. "Every time we built planes I asked him. Until one day he smashed our plane in anger, leaving broken splinters all over the low table where we knelt."

He stayed silent a long time, playing with the grass that tickled his jeans. "He apologized and offered to help me build a new plane, but I'd lost interest. I refused as politely as I could—always giving some excuse or other. For I'd lost my heart."

Jersey bit her lips. "So you see where I'm coming from?"

"Yes." Taka raised his face slowly. "But you're not the only one who suffered unjustly from the war, Jersey. Nor your grandfather."

She tipped her head and waited for him to continue.

"My mother was a prisoner here."

"Here?"

"Right here, as a matter of fact."

Jersey looked at him as if he'd lost his marbles. "I don't follow."

"In one of the Civilian Conversation Corps buildings here in Yellowstone National Park."

Jersey rocked forward and put her hand on the grass to steady herself. "Wait a second. You mean your mom was held here?" She dropped her voice. "During the war?" She squinted at Taka in disbelief. "Was she an American citizen?"

"I'm an American citizen." Taka's head came up, and his voice sounded harsh in her ears. "I'm both Japanese and American. I have dual citizenship. But I chose to stay in Fukushima after I heard how Americans treated my mother." His eyes snapped. "She was a child then, Jersey. No more than three or four years old. But because she was Japanese, she and her family were rounded up and jailed like prisoners just a few miles from here." A muscle in his jaw tightened. "Believe me, Yellowstone was the last place I wanted to come to do my research. But it was the only place left after I applied to all the others. So you'll pardon me if I harbor a few prejudices of my own."

Jersey opened her mouth to reply, in pity and in indignation, when Masao spotted Taka through the pines. He put down his saw and threw up both hands in delight, grinning and waving a handkerchief for Taka to see.

Taka stood up abruptly and strode over to Masao, greeting him in effusive Japanese and bowing repeatedly.

She crouched there among the pines, watching him go. Picturing Taka's mother as a little tear-streaked toddler, boarding a ship bound for Fukushima. Leaving the snowcapped mountains of Yellowstone behind her as a dark and frightening dream.

⁓⁂⁓

Between the hauling and the machete whacking and sanding, Jersey didn't have a single moment to speak to Taka until nightfall of the following day. He'd politely refilled her teacup, and she'd equally politely thanked him in front of the group for organizing the volunteer team.

They'd fished and fried cutthroat trout—ahem, *Oncorhynchus clarkii*—and Jersey was elbow-deep in dirty plastic bowls when Taka tapped her arm with the blunt end of a chopstick.

"Taka." Jersey looked up. "Thanks for the fish tutorial." She said it partially in jest, as he'd rattled on for nearly twenty minutes about some special predator-prey relationship with the bull trout that was supposedly key to "ecosystem integrity"—and how the species name "clarki" came from Lewis and Clark's 1804–1806 expedition into the Northwest.

He'd translated it of course, into Japanese, which took another twenty minutes.

"Fish tutorial?" Taka blinked rapidly. "Oh that." He gave a hint of a smile. "No problem. Can you walk with me?"

"Now? I'm finishing dishes."

"Ah." Taka shrugged. "You've done enough. Come on." And he started down toward the dock.

Jersey dried her hands on a towel and followed him. The sun was setting, slipping below the horizon in a blaze of orange. It sank like a dying fire, glittering on the lake water, until it disappeared in a wash of starry deep blue. They sat down on the dock, not speaking, and watched fish jump in the dark lake waters.

"You're doing great with the team, Jersey." Taka spoke without looking up.

She turned, wrinkling her nose at the stench of bug spray that wafted from his direction. He reeked of DEET and chemical repellant.

"I didn't know if you'd be able to deal with the language barrier, but you're doing just fine." He flicked a bug off his shirt. "Even if you have been avoiding me."

"No I haven't."

"Yes you have. And it's probably my fault. I'm sorry." Taka reached up to smack a whiny mosquito. "There's no excuse for prejudice of any kind—regardless of what happened to my mother. You didn't do it to her."

"No." Jersey didn't know what to say. If only it were so simple to release years of mistrust.

Jersey crossed her blue-jeaned legs on the dock, gazing up at a strip of frosty green sky on the horizon. Instead of darkening with the setting sun, it shimmered there, stretching pale arms the length of the black, pine-studded horizon.

Taka was looking at it, too. "Aurora borealis?" he gasped, jerking his glasses straight to see better. "I can't believe it. Our latitude isn't exactly conducive to sightings, is it? Most aurorae occur in the auroral zone, typically three to six degrees in latitudinal extent—normally ten to twenty degrees from the earth's magnetic pole. The pole, that is, defined by the axis of the magnetic dipole."

"Aurorae?" Jersey scrunched an eyebrow. "You're making this up as you go, aren't you?"

"Of course not. That's the plural from the Latin. You studied Latin, correct? During a geomagnetic storm, however, this auroral zone may expand to lower latitudes, including the one represented here, no?"

Jersey sank her head into her knees in exasperation. "How am I supposed to answer that?" she mumbled, rocking her head back and forth.

They lapsed into momentary silence on the creaking dock, interrupted only by the lapping of water on the pilings and the occasional whine of a mosquito and subsequent slap.

Jersey watched as the glow misted and spread, rippling around the edges like an enormous gauze curtain of filmy ghost-green. Lances of palest green, nearly white, pierced the starry sky like a searchlight, stretching over the black lake waters and shimmering, dancing, on their darkened surfaces.

A fish jumped, sending out sparkling black rings dappled with green.

"What does the *T* stand for?" Taka turned to Jersey suddenly and without warning, his whole face a wash of palest green.

"What *T*?" Jersey glanced at him uncomfortably.

"The wooden *T* you used to wear around your neck on a chain." Taka gestured, his voice uncharacteristically soft. "Where is it?"

Jersey didn't answer. She looked out over the lake and drew her feet up, stiffening a bit in the night breeze. "My son's name," she finally said, drawing the delicate cord from her pocket. "The cord broke, but. . .I had a son once."

She waited for Taka to grimace in displeasure or scoot away, but he said nothing. Didn't move. Black eyes fixed gently on her face.

Jersey started to put the necklace back in her pocket, but Taka reached out instead.

"Let me fix your necklace," he said softly. "I'm good at fixing things."

Jersey hesitated then handed him the necklace in a crumpled pile. Almost afraid to release it into someone else's hand.

"I was seventeen. My boyfriend was nineteen, and. . ." Jersey looked down at the dock, stroking a weather-worn crack in the wood with her thumbnail. "My family's a bunch of prominent designers in Chicago, and they didn't approve. They told me to. . .to get rid of my child."

"Designers?"

"Fashion designers. Haven't you ever heard of the Ana Peterson line?"

"Of course, but you can't mean. . ." Taka's mouth wobbled open.

"Yes. The same." Jersey scratched at a spot on the knee of her pants. "Ana's my mom. A famous runway model for years. My dad was her tailor, and now my twin sisters and younger brother are all models and designers. My dad makes a fortune in bespoke suits that cost tens of thousands of dollars each—all imported thread and fancy stitching. A hand-carved button in his shop on the Magnificent Mile costs two hundred bucks."

Taka leaned back on his hands, sizing her up. "You didn't care for their way of life?"

"Cocktail parties and fashion shows and inflated egos? No thanks." Jersey shook her head. "One of my sisters is still struggling with anorexia, last I heard, and my brother's trying to hide his drug habit. I don't look like them, all perfect and thin and creamy-complexioned, and they let me know it."

She looked down at her hands, her nails clipped close and clean. The thin coat of sheer polish she'd swiped on before the trip already beginning to chip along the edges.

"So what if you don't look like them? You say it as if you regret it. But you don't need to. You're you, Jersey. There's nothing wrong with that, and you don't need to apologize."

"I'm not apologizing." Jersey's voice came out a little more snappishly than she intended. "But I didn't exactly enjoy being called 'the ugly duckling' or told to suck in my gut so I could fit in something frilly like my two dainty sisters. My mom wanted me to get a nose job when I turned fourteen. I refused."

"Good for you." Taka lifted his chin.

"Yeah, well. That's easy for you to say."

Taka didn't speak for a second, and Jersey thought the conversation was over. But when she glanced over at him again, his look had darkened.

"It's not easy for me to say," he said stiffly, sitting up straight and crossing his arms. "You don't know my past."

"And you don't know mine." Jersey faced him, feeling anger flare up. "It's always easy to judge someone else from the outside of a situation, isn't it?"

"I'm not judging you." Taka raised his voice slightly—a first for him.

She turned huffily back to the northern lights, spreading misty green fingers through the pines, and watched the colors shimmer and stretch across the lake water.

"My mother was a seamstress," Taka began in a husky, faraway voice that told Jersey she was about to hear something deep. "I told you that. Who knows—maybe she even sewed some of your father's suits?"

Jersey's shoulders jumped in silent laughter at the thought. "Nah. They were mostly from New York. But I like the thought."

Taka scooted across the wooden boards next to her, dangling his socked feet over the edge. One shoulder brushing hers. She scooted away, but one long strand of her hair stayed stuck to his sleeve.

"She was an amazing seamstress. The way her hands moved with the needle, the way she pulled the thread through the fabric in a beautiful straight line, shining like. . .like one of your hairs when the sun hits it." He glanced at her with an unexpected fond expression, his eyes faraway. "And my father. He also worked with beauty."

"How so?"

"His family descends from one of the most respected houses of flower schools in all Japan—called Ikenobo. They've been practicing flower arranging for nearly five hundred years. *Ikebana*, it's called. The art of giving life to flowers so that they create poetry and symmetry with nature. My mother was proud to marry him because, being rather highborn herself, it was an honor to align her family with a man descended from the Ikenobo."

Jersey swung her feet, and her toes felt weightless. Down below her the water swirled in surprising tones of jade, not quite close enough to touch.

"And then my father did the unthinkable: he converted to Christianity."

Taka put a hand up to fix his glasses, and Jersey looked up in surprise at his calm, even emotionless tone.

"Worse yet, he converted because of a friendship he struck up with an American GI after the war, which made him more than a mere embarrassment. It made him a deserter, consorting with the enemy and rejecting his family's religious beliefs for those of a foreign invader. My mother was mortified with shame. She wept; she could scarcely show her face in public."

Jersey bristled at the words *enemy* and *foreign invader*.

"In his blinding fanaticism, as some might call it, he turned his whole style of art on its head—to the horror, or perhaps fascination, of the ikebana schools. Instead of the traditional Buddhist expressions of the beauty of nature, or the relationship between heaven, earth, and man, he created something new: an ikebana style that depicted the Gospel and the fall of man."

Jersey's eyes shot up in the darkness. "Huh?"

"He made incredible displays where the viewer could turn at different angles and see a cross, for example—as if carelessly formed between the leaves. Or a crown of thorns that bridged the gap between the traditional heaven, *ten*, and man, *jin*. He was magnificent. He used the best rare flowers, the most precise calculations and formulas for angles and leaves and stems—poring over them for hours. He knew it all, and he decided to use his medium as a mouthpiece to the world, turning his new heart and mind into his art."

"And what happened?" Jersey leaned forward.

"He was forced out of his position in disgrace. The Ikenobo sensei said he'd defied all the most cherished tenets of ikebana, and he worked a salaryman's job at a computer store chain until my mother's death."

Jersey sucked in her breath, not having the courage to ask.

"She threw herself under a train. The traditional method of suicide in Japan."

"Taka." Jersey shook her head. "I'm so sorry."

"Me, too." Taka sighed. "But. . .that's my story. Like my dad, I've thrown all my caution to the wind." He imitated a plane crashing. "All of my research is about one thing: migration. And my thesis, as it did with my kangaroo studies, leads to creation by intelligent design as opposed to the traditional evolutionary theories of order from chaos. I'll be laughed off the planet and ridiculed as a crazy man, but I can prove my points with any biochemist out there."

A stray bit of cattail fluff fluttered from one chunk of his hair. "What do I care? That's the way of the cross, Jersey. Living out your truth with all your being. And it has a cost. I lost my mother, and you lost your son."

Jersey hesitated, as if deciding whether or not to speak. "I didn't have the abortion like they ordered, if that's what you're thinking." She drew her knees up and hugged them, feeling a pain through her chest as she remembered Phyllis's tears. "I left town and lived with a friend until he was born."

"So how old is he now?"

"He's...passed away, Taka." Jersey's words came so softly she wondered if he'd heard them. "He was born with some pretty severe health issues, and I put him up for adoption. My boyfriend wanted nothing to do with either of us once he heard I was pregnant and especially not after I told him the baby wasn't well. My parents were scandalized when they heard I'd let him live. I was seventeen, without even a high school diploma. What could I do?"

Jersey's knuckles tightened against the rough wood of the dock. "But I couldn't take his life. I couldn't. He had as much right to live as I did, and if I hadn't slept with my boyfriend, he wouldn't be in this predicament. But he passed away anyway. The adoption agency let me know about two years ago."

She sighed. "That's what my mom was calling me about. She said to tell the agency to quit calling our home because it was bad publicity. I don't live there anymore anyway."

Taka turned to her, his face an ugly green in the glowing light. "You lived your truth, Jersey."

"I didn't even know God then, Taka." Jersey shook her head and gave a light laugh. "I didn't know anything. I read the Bible some, but I was clueless."

"But you knew what was right, and you stood by it. He was guiding you even then, you know that?"

Jersey drew in a shuddering breath, willing herself not to cry.

Taka touched her shoulder lightly, the only time she remembered him ever touching her.

"You did what my father did. *Kamikaze.*"

Jersey wiped her cheek. "Excuse me?"

"The cry of Japanese soldiers and pilots to fight to the death, if I may borrow an expression from a truly tragic war. 'Crash and burn,' in modern speak. Living out what's right, though it costs you everything you have. The Gospel is like that. Jesus says it'll cost you your entire life, but not many people seem to believe Him."

Taka shrugged. "It's what you do with your job every day—protecting one little corner of the environment and teaching people to do the same. It doesn't matter if they listen. It matters that you tell them. Because it's the truth."

Jersey picked at a broken piece of plank, her breath held tightly inside as if afraid to exhale and forget his words. "Yeah. Well." She tossed a broken wood splinter in the water. "It doesn't bring my son back, does it?"

"No, but you did the right thing. You gave him life." Taka smiled. "And those kids with health problems and special needs teach us so much." He leaned back on one arm and took off his glasses, massaging his face with his free hand. "There was one kid I'll never forget."

"Oh yeah. You did some fostering or something, right?"

"On and off for about six years—for kids with special needs and health issues. I'd do it again if I wasn't stuck out in the field for days at a time." He put his glasses back on. "And if I had my neurosurgery and biomedical student roommates again. They were great with medical stuff. I never needed a doctor."

"I have to hand it to you, Taka. You're sure different." Jersey shook her head.

"Why? I think more people should dare to be different, Jersey. What else do I have to do with my life anyway?" He leaned back on his hands. "All those kids were special. But that one was something extraordinary. I wish you could have met him, Jersey. He was just. . .I don't know. Alive. He reminds me of you somehow." Taka spread his fingers wide. "His eyes had this *life*, this. . .this fire. He wanted to live, conquer, explore."

"Where is he now?"

"He passed away from his health problems." Taka's voice sounded sad. "He'd just turned two—and I'd kept him almost from birth."

Jersey turned suddenly, an odd feeling welling up in her chest. "What was his health problem?"

"Spina bifida. A really severe case." Taka bit his lips. "Poor guy. Never really had a chance. Couldn't walk, probably never would."

"My son had spina bifida."

"Really? So you know about it then."

"Of course. It's a neural tube defect—a problem with the spinal column. And even with surgery, it's not really cured."

He looked away. "He didn't make it through the last surgery."

Jersey's palms felt sweaty suddenly, and she wiped them against the knees of her jeans. "You said he was two years old when he passed away?"

"Right. Just turned two that November."

A charge of cold electricity passed through Jersey's stomach, and her mouth felt dry. "November what?"

"November third. Why?"

Jersey had to grab on to the side of the dock to keep from lurching sideways into the water.

"Jersey?" Taka reached out to steady her arm. "You don't think. . ." Taka's face morphed into a blank mask of shock, and then he shook his head. "No way," he chuckled. "It's a nice thought, but it's simply not possible."

"How long ago did you foster him?" Jersey tried to keep her voice calm.

"Oh, years ago." Taka waved it away with his hand. "I was a young guy still doing my first master's. Around twenty-three, I guess. So maybe. . . fourteen years? Something like that."

Jersey started to count off on her fingers. "Wait. You're thirty-seven?"

"That sounds right."

"You don't look thirty-seven."

"Neither do you."

"Because I'm *not*." Jersey resumed counting rather coldly and then grabbed Taka's arm with shaky fingers. "Fourteen years ago, you say? You can't mean that."

"Sure. I studied the chemical composition of the planets and various chemical processes and reactions at work in the formation of rocks and soils."

Jersey waved a hand in front of his face. "Taka. Where did you foster this child?"

"It was through a private organization, Jersey. Listen to me. There's no way." He brushed a strand of hair around her ear. "Although his name did start with a *T* now that you mention it. But he couldn't have been your son. He was Japanese."

Jersey's face went white, and she felt everything spin—the green glow in the sky, the stars, the water, everything. A blur of color and brilliance. Shooting stars exploding around her head so that she could hardly think.

She felt her lips moving, slowly, like they carried a heavy weight. "My boyfriend was Japanese, Taka. His name was Hiroyuki."

Taka stared. Glasses crooked. He didn't bother to reach up and fix them.

Jersey tried to speak again, but her voice came in ragged gasps. "And I named our baby Tadashi."

"Which means honest and sincere." Taka seemed to break from his stupor, and he reached clumsily into his pocket and pulled out his fat, battered, stained wallet. Fat from business cards and pressed leaves and notes scrawled with logarithms and scientific names and a copy of the numbers in Jeremiah Wilde's logbook. Spilling them across the deck.

He thumbed through the blistered plastic pages of his wallet, which looked like he'd bargained for it at a secondhand shop, and stopped on a photo. "Here," he said, holding it up for her to see. "See for yourself."

Jersey froze there, terrified, and then reached for the wallet. She turned the faded photo up in the frosty overhead glow.

Jersey sat alone on the sand, knees drawn up, when the sun spread pale pink light across the horizon, turning the black pines a smoky gray. Mist rose up from the lake like clouds, impossibilities—hovering just over the water.

She'd left Taka there on the dock in the middle of the aurora and found a spot on the beach by herself. Not wanting to speak another word.

She'd watched the sky flow like green rivers, streaking over the lake, and then softly fold into itself and fade into the silent black of night. The green glow had slowly died back into stars and pines like a retreating elk, its life and energy spilling out from an ignominious arrow wound.

The magic had vanished, withdrawn.

Except Taka's words. His story, too preposterous to be true. And the little photo of a boy with dark eyes who had, by some miracle, her dimpled chin. Her ears that stuck out, her heart-shaped birthmark.

Jersey's nose was stuffy from tears as she shuffled her bare feet against the sand, squeezing it between her toes. She slapped at mosquitoes who were so intent on human blood that they stung her flesh through her long-sleeved ranger's shirt, a gray cotton undershirt, and a thick layer of supposedly noxious DEET repellent that seemed no more threatening to mosquitoes than strawberry jam.

Taka had held her child.

It seemed improbable—that fourteen years ago the story of her own son would come back to her, like a message in a bottle chucked in the vast waters of Yellowstone Lake.

And yet not so improbable after all. It wasn't like people were breaking down the doors of adoption and foster agencies to take children with severe special needs. Children that may never live more than a few years, or children who might never speak or walk.

Perhaps Taka was the only one willing.

Jersey was sure of one thing: it was Tadashi, all right. His pale skin and thick black hair, and the little heart-shaped birthmark on his upper arm. His curved black eyes and long lashes.

Jersey had memorized them—memorized his milky baby-powder scent—as a final good-bye before the nurses whisked him away. Trusting him to a God she'd only met in bits and pieces, like scattered stones from a mosaic that depicted nothing until ordered and shaped.

Her son had been loved. Fed. Cared for. Given medical care. And now—what else was there to say except thanks?

Jersey bowed her head there on the beach and tried to pray, feeling the breeze pick up as peachy light flowed across the water. Her heart still felt empty, a Tadashi-shaped hole, but she could embrace it now. Could kiss it and let it go, like one of the broken cattail fronds floating on glassy ripples. Farther and farther, borne on a strength not her own. Shifting softly into the misty distance until she could no longer see it.

"Now you know," she'd whispered, tear-choked. *"Why I vowed I'd never trust Japanese people again. Hiroyuki was Japanese. And he left me."*

"I am Japanese," Taka had said, drawing himself up. His eyes black and luminous. *"And I didn't leave your son."*

The beach smelled of sand and water, of moist pines and lingering smoke.

Jersey rested her head on her knees, listening to distant trumpeter swans cry out to the spreading glow of morning.

Chapter 8

I think I've figured it out." Taka held out a piece of paper full of mathematical scribbles—covering both sides of the page.

Jersey looked up from her bowl of cool *soba* noodles and swatted away gnats. The sun was sinking gold on the horizon, and she'd just mastered the art of lifting a noodle with clumsy chopsticks.

"You've figured what out?" She turned in her folding chair and put her bowl down, bobbing her head in a slight bow to the volunteers she was chatting with.

"The numbers in Jeremiah Wilde's logbook." Taka squatted next to her and pointed to the paper. "I believe he wrote them intentionally, but I need to ask a few more questions to explore my theory fully."

"Shoot." Jersey crammed a mouthful of noodles into her mouth, relishing the flavors of ginger and green onion in a cold brown dipping sauce. The thin buckwheat noodles were chewy and flavorful, refreshing. If she sold soba on the streets during Wyoming's ninety-degree summer heat waves, she wouldn't need Ezra Kind's gold.

"Tell me something. When did Jeremiah Wilde die?"

Jersey wiped her mouth on a napkin and put down her chopsticks, reaching for her cup of green tea before speaking. "In 1903."

"After President Theodore Roosevelt dedicated the park in April, right?"

"Right. The info I have says he died of a snakebite just a week later."

"A week, huh?" Taka rubbed his jaw and sat back on his heels.

Jersey dug a gnat out of her hot green tea with her finger and then shook her hand from the searing heat. She sucked on the tip of her finger. "What are you getting at, Taka?"

Taka picked up a notebook and flipped through pages, each one crammed from top to bottom with tiny mathematical calculations.

"Did you do all that?" Jersey lifted a page in horror. "I only sent you the numbers a couple days ago."

"This? Yeah." Taka shrugged, adjusting his nerdy glasses. "Observe." He drew a perfect graph on his paper with a thin, clear plastic slide rule and began carefully plotting points.

Jersey sipped her tea in silence as he flipped back to his calculations, comparing numbers, and then dotted new points on the graph. "Connect the dots?" she raised an eyebrow.

"It's a matrix code." Taka evened his slide rule, sticking his tongue out slightly as he edged it into place.

"What, Jeremiah Wilde's numbers?" Jersey jerked her head up.

"An odd one, but I think I've solved it." He pointed to the pages of calculations. "Instead of replacing a letter or a symbol one at a time, a matrix code replaces groups of letters—which is much more difficult to solve than a traditional numerical code."

Taka drew another point on the graph and connected it with a straight line, using his slide rule for a straight edge. "Jeremiah didn't leave a written message using letters. He created a list of points to plot on a graph."

Jersey leaned forward. "As in. . .a location?"

"Precisely." Taka drew in two more dots, and suddenly the points on the graph began to curve. Straight on the sides and domed at the top, like a candy cane. An arrow, and a small rectangle below.

"Oh my goodness." Jersey's pulse raced, and she nearly dropped her tea as she rushed to set it down on the grass. "Is it what I'm thinking?"

"You tell me." Taka drew three more points, completing the curve and continuing downward with another straight line. Making a squared-off arch with thick bases.

"The Roosevelt Arch." Jersey's heart stood still.

Taka raised his head and evenly met her gaze. "Exactly."

⸺⁂⸺

"So what's with all the questions about when Jeremiah Wilde died?" Jersey lifted her paddle in the rust-gold sunset, coppery sparks glittering in the last rays of sun over Yellowstone Lake. The nearest Park Service speedboat lay just a few miles to the east, and Jersey couldn't row fast enough.

"It goes along with my theory." Taka fumbled with the paddle, and his life jacket came open again. He shifted his paddle awkwardly to the other hand and stuffed the two halves of the plastic buckle together again. He leaned too far, and the canoe shifted.

"Watch it, will you?" Jersey grabbed the side of the canoe, nearly dropping her paddle. "These things can flip on a dime. And with the cold lake temps, you've got about. . .oh, ten minutes to get out before hypothermia sets in."

"Sorry." Taka fixed his lake-water-spattered glasses.

"Haven't you ever canoed before?" Jersey laid her paddle carefully across the canoe and reached behind her, tugging his buckle closed.

"Me? No." Taka flashed an embarrassed smile.

"So you can solve matrix codes and sew and ride a unicycle, but not paddle."

"I guess." Taka reached clumsily for his paddle. "I. . .I can doggie paddle. Is that the same thing?"

"Not at all." Jersey's mouth twisted with laughter. "So what's your theory about Jeremiah Wilde?"

"He died shortly after Theodore Roosevelt dedicated the park and laid the cornerstone for the arch, correct?" He flipped a paddle in the wrong direction, spraying water. "The ground was already disturbed from the construction, so no one would notice if he dug up the same spot and buried the gold. It's near the entrance of the park, so he could get away quickly with the gold without being spotted."

"Like maybe he intended to come back and get it later?"

"That's my theory."

"Well, what about the note in the jar that kid found back in the '30s? Didn't he write his cousin a letter in 1893?"

"Maybe his first theory was wrong. Maybe the cousin left the letter behind—or Jeremiah never mailed it." Taka shrugged. "But he seemed pretty certain in his logbook. A matrix takes a long time to write."

Jersey twisted her head to see the sinking sun. "For goodness' sake, Taka—row faster!" She shielded her eyes to see the Park Service speedboat tethered to the shore, just up ahead.

⌘

Starlight glimmered behind Roosevelt Arch as Jersey and Taka pulled up in a Park Service pickup truck, loaded up with shovels and pickaxes and Coleman lanterns. Two other Park Service trucks pulled up behind her, full of Park Service higher-ups, followed by an excavator, a crane, and a local news crew who'd gotten wind of the story.

The heavy stone arch glimmered in the news crew lights and lanterns, towering into the night sky. FOR THE BENEFIT AND ENJOYMENT OF THE

People, read the stone inscription at the top.

Don, the head ranger, scowled as he slammed the truck door shut. "There better be lots of enjoyment for the people when we dig, Jersey," he growled, "or you'll definitely lose some benefits."

"Trust me." Jersey handed him a sheaf of papers. Copies she'd made of Taka's calculations and Jeremiah Wilde's logbook.

"That's exactly what I'm afraid of." Don shook his head.

"You should never be afraid of truth, Don," Jersey heard herself say, cool night wind blowing strands of hair across her cheek. Thinking of Tadashi, and thinking of Phyllis. "Sometimes what we cover up needs to be unearthed."

Somebody gave the signal, and the excavator roared, lowering the bucket to scoop into dry earth.

Chapter 9

S o your tour group is gone, Jersey?" Phyllis looked up from the ranger's office desk in surprise, stacking papers together in a bunch. "Yep. Left this morning." Jersey pulled out the computer chair and swiveled around, enjoying the familiar pine planks and sweet coffee scent of the ranger's station. "I bawled like a baby."

Phyllis crooked an eyebrow. "You didn't."

"I did so. They were amazing." Jersey switched on the computer. "They finished not just the entire cabin and the grounds, but they asphalted some trails, too—and built some bridges and benches. Picking up trash everywhere they went."

She clicked on the Internet icon. "The volunteers left me so many Japanese snacks and packets of green tea I don't know what to do with them. Here." She dug through her backpack and produced a foil bag. "Try some of these."

Phyllis wrinkled up her nose. "They smell like fish."

"I think they are made of fish. Fish. . .something. Crackers, I think." Jersey squinted at the kanji characters on the wrinkled label. "They're pretty good though. Even if they do look like dog food."

"I dunno. I'll try just one." Phyllis nudged one with the tip of her fingernail, which she'd painted a livid pink. "Hmm." She stuck one in her mouth and crunched. "Fishy, yes, but not bad. What are they called?"

"Beats me. Ask Taka."

Phyllis gave a sly smirk. "The guy's always asking you for rides." She tipped her head. "Funny thing is, Jersey, he never asked me for a ride. Or Nelson, or anybody else."

Jersey glanced up. "I think I know why now." She pressed her lips together to keep from smiling.

"Well, Taka left this morning. I came in early to finish up some work, and he was packing up to leave for Montana. Following the elk, he said." Phyllis rolled her eyes. "What a weirdo. Is he coming back?"

"He'd better." Jersey reached instinctively for the T-shaped necklace around her neck. "He made a few promises to me before he left, and I'll be here waiting for him to keep them." A corner of her lips turned up in a smile. "And he fixed our computer, too. Remotely. The little sneak."

"Oh, so Nelson *was* right about you and Taka." Phyllis shook her head and glanced out into the lobby, dropping her voice to a whisper. "Sore loser." She turned back to the computer. "And Taka was right about the gold."

Jersey's hands stopped on the keyboard, remembering the sound of scraping metal when the excavator bucket swung deep into the earth. The shouts, and the sprays of light as news crews focused floodlights down into the hole.

Jersey had crouched, motionless, as the crane lifted a dirty pine box, which was rotting through in several places and sagged open at one end. The lift hoisted the box gently onto the ground, and the pine boards fell apart.

Revealing a dirty burlap sack, muddied and stiffened from a hundred years of rains and snows. Someone pulled at the mildewed cord around the neck of the bag, and Jersey saw gold.

Brilliant nuggets, too many to count. Spilling sideways onto the grass as cameras flashed, making a golden waterfall of iridescent yellow bits.

"So what's going to happen to the gold?"

"That's all up in the air. It'll probably take them years to determine. But Yellowstone National Park will get a big cut because it was found on park property. Which makes my funding report much easier to write, doesn't it?" Jersey smiled. "Some of the gold will probably be returned to the Sioux reservations near the Black Hills, where they think the gold originated."

"So it was Ezra Kind's gold." Phyllis's eyes widened. "The Thoen Stone was the real thing then, huh?"

"Apparently so. There'll probably be all kinds of people coming out of the woodwork to claim inheritance."

"What about you?" Phyllis put her hands on her hips.

"I've asked Don for a raise." Jersey bobbed her eyebrows. "And we'll take it from there."

"Hmph. I'd ask him for a lot more than a raise." Phyllis turned on the fax machine and straightened some files. "It's so exciting, you know that? All this arch publicity makes me want to open the time capsule buried in the cornerstone. What's in it?"

"A picture of Roosevelt, some local newspapers, and—wonder of wonders—a Bible." Jersey turned to look at Phyllis over her shoulder. "Funny how everything seems to go back to the Bible, doesn't it, Phyllis? Even after all these years."

Phyllis didn't answer. She just pierced Jersey with a keen look, tears sparkling in her eyes.

"What's wrong?" Jersey swiveled the squeaky chair to face her.

"Nothing." Phyllis laughed and wiped her eyes, turning her back and stacking her papers again. "Forget it."

"Not when you're crying." Jersey got up and marched over to Phyllis's desk, resting a hand on a wooden chair back. "What's going on?" She bit her lip. "More dreams again? I hope not. I've been praying for you."

Phyllis seemed absorbed in her paperwork, shifting one sheet from the front to the back in an endless succession. Jersey finally grabbed them out of her hands and slapped them down on the table then pulled out the chair across from her and plopped down.

"Phyllis." She reached over and took her hands. "Talk to me." She glanced down at Phyllis's nails. "Nice nail polish, by the way. Did you do it yourself?"

"Me? Yeah. Terrance picked it out." Phyllis gave a shy smile. "I guess you could say I was inspired." She flicked one of Jersey's delicate hoop earrings.

"Great. There goes the office." Jersey smoothed her hair back over her shoulder. It smelled nice; she'd actually shelled out a few bucks to buy a hot-oil treatment. "So what's eating you?"

"Eating me? Nothing." Phyllis squeezed Jersey's hands as her tears welled up again. "But I did have another...dream. Like I told you before."

Jersey moaned, rolling her head back on her shoulders in frustration. "Not again! I hoped you would find some peace. That God would help you move past it."

"No, no. It wasn't bad this time," said Phyllis quickly. "It was a good dream. A really good one. I can't get it out of my mind." She turned toward the window, the lined curves of her face illuminated in a soft blue glow.

Jersey waited in silence until Phyllis turned back, playing with a paper clip with her free hand.

"I saw her," she finally said, looking up abruptly and meeting Jersey's gaze with tear-swollen eyes. "My daughter. We never gave her a name." A tear streaked down her cheek, and she sponged her face with her hand. "She was about twelve years old, and she was. . .was. . ."

"Was what?" Jersey stroked the lines in Phyllis's hand.

"She was laughing." Phyllis gasped the words out. "Laughing, Jersey. Can you believe it?" Her eyes spilled over. "She called out to me. 'Mom!' she said. 'Mom! Can you see me? Look how tall I am. Taller than you, huh?'"

Jersey couldn't breathe. She sat there, riveted to Phyllis's tear-soaked face. A glow lighting up the red corners of her eyes.

"She was beautiful, Jersey. Just like I dreamed. So perfect. So. . .at peace." Phyllis gasped back a sob, her tears dripping in wet circles on the table. "She hugged me. It was so real, so. . ." She groped for words, gesturing with her free arm. "The sunlight. Her curly hair. Everything. So amazing. I can't begin to describe it."

Jersey scooted her chair back and reached for a stash of Hardee's napkins somebody had stuffed in the computer drawer. She passed some to Phyllis and then wiped at her own wet cheeks.

"Phyllis. That's amazing." She squeezed Phyllis's hand with trembling fingers. "God answered your prayer. He gave you peace." She grinned, delighting in the feel of eyelashes wet with joyful tears. "I told you she's all right. I told you."

Phyllis nodded, laughing, her earrings clinking as she tipped her head forward to blow her nose. "And there's something else I couldn't figure out, but I guess God knows why He showed me." She shrugged and wiped her nose again. "It didn't make sense to me though."

"What didn't make sense?"

"The boy she was with." Phyllis's hands shook as she reached for a new napkin. "An Asian-looking kid. Japanese maybe. Who knows? At least that's what I thought he was, for some strange reason."

"He?" Jersey froze in mid-wipe of her nose. "What do you mean 'he'?"

"I don't know who he was, Jersey. Some little Japanese boy, cute as a button. But my daughter was playing with him. Pulling him by the arm and laughing with him. She said he was her best friend."

Phyllis shook out one of the napkins. "These new recycled things don't soak up water worth anything, do they?" she fussed. "Apologies to the environment, but give me the old tree-shredders. At least I could clean my face with those."

Jersey jolted with unexpected laughter. "I'm with you on the napkins.

And lightbulbs." She rolled her eyes. "Please. I hate these energy-efficient beasts."

"Don't even go there."

Jersey wiped her nose and balled up her napkin, suppressing the urge to fold it in tiny triangles like the Japanese volunteers. "But tell me more about this boy who was with your daughter. What did he look like? Did he say anything?"

"I don't remember much. But the odd thing is that he looked like you, Jersey. I know that sounds crazy." She put up a hand. "But he did. You're not Japanese, but he had some of your features. The chin." Tears filled her eyes as she pointed. "He said to say hi to you—and he blew a kiss."

Jersey had been rolling her chair legs to one side while she listened, and the chair dropped with a loud thunk. "He said hi to *me*?"

"I know, I know. It makes no sense. But that's what happened. He pulled up his shirt to show me a little scar on his back, the faintest of lines in perfect skin. It was sweet." Phyllis twisted her napkin back and forth. "All of it. The best dream I've ever had."

"Tell me something." Jersey's voice dropped to a whisper. "Was his back straight?"

"Straight. It was just like yours and mine. Perfect." Phyllis closed her eyes as if trying to remember. " 'Truth,' he said his name was. Isn't that a funny thing to say?"

"My living truth," Jersey whispered, turning the *T* necklace over in her hand. "Tadashi."

She let her breath out. Remembering the green aurora exploding over lake water. "Did he. . .walk?"

"Of course he walked." Phyllis looked up. "He ran! Why?"

And Jersey reached for another napkin, covering her tears with her hand.

ABOUT THE AUTHOR

Jennifer Rogers Spinola, a Virginia/South Carolina native and graduate of Gardner-Webb University in North Carolina, just moved to the Black Hills of South Dakota with her Brazilian husband, Athos, son Ethan, and second miracle boy on the way. Jennifer lived in Brazil for nearly eight years after meeting her husband in Sapporo, Japan, where she worked as a missionary. During college, she served as a National Park Service volunteer at Yellowstone and Grand Teton National Parks. In between waddling to ultrasounds and homeschooling high-energy Ethan, Jennifer loves adoption, gardening (her first garden!), snow, hiking, camping, and—of course—Yellowstone.

Southern Fried
SUSHI

From Tokyo to rural Virginia, Shiloh takes the long road home.

Southern Fried
SUSHI
Jennifer Rogers Spinola

978-1-61626-364-5

Ride the rollercoaster of Shiloh Jacobs's life as her dreams derail, sending her on a downward spiral from the heights of an AP job in Tokyo to penniless in rural Virginia. Trapped in a world so foreign to her sensibilities and surrounded by a quirky group of friends, will she break through her hardened prejudices before she loscs those who want to help her? Can she find the key to what changed her estranged mother's life so powerfully before her death that she became a different woman—and can it help Shiloh, too?

Available wherever books are sold.

'Til GRITS DO US Part

978-1-61626-366-9

In Book 3 of the Southern Fried Sushi series, Shiloh Jacobs is planning her wedding, hiding from her past—and dodging a stalker. When the madman threatens to stop her wedding at any cost, Shiloh wonders if small-town life is more trouble than she anticipated.

Available wherever books are sold.